RIPLEY'S GAME

Patricia Highsmith was born in Fort Worth, Texas, in 1921. Her parents moved to New York when she was six, and she attended the Julia Richmond High School and Barnard College. In her senior year she edited the college magazine, having decided at the age of sixteen to become a writer. Her first novel, *Strangers on a Train*, was made into the famous film by Alfred Hitchcock in 1951. *The Talented Mr Ripley*, published in 1955, was awarded the Edgar Allan Poe Scroll by the Mystery Writers of America and introduced the fascinating anti-hero Tom Ripley, who was to appear in many of her later crime novels. Patricia Highsmith died in Locarno, Switzerland, in February 1995. Her last novel, *Small g: A Summer Idyll*, was published posthumously just over a month later.

YOOX

ALSO BY PATRICIA HIGHSMITH

Patricia Highsmith

RIPLEY'S GAME

V

VINTAGE

Published by Vintage 1999

6 8 10 9 7 5

First published in Great Britain in 1974 by
William Heinemann Ltd

Vintage
Random House, 20 Vauxhall Bridge Road,
London SW1V 2SA

Random House Australia (Pty) Limited
20 Alfred Street, Milsons Point, Sydney
New South Wales 2061, Australia

Random House New Zealand Limited
18 Poland Road, Glenfield,
Auckland 10, New Zealand

Random House (Pty) Limited
Endulini, 5a Jubilee Road, Parktown 2193,
South Africa

The Random House Group Limited Reg. No. 954009

www.randomhouse.co.uk

A CIP catalogue record for this book
is available from the British Library

ISBN 0 09 928368 9

Papers used by Random House are natural, recyclable
products made from wood grown in sustainable forests.
The manufacturing processes conform to the environ-
mental regulations of the country of origin.

Printed and bound in Great Britain by
Bookmarque Ltd, Croydon, Surrey

1

'There's no such thing as a perfect murder,' Tom said to Reeves. 'That's just a parlour game, trying to dream one up. Of course you could say there are a lot of unsolved murders. That's different.' Tom was bored. He walked up and down in front of his big fireplace, where a small but cosy fire crackled. Tom felt he had spoken in a stuffy, pontificating way. But the point was, he couldn't help Reeves, and he'd already told him that.

'Yes, sure,' said Reeves. He was sitting in one of the yellow silk armchairs, his lean figure hunched forward, hands clasped between his knees. He had a bony face, short, light-brown hair, cold grey eyes – not a pleasant face but a face that might have been rather handsome if not for a scar that travelled five inches from his right temple across his cheek almost to his mouth. Slightly pinker than the rest of his face, the scar looked like a bad job of stitching, or as if perhaps it had never been stitched. Tom had never asked about the scar, but Reeves had volunteered once, 'A girl did it with her compact. Can you imagine?' (No, Tom couldn't.) Reeves had given Tom a quick. sad smile, one of the few smiles Tom could recall from Reeves. And on another occasion, 'I was thrown from a horse – dragged by the stirrup for a few yards.' Reeves had said that to someone else, but Tom had been present. Tom suspected a dull knife in a very nasty fight somewhere.

Now Reeves wanted Tom to provide someone, suggest someone to do one or perhaps two 'simple murders' and perhaps one theft, also safe and simple. Reeves had come from Hamburg to Villeperce to talk to Tom, and he was going to stay the night and go to Paris tomorrow to talk to someone else about it, then return to his home in Hamburg, presumably to do some more thinking if he failed. Reeves was primarily a fence, but lately was dabbling in the illegal gambling world of Hamburg, which he was now undertaking to protect. Protect from what? Italian sharks who wanted to come in. One Italian in Hamburg was a Mafia button man, sent out as a feeler, Reeves thought, and the other might be, from a different family. By eliminating one or both of these intruders, Reeves hoped to discourage further Mafia attempts, and also to draw the attention of the Hamburg police to a Mafia threat, and let the police handle the rest, which was to say, throw the Mafia out. 'These Hamburg boys are a decent batch,' Reeves had declared fervently. 'Maybe what they're doing is illegal, running a couple of private casinos, but as clubs they're not illegal, and they're not taking outrageous profits. It's not like Las Vegas, *all* Mafia-corrupted, and right under the noses of the American cops!'

Tom took the poker and pushed the fire together, put another neatly cut third-of-a-log on. It was nearly 6 p.m. Soon be time for a drink. And why not now? 'Would you –'

Mme Annette, the Ripley's housekeeper, came in from the kitchen hall just then. 'Excuse me, messieurs. Would you like your drinks now, M. Tome, since the gentleman has not wanted any tea?'

'Yes, thank you, Mme Annette. Just what I was thinking. And ask Mme Heloise to join us, would you?' Tom wanted Heloise to lighten the atmosphere a little. He had said to Heloise, before he went to Orly at 3 p.m. to fetch Reeves, that Reeves wanted to talk to him about something, so Heloise had pottered about in the garden or stayed upstairs all afternoon.

'You wouldn't,' Reeves said with a last-minute urgency and hope, 'consider taking it on yourself? You're not connected, you see, and that's what we want. Safety. And after all, the money, ninety-six thousand bucks, isn't bad.'

Tom shook his head. 'I'm connected with *you* – in a way.' Dammit, he'd done little jobs for Reeves Minot, like posting on small, stolen items, or recovering from toothpaste tubes, where Reeves had planted them, tiny objects like microfilm rolls from the unsuspecting toothpaste carriers. 'How much of this cloak and dagger stuff do you think I can get away with? I've got my reputation to protect, you know.' Tom felt like smiling at that, but at the same time his heart had quickened with genuine feeling, and he stood taller, conscious of the fine house in which he lived, of his secure existence now, six whole months after the Derwatt episode, a near-catastrophe from which he had escaped with no worse than a bit of suspicion upon him. Thin ice, yes, but the ice hadn't broken through. Tom had accompanied the English Inspector Webster and a couple of forensic men to the Salzburg woods where he had cremated the body of the man presumed to be the painter Derwatt. Why had he crushed the skull, the police had asked. Tom could still wince when he thought of it, because he had done it to try to scatter and hide the upper teeth. The lower jaw had easily come away, and Tom had buried it at a distance. But the upper teeth – Some of them had been gathered by one of the forensic men, but there had been no record of Derwatt's teeth with any dentist in London, Derwatt having been living (it was believed) in Mexico for the preceding six years. 'It seemed part of the cremation, part of the idea of reducing him to ashes,' Tom had replied. The cremated body had been Bernard's. Yes, Tom could still shudder, as much at the danger of that moment as at the horror of his act, dropping a big stone on the charred skull. But at least he hadn't killed Bernard. Bernard Tufts had been a suicide.

Tom said, 'Surely among all the people you know, you can find somebody who can do it.'

'Yes, and that would be a connection – more than you. Oh, the people I know are sort of known,' Reeves said with a sad defeat in his voice. 'You know a lot of respectable people, Tom, people really in the clear, people above reproach.'

Tom laughed. 'How're you going to *get* such people? Sometimes I think you're out of your mind, Reeves.'

'No! You know what I mean. Someone who'd do it for the money, just the money. They don't have to be experts. We'd prepare the way. It'd be like – public assassinations. Someone who if he was questioned would look – absolutely incapable of doing such a thing.'

Mme Annette came in with the bar cart. The silver ice bucket shone. The cart squeaked slightly. Tom had been meaning to oil it for weeks. Tom might have gone on bantering with Reeves because Mme Annette, bless her soul, didn't understand English, but Tom was tired of the subject, and delighted by Mme Annette's interruption. Mme Annette was in her sixties, from a Normandy family, fine of feature and sturdy of body, a gem of a servant. Tom could not imagine Belle Ombre functioning without her.

Then Heloise came in from the garden, and Reeves got to his feet. Heloise was wearing bell-bottom pink-and-red-striped dungarees with LEVI printed vertically down all the stripes. Her blonde hair swung long and loose. Tom saw the firelight glow in it and thought, 'What purity compared to what we've been talking about!' The light in her hair was gold, however, which made Tom think of money. Well, he didn't really need any more money, even if the Derwatt picture sales, of which he got a percentage, would soon come to an end because there would be no more pictures. Tom still got a percentage from the Derwatt art supplies company, and that would continue. Then there was the modest but slowly increasing income from the Greenleaf securities which he had inherited by means of a will forged by Tom himself. Not to mention Heloise's generous allowance from her father. No use being greedy. Tom detested murder unless it was absolutely necessary.

'Did you have a good talk?' Heloise asked in English, and fell back gracefully on to the yellow sofa.

'Yes, thank you,' said Reeves.

The rest of the conversation was in French, because Heloise was not comfortable in English. Reeves did not know much French but he got along, and they were not talking about anything important : the garden, the mild winter that seemed really to have passed, because here it was early March and the daffodils were opening. Tom poured champagne for Heloise from one of the little bottles on the cart.

'How ees eet in Hambourg?' Heloise ventured again in English, and Tom saw amusement in her eyes as Reeves struggled to get out a conventional response in French.

It was not too cold in Hamburg either, and Reeves added that he had a garden also, as his 'petite maison' found itself on the Alster which was water, that was to say a sort of bay where many people had homes with gardens and water, meaning they could have small boats if they wished.

Tom knew that Heloise disliked Reeves Minot, mistrusted him, that Reeves was the kind of person Heloise wanted Tom to avoid. Tom reflected with satisfaction that he could honestly say to Heloise tonight that he had declined to cooperate in the scheme that Reeves had proposed. Heloise was always worried about what her father would say. Her father, Jacques Plisson, was a millionaire pharmaceutical manufacturer, a Gaullist, the essence of French respectability. And he had never cared for Tom. 'My father will not stand for much more!' Heloise often warned Tom, but Tom knew she was more interested in his own safety than in hanging on to the allowance her father gave her, an allowance he frequently threatened to cut off, according to Heloise. She had lunch with her parents at their home in Chantilly once a week, usually Friday. If her father ever severed her allowance, they could not quite make it at Belle Ombre, Tom knew.

The dinner menu was *médaillons de bœuf*, preceded by cold artichokes with Mme Annette's own sauce. Heloise had changed into a simple dress of pale blue. She sensed already, Tom thought, that Reeves had not got what he had come for. Before they all retired, Tom made sure that Reeves had everything he needed, and at what hour he would like tea or coffee brought to his room. Coffee at 8 a.m., Reeves said. Reeves had the guest room in the left centre of the house, which gave Reeves the bathroom that was usually Heloise's, but from which Mme Annette had already removed Heloise's toothbrush to Tom's bathroom, off his own room.

'I am glad he is going tomorrow. Why is he so tense?' Heloise asked, while brushing her teeth.

'He's always tense.' Tom turned off the shower, stepped out and quickly enveloped himself in a big yellow towel. 'That's why he's thin – maybe.' They were speaking in English, because Heloise was not shy about speaking English with him.

'How did you meet him?'

Tom couldn't remember. When? Maybe five or six years ago. In Rome? Who was Reeves a friend of? Tom was too tired to think hard, and it didn't matter. He had five or six such acquaintances, and would have been hard pressed to say where he had met each and every one.

'What did he want from you?'

Tom put his arm around Heloise's waist, pressing the loose

9

nightdress close to her body. He kissed her cool cheek. 'Something impossible. I said no. You can see that. He is disappointed.'

That night there was an owl, a lonely owl calling somewhere in the pines of the communal forest behind Belle Ombre. Tom lay with his left arm under Heloise's neck, thinking. She fell asleep, and her breathing became slow and soft. Tom sighed, and went on thinking. But he was not thinking in a logical, constructive way. His second coffee was keeping him awake. He was remembering a party he had been to a month ago in Fontainebleau, an informal birthday for a Mme – who? It was her husband's name that Tom was interested in, an English name that might come to him in a few seconds. The man, the host, had been in his early thirties, and they had a small son. The house was a straight-up-and-down three-storey, on a residential street in Fontainebleau, a patch of garden behind it. The man was a picture framer, that was why Tom had been dragged along by Pierre Gauthier, who had an art supply shop in the Rue Grande, where Tom bought his paints and brushes. Gauthier had said, 'Oh, come along with me, M. Reeply. Bring your wife! He wants a lot of people. He's a little depressed . . . And anyway, since he makes frames, you might give him some business.'

Tom blinked in the darkness, and moved his head back a little so his eyelashes would not touch Heloise's shoulder. He recalled a tall blond Englishman with a certain resentment and dislike, because in the kitchen, that gloomy kitchen with worn-out linoleum, smoke-stained tin ceiling with a nineteenth-century bas-relief pattern, this man had made an unpleasant remark to Tom. The man – Trewbridge, Tewksbury? – had said in an almost sneering way, 'Oh yes, I've heard of you.' Tom had said, 'I'm Tom Ripley. I live in Villeperce,' and Tom had been about to ask him how long he'd been in Fontainebleau, thinking that perhaps an Englishman with a French wife might like to make acquaintance with an American with a French wife living not far away, but Tom's venture had been met with rudeness. Trevanny? Wasn't that his name? Blond, straight hair, rather Dutch-looking, but then the English often looked Dutch and vice versa.

What Tom was thinking of now, however, was what Gauthier had said later the same evening. 'He's depressed. He doesn't

mean to be unfriendly. He's got some kind of blood disease –
leukaemia, I think. Pretty serious. Also as you can see from the
house, he's not doing too well.' Gauthier had a glass eye of a
curious yellow-green colour, obviously an attempt to match the
real eye, but rather a failure. Gauthier's false eye suggested the
eye of a dead cat. One avoided looking at it, yet one's eyes were
hypnotically drawn to it, so Gauthier's gloomy words, combined
with his glass eye, had made a strong impression of Death
upon Tom, and Tom had not forgotten.

Oh, yes, I've heard of you. Did that mean that Trevanny or
whatever his name was thought he was responsible for Bernard
Tuft's death, and before that Dickie Greenleaf's? Or was the
Englishman merely embittered against everyone because of his
ailment? Dyspeptic, like a man with a constant stomach ache?
Now Tom recalled Trevanny's wife, not a pretty but a rather
interesting-looking woman with chestnut hair, friendly and out-
going, making an effort at that party in the small living-room
and the kitchen where no one had sat down on the few chairs
available.

What Tom was thinking was : would this man take on such a
job as Reeves was proposing? An interesting approach to
Trevanny had occurred to Tom. It was an approach that might
work with any man, if one prepared the ground, but in this case
the ground was already prepared. Trevanny was seriously
worried about his health. Tom's idea was nothing more than a
practical joke, he thought, a nasty one, but the man had been
nasty to him. The joke might not last more than a day or so,
until Trevanny could consult his doctor.

Tom was amused by his thoughts, and eased himself gently
from Heloise, so that if he shook with repressed laughter for an
instant, he wouldn't awaken her. Suppose Trevanny was vulnerable, and carried out Reeves' plan like a soldier, like a dream?
Was it worth a try? Yes, because Tom had nothing to lose.
Neither had Trevanny. Trevanny might gain. Reeves might gain
– according to Reeves, but let Reeves figure that out, because
what Reeves wanted seemed as vague to Tom as Reeves' microfilm activities, which presumably had to do with international
spying. Were governments aware of the insane antics of some of
their spies? Or those whimsical, half-demented men flitting from

Bucharest to Moscow and Washington with guns and microfilm
– men who might with the same enthusiasm have put their
energies to international warfare in stamp-collecting, or in
acquiring secrets of miniature electric trains?

2

So it was that some ten days later, on 22 March, Jonathan Trevanny, who lived in the Rue St Merry, Fontainebleau, received a curious letter from his good friend Alan McNear. Alan, a Paris representative of an English electronics firm, had written the letter just before leaving for New York on a business assignment, and oddly the day after he had visited the Trevannys in Fontainebleau. Jonathan had expected – or rather not expected – a sort of thank-you letter from Alan for the send-off party Jonathan and Simone had given him, and Alan did write a few words of appreciation, but the paragraph that puzzled Jonathan went :

Jon, I was shocked at the news in regard to the old blood ailment, and am even now hoping it isn't so. I was told that you knew, but weren't telling any of your friends. Very noble of you, but what are friends for? You needn't think we'll avoid you or that we'll think you'll become so melancholy that we won't want to see you. Your friends (and I'm one) are here – always. But I can't write anything I want to say, really. I'll do better when I see you next, in a couple of months when I wangle myself a vacation, so forgive these inadequate words.

What was Alan talking about? Had his doctor, Dr Perrier, said something to his *friends*, something he wouldn't tell him? Something about not living much longer? Dr Perrier hadn't been to the party for Alan, but could Dr Perrier have said something to someone else?

Had Dr Perrier spoken to Simone? And was Simone keeping it from him, too?

As Jonathan thought of these possibilities, he was standing in his garden at 8.30 a.m., chilly under his sweater, his fingers smudged with earth. He'd best speak with Dr Perrier today. No use with Simone. She might put up an act. *But darling, what're you talking about?* Jonathan wasn't sure he'd be able to tell if she was putting up an act or not.

And Dr Perrier – could he trust him? Dr Perrier was always bouncing with optimism, which was fine if you had something minor – you felt fifty per cent better, even cured. But Jonathan knew he hadn't anything minor. He had myeloid leukaemia, characterized by an excess of yellow matter in the bone marrow. In the past five years, he'd had at least four blood transfusions per year. Every time he felt weak, he was supposed to get to his doctor, or to the Fontainebleau hospital for a transfusion. Dr Perrier had said (and so had a specialist in Paris) that there would come a time when the decline might be swift, when transfusions wouldn't do the trick any longer. Jonathan had read enough about his ailment to know that himself. No doctor as yet had come up with a cure for myeloid leukaemia. On the average, it killed after six to twelve years, or six to eight even. Jonathan was entering his sixth year with it.

Jonathan set his fork back in the little brick structure, formerly an outside toilet, that served as a tool shed, then walked to his back steps. He paused with one foot on the first step and drew the fresh morning air into his lungs, thinking, 'How many weeks will I have to enjoy such mornings?' He remembered thinking the same thing last spring, however. Buck up, he told himself, he'd known for six years that he might not live to see thirty-five. Jonathan mounted the eight iron steps with a firm tread, already thinking that it was 8.52 a.m., and that he was due in his shop at 9 a.m. or a few minutes after.

Simone had gone off with Georges to the Ecole Maternelle, and the house was empty. Jonathan washed his hands at the sink and made use of the vegetable brush, which Simone would not have approved of, but he left the brush clean. The only other sink was in the bathroom on the top floor. There was no telephone in the house. He'd ring Dr Perrier from his shop the first thing.

Jonathan walked to the Rue de la Paroisse and turned left, then went on to the Rue des Sablons which crossed it. In his shop, Jonathan dialled Dr Perrier's number, which he knew by heart.

The nurse said the doctor was booked up today, which Jonathan had expected.

'But this is urgent. It's something that won't take long. Just a question really – but I must see him.'

'You are feeling weak, M. Trevanny?'

'Yes, I am,' Jonathan said at once.

He got an appointment for twelve noon. The hour had a certain doom about it.

Jonathan was a picture framer. He cut mats and glass, made frames, chose frames from his stock for clients who were undecided, and once in a blue moon, in buying old frames at auctions and from junk dealers, he got a picture that was of some interest with the frame, a picture which he could clean and put in his window and sell. But it wasn't a lucrative business. He scraped along. Seven years ago he'd had a partner, another Englishman, from Manchester, and they had started an antique shop in Fontainebleau, dealing mainly in junk which they refurbished and sold. This hadn't paid enough for two, and Roy had pushed off and got a job as a garage mechanic somewhere near Paris. Shortly after that, a Paris doctor had said the same thing that a London doctor had told Jonathan: 'You're inclined to anaemia. You'd better have frequent check-ups, and it's best if you don't do any heavy work.' So from handling armoires and sofas, Jonathan had turned to the lighter work of handling picture frames and glass. Before Jonathan had married Simone, he had told her that he might not live more than another six years, because just at the time he met Simone, he'd had it confirmed by two doctors that his periodic weakness was caused by myeloid leukaemia.

Now, Jonathan thought as he calmly, very calmly began his day, Simone might remarry if he died. Simone worked five afternoons a week from 2.30 p.m. until 6.30 p.m. at a shoe shop in the Avenue Franklin Roosevelt, which was within walking distance of their house, and this was only in the past year when Georges had been old enough to be put into the French equivalent of kindergarten. He and Simone needed the two hundred francs per week that Simone earned, but Jonathan was irked by the thought that Brezard, her boss, was a bit of a lecher, liked to pinch his employees' behinds, and doubtless try his luck in the back room where the stock was. Simone was a married woman, as Brezard well knew, so there was a limit as to how far he

15

could go, Jonathan supposed, but that never stopped his type from trying. Simone was not at all a flirt – she had a curious shyness, in fact, that suggested that she thought herself not attractive to men. It was a quality that endeared her to Jonathan. In Jonathan's opinion, Simone was supercharged with sex appeal, though of the kind that might not be apparent to the average man, and it annoyed Jonathan especially that the cruising swine Brezard must have become aware of Simone's very different kind of attractiveness, and that he wanted some of it for himself. Not that Simone talked much about Brezard. Only once had she mentioned that he tried it on with his women employees who were two besides Simone. For an instant that morning, as Jonathan presented a framed watercolour to a client, he imagined Simone, after a discreet interval, succumbing to the odious Brezard, who after all was a bachelor and financially better off than Jonathan. Absurd, Jonathan thought. Simone hated his type.

'Oh, it's lovely! Excellent!' said the young woman in a bright red coat, holding the watercolour at arm's length.

Jonathan's long, serious face slowly smiled, as if a small and private sun had come out of clouds and begun to shine within him. She was so genuinely pleased! Jonathan didn't know her, in fact she was picking up the picture that an older woman, perhaps her mother, had brought in. The price should have been twenty francs more than he had first estimated, because the frame was not the same as the older woman had chosen (Jonathan had not had enough in stock), but Jonathan didn't mention this and accepted the eighty francs agreed upon.

Then Jonathan pushed a broom over his wooden floor, and feather-dusted the three or four pictures in his small front window. His shop was positively shabby, Jonathan thought that morning. No colour anywhere, frames of all sizes leaning against unpainted walls, samples of frame wood hanging from the ceiling, a counter with an order book, ruler, pencils. At the back of the shop stood a long wooden table where Jonathan worked with his mitre boxes, saws and glass cutters. Also on the big table were his carefully protected sheets of mat board. a great roll of brown paper, rolls of string, wire, pots of glue, boxes of variously sized nails, and above the table on the wall were racks of knives and hammers. In principle, Jonathan liked the nineteenth-century atmosphere, the lack of commercial frou-frou. He wanted his shop to look as if a good craftsman ran it, and in that he had succeeded, he thought. He never overcharged, did his work on time, or if he was going to be late, he notified his clients by postcard or a telephone call. People appreciated that, Jonathan had found.

At 11.35 a.m., having framed two small pictures and fixed their owners' names to them, Jonathan washed his hands and face at the cold water tap in his sink, combed his hair, stood up straight and tried to brace himself for the worst. Dr Perrier's office was not far away in the Rue Grande. Jonathan turned his door card to OUVERT at 14.30, locked his front door, and set out.

Jonathan had to wait in Dr Perrier's front room with its sickly, dusty rose laurel plant. The plant never flowered, it didn't die, and never grew, never changed. Jonathan identified himself with the plant. Again and again his eyes were drawn to it, though he tried to think of other things. There were copies of *Paris Match* on the oval table, out of date and much thumbed, but Jonathan found them more depressing than the laurel plant. Dr Perrier also worked at the big Hôpital de Fontainebleau, Jonathan reminded himself, otherwise it would have seemed an absurdity to entrust one's life, to believe an opinion of whether one lived or died, to a doctor who worked in such a wretched little place as this looked.

The nurse came out and beckoned.

'Well, well, how's the interesting patient, my most interesting patient?' said Dr Perrier, rubbing his hands, then extending one to Jonathan.

Jonathan shook his hand. 'I feel quite all right, thank you. But what is this about – I mean the tests of two months ago. I understand they are not so favourable?'

Dr Perrier looked blank, and Jonathan watched him intently. Then Dr Perrier smiled, showing yellowish teeth under his carelessly trimmed moustache.

'What do you mean unfavourable? You saw the results.'

'But – you know I'm not an expert in understanding them – perhaps.'

'But I explained them to you – Now what is the matter? You're feeling tired again?'

'In fact no.' Since Jonathan knew the doctor wanted to get away for lunch, he said hastily, 'To tell the truth, a friend of mine has learned somewhere that – I'm due for a crisis. Maybe I haven't long to live. Naturally, I thought this information must have come from you.'

Dr Perrier shook his head, then laughed, hopped about like a bird and came to rest with his skinny arms lightly outspread on the top of a glass-enclosed bookcase. 'My dear sir – first of all, if it were true, I would not have said it to anybody. That is not ethical. Second, it is not true, as far as I know from the last test. – Do you want another test today? Late this afternoon at the hospital, maybe I – '

'Not necessarily. What I really wanted to know is – is it true? You wouldn't just not tell me?' Jonathan said with a laugh. 'Just to make me feel better?'

'What nonsense! Do you think I'm that kind of a doctor?'

Yes, Jonathan thought, looking Dr Perrier straight in the eye. And God bless him, maybe, in some cases, but Jonathan thought he deserved the facts, because he was the kind of man who could face the facts. Jonathan bit his underlip. He could go to the lab in Paris, he thought, insist on seeing the specialist Moussu again. Also he might get something out of Simone today at lunch-time.

Dr Perrier was patting his arm. 'Your friend – and I won't ask who he is! – is either mistaken or not a very nice friend, I think. Now then, you should tell me when and if you become tired, *that* is what counts . . . '

Twenty minutes later, Jonathan was climbing the front steps of his house, carrying an apple tart and a long loaf of bread. He let himself in with his key, and walked down the hall to the kitchen. He smelled frying potatoes, a mouth-watering smell always signifying lunch, not dinner, and Simone's potatoes would be in long slender pieces, not short chunks like the chips in England. Why had he thought of English chips?

Simone was at the stove, wearing an apron over her dress, wielding a long fork. 'Hello, Jon. You're a little late.'

Jonathan put an arm around her and kissed her cheek, then

held up the paper box, swung it towards Georges who was sitting at the table, blond head bent, cutting out parts for a mobile from an empty box of cornflakes.

'Ah, a cake! What kind?' Georges asked.

'Apple.' Jonathan set the box on the table.

They had a small steak each, the delicious fried potatoes, a green salad.

'Brezard is starting inventory,' Simone said. 'The summer stock comes in next week, so he wants to have a sale Friday and Saturday. I might be a little late tonight.'

She had warmed the apple tart on the asbestos plate. Jonathan waited impatiently for Georges to go in the living-room where a lot of his toys were, or out to the garden. When Georges left finally Jonathan said:

'I had a funny letter today from Alan.'

'Alan? Funny how?'

'He wrote it just before he went to New York It seems he's heard – ' Should he show her Alan's letter? She could read English well enough. Jonathan decided to go on. 'He's heard somewhere that I'm worse, due for a bad crisis – or something. Do you know anything about it?' Jonathan watched her eyes.

Simone looked genuinely surprised. 'Why no, Jon. How would I hear – except from you?'

'I spoke with Dr Perrier just now. That's why I was a bit late. Perrier says he doesn't know of any change in the situation, but you know Perrier!' Jonathan smiled, still watching Simone anxiously. 'Well, here's the letter,' he said, pulling it from his back pocket. He translated the paragraph.

'Mon dieu! – Well, where did he hear it from?'

'Yes, that's the question. I'll write him and ask. Don't you think?' Jonathan smiled again, a more genuine smile. He was sure Simone didn't know anything about it.

Jonathan carried a second cup of coffee into the small square living-room where Georges was now sprawled on the floor with his cut-outs. Jonathan sat down at the writing desk, which always made him feel like a giant. It was a rather dainty French écritoire, a present from Simone's family. Jonathan was careful not to put too much weight on the writing shelf. He addressed an air-letter to Alan McNear at the Hotel New Yorker, began the letter breezily enough, and wrote a second paragraph:

I don't know quite what you mean in your letter about the news (about me) which shocked you. I feel all right, but this morning spoke with my doctor here to see if he was giving me the whole story. He disclaims any knowledge of a worse condition. So dear Alan, what does interest me is where did you hear it? Could you possibly drop me a line soon? It sounds like a misunderstanding, I'd be delighted to forget it, but I hope you can understand my curiosity as to where you heard it.

He dropped the letter in a yellow box *en route* to his shop. It would probably be a week before he heard from Alan.

That afternoon, Jonathan's hand was as steady as ever as he pulled his razor knife down the edge of his steel ruler. He thought of his letter, making its progress to Orly airport, maybe by this evening, maybe by tomorrow morning. He thought of his age, thirty-four, and of how pitifully little he would have done if he were to die in another couple of months. He'd produced a son, and that was something, but hardly an achievement worthy of special praise. He would not leave Simone very secure. If anything, he had lowered her standard of living slightly. Her father was only a coal merchant, but somehow over the years her family had gathered a few conveniences of life around them, a car for instance, decent furniture. They vacationed in June or July down south in a villa which they rented, and last year they had paid a month's rent so that Jonathan and Simone could go there with Georges. Jonathan had not done as well as his brother Philip, two years older than himself, though Philip had looked physically weaker, had been a dull, plodding type all his life. Now Philip was a professor of anthropology at Bristol University, not brilliant, Jonathan was sure, but a good solid man with a solid career, a wife and two children. Jonathan's mother, a widow now, had a happy existence with her brother and sister-in-law in Oxfordshire, taking care of the big garden there and doing all the shopping and cooking. Jonathan felt himself the failure of his family, both physically and as to his work. He had first wanted to be an actor. At eighteen he'd gone to a drama school for two years. He'd not a bad face for an actor, he thought, not too handsome with a big nose and wide mouth, yet good-looking enough to play romantic roles, and at the same time heavy enough to play heavier roles in time. What pipe dreams! He'd hardly got two walk-on parts in the three years he'd hung around London and Manchester theatres – always supporting himself, of course, by odd jobs, including one as a veterinary's assistant. 'You take up a lot of space and you're not even sure of yourself,' a director once said to him. And then, working for an antique dealer in another of his odd jobs, Jonathan had thought he might like the antique business. He had learned all he could from his boss, Andrew Mott. Then the grand move to France with his chum Roy Johnson, who had also had enthusiasm, if not much knowledge, for starting an antique shop via the junk trade. Jonathan remembered his dreams of glory and adventure in a new country, France, dreams of freedom, of success. And instead of success, instead of a series of educational mistresses, instead of making friends with the bohemians, or with some stratum of French society which Jonathan had imagined existed but perhaps didn't – instead of all this Jonathan had continued to limp along, no better off really than when he'd been trying to get jobs as an actor and had supported himself any old way.

The only successful thing in his whole life was his marriage to Simone, Jonathan thought. The news of his disease had come in the same month he had met Simone Foussadier. He'd begun to feel strangely weak and had romantically thought that it might be due to falling in love. But a little extra rest hadn't shaken the weakness, he had fainted once in a street of Nemours, so he had gone to a doctor – Dr Perrier in Fontainebleau, who had suspected a blood condition and sent him to a Dr Moussu in Paris. The specialist Moussu, after two days of tests, had confirmed myeloid leukaemia, and said that he might have from six to eight, with luck twelve years to live. There would be an enlargement of the spleen, which in fact Jonathan already had without having noticed it. Thus Jonathan's proposal to Simone had been a declaration of love and death in the same awkward speech. It would have been enough to put most young women off, or to have made them say they needed time to think about it. Simone had said yes, she loved him too. 'It is the love that is important, not the time,' Simone had said. None of the calculations that Jonathan had associated with the French, and with Latins in general. Simone said she had already spoken to her family. And this after they had known each other only two weeks. Jonathan felt himself suddenly in a world more secure than any he had ever known. Love, in a real and not a merely romantic sense, love that he had no control over, had miraculously rescued him. In a way, he felt that it had rescued him from death, but he realized that he meant that love had taken the terror out of death. And here was death six years later, as Dr Moussu in Paris had predicted. Perhaps. Jonathan didn't know what to believe.

He must make another visit to Moussu in Paris, he thought. Three years ago, Jonathan had had a complete change of blood under Dr Moussu's supervision in a Paris hospital. The treatment was called Vincainestine, the idea or the hope being that the excess of white with accompanying yellow components would not return to the blood. But the yellow excess had reappeared in about eight months.

Before he made an appointment with Dr Moussu, however, Jonathan preferred to wait for a letter from Alan McNear. Alan would write at once, Jonathan felt sure. One could count on Alan.

Jonathan, before he left his shop, cast one desperate glance around its Dickensian interior. It wasn't really dusty, it was just that the walls needed repainting. He wondered if he should make an effort to spruce the place up, start soaking his customers as so many picture framers did, sell lacquered brass items with big mark-ups? Jonathan winced. He wasn't the type.

That day was Wednesday. On Friday, while bending over a stubborn screw-eye that had been in an oak frame for perhaps a hundred and fifty years and had no intention of yielding to his pliers, Jonathan had suddenly to drop the pliers and look for a seat. The seat was a wooden box against a wall. He got up almost at once and wet his face at the sink, bending as low as he could. In five minutes or so, the faintness passed, and by lunch-time he had forgotten about it. Such moments came every two or three months, and Jonathan was glad if they didn't catch him on the street.

On Tuesday, six days after he had posted his letter to Alan, he received a letter from the Hotel New Yorker.

Dear Jon,

Believe me, I'm glad you spoke with your doctor and that the news is good! The person who told me you were in a serious way was a little balding fellow with moustache and a glassy eye, early forties maybe. He seemed really concerned, and perhaps you shouldn't hold it too much against him, as he may have heard it from someone else.

I'm enjoying this town and wish you and Simone were here, esp. as I'm on an expense account ...

The man Alan meant was Pierre Gauthier, who had an art supply shop in the Rue Grande. He was not a friend of Jonathan's, just an acquaintance. Gauthier often sent people to Jonathan to have their pictures framed. Gauthier had been at the house the night of Alan's send-off party, Jonathan remembered distinctly, and must have spoken to Alan then. It was out of the question that Gauthier had spoken maliciously. Jonathan was only a little surprised that Gauthier even knew he had a blood ailment, though the word did get around, Jonathan realized. Jonathan thought the thing to do was speak to Gauthier and ask him where he'd heard the story.

It was 8.50 a.m. Jonathan had waited for the post, as he had yesterday morning also. His impulse was to go straight to Gauthier's, but he felt this would show unseemly anxiety, and that he'd better get his bearings by going to his shop and opening as usual.

Because of three or four customers, Jonathan hadn't a break till 10.25 a.m. He left his clock card in the glass of his door indicating that he would be open again at 11 a.m.

When Jonathan entered the art supply shop, Gauthier was busy with two women customers. Jonathan pretended to browse among racks of paint brushes until Gauthier was free. Then he said:

'M. Gauthier! How goes it?' Jonathan extended a hand.

Gauthier clasped Jonathan's hand in both his own and smiled. 'And you, my friend?'

'Well enough, thank you . . . *Ecoutez*. I don't want to take your time – but there is something I would like to ask you.'

'Yes? What's that?'

Jonathan beckoned Gauthier farther away from the door

which might open at any minute. There was not much standing room in the little shop. 'I heard from a friend – my friend Alan, you remember? The Englishman. At the party at my house a few weeks ago.'

'Yes! Your friend the Englishman. Alain.' Gauthier remembered and looked attentive.

Jonathan tried to avoid even glancing at Gauthier's false eye, but to concentrate on the other eye. 'Well, it seems you told Alan that you'd heard I was very ill, maybe not going to live much longer.'

Gauthier's soft face grew solemn. He nodded. 'Yes, m'sieur, I did hear that. I hope it's not true. I remember Alain, because you introduced him to me as your best friend. So I assumed he knew. Perhaps I should have said nothing. I am sorry, it was perhaps tactless. I though you were – in the English style – putting on a brave face.'

'It's nothing serious, M. Gauthier, because as far as I know, it's not true! I've just spoken with my doctor. But – '

'*Ah, bon!* Ah well, that's different! I'm delighted to hear that, M. Trevanny! Ha! Ha!' Pierre Gauthier gave a clap of laughter as if a ghost had been laid, and he found not only Jonathan but himself back among the living.

'But I'd like to know where you heard this. Who told you I was ill?'

'Ah – yes!' Gauthier pressed a finger to his lips, thinking. 'Who? A man. Yes – of *course*!' He had it, but he paused.

Jonathan waited.

'But I remember he said he wasn't sure. He'd heard it, he said. An incurable blood disease, he said.'

Jonathan felt warm with anxiety again, as he had felt several times in the past week. He wet his lips. 'But who? How did he hear it? Didn't he say?'

Gauthier again hesitated. 'Since it isn't true – shouldn't we best forget it?'

'Someone you know very well?'

'No! Not at all well, I assure you.'

'A customer.'

'Yes. Yes, he is. A nice man, a gentleman. But since he *said* he wasn't sure – Really, *m'sieur*, you shouldn't bear a resentment,

24

although I can understand how you could resent such a remark.'

'Which leads to the interesting question how did the gentleman come to hear I was very ill,' Jonathan went on, laughing now.

'Yes. Exactly. Well, the point is, it isn't true Isn't that the main thing?'

Jonathan saw in Gauthier a French politeness, and unwillingness to alienate a customer, and – which was to be expected – an aversion to the subject of death. 'You're right. That's the main thing.' Jonathan shook hands with Gauthier, both of them smiling now, and bade him adieu.

That very day at lunch, Simone asked Jonathan if he had heard from Alan. Jonathan said yes.

'It was Gauthier who said something to Alan.'

'Gauthier? The art shop man?'

'Yes.' Jonathan was lighting a cigarette over his coffee. Georges had gone out into the garden. 'I went to see Gauthier this morning and I asked him where he'd heard it. He said from a customer. A man. – Funny, isn't it? Gauthier wouldn't tell me who, and I can't really blame him. It's some mistake, of course. Gauthier realizes that.'

'But it's a shocking thing,' said Simone.

Jonathan smiled, knowing Simone wasn't really shocked, since she knew Dr Perrier had given him rather good news. 'As we say in English, one must not make a mountain out of a molehill.'

In the following week, Jonathan bumped into Dr Perrier in the Rue Grande, the doctor in a hurry to enter the Société Générale before it shut at twelve sharp. But he paused to ask how Jonathan was.

'Quite well, thank you,' said Jonathan, whose mind was on buying a plunger for the toilet from a shop a hundred yards away which also shut at noon.

'M. Trevanny – ' Dr Perrier paused with one hand on the big knob of the bank's door. He moved away from the door, closer to Jonathan. 'In regard to what we were talking about the other day – no doctor can be *sure*, you know. In a situation like yours. I didn't want you to think I'd given you a guarantee of perfect health, immunity for years. You know yourself – '

'Oh, I didn't assume that!' Jonathan interrupted.

'Then you understand,' said Dr Perrier, smiling, and dashed at once into his bank.

Jonathan trotted on in quest of the plunger. It was the kitchen sink stopped up, not the toilet, he remembered, and Simone had lent a neighbour their plunger months ago and – Jonathan was thinking of what Dr Perrier had said. *Did* he know something, suspect something from the last test, something not sufficiently definite to warrant telling him about?

At the door of the droguerie, Jonathan encountered a smiling, dark-haired girl who was just locking up, removing the outside door handle.

'I am sorry. It is five minutes past twelve,' she said.

3

Tom, during the last week in March, was engaged in painting a full-length portrait of Heloise horizontal on the yellow satin sofa. And Heloise seldom agreed to pose. But the sofa stayed still, and Tom had it satisfactorily on his canvas. He had also made seven or eight sketches of Heloise with her head propped upon her left hand, her right hand resting on a big art book. He kept the two best sketches and threw the others away.

Reeves Minot had written him one letter, asking Tom if he had come up with a helpful idea – as to a person, Reeves meant. The letter had arrived a couple of days after Tom had spoken with Gauthier, from whom Tom usually bought his paints. Tom had replied to Reeves: 'Am trying to think, but meanwhile you should go ahead with your own ideas, if you have any.' The 'am trying to think' was merely polite, even false, like a lot of phrases that served to oil the machinery of social intercourse, as Emily Post might say. Reeves hardly kept Belle Ombre oiled financially, in fact Reeves' payments to Tom for occasional services as go-between and fence would hardly cover the dry-cleaning bills, but it never hurt to maintain friendly relations. Reeves had procured a false passport for Tom and had got it to Paris fast when Tom had needed it to help defend the Derwatt industry. Tom might one day need Reeves again.

But the business with Jonathan Trevanny was merely a game for Tom. He was not doing it for Reeves' gambling interests. Tom happened to dislike gambling, and had no respect for people who chose to earn their living, or even part of their living from it. It was pimping, of a sort. Tom had started the Trevanny game out of curiosity, and because Trevanny had once sneered at him – and because Tom wanted to see if his own wild shot would find its mark, and make Jonathan Trevanny, who Tom sensed was priggish and self-righteous, uneasy for a time. Then Reeves could offer his bait, hammering the point of course that Trevanny was soon to die anyway. Tom doubted that Trevanny would bite, but it would be a period of discomfort for Trevanny, certainly. Unfortunately Tom couldn't guess how soon the rumour would get to Jonathan Trevanny's ears. Gauthier was gossipy enough, but it just might happen, even if Gauthier told two or three people, that no one would have the courage to broach the subject to Trevanny himself.

So Tom, although busy as usual with his painting, his spring planting, his German and French studies (Schiller and Molière now), plus supervising a crew of three masons who were constructing a greenhouse along the right side of Belle Ombre's back lawn, still counted the passing days and imagined what might have happened after that afternoon in the middle of March, when he had said to Gauthier that he'd heard that Trevanny wasn't long for this world. Not too likely that Gauthier would speak to Trevanny directly, unless they were closer than Tom thought. Gauthier would more likely tell someone else about it. Tom counted on the fact (he was sure it was a fact) that the possibility of anyone's imminent death was a fascinating subject to everyone.

Tom went to Fontainebleau, some twelve miles from Villeperce, every two weeks or so. Fontainebleau was better than Moret for shopping, for having suède coats cleaned, for buying radio batteries and the rarer things that Mme Annette wished for her cuisine. Jonathan Trevanny had a telephone in his shop, Tom had noted in the directory, but apparently not in his house in the Rue St Merry. Tom had been trying to look up the house number, but he thought he would recognize the house when he saw it. Around the end of March, Tom became curious to see Trevanny again, from a distance, of course, and so on a trip to Fontainebleau one Friday morning, a market day, for the purpose of buying two round terracotta flower tubs, Tom, after putting these items in the back of the Renault station wagon, walked through the Rue des Sablons where Trevanny's shop was. It was nearly noon.

Trevanny's shop looked in need of paint and a bit depressing, as if it belonged to an old man, Tom thought. Tom had never patronized Trevanny, because there was a good framer in Moret, closer to Tom. The little shop with 'Encadrement' in fading red letters on the wood over the door stood in a row of shops – a launderette, a cobbler's, a modest travel agency –with its door on the left side and to the right a square window with assorted frames and two or three paintings with handwritten price tags on them. Tom crossed the street casually, glanced into the shop and saw Trevanny's tall, Nordic-looking figure behind the counter some twenty feet away. Trevanny was showing a man a length of frame, slapping it into his palm, talking. Then Trevanny glanced at the window, saw Tom for an instant, but continued talking to the customer with no change in his expression.

Tom strolled on. Trevanny hadn't recognized him, Tom felt. Tom turned right, into the Rue de France, the next more important street after the Rue Grande, and continued till he came to the Rue St Merry where he turned right. Or had Trevanny's house been to the left? No, right.

Yes, there it was, surely, the narrow, cramped-looking grey house with slender black handrails going up the front steps. The tiny areas on either side of the steps were cemented, and no flower pots relieved the barrenness. But there was a garden behind, Tom recalled. The windows, though sparkling clean, showed rather limp curtains. Yes, this was where he'd come on the invitation of Gauthier that evening in February. There was a narrow passage on the left side of the house which must lead to the garden beyond. A green plastic garbage bin stood in front of the padlocked iron gate to the garden, and Tom imagined that the Trevannys usually got to the garden via the back door off the kitchen, which Tom remembered.

Tom was on the other side of the street, walking slowly, but careful not to appear to be loitering, because he could not be sure that the wife, or someone, was not even now looking out one of the windows.

Was there anything else he needed to buy? Zinc white. He was nearly out of it. And that purchase would take him to Gauthier the art supply man. Tom quickened his step, congratulating himself because his need of zinc white was a real need, so he'd be entering Gauthier's on a real errand, while at the same time he might be able to satisfy his curiosity.

Gauthier was alone in the shop.

'*Bonjour*, M. Gauthier!' said Tom.

'*Bonjour*, M. Reepley!' Gauthier replied, smiling. 'And how are you?'

'Very well, thank you, and you? – I find I need some zinc white.'

'Zinc white.' Gauthier pulled a flat drawer from his cabinet against a wall. 'Here they are. And you like the Rembrandt, as I recall.'

Tom did. Derwatt zinc white and other Derwatt-made colours were available, too, their tubes emblazoned with the bold, downward slanting signature of Derwatt in black on the label, but somehow Tom did not want to paint at home with the name Derwatt catching his eye every time he reached for a tube of anything. Tom paid, and as Gauthier was handing him his change and the little bag with the zinc white in it. Gauthier said:

'Ah, M. Reepley, you recall M. Trevanny, the framer of the Rue St Merry?'

'Yes, of course,' said Tom who had been wondering how to bring Trevanny up.

'Well, the rumour that you heard, that he is going to die soon, is not true at all.' Gauthier smiled.

'No? Well, very good! I'm glad to hear that.'

'Yes. M. Trevanny went to see his doctor even. I think he was a bit upset. Who wouldn't be, eh? Ha-ha! – But you said somebody told *you*, M. Reepley?'

'Yes. A man who was at the party – in February. Mme Trevanny's birthday party. So I assumed it was a fact and everybody knew it, you see.'

Gauthier looked thoughtful.

'You spoke to M. Trevanny?'

'No – no. But I did speak to his best friend one evening, another evening at the Trevannys' house, this month. Evidently he spoke to M. Trevanny. How these things get around!'

'His best friend?' Tom asked with an air of innocence.

'An Englishman. Alain something. He was going to America next day. But – do you recall who told *you*, M. Reepley?'

Tom shook his head slowly. 'Can't recall his name and not even how he looked. There were so many people that night.'

'Because – ' Gauthier bent closer and whispered, as if there were someone else present. 'M. Trevanny asked *me*, you see, who had told me, and of course I didn't say it was *you*. These things can be misinterpreted. I didn't want to get *you* into trouble. Ha !' Gauthier's shiny glass eye did not laugh but looked out from his head with a bold stare, as if there were a different brain from Gauthier's behind that eye, a computer kind of brain that at once could know everything, if someone just set the programming.

'I thank you for that, because it is not nice to make remarks which are not true about people's health, eh ?' Tom was grinning now, ready to take his leave, but he added, 'M. Trevanny does have a blood condition, however, didn't you say ?'

'That is true. I think it's leukaemia. But that is something he lives with. He once told me he'd had it for years.'

Tom nodded. 'At any rate, I'm glad he's not in danger. *A bientôt*, M. Gauthier. Many thanks.'

Tom walked in the direction of his car. Trevanny's shock, though it may have lasted just a few hours until he consulted his doctor, must at least have put a little crack in his self-confidence. A few people had believed, and maybe Trevanny himself had believed, that he was not going to live more than a few weeks. That was because such a possibility wasn't out of the question for a man with Trevanny's ailment. A pity Trevanny was now reassured, but that little crack might be all that Reeves needed. The game could now enter its second stage. Trevanny would probably say no to Reeves. End of game, in that case. On the other hand Reeves would approach him as if of course he was a doomed man. It would be amusing if Trevanny weakened. That day after lunch with Heloise and her Paris friend Noëlle, who was going to stay overnight, Tom left the ladies and wrote a letter to Reeves on his typewriter.

March 28, 19—

Dear Reeves,

I have an idea for you, in case you have not yet found what you are looking for. His name is Jonathan Trevanny, early thirties, English, a picture-framer, married to Frenchwoman with small son. [Here Tom gave Trevanny's home and shop addresses and shop telephone number.] He looks as if he could use some money, and although he may not be the *type* you want, he looks the picture of decency and innocence, and what is more important for you, he has only a few more months or weeks to live, I have found out. He's got leukaemia, and has just heard the bad news. He might be willing to take on a dangerous job to earn some money now.

I don't know Trevanny personally, and need I emphasize that I don't wish to make his acquaintance, nor do I wish you to mention my name. My suggestion is, if you want to sound him out come to F'bleau, put yourself up at a charming hostelry called the Hôtel de L'Aigle Noir for a couple of days, contact Trevanny by ringing his shop, make an appointment and talk it over. And do I have to tell you to give another name besides your own?

Tom felt a sudden optimism about the project The vision of Reeves with his disarming air of uncertainty and anxiety – almost suggestive of probity – laying such an idea before Trevanny who looked as upright as a saint, made Tom laugh. Did he dare occupy another table in the Hôtel de L'Aigle Noir's dining-room or bar when Reeves made his date with Trevanny? No, that would be too much. This reminded Tom of another point, and he added to his letter:

If you come to F'bleau, please don't telephone or write a note to me under any circumstances. Destroy my letter here, please.

Yours ever,
Tom

4

The telephone rang in Jonathan's shop on Friday afternoon 31 March. He was just then gluing brown paper to the back of a large picture, and he had to find suitable weights – an old sandstone saying LONDON, the glue pot itself, a wooden mallet – before he could lift the telephone.

'Hello?'

'*Bonjour, m'sieur.* M. Trevanny? . . . You speak English, I think. My name is Stephen Wister, W-i-s-t-e-r. I'm in Fontainebleau for a couple of days, and I wonder if you could find a few minutes to talk with me about something – something that I think would interest you.'

The man had an American accent. 'I don't buy pictures,' Jonathan said. 'I'm a framer.'

'I didn't want to see you about anything connected with your work. It's something I can't explain over the phone. – I'm staying at the Aigle Noir.'

'Oh?'

'I was wondering if you have a few minutes this evening after you close your shop. Around seven? Six-thirty? We could have a drink or a coffee.'

'But – I'd like to know why you want to see me.' A woman had come into the shop – Mme Tissot, Tissaud? – to pick up a picture. Jonathan smiled apologetically to her.

'I'll have to explain when I see you,' said the soft, earnest voice. 'It'll take only ten minutes. Have you any time at seven today, for instance?'

Jonathan shifted. 'Six-thirty would be all right'

'I'll meet you in the lobby. I'm wearing a grey plaid suit. But I'll speak to the porter. It won't be difficult.'

Jonathan usually closed around 6.30 p.m. At 6.15 p.m., he stood at his cold-water sink, scrubbing his hands. It was a mild day and Jonathan had worn a polo-neck sweater with an old beige corduroy jacket, not elegant enough for l'Aigle Noir, and the addition of his second-best mac would have made things worse. Why should he care? The man wanted to sell him something. It couldn't be anything else.

The hotel was only a five-minute walk from the shop. It had a small front court enclosed by high iron gates, and a few steps led up to its front door. Jonathan saw a slender, tense-looking man with crew-cut hair move towards him with a faint uncertainty, and Jonathan said:

'Mr Wister?'

'Yes.' Reeves gave a twitch of a smile and extended his hand. 'Shall we have a drink in the bar here, or do you prefer somewhere else?'

The bar here was pleasant and quiet. Jonathan shrugged. 'As you like.' He noticed an awful scar the length of Wister's cheek.

They went to the wide door of the hotel's bar, which was empty except for one man and woman at a small table. Wister turned away as if put off by the quietude, and said:

'Let's try somewhere else.'

They walked out of the hotel and turned right. Jonathan knew the next bar, the Café du Sport or some such, roistering at this hour with boys at the pinball machines and workmen at the counter, and on the threshold of the bar-café Wister stopped as if he had come unexpectedly upon a battlefield in action.

'Would you mind,' Wister said, turning away, 'coming up to my room? It's quiet and we can have something sent up.'

They went back to the hotel, climbed one flight of stairs, and entered an attractive room in Spanish décor – black ironwork, a raspberry-coloured bedspread, a pale green carpet. A suitcase on the rack was the only sign of the room's occupancy. Wister had entered without a key.

'What'll you have?' Wister went to the telephone. 'Scotch?'

'Fine.'

The man ordered in clumsy French. He asked for the bottle to be brought up, and for plenty of ice, please.

Then there was a silence. Why was the man uneasy, Jonathan wondered. Jonathan stood by the window where he had been looking out. Evidently Wister didn't want to talk until the drinks arrived. Jonathan heard a discreet tap at the door.

A white-jacketed waiter came in with a tray and a friendly smile. Stephen Wister poured generous drinks.

'Are you interested in making some money?'

Jonathan smiled, settled in a comfortable armchair now, with the huge iced scotch in his hand. 'Who isn't?'

'I have a dangerous job in mind – well, an important job – for which I'm prepared to pay quite well.'

Jonathan thought of drugs: the man probably wanted something delivered, or held. 'What business are you in?' Jonathan inquired politely.

'Several. Just now one you might call – gambling. Do you gamble?'

'No.' Jonathan smiled.

'I don't either. That's not the point.' The man got up from the side of the bed and walked slowly about the room. 'I live in Hamburg.'

'Oh?'

'Gambling isn't legal in city limits, but it goes on in private clubs. However, that's not the point, whether it's legal or not. I need one person eliminated, possibly two, and possibly a theft – to be done. Now that's putting my cards on the table.' He looked at Jonathan with a serious, hopeful expression.

Killed, the man meant. Jonathan was startled, then he smiled and shook his head. 'I wonder where you got my name!'

Stephen Wister didn't smile. 'Never mind that.' He continued walking up and down with his drink in his hand, and his grey eyes glanced at Jonathan and away again. 'I wonder if you're interested in ninety-six thousand dollars? That's forty thousand pounds, and about four hundred and eighty thousand francs – new francs. Just for shooting only one man, maybe two, we'll have to see how it goes. It'll be an arrangement that's safe and foolproof for you.'

Jonathan shook his head again. 'I don't know where you heard that I'm a – a gunman. You've got me confused with someone else.'

'No. Not at all.'

Jonathan's smile faded under the man's intense stare. 'It's a mistake . . . Do you mind telling me how you came to ring me?'

'Well, you're – ' Wister looked more pained than ever. 'You're not going to live more than a few weeks. You know that. You've got a wife and a small son – haven't you? Wouldn't you like to leave them a little something when you're gone?'

Jonathan felt the blood drain from his face. How did Wister know so much? Then he realized it was all connected, that whoever told Gauthier he was going to die soon knew this man, was connected with him somehow. Jonathan was not going to mention Gauthier. Gauthier was an honest man, and Wister was a crook. Suddenly Jonathan's scotch did not taste so good. 'There was a crazy rumour – recently – '

Now Wister shook his head. 'It is not a crazy rumour. It may be that your doctor hasn't told you the truth.'

'And you know more than my doctor? My doctor doesn't lie to me. It's true I have a blood disease, but – I'm in no worse a state now – ' Jonathan broke off. 'The essential thing is, I'm afraid I can't help you, Mr Wister.'

As Wister bit on his underlip, the long scar moved in a distasteful way, like a live worm.

Jonathan looked away from him. Was Dr Perrier lying after all? Jonathan thought he should ring up the Paris laboratory tomorrow morning and ask some questions, or simply go to Paris and demand another explanation.

'Mr Trevanny, I'm sorry to say it's you who aren't informed, evidently. At least you've heard what you call the rumour, so I'm not the bearer of bad tidings. It's a matter for your own free choice, but under the circumstances, a considerable sum like this, I would think, sounds rather pleasant. You could stop working and enjoy your – Well, for instance, you could take a cruise around the world with your family and still leave your wife . . .'

Jonathan felt slightly faint, and stood up and took a deep breath. The sensation passed, but he preferred to be on his feet. Wister was talking, but Jonathan barely listened.

' . . . my idea. There're a few men in Hamburg who would contribute towards the ninety-six thousand dollars. The man or men we want out of the way are Mafia men.'

Jonathan had only half recovered. 'Thanks, I am not a killer. You may as well get off the subject.'

Wister went on. 'But exactly what we want is someone not connected with any of us, or with Hamburg. Although the first man, only a button man, must be shot in Hamburg. The reason is, we want the police to think that two Mafia gangs are fighting each other in Hamburg. In fact, we want the police to step in on our side.' He continued to walk up and down, looking at the floor mostly. 'The first man ought to be shot in a crowd, a U-Bahn crowd. That's our subway, underground you'd call it. The gun would be dropped at once, the – the assassin blends into the crowd and vanishes. An Italian gun, with no fingerprints on it. No clues.' He brought his hands down like a conductor finishing.

Jonathan moved back to the chair, in need of it for a few seconds. 'Sorry. No.' He would walk to the door, as soon as he got his strength back.

'I'm here all tomorrow, and probably till late Sunday afternoon. I wish you'd think about it. – Another scotch? Might do you good.'

'No, thanks.' Jonathan hauled himself up. 'I'll be pushing off.'

Wister nodded, looking disappointed.

'And thanks for the drink.'

'Don't mention it.' Wister opened the door for Jonathan.

Jonathan went out. He had expected Wister to press a card with his name and address into his hand. Jonathan was glad he hadn't.

The street lights had come on in the Rue de France. 7.22 p.m. Had Simone asked him to buy anything? Bread, perhaps. Jonathan went into a boulangerie and bought a long stick. The familiar chore was comforting.

The supper consisted of a vegetable soup, a couple of slices of leftover *fromage de tête*, a salad of tomatoes and onions. Simone talked about a wallpaper sale at a shop near where she worked. For a hundred francs, they could paper the bedroom, and she had seen a beautiful mauve and green pattern, very light and art nouveau.

'With only one window that bedroom's very dark, you know, Jon.'

'Sounds fine,' Jonathan said. 'Especially if it's a sale.'

'It *is* a sale. Not one of these silly sales where they reduce something five per cent – like my stingy boss.' She wiped bread-crust in her salad oil and popped it into her mouth. 'You're worried about something? Something happened today?'

Jonathan smiled suddenly. He wasn't worried about anything. He was glad Simone hadn't noticed he was a little late, and that he'd had a big drink. 'No, darling. Nothing happened. The end of the week, maybe. Almost the end.'

'You feel tired?'

It was like a question from a doctor, routine now. 'No . . . I've got to telephone a customer tonight between eight and nine.' It was 8.37 p.m. 'I may as well do it now, my dear. Maybe I'll have some coffee later.'

'Can I go with you?' Georges asked, dropping his fork, sitting back ready to leap out of his chair.

'Not tonight, *mon petit vieux*. I'm in a hurry. And you just want to play the pinball machines, I know you.'

'Hollywood Chewing Gum!' Georges shouted, pronouncing it in the French manner : *'Ollyvoo Schvang Gom!'*

Jonathan winced as he lifted his jacket from the hall hook. Hollywood Chewing Gum, whose green and white wrappers littered the gutters and occasionally Jonathan's garden, had mysterious attractions for infants of the French nation. *'Oui, m'sieur,'* Jonathan said, and went out the door.

Dr Perrier had a home number in the directory, and Jonathan hoped he was in tonight. A certain *tabac*, which had a telephone, was closer than Jonathan's shop. A panic was taking hold of Jonathan, and he began to trot towards the slanted lighted red cylinder that marked the *tabac* two streets away. He would insist on the truth. Jonathan nodded a greeting to the young man behind the bar, whom he knew slightly, and pointed to the telephone and also to the shelf where the directories lay. *'Fontainebleau!'* Jonathan shouted. The place was noisy, with a juke box going besides. Jonathan searched out the number and dialled.

Dr Perrier answered, and recognized Jonathan's voice.

'I would like very much to have another test. Even tonight. Now – if you could take a sample.'

'Tonight?'

'I could come to see you at once. In five minutes.'

'Are you – You are weak?'

'Well – I thought if the test went to Paris tomorrow – ' Jonathan knew that Dr Perrier was in the habit of sending various samples to Paris on Saturday morning. 'If you could take a sample either tonight or early tomorrow morning – '

'I am not in my office tomorrow morning. I have visits to make. If you are so upset, M. Trevanny, come to my house now.'

Jonathan paid for his call, and remembered just before he went out the door to buy two packages of Hollywood Chewing Gum, which he dropped into his jacket pocket. Perrier lived way over on the Boulevard Maginot, which would take nearly ten minutes. Jonathan trotted and walked. He had never been to the doctor's home.

It was a big, gloomy building, and the concièrge was an old, slow, skinny woman watching television in a little glass-enclosed room full of plastic plants. While Jonathan waited for the lift to descend into the rickety cage, the concièrge crept into the hall and asked curiously:

'Your wife is having a baby, m'sieur?'

'No. No,' Jonathan said, smiling, and recalled that Dr Perrier was a general practitioner.

He rode up.

'Now what is the matter?' Dr Perrier asked, beckoning him through the dining-room. 'Come into this room.'

The house was dimly lighted. The television set was on somewhere. The room they went into was like a little office, with medical books on the shelves, and a desk on which the doctor's black bag now sat.

'*Mon dieu*, one would think you are on the brink of collapse and you've just been running, obviously, and your cheeks are pink. Don't tell me you've heard another rumour that you're on the edge of the grave!'

Jonathan made an effort to sound calm. 'It's just that I want to be sure. I don't feel so splendid, to tell the truth. I know it's been only two months since the last test but – since the next is due the end of April, what's the harm – ' He broke off, shrugging. 'Since it's easy to take some marrow, and since it can go off tomorrow early – ' Jonathan was aware that his French was clumsy at that moment, aware of the word *moelle*, marrow,

39

which had become revolting, especially when Jonathan thought of his as being abnormally yellow. He sensed Dr Perrier's attitude that he must humour his patient.

'Yes, I can take the sample. The result will probably be the same as last time. You can never have complete assurance from the medical men, M. Trevanny . . . ' The doctor continued to talk, while Jonathan removed his sweater, obeyed Dr Perrier's gesture and lay down on an old leather sofa. The doctor jabbed the anaesthetizing needle in. 'But I can appreciate your anxiety,' Dr Perrier said seconds later, pressing and tapping on the tube that was going into Jonathan's sternum.

Jonathan disliked the crunching sound of it, but found the slight pain quite bearable. This time, perhaps, he'd learn something. Jonathan could not refrain from saying, before he left, 'I must know the truth, Dr Perrier. You don't think, really, that the laboratory might not be giving us a proper summing up? I'm ready to believe their figures are correct –'

'This summing up or prediction is what you can't get, my dear young man!'

Jonathan then walked home. He had thought of telling Simone that he'd gone to see Perrier, that he again felt anxious, but Jonathan couldn't: he'd put Simone through enough. What could she say, if he told her? She would only become a little more anxious herself, like him.

Georges was already in bed upstairs, and Simone was reading to him. Astérix again. Georges, propped against his pillows, and Simone on a low stool under the lamplight, were like a tableau vivant of domesticity, and the year might have been 1880, Jonathan thought, except for Simone's slacks. Georges' hair was as yellow as cornsilk under the light.

'Le schvang gom?' Georges asked, grinning.

Jonathan smiled and produced one packet. The other could wait for another occasion.

'You were a long time,' said Simone.

'I had a beer at the café,' Jonathan said.

The next afternoon between 4.30 and 5 p.m., as Dr Perrier had told him to do, Jonathan telephoned the Ebberle-Valent Laboratoires in Neuilly. He gave his name and spelt it and said he was a patient of Dr Perrier's in Fontainebleau. Then he waited to be connected with the right department, while the telephone gave a *blup* every minute for the pay units. Jonathan had pen and paper ready. Could he spell his name again, please? Then a woman's voice began to read the report, and Jonathan jotted figures down quickly. Hyperleucocytose 190,000. Wasn't that bigger than before?

'We shall of course send a written report to your doctor which he should receive by Tuesday.'

'This report is less favourable than the last, is it not?'

'I have not the previous report here, *m'sieur.*'

'Is there a doctor there? Could I speak with a doctor, perhaps?'

'*I* am a doctor, *m'sieur.*'

'Oh. Then this report – whether you have the old one or not there, is not a good one, is it?'

Like a textbook, she said, 'This is a potentially dangerous condition involving lowered resistance . . .'

Jonathan had telephoned from his shop. He had turned his sign to FERME and drawn his door curtain, though he had been visible through the window, and now as he went to remove the sign, he realized he hadn't locked his door. Since no one else was due to call for a picture that afternoon, Jonathan thought he could afford to close. It was 4.55 p.m.

He walked to Dr Perrier's office, prepared to wait more than an hour if he had to. Saturday was a busy day, because most people didn't work and were free to see the doctor. There were three people ahead of Jonathan, but the nurse spoke to him and asked if he would be long, Jonathan said no, and the nurse squeezed him in with an apology to the next patient. Had Dr Perrier spoken to his nurse about him, Jonathan wondered?

Dr Perrier raised his black eyebrows at Jonathan's scribbled notes, and said, 'But this is incomplete.'

'I know, but it tells something, doesn't it? It's slightly worse – isn't it?'

'One would think you want to get worse!' Dr Perrier said with his customary cheer, which now Jonathan mistrusted. 'Frankly, yes, it is worse, but only a little worse. It is not crucial.'

'In percentage – ten per cent worse, would you say?'

'M. Trevanny – you are not an automobile! Now it is not

reasonable for me to make a remark until I get the full report on Tuesday.'

Jonathan walked homeward rather slowly, walked through the Rue des Sablons just in case he saw someone who wanted to go into his shop. There wasn't anyone. Only the launderette was doing a brisk business, and people with bundles of laundry were bumping into each other at the door. It was nearly 6 p.m. Simone would be quitting the shoe shop sometime after 7 p.m., later than usual, because her boss Brezard wanted to take in every franc possible before closing for Sunday and Monday. And Wister was still at l'Aigle Noir. Was he waiting only for him, waiting for him to change his mind and say yes? Wouldn't it be funny if Dr Perrier was in conspiracy with Stephen Wister, if between them they might have fixed the Ebberle-Valent Laboratories to give him a bad report? And if Gauthier were in on it, too, the little messenger of bad tidings? Like a nightmare in which the strangest elements join forces against – against the dreamer. But Jonathan knew he was not dreaming. He knew that Dr Perrier was not in the pay of Stephen Wister. Nor was Ebberle-Valent. And it was not a dream that his condition was worse, that death was a little closer, or sooner, than he had thought. True of everyone, however, who lived one more day, Jonathan reminded himself. Jonathan thought of death, and the process of ageing, as a decline, literally a downward path. Most people had a chance to take it slowly, starting at fifty-five or whenever they slowed up, descending until seventy or whatever year was their number. Jonathan realized that his death was going to be like falling over a cliff. When he tried to 'prepare' himself, his mind wavered and dodged. His attitude, or his spirit, was still thirty-four years old and wanted to live.

The Trevannys' narrow house, blue-grey in the dusk, showed no lights. It was a rather sombre house, and that fact had amused Jonathan and Simone when they had bought it five years ago. 'The Sherlock Holmes house', Jonathan had used to call it, when they were debating his house versus another in Fontainebleau. 'I still prefer the Sherlock Holmes house,' Jonathan remembered saying once. The house had an 1890 air, suggestive of gas lights and polished banisters, though none of the wood anywhere in the house had been polished when they had moved in. The house had looked as if it could be made into something with turn-of-the-century charm, however. The rooms were smallish but interestingly arranged, the garden a rectangular patch full of wildly overgrown rose bushes, but at least the rose bushes had been there, and all the garden had needed was a clearing out. And the scalloped glass portico over the back steps, its little glass enclosed porch, had made Jonathan think of Vuillard, and Bonnard. But now it struck Jonathan that five years of their occupancy hadn't really defeated the gloom. New wallpaper would brighten the bedroom, yes, but that was only one room. The house wasn't yet paid for : they had three more years to go on the mortgage. An apartment, such as they'd had in Fontainebleau in the first year of their marriage, would have been cheaper, but Simone was used to a house with a bit of garden – she'd had a garden all her life in Nemours – and as an Englishman, Jonathan liked a bit of garden too. Jonathan never regretted that the house took such a hunk of their income.

What Jonathan was thinking, as he climbed the front steps, was not so much of the remaining mortgage, but the fact that he was probably going to die in this house. More than likely, he would never know another, more cheerful house with Simone. He was thinking that the Sherlock Holmes house had been standing for decades before he had been born, and that it would stand for decades after his death. It had been his fate to choose this house, he felt. One day they would carry him out feet first, maybe still alive but dying, and he would never enter the house again.

To Jonathan's surprise, Simone was in the kitchen, playing some kind of card game with Georges at the table. She looked up, smiling, then Jonathan saw her remember : he was to have rung the Paris laboratory this afternoon. But she couldn't mention that in front of Georges.

'The old creep closed early today,' Simone said 'No business.'

'Good!' Jonathan said brightly. 'What goes on in this gambling den?'

'I'm winning!' Georges said in French.

Simone got up and followed Jonathan into the hall as he hung his raincoat. She looked at him inquiringly.

'Nothing to worry about,' Jonathan said, but she beckoned

him farther down the hall to the living-room. 'It seems to be a trifle worse, but I don't feel worse, so what the hell? I'm sick of it. Let's have a Cinzano.'

'You were worried because of that story, weren't you, Jon?'

'Yes. That's true.'

'I wish I knew who started that.' Her eyes narrowed bitterly. 'It's a nasty story. Gauthier never told you who said it?'

'No. As Gauthier said, it was some mistake somewhere, some kind of exaggeration.' Jonathan was repeating what he had said to Simone before. But he knew it was no mistake, that it was a story quite calculated.

5

Jonathan stood at the first-floor bedroom window, watching Simone hang the wash on the garden line. There were pillow-cases, Georges' sleep suits, a dozen pairs of Georges' and Jonathan's socks, two white nightdresses, bras, Jonathan's beige work trousers – everything except sheets, which Simone sent to the laundry, because well-ironed sheets were important to her. Simone wore tweed slacks and a thin red sweater that clung to her body. Her back looked strong and supple as she bent over the big oval basket, pegging out dishcloths now. It was a fine, sunny day with a hint of summer in the breeze.

Jonathan had wriggled out of going to Nemours to have lunch with Simone's parents, the Foussadiers. He and Simone went every other Sunday as a rule. Unless Simone's brother Gérard fetched them, they took the bus to Nemours. Then at the Foussadiers' home, they had a big lunch with Gérard and his wife and two children, who also lived in Nemours. Simone's parents always made a fuss over Georges, always had a present for him. Around 3 p.m., Simone's father Jean-Noël would turn on the TV. Jonathan was frequently bored, but he went with Simone because it was the correct thing to do, and because he respected the closeness of French families.

'Do you feel all right?' Simone had asked, when Jonathan had begged out.

'Yes, darling. It's just that I'm not in the mood today, and I'd also like to get that patch ready for the tomatoes. So why don't you go with Georges?'

So Simone and Georges went on the bus at noon. Simone had put the remains of a *bœuf bourguignon* into a small red casserole on the stove, so all Jonathan had to do was heat it when he felt hungry.

Jonathan had wanted to be alone. He was thinking about the

mysterious Stephen Wister and his proposal. Not that Jonathan meant to telephone Wister today at l'Aigle Noir, though Jonathan was very much aware that Wister was still there, not three hundred yards away. He had no intention of getting in touch with Wister, though the idea was curiously exciting and disturbing, a bolt from the blue, a shaft of colour in his uneventful existence, and Jonathan wanted to observe it, to enjoy it in a sense. Jonathan also had the feeling (it had been proven quite often) that Simone could read his thoughts, or at least knew when something was preoccupying him. If he appeared absent-minded that Sunday, he didn't want Simone to notice it and ask him what was the matter. So Jonathan gardened with a will, and day-dreamed. He thought of forty thousand pounds, a sum which meant the mortgage paid off at once, a couple of hire-purchase items paid off, the interior of his house painted where it needed to be painted, a television set, a nest-egg put aside for Georges' university, a few new clothes for Simone and himself – ah, mental ease! Simply freedom from anxiety! He thought of one, maybe two Mafia figures – burly, dark-haired thugs exploding in death, arms flailing, their bodies falling. What Jonathan was incapable of imagining, as his spade sank into the earth of his garden, was himself pulling a trigger, having aimed a gun at a man's back, perhaps. More interesting, more mysterious, more dangerous, was how Wister had got hold of his name. There was a plot against him in Fontainebleau, and it had somehow got to Hamburg. Impossible that Wister had him mixed up with someone else, because even Wister had spoken of his illness, of his wife and small son. Someone, Jonathan thought, who he considered a friend or at least a friendly acquaintance, was not friendly at all towards him.

Wister would probably leave Fontainebleau around 5 p.m. today, Jonathan thought. By 3 p.m., Jonathan had eaten his lunch, tidied up papers and old receipts in the catch-all drawer of the round table in the centre of the living-room. Then – he was happily aware that he was not tired at all – he tackled with broom and dustpan the exterior of the pipes and the floor around their *mazout* furnace.

A little after 5 p.m., as Jonathan was scrubbing soot from his hands at the kitchen sink, Simone arrived with Georges and

46

her brother Gérard and his wife Yvonne, and they all had a drink in the kitchen. Georges had been presented by his grandparents with a round box of Easter goodies including an egg wrapped in gold foil, a chocolate rabbit, coloured gumdrops, all under yellow cellophane and as yet unopened, because Simone forbade him to open it, in view of the other sweets he had eaten in Nemours. Georges went with the Foussadier children into the garden.

'Don't step on the soft part, Georges!' Jonathan shouted. He had raked the turned ground smooth, but left the pebbles for Georges to pick up. Georges would probably get his two chums to help him fill the red wagon. Jonathan gave him fifty centimes for a wagonful of pebbles – not ever full, but full enough to cover the bottom.

It was starting to rain. Jonathan had taken the laundry in a few minutes ago.

'The garden looks marvellous!' Simone said. 'Look, Gérard!' She beckoned her brother on to the little back porch.

By now, Jonathan thought, Wister was probably on a train from Fontainebleau to Paris, or maybe he'd take a taxi from Fontainebleau to Orly, considering the money he seemed to have. Maybe he was already in the air, *en route* to Hamburg. Simone's presence, the voices of Gérard and Yvonne, seemed to erase Wister from the Hôtel de l'Aigle Noir, at any rate, seemed to turn Wister almost into a quirk of Jonathan's imagination. Jonathan felt also a mild triumph in the fact that he had not telephoned Wister, as if by not telephoning him he had successfully resisted some kind of temptation.

Gérard Foussadier, an electrician, was a neat, serious man a little older than Simone, with fairer hair than hers, and a carefully clipped brown moustache. His hobby was naval history, and he made model nineteenth-century and eighteenth-century frigates in which he installed miniature electric lights that he could put completely or partially on by a switch in his living-room. Gérard himself laughed at the anachronism of electric lights in his frigates, but the effect was beautiful when all the other lights in the house were turned out. and eight or ten ships seemed to be sailing on a dark sea around the living-room.

'Simone said you were a little worried – as to your health, Jon,' Gérard said earnestly. 'I am sorry.'

'Not particularly. Just another check-up,' Jonathan said. 'The report's about the same.' Jonathan was used to these clichés, which were like saying, 'Very well, thank you,' when someone asked you how you felt. What Jonathan said seemed to satisfy Gérard, so evidently Simone had not said much.

Yvonne and Simone were talking about linoleum. The kitchen linoleum was wearing out in front of the stove and the sink. It hadn't been new when they bought the house.

'You're really feeling all right, darling?' Simone asked Jonathan, when the Foussadiers had left.

'Better than all right. I even attacked the boiler-room. The soot.' Jonathan smiled.

'You are mad. – Tonight you'll have a decent dinner at least. Mama insisted that I bring home three *paupiettes* from lunch and they're delicious!'

Then close to 11 p.m., as they were about to go to bed, Jonathan felt a sudden depression, as if his legs, his whole body had sunk into something viscous – as if he were walking hip-deep in mud. Was he simply tired? But it seemed more mental than physical. He was glad when the light was turned out, when he could relax with his arms around Simone, her arms around him, as they always lay when they fell asleep. He thought of Stephen Wister (or was that his real name?) maybe flying eastward now, his thin figure stretched out in an aeroplane seat. Jonathan imagined Wister's face with the pinkish scar, puzzled, tense, but Wister would no longer be thinking of Jonathan Trevanny. He'd be thinking of someone else. He must have two or three more prospects, Jonathan thought.

The morning was chill and foggy. Just after 8 a.m., Simone went off with Georges to the Ecole Maternelle, and Jonathan stood in the kitchen, warming his fingers on a second bowl of *café au lait*. The heating system wasn't adequate. They'd got rather uncomfortably through another winter, and even now in spring the house was chilly in the mornings. The furnace had been in the house when they bought it, adequate for the five radiators downstairs, but not for the other five upstairs which they had installed hopefully. They'd been warned, Jonathan remembered, but a bigger furnace would have cost three thousand new francs, and they hadn't had the money.

Three letters had fallen through the slot in the front door. One was an electricity bill. Jonathan turned a square white envelope over and saw Hôtel de l'Aigle Noir on its back. He opened the envelope. A business card fell out and dropped. Jonathan picked it up and read 'Stephen Wister chez', which had been written above:

Reeves Minot
159 Agnesstrasse
Winterhude (Alster)
Hamburg 56
629–6757

There was a letter also.

1 Apr. 19—

Dear Mr Trevanny,

I was sorry not to hear from you this morning or so far this afternoon. But in case you change your mind, I enclose a card with my address in Hamburg. If you have second thoughts about my proposition, please telephone me collect at any hour. Or come to talk to me in Hamburg. Your round-trip transportation can be wired to you at once when I hear from you.

In fact, wouldn't it be a good idea to see a Hamburg specialist about your blood condition and get another opinion? This might make you feel more comfortable.

I am returning to Hamburg Sunday night,

Yours sincerely,
Stephen Wister

Jonathan was surprised, amused, annoyed all at once. *More comfortable.* That was a bit funny, since Wister was sure he was going to die soon. If a Hamburg specialist said, '*Ach, ja,* you have just one or two more months,' would that make him feel more comfortable? Jonathan pushed the letter and the card into a back pocket of his trousers. A return trip to Hamburg gratis. Wister was thinking of every enticement. Interesting that he'd sent the letter Saturday afternoon, so he would receive it early Monday, though Jonathan might have rung him at any time Sunday. But there was no collection from post boxes in town on Sunday.

49

It was 8.52 a.m. Jonathan thought of what he had to do. He needed more mat paper from a firm in Melun. There were at least two clients he should write a postcard to, because their pictures had been ready for more than a week. Jonathan usually went to his shop on Mondays, and spent his time doing odds and ends, though the shop was not open, as it was against French law to be open six days a week.

Jonathan got to his shop at 9.15 a.m., drew the green shade of his door, and locked the door again, leaving the FERME sign in it. He pottered about, thinking still about Hamburg. The opinion of a German specialist might be a good thing. Two years ago Jonathan had consulted a specialist in London. His report had been the same as the French, which had satisfied Jonathan that the diagnoses were true. Mightn't the Germans be a little more thorough or up to date? Suppose he accepted Wister's offer of a round trip? (Jonathan was copying an address on to a postcard.) But then he'd be beholden to Wister. Jonathan realized he was toying with the idea of killing someone for Wister – not for Wister, but for the money. A Mafia member. They were all criminals themselves, weren't they? Of course, Jonathan reminded himself, he could always pay Wister back, if he accepted his round-trip fare. The point was, Jonathan couldn't pull the money out of the bank funds just now, there wasn't enough. If he really wanted to make sure of his condition, Germany (or Switzerland for that matter) could tell him. They still had the best doctors in the world, hadn't they? Jonathan was now putting the card of the paper supplier of Melun beside his telephone to remind him to ring tomorrow, because the paper place wasn't open today either. And who knew, mightn't Stephen Wister's proposal be feasible? For an instant, Jonathan saw himself blown to bits by the crossfire of German police officers : they'd caught him just after he fired on the Italian. But even if he were dead, Simone and Georges would get the forty thousand quid. Jonathan came back to reality. He wasn't going to kill anybody, no. But Hamburg, going to Hamburg seemed a lark, a break, even if he learned some awful news there. He'd learn *facts*, anyway. And if Wister paid now, Jonathan could pay him back in a matter of three months, if he scrimped, didn't buy any clothes, not even a beer in a café. Jonathan rather dreaded telling Simone, though she'd agree, of course, since it had to do with seeing another doctor, presumably an excellent doctor. The scrimping would come out of Jonathan's own pocket.

Around 11 a.m., Jonathan put in a call to Wister's number in Hamburg, direct, not collect. Three or four minutes later, his telephone rang, and Jonathan had a clear connection, much better than Paris usually sounded.

' . . . Yes, this is Wister,' Wister said in his light, tense voice.

'I had your letter this morning,' Jonathan began. 'The idea of going to Hamburg – '

'Yes, why not?' said Wister casually.

'But I mean the idea of seeing a specialist – '

'I'll cable you the money right away. You can pick it up at the Fontainebleau post office. It should be there in a couple of hours.'

'That's – that's kind of you. Once I'm there, I can – '

'Can you come today? This evening? There's room here for you to stay.'

'I don't know about today.' And yet, why not?

'Call me again when you've got your ticket. Tell me what time you're coming in. I'll be in all day.'

Jonathan's heart was beating a little fast when he hung up.

At home during lunch-time, Jonathan went upstairs to the bedroom to see if his suitcase was handy. It was, on top of the wardrobe where it had been since their last holiday, nearly a year ago, in Arles.

He said to Simone, 'Darling, something important. I've decided to go to Hamburg and see a specialist.'

'Oh, yes? – Perrier suggested it?'

'Well – in fact, no. My idea. I wouldn't mind having a German doctor's opinion. I know it's an expense.'

'Oh, Jon! Expense! – Did you have any news this morning? But the laboratory report comes tomorrow, doesn't it?'

'Yes. What they say is always the same, darling. I want a fresh opinion.'

'When do you want to go?'

'Soon. This week.'

Just before 5 p.m. Jonathan called at the Fontainebleau post office. The money had arrived. Jonathan presented his *carte*

51

d'identité and received six hundred francs. He went from the post office to the Syndicat d'Initiatives in the Place Franklin Roosevelt, just a couple of streets away, and bought a round-trip ticket to Hamburg on a plane that left Orly airport at 9.25 p.m. that evening. He would have to hurry, he realized, and he liked that, because it precluded thinking, hesitating. He went to his shop and telephoned Hamburg, this time collect.

Wister again answered. 'Oh, that's fine. At eleven fifty-five, right. Take the airport bus to the city terminus, would you? I'll meet you there.'

Then Jonathan made one telephone call to a client who had an important picture to pick up, to say that he would be closed Tuesday and Wednesday for 'reasons of family', a common excuse. He'd have to leave a sign to that effect in his door for a couple of days. Not a very important matter, Jonathan thought, since shopkeepers in town frequently closed for a few days for one reason or another. Jonathan had once seen a sign saying 'closed due to hangover'.

Jonathan shut up shop and went home to pack It would be a two-day stay at most, he thought, unless the Hamburg hospital or whatever insisted that he stay longer for tests. He had checked the trains to Paris, and there was one around 7 p.m. that would do nicely. He had to get to Paris, then to Les Invalides for a bus to Orly. When Simone came home with Georges, Jonathan had his suitcase downstairs.

'Tonight?' Simone said.

'The sooner the better, darling. I had an impulse. I'll be back Wednesday, maybe even tomorrow night.'

'But – where can I reach you? You arranged for a hotel?'

'No. I'll have to telegraph you, darling. Don't worry.'

'You've got everything arranged with the doctor? Who is the doctor?'

'I don't know yet. I've only heard of the hospital.' Jonathan dropped his passport, trying to stick it into the inside pocket of his jacket.

'I never saw you like this,' said Simone.

Jonathan smiled at her. 'At least – obviously I'm not collapsing!'

Simone wanted to go with him to the Fontainebleau-Avon

station, and take the bus back, but Jonathan begged her not to.
'I'll telegraph right away,' Jonathan said.
'Where is Hamburg?' Georges demanded for the second time.
'*Allemagne!* – Germany!' Jonathan said.

Jonathan found a taxi in the Rue de France, luckily. The train was pulling into the Fontainebleau-Avon station as he arrived, and he barely had time to buy his ticket and hop on. Then it was a taxi from the Gare de Lyon to Les Invalides. Jonathan had some money left over from the six hundred francs. For a while, he was not going to worry about money.

On the plane, he half slept, with a magazine in his lap. He was imagining being another person. The rush of the plane seemed to be rushing this new person away from the man left behind in the dark grey house in the Rue St Merry. He imagined another Jonathan helping Simone with the dishes at this moment, chatting about boring things such as the price of linoleum for the kitchen floor.

The plane touched down. The air was sharp and much colder. There was a long lighted motorway, then the city's streets, massive buildings looming up into the night sky, street lights of different colour and shape from those of France.

And there was Wister smiling, walking towards him with his hand extended. 'Welcome, Mr Trevanny! Had a good trip? . . . My car is just outside. Hope you didn't mind coming to the terminus. My driver – not my driver but one I use sometimes – he was tied up till just a few minutes ago.'

They were walking out to the kerb. Wister droned on in his American accent. Except for his scar, nothing about Wister suggested violence. He was, Jonathan decided, too calm, which from a psychiatric point of view might be ominous. Or was he merely nursing an ulcer? Wister stopped beside a well-polished black Mercedes-Benz. An older man, wearing no cap, took care of Jonathan's medium-sized suitcase, and held the door for him and Wister.

'This is Karl,' Wister said.

'Evening,' Jonathan said.

Karl smiled, and murmured something in German.

It was quite a long drive. Wister pointed out the Rathaus, 'the oldest in all Europe, and the bombs didn't get it,' and a great church or cathedral whose name Jonathan didn't get. He and Wister were sitting together in the back. They entered a part of the town with a more countrylike atmosphere, went over still another bridge, and on to a darker road.

'Here we are,' Wister said. 'My place.'

The car had turned into a climbing driveway and stopped beside a large house with a few lighted windows and a lighted, well-kept entrance.

'It's an old house with four flats, and I have one,' Wister explained. 'Lots of such houses in Hamburg. Converted. Here I have a nice view of the Alster. It's the Aussen Alster, the big one. You'll see more tomorrow.'

They rode up in a modern lift, Karl taking Jonathan's suitcase. Karl pressed a bell, and a middle-aged woman in a black dress and white apron opened the door, smiling.

'This is Gaby,' said Wister to Jonathan. 'My part-time housekeeper. She works for another family in the house and sleeps with them, but I told her we might want some food tonight. Gaby, Herr Trevanny aus Frankreich.'

The woman greeted Jonathan pleasantly, and took his coat. She had a round, pudding-like face, and looked the soul of goodwill.

'Wash in here, if you like,' said Wister, gesturing to a bathroom whose light was already on. 'I'll get you a scotch. Are you hungry?'

When Jonathan came out of the bathroom, the lights – four lamps – were on in the big square living-room. Wister was sitting on a green sofa, smoking a cigar. Two scotches stood on the coffee-table in front of Wister. Gaby came in at once with a tray of sandwiches and a round, pale-yellow cheese.

'Ah, thank you, Gaby.' Wister said to Jonathan, 'Late for Gaby, but when I told her I had a guest coming, she insisted on staying on to serve the sandwiches.' Wister, though making a cheerful remark, still didn't smile. In fact his straight eyebrows drew together anxiously as Gaby arranged the plates and the silverware. When she departed, he said, 'You're feeling all right? Now the main thing is – the visit to the specialist I have a good man in mind, Dr Heinrich Wentzel, a haematologist at the Eppendorfer Krankenhaus, which is the main hospital here. World famous. I've made an appointment for you for tomorrow at two, if that's agreeable.'

'Certainly. Thank you,' Jonathan said.

'That gives you a chance to catch up on your sleep. Your wife didn't mind too much, I hope, your taking off on such short notice? . . . After all it's only intelligent to consult more than one doctor about a serious ailment . . .'

Jonathan was only half listening. He felt dazed, and he was also a bit distracted by the décor, by the fact it was all supposed to be *German*, and that it was the first time he'd been in Germany. The furnishings were quite conventional and more modern than antique, though there was a handsome Biedermeier desk against the wall opposite Jonathan. There were low book-shelves along all the walls, long green curtains at the windows, and the lamps in corners spread the light pleasantly. A purple wooden box lay open on the glass coffee-table, presenting a variety of cigars and cigarettes in compartments. The white fire-place had brass accessories, but there was no fire now. A rather interesting painting which looked like a Derwatt hung over the fireplace. And where was Reeves Minot? Wister was Minot, Jonathan supposed. Was Wister going to announce this or assume that Jonathan realized it? It occurred to Jonathan that he and Simone ought to paint or paper their whole house white. He should discourage the idea of the art nouveau wallpaper in the bedroom. If they wanted to achieve more light, white was the logical –

' . . . You might've given some thought to the other proposition,' Wister was saying in his soft voice. 'The idea I was talking about in Fontainebleau.'

'I'm afraid I haven't changed my mind about that,' Jonathan said. 'And so this leads to – obviously I owe you six hundred francs.' Jonathan forced a smile. Already he felt the scotch, and as soon as he realized this, he nervously drank a little more from his glass. 'I can repay you within three months. The specialist is the essential thing for me now. First things first.'

'Of course,' said Wister. 'And you mustn't think about any repayment. That's absurd.'

Jonathan didn't want to argue, but he felt vaguely ashamed. More than anything, Jonathan felt odd, as if he were dreaming, or somehow not himself. It's only the foreignness of everything, he thought.

'This Italian we want eliminated,' Wister said, folding his hands behind his head and looking up at the ceiling, 'has a routine job. – Ha! That's funny! He only pretends it's a job with regular hours. He's hanging around the clubs off the Reeperbahn, pretending he has a taste for gambling, and he's pretending he has a job as a oenologist, and I'm sure he has a chum at the – whatever they call the wine factory here. He goes to the wine factory every afternoon, but he spends his evenings in one or another of the private clubs, playing the tables a little and seeing who he can meet. Mornings he sleeps, because he's up all night. Now the point is,' Wister said, sitting up, 'he takes the U-bahn every afternoon to get home, home being a rented flat. He's got a six-months lease and a real six-month job with the wine place to make it look legitimate. – Have a sandwich!' Wister extended the plate, as if he had just realized the sandwiches were there.

Jonathan took a tongue sandwich. There were also cole slaw and dill pickle.

'The important point is he gets off the U-bahn at the Steinstrasse station every day around six-fifteen by himself, looking like any other businessman coming back from the office. That's the time we want to get him.' Wister spread his bony hands palm downward. 'The assassin fires once if you can get the middle of his back, twice for sure maybe, drops the gun and – Bob's your uncle as the English say, isn't that right?'

The phrase was indeed familiar, out of the long ago past. 'If it's so easy, why do you need me?' Jonathan managed a polite smile. 'I'm an amateur to say the least. I'd botch it.'

Wister might not have heard. 'The crowd in the U-bahn *may* be rounded up. Some of them. Who can tell? Thirty, forty people maybe, if the cops get there fast enough. It's a huge station, the station for the main railway terminus. They might look people over. But suppose they look you over?' Wister shrugged. 'You'll have dropped the gun. You'll have used a thin stocking over your hand, and you'll drop the stocking a few seconds after you fire. No powder marks on you, no fingerprints on the gun. You have no connection with the man who's dead. Oh, it really won't come to all that. But one look at your French identity card, the fact of your appointment with Dr Wentzel, you're in the clear. My point is, *our* point, we don't want anyone connected with us or the clubs . . . '

Jonathan listened and made no comment. On the day of the shooting, he was thinking, he would have to be in a hotel, he could hardly be a house-guest of Wister, in case a policeman asked him where he was staying. And what about Karl and the housekeeper? Did they know anything about this? Were they trustworthy? *It's all a lot of nonsense*, Jonathan thought, and wanted to smile, but he wasn't smiling.

'You're tired,' Wister informed him. 'Want to see your room? Gaby already took your suitcase in.'

Fifteen minutes later, Jonathan was in pyjamas after a hot shower. His room had a window at the front of the house, like the living-room which had two windows on the front, and Jonathan looked out on a surface of water where there were lights along the near shore, and some red and green lights of tied-up boats. It looked dark, peaceful and spacious. A searchlight's beam swept protectively across the sky. His bed was a three-quarter width, neatly turned down. There was a glass of what looked like water on his bed-table and a package of Gitane *maïs*, his brand, and an ashtray and matches. Jonathan took a sip from the glass and found that it was indeed water.

6

Jonathan sat on the edge of his bed, sipping coffee which Gaby
had just brought. It was coffee the way he liked it, strong with a
dash of thick cream. Jonathan had awakened at 7 a.m., then gone
back to sleep until Wister had knocked on the door at 10.30 a.m.

'Don't apologize, I'm glad you slept,' said Wister. 'Gaby is
ready to bring you some coffee. Or do you prefer tea?'

Wister had also added that he had made a reservation for
Jonathan at the Hotel — Victoria was its name in English, anyway, where they would go before lunch. Jonathan thanked him.
No further conversation about the hotel. But that was the beginning, Jonathan thought, as he had thought last night. If he
were to carry out Wister's plan, he mustn't be a house-guest
here. Jonathan, however, felt glad he was going to be out from
under Wister's roof in a couple of hours.

A friend or acquaintance of Wister's named Rudolf something
arrived at noon. Rudolf was young and slender with straight
black hair, nervous and polite. Wister said he was a medical
student. Evidently he did not speak English. He reminded Jonathan of photographs of Franz Kafka. They all got into the car,
driven by Karl, and set off for Jonathan's hotel. Everything looked
so new compared to France, Jonathan thought, and then recalled
that Hamburg had been flattened by bombs. The car stopped in
a commercial-looking street. It was the Hotel Victoria.

'They all speak English,' Wister said. 'We'll wait for you.'

Jonathan went in. A bellhop had taken his suitcase at the door.
He registered, looking at his English passport to get the number
right. He asked for his suitcase to be sent up to his room, as
Wister had told him to do. The hotel was of middle category,
Jonathan saw.

Then they drove to a restaurant for lunch, where Karl did not
join them. They had a bottle of wine at their table before the

meal, and Rudolf became more merry. Rudolf spoke in German and Wister translated a few of his pleasantries. Jonathan was thinking of the hour 2 p.m., when he was due at the hospital.

'Reeves – ' said Rudolf to Wister.

Jonathan thought Rudolf had said it once before, and this time there was no mistake. Wister – Reeves Minot – took it calmly. And so did Jonathan.

'Anaemic,' said Rudolf to Jonathan.

'Worse.' Jonathan smiled.

'Schlimmer,' said Reeves Minot, and continued to Rudolf in German, which seemed to Jonathan as clumsy as his French, but was probably equally adequate.

The food was excellent, the portions enormous. Reeves had brought his cigars. But before they could finish the cigars, they had to leave for the hospital.

The hospital was a vast assembly of buildings set among trees and pathways lined with flowers. Karl had again driven them. The wing of the hospital where Jonathan had to go looked like a laboratory of the future – rooms on either side of a corridor as in a hotel, except that these rooms held chromium chairs or beds and were illuminated by fluorescent or variously coloured lamps. There was a smell not of disinfectant but as of some unearthly gas, somewhat resembling the smell Jonathan had known under the X-ray machine which five years ago had done him no good with the leukaemia. It was the kind of place where laymen surrendered utterly to the omniscient specialists, Jonathan thought, and at once he felt weak enough to faint. Jonathan was walking at that moment down a seemingly endless corridor of soundproofed floor surface with Rudolf, who was to interpret if Jonathan needed it. Reeves had remained in the car with Karl, but Jonathan was not sure if they were going to wait, or of how long the examination would take.

Dr Wentzel, a heavy man with grey hair and walrus moustaches, knew a little English, but he did not try to construct long sentences. 'How long?' Six years. Jonathan was weighed, asked if he had had any weight loss recently, stripped to the waist, his spleen palpated. All the while, the doctor murmured in German to a nurse who was taking notes. His blood pressure was taken, his eyelids looked at, urine and blood samples taken, finally the sternum marrow sample taken with a punch-like instrument that operated faster and with less discomfort than Dr Perrier's. Jonathan was told he could have the results tomorrow morning. The examination had taken only about forty-five minutes.

Jonathan and Rudolf walked out. The car was several yards away among some other cars in a parking area.

'How was it? . . . When will you know?' Reeves asked. 'Would you like to come back to my place or go to your hotel?'

'I think to my hotel, thanks.' Jonathan sank with relief into a corner seat of the car.

Rudolf seemed to be singing Wentzel's praises to Reeves. They arrived at the hotel.

'We'll pick you up for dinner,' said Reeves cheerfully. 'At seven.'

Jonathan got his key and went to his room. He took off his jacket and fell on to the bed face down. After two or three minutes, he pushed himself up and went to the writing desk. There was notepaper in a drawer. He sat down and wrote:

April 4, 19—

My dear Simone,

I have just had an examination and will know the results tomorrow morning. Very efficient hospital, doctor looking like Emp. Franz Josef, said to be the best haematologist in the world! Whatever the result tomorrow I shall feel more at ease knowing it. With luck I may be home tomorrow before you get this, unless Dr Wentzel wants to do some other tests.

Will telegraph now, just to say I am all right. I miss you, I think of you and Cailloux.

A bientôt with all my love,

Jon

Jonathan hung up his best suit, which was a dark blue, left the rest of his things in his suitcase, and went downstairs to post his letter. He had changed a ten-pound traveller's cheque, from an ancient book of three or four, last evening at the airport. He wrote a short telegram to Simone saying he was all right and that a letter was arriving. Then he went out, took note of the street's name and of the look of the neighbourhood – a huge

60

beer advertisement struck him most forcibly – then went out for a walk.

The pavements bustled with shoppers and pedestrians, with dachshunds on leads, with hawkers of fruit and newspapers at the corners. Jonathan gazed into a window full of beautiful sweaters. There was also a handsome blue-silk dressing-gown set off against a background of creamy white sheep pelts. He started to figure out its price in francs and gave it up, not being really interested. He crossed a busy avenue where there were both tramways and buses, came to a canal with a footbridge, and decided not to cross it. A coffee, perhaps. Jonathan approached a pleasant-looking coffee bar which had pastry in the window, a counter as well as small tables inside, and then could not bring himself to go in. He realized that he was terrified of what the report tomorrow morning would say. He had suddenly a hollow feeling with which he was familiar, a feeling of thinness as if he had become tissue paper, a coolness on his forehead as if his life itself were evaporating.

What Jonathan knew also, or at least suspected, was that tomorrow morning he would receive a phoney report. Jonathan mistrusted Rudolf's presence. A medical student. Rudolf had been no help, because he hadn't been needed. The doctor's nurse had spoken English. Mightn't Rudolf write up a phoney report tonight? Substitute it somehow? Jonathan even imagined Rudolf pinching hospital stationery that after-noon. Or maybe he was losing his mind, Jonathan warned him-self.

He turned back in the direction of his hotel, taking the shortest way possible. He reached the Victoria, claimed his key, and let himself into his room. Then he took his shoes off, went into the bathroom and wet a towel, and lay down with the towel across his forehead and his eyes. He did not feel sleepy, just somehow odd. Reeves Minot was odd. To advance a total stranger six hundred francs, to make the insane proposal that he had – promising more than forty thousand pounds. It couldn't be true. Reeves Minot would never deliver. Reeves Minot seemed to live in a world of fantasy. Maybe he wasn't even a crook, but merely a bit cracked, a type that lived on delusions of im-portance and power.

The telephone awakened Jonathan. A man's voice said in English :

'A chentleman waits on you below, sir.'

Jonathan looked at his watch and saw that it was a minute or two past 7 p.m. 'Would you tell him I'll be down in two minutes?'

Jonathan washed his face, put on a polo-neck sweater, then a jacket. He also took his topcoat.

Karl was alone with the car. 'You had a nice afternoon, sir?' he asked in English.

In the course of the small talk, Jonathan found that Karl had quite a vocabulary in English. How many other strangers had Karl ferried around for Reeves Minot, Jonathan wondered? What business did Karl think Reeves was in? Maybe it simply didn't matter to Karl. What business was Reeves supposed to be in?

Karl stopped the car in the sloping driveway again, and this time Jonathan took the lift alone to the second floor.

Reeves Minot, in grey flannels and a sweater, greeted Jonathan at the door. 'Come in! – Did you take it easy this afternoon?'

They had scotches. A table was set for two. and Jonathan assumed that they were going to be alone this evening.

'I would like you to see a picture of this man I have in mind,' Reeves said, hauling his thin form from the sofa, going to his Biedermeier desk. He took something from a drawer. He had two photographs, one a front view, the other a profile in a group of several people bending over a table.

The table was a roulette-table. Jonathan looked at the front-view picture, which was as clear as a passport photograph. The man looked about forty, with the square, fleshy face of lots of Italians, creases already curving from the flanges of his nose down to the level of his thick lips. His dark eyes looked wary, almost startled, yet in the faint smile there was an air also of 'So what've I done, eh?' Salvatore Bianca, Reeves said his name was.

'This picture,' Reeves said, pointing to the group picture, 'was taken in Hamburg about a week ago. He doesn't even gamble, just watches. This is a rare moment when he's looking at the wheel . . . Bianca's probably killed half a dozen men himself or he wouldn't even be a button man. But he's not important as a

Mafioso. He's expendable. Just to start the ball rolling, you see . . . ' Reeves went on, while Jonathan finished his drink, and Reeves made him another. 'Bianca wears a hat all the time – outdoors that is – a homburg. A tweed overcoat usually . . . '

Reeves had a gramophone, and Jonathan would have enjoyed some music, but felt it would have been rude to ask, though he could imagine Reeves flying to the gramophone to play precisely what he wanted. Jonathan interrupted finally, 'An ordinary-looking man, homburg pulled down and coat collar turned up – and one's supposed to spot him in a crowd after seeing these two pictures?'

'A friend of mine is going to ride the same underground from the Rathaus stop, where Bianca gets on, to the Messberg, which is the next stop and the only stop before the Steinstrasse. Look!'

This had set Reeves off again, and he showed Jonathan a street map of Hamburg which folded like an accordion and showed the U-bahn routes in blue dots.

'You'll get on the U-bahn with Fritz at the Rathaus. Fritz is coming over after dinner.'

I'm sorry to disappoint you, Jonathan wanted to say. He felt a twinge of guilt for having led Reeves on to this extent. Or had he led him on? No. Reeves had taken a crazy gamble. Reeves was probably used to such things, and he might not be the first person Reeves had approached. Jonathan was tempted to ask if he were the first person, but Reeves' voice droned on.

'There is definitely the possibility of a second shooting. I don't want to mislead you . . . '

Jonathan was glad of the bad side of it. Reeves had been presenting it all in a rosy light, the Bob's-your-uncle shooting followed by pockets full of money and a better life in France or wherever, a cruise around the world, the best of everything for Georges (Reeves had asked his son's name), a more secure life for Simone. *How would I ever explain all the lolly to her?* Jonathan wondered.

'This is *Aalsuppe*,' Reeves said, as he picked up his spoon. 'Specialty of Hamburg and Gaby loves to make it '

The eel soup was very good. There was an excellent cool Moselle.

'Hamburg has a famous zoo, you know. Hagenbeck's Tierpark

in Settlingen. A nice drive from here. We might go tomorrow morning. That is' – Reeves looked suddenly more troubled – 'if something doesn't turn up for me. I'm half-way expecting something. I should know by tonight or early tomorrow.'

One would have thought the zoo was an important matter. Jonathan said, 'Tomorrow morning I get the results from the hospital. I'm supposed to be there at eleven.' Jonathan felt a despair, as if 11 a.m. might be the hour of his death.

'Yes of course. Well, the zoo maybe in the afternoon. The animals are in a natural – natural habitat . . .'

Sauerbraten. Red cabbage.

The doorbell rang. Reeves did not get up, and in a moment Gaby came in and announced that Herr Fritz had arrived.

Fritz had a cap in his hand, and wore a rather shabby overcoat. He was about fifty.

'This is Paul,' said Reeves to Fritz, indicating Jonathan. 'An Englishman. Fritz.'

'Good evening,' Jonathan said.

Fritz gave a friendly wave to Jonathan. Fritz was a tough one, Jonathan thought, but he had an amiable smile.

'Sit down, Fritz,' said Reeves. 'Glass of wine? Scotch?' Reeves spoke in German. 'Paul is our man,' he added in English to Fritz. He handed Fritz a tall, stemmed glass of white wine.

Fritz nodded.

Jonathan was amused. The oversized wine glasses looked like something out of Wagnerian opera. Reeves was sitting sideways in his chair now.

'Fritz is a taxi-driver,' Reeves said. 'Taken Herr Bianca home many an evening, eh, Fritz?'

Fritz murmured something, smiling.

'Not many an evening, twice,' Reeves said. 'Sure, we don't – Reeves hesitated, as if not knowing in what language to speak, then continued to Jonathan, 'Bianca probably doesn't know Fritz by sight. It doesn't matter too much if he does, because Fritz gets off at Messberg. The point is, you and Fritz will meet outside the Rathaus U-bahn station tomorrow, and then Fritz will indicate our – our Bianca.'

Fritz nodded, apparently understanding everything.

Tomorrow now. Jonathan listened in silence.

'Now you both get on at the Rathaus stop, that'll be around six-fifteen. Best to be there just before six, because Bianca for some reason might be early, though he's pretty regular at six-fifteen. Karl will drive you, Paul, so there's nothing to worry about. You don't go anywhere near each other, you and Fritz, but it may be that Fritz has to get on the train, the same train as Bianca and you, in order to point him out definitely. In any case, Fritz gets off at Messberg, the next stop.' Then Reeves said something in German to Fritz and extended a hand.

Fritz produced from an inside pocket a small black gun and gave it to Reeves. Reeves looked at the door, as if anxious lest Gaby came in, but he didn't seem very anxious, and the gun was hardly bigger than his palm. After fumbling a little, Reeves got the gun open and peered at its cylinders.

'It's loaded. Has a safety. Here. You know a little about guns, Paul?'

Jonathan had a smattering. Reeves showed him, with assistance from Fritz. The safety, that was the important thing. Be sure how to get it off. This was the Italian gun.

Fritz had to leave. He said good-bye, nodding to Jonathan. *'Bis morgen! Um sechs!'*

Reeves walked with him to the door. Then Reeves came back from the hall with a brownish-red tweed topcoat, not a new coat. 'This is very loose,' he said. 'Try it on.'

Jonathan didn't want to try it on, but he got up and put the coat on. The sleeves were longish. Jonathan put his hands into the pockets, and found, as Reeves was now informing him, that the right-hand pocket was cut through. He was to carry the gun in his jacket pocket, and reach for it through the pocket of the coat, fire the gun preferably once and drop the gun.

'You'll see the crowd,' Reeves said, 'a couple of hundred people. You step back afterwards, like everybody else, recoiling from an explosion.' Reeves illustrated, his body leaning backward, walking backward.

They drank Steinhäger with their coffee. Reeves asked him about his home life, Simone, Georges. Did Georges speak English or only French?

'He's learning some English,' Jonathan said. 'I'm at a disadvantage, since I'm not with him a lot.'

7

Reeves telephoned Jonathan at his hotel the next morning just after 9 a.m. Karl would pick him up at 10.40 a.m. to drive him to the hospital. Rudolf would come along too. Jonathan had been sure of that.

'Good luck,' said Reeves. 'I'll see you later.'

Jonathan was downstairs in the lobby, reading a London *Times*, when Rudolf walked in a few minutes early. Rudolf was smiling a shy, mouselike smile, looking more like Kafka than ever.

'Morning, Herr Trevanny!' he said.

Rudolf and Jonathan got into the back of the big car.

'Luck with report!' said Rudolf pleasantly.

'I intend to speak with the doctor too,' said Jonathan just as pleasantly.

He was sure Rudolf understood this, but Rudolf looked a little confused and said, '*Wir werden versuchen –*'

Jonathan went with Rudolf into the hospital, though Rudolf had said he could fetch the report and also find out if the doctor was free. Karl had helpfully translated, so that Jonathan understood perfectly. Karl, in fact, seemed neutral, Jonathan thought, and probably was. The atmosphere to Jonathan was strange, however, as if everyone were acting, acting badly, even himself. Rudolf spoke with a nurse at a desk in the front hall, and asked for the report of Herr Trevanny.

The nurse looked at once in a box of sealed envelopes of various sizes, and produced one of business-letter size with Jonathan's name on it.

'And Dr Wentzel? Is it possible to see him?' Jonathan asked the nurse.

'Dr Wentzel?' She consulted a ledger with isinglass slots, pushed a button and lifted a telephone. Then she spoke in

German for a minute, put the telephone down and said to Jonathan in English, 'Dr Wentzel is busy all day today, his nurse says. Would you care to make an appointment for tomorrow morning at ten-thirty?'

'Yes, I would,' Jonathan said.

'Very good, I will make it. But his nurse says you will find a – a lot of information in the report.'

Then Jonathan and Rudolf walked back to the car. Rudolf was disappointed, Jonathan thought, or was he imagining? Anyway, Jonathan had the thick envelope in his hand, the genuine report.

In the car, Jonathan said, 'Excuse me,' to Rudolf, and opened the envelope. It was three typewritten pages, and Jonathan saw at a glance that many of the words were the same as the French and English terms he was familiar with. The last page, however, was two long paragraphs in German. There was the same long word for the yellow components. Jonathan's pulse faltered at 210,000 leucocytes, which was higher than the last French report, and higher than it had ever been. Jonathan did not struggle with the last page. As he refolded the sheets, Rudolf said something in a polite tone, extending his hand, and Jonathan handed him the report, hating it, and yet what else could he do, and what did it matter?

Rudolf told Karl to drive on.

Jonathan looked out the window. He had no intention of asking Rudolf to explain anything. Jonathan preferred to work it out with a dictionary, or to ask Reeves. Jonathan's ears began to ring, and he leaned back and made an effort to breathe deeply. Rudolf glanced at him and at once lowered a window.

Karl said over his shoulder, '*Meine Herrn*, Herr Minot expects you both to come to lunch. Then perhaps to the zoo.'

Rudolf gave a laugh and replied in German.

Jonathan thought of asking to be driven back to his hotel. But to do what? Stew over the report, not understanding all of it? Rudolf wanted to be let out somewhere. Karl dropped him beside a canal, and Rudolf extended his hand to Jonathan, shook Jonathan's hand firmly. Then Karl drove on to Reeves Minot's house. Sunlight twinkled on the Alster's water. Little boats bobbed gaily at anchor, and two or three boats were sailing about, simple and clean as brand-new toys.

Gaby opened the door for Jonathan. Reeves was on the telephone, but he soon finished.

'Hello, Jonathan! What's the news?'

'Not too good,' said Jonathan, blinking. The sunlight in the white room was dazzling.

'And the report? Can I see it? Can you understand all of it?'

'No – not all of it.' Jonathan handed the envelope to Reeves.

'You saw the doctor too?'

'He was busy.'

'Sit down, Jonathan. Maybe you could use a drink.' Reeves went to the bottles on one of his bookshelves.

Jonathan sat on the sofa and put his head back. He felt blank and discouraged, but at least not faint at the moment.

'A worse report than you've been getting from the French?' Reeves returned with a scotch and water.

'That's about it,' Jonathan said.

Reeves looked at the back page, the prose. 'You've got to watch out about minor wounds. That's interesting.'

And nothing new, Jonathan thought. He bled easily. Jonathan waited for Reeves' comment, in fact for Reeves' translation.

'Rudolf translated this for you?'

'No. But then I didn't ask him to.'

' " . . . cannot tell if this represents a worsened condition, not having seen a former – diagnosis . . . sufficiently dangerous in view of the length of time – *et cetera*". I'll go through it word for word, if you like,' said Reeves. 'One or two words I'll need the dictionary for, these compound words, but I've got the essentials.'

'Then just tell me the essentials.'

'I must say they might've written this out for you in English,' Reeves said, then scanned the page again. ' " . . . a considerable granulation of cells as well as – of the yellow – matter. As you have had X-ray treatment, this is not to be advised again at the moment, as the leukaemia cells become resistant to it . . . " '

Reeves went on for a few moments. There was no prediction of remaining time, Jonathan noticed, no hint of a deadline.

'Since you couldn't see Wentzel today, would you like me to try to make an appointment for you tomorrow?' Reeves sounded genuinely concerned.

'Thanks, but I made an appointment for tomorrow morning. Ten-thirty.'

'Good. And you said his nurse speaks English, so you don't need Rudolf. – Why don't you stretch out for a few minutes?' Reeves pulled a pillow to the corner of the sofa.

Jonathan lay back with one foot on the floor, the other foot dangling over the sofa's edge. He felt weak and drowsy, as if he could sleep for several hours. Reeves strolled towards the sunny window, talking about the zoo. He spoke of a rare animal – the name went out of Jonathan's mind as soon as he heard it – that had recently been sent from South America. A pair of them. Reeves said they must see these animals. Jonathan was thinking of Georges tugging his wagon of pebbles. *Cailloux.* Jonathan knew he would not live to see Georges much older, never by any means see him grow tall, hear his voice break. Jonathan sat up abruptly, clenched his teeth, and tried to will his strength back.

Gaby came in with a large tray.

'I asked Gaby to make a cold lunch, so we can eat whenever you feel up to it,' Reeves said.

They had cold salmon with mayonnaise. Jonathan could not eat much, but the brown bread and butter and the wine tasted good. Reeves was talking about Salvatore Bianca, of the Mafia's connection with prostitution, of their custom of employing prostitutes in their gambling establishments, and of taking 90 per cent of the girls' earnings from them. 'Extortion,' Reeves said. 'Money's their objective – terror's their method. See Las Vegas! For example, the Hamburg boys want *no* prostitutes,' Reeves said with an air of righteousness. 'Girls are there, a few, helping at the bar, for instance. Maybe they're available, but not on the premises, no indeed.' Jonathan was hardly listening, certainly not thinking about what Reeves was saying. He poked at his food, felt the blood rise to his cheeks, and held a quiet debate with himself. He would try the shooting. And it was not because he thought he was going to die in a few days or weeks, it was simply because the money was useful, because he wanted to give it to Simone and Georges. Forty thousand pounds, or ninety-six thousand dollars or – Jonathan supposed – only half of that, if there wasn't another shooting to do, or if he got caught on the first shooting.

'But you will, I think, won't you?' Reeves asked, wiping his lips on a crisp white napkin. He meant fire the gun this evening.

'If something happens to me,' Jonathan said, 'can you see that my wife gets the money?'

'But – ' Reeves' scar twitched as he smiled. 'What can happen? Yes, I'll see that your wife gets the money.'

'But if something does happen – if there's only one shooting – '

Reeves pressed his lips together as if he didn't like replying. 'Then it's half the money. – But there'll likely be two, to be honest. Full payment after the second. – But that's splendid!' He smiled, and it was the first time Jonathan had seen a real smile from him. 'You'll see how easy it is tonight. And later we'll celebrate – if you're in the mood.' He clapped his hands over his head, Jonathan thought as a gesture of jubilation, but it was a signal to Gaby.

Gaby arrived and took away the plates.

Twenty thousand pounds, Jonathan was thinking. Not so impressive, but better than a dead man with funeral expenses.

Coffee. Then the zoo. The animals Reeves had wanted him to see were two small bearlike creatures the colour of butterscotch. There was a small crowd in front of them, and Jonathan never got a good view. He was also not interested. Jonathan had a good view of some lions walking in apparent freedom. Reeves was concerned that Jonathan did not become tired. It was nearly 4 p.m.

Back at Reeves' house, Reeves insisted on giving Jonathan a tiny white pill which he called a 'mild sedative'.

'But I don't need a sedative,' Jonathan said. He felt quite calm, in fact, quite well.

'It's best. Please take my word for it.'

Jonathan swallowed the pill. Reeves told him to lie down in the guest-room for a few minutes. He did not fall asleep, and Reeves came in at 5 p.m. to say it would soon be time for Karl to drive him to his hotel. The topcoat was at Jonathan's hotel. Reeves gave him a cup of tea with sugar, which tasted all right, and Jonathan assumed there was nothing in it but tea. Reeves gave him the gun, and showed him the safety-catch again. Jonathan put the gun in his trousers pocket.

'See you tonight!' Reeves said cheerily.

Karl drove him to his hotel, and said he would wait. Jonathan supposed he had five or ten minutes. He brushed his teeth – with soap, because he'd left the toothpaste at home for Simone and Georges and hadn't bought any as yet – then lit a Gitane and stood looking out the window until he realized he wasn't seeing anything, wasn't even thinking of anything, and then he went to the closet and got the largish coat. The coat had been worn, but not much. Whose had it been? Appropriate, Jonathan thought, because he could pretend to be acting, in someone else's clothes, pretend the gun was a blank gun in a play. But Jonathan knew he knew exactly what he was doing. Towards the Mafioso he was going to kill (he hoped) he felt no mercy. And Jonathan realized he felt no pity for himself, either. Death was death. For different reasons, Bianca's life and his own life had lost value. The only interesting detail was that Jonathan stood to be paid for his action of killing Bianca. Jonathan put the gun in his jacket pocket and the nylon stocking in the same pocket with it. He found he could draw the stocking on to his hand with the fingers of the same hand. Nervously, he wiped the gun of fingerprints real and imaginary with the stocking-covered fingers. He would have to hold the coat aside slightly when he fired, otherwise there'd be a bullet-hole in the coat. He had no hat. Curious that Reeves hadn't thought of a hat. It was too late now to worry about it.

Jonathan went out of his room door and pulled it firmly shut.

Karl was standing on the pavement by his car. He held the door for Jonathan. Jonathan wondered how much Karl knew, and if he knew everything? Jonathan was leaning forward in the back seat, to ask Karl to go to the Rathaus U-bahn station, when Karl said over his shoulder:

'You are to meet Fritz at the Rathaus station. That is correct, sir?'

'Yes,' said Jonathan, relieved. He sat back in a corner and lightly fingered the little gun. He pushed the safety on and off, remembering that forward was off.

'Herr Minot suggested here, sir. The entrance is across the street.' Karl opened the door but did not get out, because the street was crowded with cars and people. 'Herr Minot said I am to find you at your hotel at seven-thirty, sir,' said Karl.

'Thank you.' Jonathan felt lost for an instant, hearing the thud of the car door closing. He looked around for Fritz. Jonathan was at a huge intersection marked Gr. Johannesstrasse and Rathausstrasse. As in London, Piccadilly for instance, there seemed to be at least four entrances to the U-bahn here because of so many streets intersecting. Jonathan looked around for the short figure of Fritz with his cap on his head. A group of men, like a football team in topcoats, dashed down the U-bahn steps, revealing Fritz standing calmly by the metal post of the stairs, and Jonathan's heart gave a leap as if he had met a lover at a secret rendezvous. Fritz gestured towards the steps, and went down himself.

Jonathan kept an eye on Fritz's cap, though there were now fifteen or more people between them. Fritz moved to one side of the throng. Evidently Bianca had not come on the scene yet, and they were to await him. There was a hubbub of German around Jonathan, a burst of laughter, a shouted 'Wiedersehen, Max!'

Fritz stood against a wall some twelve feet away, and Jonathan drifted in his direction but kept a safe distance away from him, and before Jonathan reached the wall, Fritz nodded and moved diagonally away from the wall, towards a ticket gate. Jonathan bought a ticket. Fritz shuffled on in the crowd. Tickets were punched. Jonathan knew Fritz had sighted Bianca, but Jonathan didn't see him.

A train was standing. When Fritz made a dash for a certain carriage, Jonathan dashed too. In the carriage, which was not particularly crowded, Fritz remained standing, holding to a chromium, vertical bar. He pulled a newspaper from his pocket. Fritz nodded forward, not looking at Jonathan.

Then Jonathan saw the Italian, closer to Jonathan than to Fritz – a dark, square-faced man in a smart grey topcoat, with brown leather buttons, a grey homburg, staring rather angrily straight ahead of him as if lost in thought. Jonathan looked again at Fritz who was only pretending to read his newspaper, and when Jonathan's eyes met his, Fritz nodded and smiled slightly in confirmation.

At the next stop, Messberg, Fritz got off. Jonathan looked again at the Italian, briefly, although Jonathan's glance seemed in no danger of distracting the Italian from the rigid stare into space. Suppose Bianca didn't get off at the next stop, but rode on and on to a remote stop where there'd be almost no people getting off?

But Bianca moved to the door as the train slowed. Steinstrasse. Jonathan had to make an effort, without bumping anyone, to stay just behind Bianca. There was a flight of steps up. The crowd, perhaps eighty to a hundred people, flowed together more tightly in front of the stairway, and began to creep upward. Bianca's grey topcoat was just in front of Jonathan, and they were still a couple of yards from the stairs. Jonathan could see grey hairs among the black at the back of the man's neck, and a jagged dent in his flesh like a carbuncle scar

Jonathan had the gun in his right hand, out of his jacket pocket. He removed the safety. Jonathan pushed his coat aside and aimed at the centre of the man's topcoat.

The gun made a raucous 'Ka-boom!'

Jonathan dropped the gun. He had stopped, and now he recoiled, backward and to the left, as a collective 'Oh-h-a – Ah-h-h!' rose from the crowd. Jonathan was perhaps one of the few people who did not utter an exclamation.

Bianca had sagged and fallen.

An uneven circle of space surrounded Bianca.

'...Pistole...'

'...erschossen...!'

The gun lay on the cement, someone started to pick it up, and was stopped by at least three people from touching it. Many people, not enough interested or in a hurry, were going up the stairs. Jonathan was moving a little to the left to circle the group around Bianca. He reached the stairs. A man was shouting for the 'Polizei!' Jonathan walked briskly, but no faster than several other people who were making their way to pavement level.

Jonathan arrived on the street, and simply walked on, straight ahead, not caring where he walked. He walked at a moderate pace and as if he knew where he was going, though he didn't. He saw a huge railway station on his right. Reeves had mentioned that. There were no footsteps behind him, no sound of pursuit. With the fingers of his right hand, he wriggled the piece of stocking off. But he did not want to drop it so close to the underground station.

'Taxi!' Jonathan had seen a free one, making for the railway station. It stopped, and he got in. Jonathan gave the name of the street where his hotel was.

Jonathan sank back, but he found himself glancing to right and left out the windows of the cab, as if expecting to see a policeman gesticulating, pointing to the cab, demanding that the driver stop. Absurd! He was absolutely in the clear.

Yet the same sensation came to him as he entered the Victoria – as if the law must have got his address somehow and would be in the lobby to meet him. But no. Jonathan walked quietly into his own room and closed the door. He felt in his pocket, the jacket pocket, for the bit of stocking. It was gone, had fallen somewhere.

7.20 p.m. Jonathan took off the topcoat, dropped it in an upholstered chair, and went for his cigarettes which he had forgotten to take with him. He inhaled the comforting smoke of Gitane. He put the cigarette on the edge of the basin in the bathroom, washed his hands and face, then stripped to the waist and washed with a face towel and hot water.

As he was pulling on a sweater, the telephone rang.

'Herr Karl waits on you below, sir.'

Jonathan went down. He carried the topcoat over his arm. He wanted to give it back to Reeves, wanted to see the last of it.

'*Good* evening, sir!' said Karl, beaming, as if he had heard the news and deemed it good.

In the car, Jonathan lit another cigarette. It was Wednesday evening. He'd said to Simone that he might be home tonight, but she probably wouldn't have his letter till tomorrow. He thought of two books due back Saturday at the Bibliothèque pour Tous by the church in Fontainebleau.

Jonathan was again in Reeves' comfortable apartment. He handed the topcoat to Reeves, rather than to Gaby. Jonathan felt awkward.

'*How* are you, Jonathan?' Reeves asked, tense and concerned. 'How did it go?'

Gaby went away. Jonathan and Reeves were in the living-room.

'All right,' Jonathan said. 'I think.'

Reeves smiled a little – even the little making his face look

74

radiant. 'Very good. Fine! I hadn't heard, you know? – May I offer you champagne, Jonathan? Or scotch? Sit down!'

'A scotch.'

Reeves bent over the bottles. He asked in a soft voice, 'How many – how many shots, Jonathan?'

'One.' And what if he wasn't dead, Jonathan thought suddenly. Wasn't that quite possible? Jonathan took the scotch from Reeves.

Reeves had a stemmed glass of champagne, and he raised the glass to Jonathan and drank. 'No difficulties? – Fritz did well?'

Jonathan nodded, and glanced at the door where Gaby would appear if she came back. 'Let's hope he's dead. It just occurs to me – he might not be.'

'Oh, this'll do all right if he's *not* dead. You saw him fall?'

'Oh, yes.' Jonathan gave a sigh, and realized he had been hardly breathing for several minutes.

'The news may have reached Milan already,' Reeves said cheerfully. 'An Italian bullet. Not that the Mafia always use Italian guns, but it was a nice little touch, I thought. He was of the Di Stefano family. There are a couple of the Genotti family here in Hamburg now too, and we hope these two families will start shooting at each other.'

Reeves had said that before. Jonathan sat down on the sofa. Reeves walked about in a glow of satisfaction.

'If it suits you, we'll have a quiet evening here,' Reeves said. 'If anyone telephones, Gaby's going to say I'm out.'

'Does Karl or Gaby – How much do they know?'

'Gaby – nothing. Karl, it doesn't matter if he does. Karl simply isn't interested. He works for other people besides me, and he's well paid. It's in his interest *not* to know anything, if you follow me.'

Jonathan understood. But Reeves' information did not make Jonathan feel any more comfortable. 'By the way – I'd like to go back to France tomorrow.' This meant two things, that Reeves could pay him or make the arrangement to pay him tonight, and that any other assignment ought to be discussed tonight. Jonathan intended to say no to any other assignment, whatever the financial arrangement, but he thought he should be entitled to half the forty thousand pounds for what he had done.

'Why not, if you like,' said Reeves. 'Don't forget you have the appointment tomorrow morning.'

But Jonathan didn't want to see Dr Wentzel again. He wet his lips. His report was bad, and his condition was worse. And there was another element : Dr Wentzel with his walrus moustaches represented 'authority' somehow, and Jonathan felt that he would be putting himself in a dangerous position by confronting Wentzel again. He knew he wasn't thinking logically, but that was the way he felt. 'I don't really see any reason to see him again – since I'm not staying any longer in Hamburg. I'll cancel the appointment early tomorrow. He's got my Fontainebleau address for the bill.'

'You can't send francs out of France,' Reeves said with a smile. 'Send me the bill when you get it. Don't worry about that.'

Jonathan let it go. He certainly didn't want Reeves' name on a cheque to Wentzel, however. He told himself to come to the point, which was his own payment from Reeves. Instead, Jonathan sat back on the sofa and asked rather pleasantly, 'What do you do here – as to work, I mean?'

'Work – ' Reeves hesitated, but looked not at all disturbed by the question. 'Various things. I scout for New York art dealers, for example. All those books over there – ' He indicated the bottom row of books in a bookshelf. 'They're art books, mainly German art, with names and addresses of individuals who own things. There's a demand in New York for German painters. Then, of course, I scout among the young painters here, and recommend them to galleries and buyers in the States. Texas buys a lot. You'd be surprised.'

Jonathan was surprised. Reeves Minot – if what he said was true – must judge paintings with the coldness of a Geiger counter. Was Reeves possibly a *good* judge? Jonathan had realized that the painting over the fireplace, a pinkish scene of a bed with an old person lying in it – male or female? – apparently dying, really *was* a Derwatt. It must be extremely valuable, Jonathan thought, and evidently Reeves owned it.

'Recent acquisition,' Reeves said, seeing Jonathan looking at his painting. 'A gift – from a grateful friend, you might say.' He had an air of wanting to say more, but of thinking he shouldn't.

During the dinner, Jonathan wanted to bring up the money

again, and couldn't, and Reeves started talking about something else. Ice-skating on the Alster in winter, and iceboats that went like the wind and occasionally collided. Then nearly an hour later, when they were sitting on the sofa over coffee, Reeves said:

'This evening I can't give you more than five thousand francs, which is absurd. No more than pocket money.' Reeves went to his desk and opened a drawer. 'But at least it's in francs.' He came back with the francs in his hand. 'I could give you an equal amount in marks tonight too.'

Jonathan didn't want marks, didn't want to have to change them in France. The francs, he saw, were in hundred-franc notes in pinned together batches of ten, the way French banks issued them. Reeves laid the five stacks on the coffee-table, but Jonathan did not touch them.

'You see I can't get any more until the rest contribute. Four or five people,' Reeves said. 'But there's no doubt at all that I can get the marks.'

Jonathan was thinking, somewhat vaguely because he was anything but a bargainer himself, that Reeves was in a weak position asking other people for money after the deed was done. Shouldn't his friends have put up the money first, in trust somehow, or at least more money? 'I don't want it in marks, thanks,' said Jonathan.

'No, of course. I understand. That's another thing, your money ought to be in Switzerland in a secret account, don't you think? You don't want it showing on your account in France, or you don't want to keep it in a sock like the French, do you?'

'Hardly. – When can you get the half?' Jonathan asked, as if he was sure it was coming.

'Within a week. Don't forget there might be a second job – in order to make the first job count for something. We'll have to see.'

Jonathan was irked and tried to conceal it. 'When will you know that?'

'Also within a week. Maybe even in four days. I'll be in touch.'

'But – to be frank – I think more money than this is only fair, don't you? Now, I mean.' Jonathan felt his face grow warm.

'I do. That's why I apologized for this paltry sum. I tell you what. I shall do the very best I can, and the next you will hear from me – via me – is the pleasant news of a Swiss bank account and a statement of the sum you have in it.'

That sounded better. 'When?' Jonathan asked.

'Within a week. My word of honour.'

'That is – a half?' Jonathan said.

'I'm not sure I can get a half before – You know I explained to you, Jonathan, this was a double-barrelled deal. The boys who are paying this kind of money want a certain kind of result.' Reeves looked at him.

Jonathan could see Reeves was asking, silently, was he going to do the second shooting or was he not? And if he wasn't, say so now. 'I understand,' Jonathan said. A little more, a third of the money even, wouldn't be bad, Jonathan was thinking. Something like fourteen thousand pounds. For the work he had done, that was a comfortable little sum. Jonathan decided to sit tight and stop arguing tonight.

He flew back to Paris the next day on a midday plane. Reeves had said he would cancel Dr Wenztel, and Jonathan had left it to him to do. Reeves had also said he would telephone him Saturday, day after tomorrow, in his shop. Reeves had accompanied Jonathan to the airport, and had shown him the morning paper with a picture of Bianca on the U-bahn platform. Reeves had an air of quiet triumph: there was not a clue except the Italian gun, and a Mafia killer was suspected. Bianca was labelled a Mafia soldier or button man. Jonathan had seen the front pages of the newspapers on the stands that morning when he went out to buy cigarettes, but he had had no desire to buy a newspaper. Now in the plane, he was handed a newspaper by the smiling stewardess. Jonathan left the paper folded on his lap, and closed his eyes.

It was nearly 7 p.m. when Jonathan got home, via train and taxi, and he let himself into the house with his key.

'Jon!' Simone came down the hall to greet him.

He put his arms around her. 'Hello, darling!'

'I was expecting you!' she said, laughing. 'Somehow. Just now – What's the news? Take off your coat. I had your letter this morning that you might be home last night. Are you out of your mind?'

Jonathan flung his overcoat on the hook, and picked up Georges who had just crashed against his legs. 'And how's my little pest? How's Cailloux?' He kissed Georges' cheek. Jonathan had brought Georges a truck which dumped things and this was in the plastic bag with the whisky, but Jonathan thought the truck could wait, and he pulled out the drink.

'Ah, *quel luxe!*' Simone said. 'Shall we open it now?'

'I insist!' said Jonathan.

They went into the kitchen. Simone liked ice with scotch and Jonathan was indifferent.

'Tell me what the doctors said.' Simone took the ice tray to the sink.

'Well – they say about the same as the doctors here. But they want to try out some drugs on me. They're going to let me know.' Jonathan had, on the plane, decided to say this to Simone. It would leave the way open for another trip to Germany. And what was the real *use* of telling her things were a trifle worse, or looked worse? What could she do about it but worry a little more? Jonathan's optimism had risen on the plane: if he'd come well through the first episode, he might make it through the second.

'You mean you'll have to go back?' she asked.

'That's possible.' Jonathan watched her pour the two scotches, generous ones. 'But they're willing to pay me for it. They're going to let me know.'

'Really?' said Simone, surprised.

'Is that scotch? What do *I* get?' Georges said in English, with such clarity that Jonathan burst out laughing.

'Want some? Take a sip,' Jonathan said, holding out his glass.

Simone restrained his hand. 'There's orange juice, Georgie!' She poured orange juice for him. 'They're trying a certain cure, you mean?'

Jonathan frowned, but he still felt master of the situation. 'Darling, there's no cure. They're – they're going to try a lot of new pills. That's about all I know. Cheers!' Jonathan felt a bit euphoric. He had the five thousand francs in his inside jacket pocket. He was safe, for the moment, safe in the bosom of his family. If all went well, the five thousand was merely pocket money, as Reeves Minot had said.

Simone leaned on the back of one of the straight chairs. 'They'll *pay* for your going back? That means there's some danger attached?'

'No. I think – there's some inconvenience attached. Going back to Germany. I only mean they'll pay my transportation.' Jonathan hadn't worked it out: he could say that Dr Perrier would give the injections, administer the pills. But for the moment he thought he was saying the right thing.

'You mean – they consider you a special case?'

'Yes. In a way. Of course I'm not,' he said, smiling. He wasn't, and Simone knew he wasn't. 'They just *might* want to try some tests. I don't know yet, darling.'

'Anyway you look awfully happy about it. I'm glad, darling.'

'Let's go out to dinner tonight. The restaurant on the corner here. We can take Georges,' he protested over her voice. 'Come on, we can afford it.'

8

Jonathan put four thousand of the francs into an envelope in a certain drawer among eight such drawers in a wooden cabinet at the back of his shop. This drawer was the next from the bottom drawer, and held nothing but ends of wire and string and some tags with reinforced holes – junk that only a frugal person or an eccentric would save, Jonathan thought. It was a drawer, like the one below it (Jonathan had no idea what that contained) which Jonathan never opened ordinarily, therefore neither would Simone open it, he thought, on the rare occasions when she helped out in the shop. Jonathan's real cash drawer was the top one on the right under his wooden counter. The remaining thousand francs Jonathan put into the joint account at the Société Générale on Friday morning. It could be two or three weeks before Simone noticed the extra thousand, and she might not comment, even if she saw it in their cheque book. And if she did, Jonathan could say that a few customers had suddenly paid up. Jonathan usually signed cheques to pay their bills, and the bankbook lived in the drawer of the *écritoire* in the living-room, unless one or the other of them had to take it out of the house to pay for something, which happened only about once a month.

And by Friday afternoon, Jonathan had found a way to use a little of the thousand. He bought a mustard-coloured tweed suit for Simone from a shop in the Rue de France for 395 francs. He'd seen the suit days ago, before Hamburg, and thought of Simone – the rounded collar, the dark yellow tweed flecked with brown, the four brown buttons set in a square on the jacket had seemed created just for Simone. The price had been shocking to his eyes, more than a bit out of line, he'd thought. Now it seemed almost a bargain, and Jonathan gazed with pleasure at the new material being folded with care between snowy sheets of tissue paper. And Simone's appreciation gave Jonathan pleasure all over again. Jonathan thought it was the first new thing she'd had, the first pretty clothes, in a couple of years, because the dresses from the market or the Prisunic didn't count.

'But it must've been terribly expensive, Jon!'

'No – not really. The Hamburg doctors gave me an advance – in case I have to go back. Quite generous. Don't think about that.'

Simone smiled. She didn't want to think about money, Jonathan saw. Not just now. 'I'll count this as one of my birthday presents.'

Jonathan smiled too. Her birthday had been almost two months ago.

On Saturday morning Jonathan's telephone rang. It had rung a few times that morning, but this was the irregular ring of a long distance call.

'This is Reeves . . . How is everything?'

'All right, thanks.' Jonathan was suddenly tense and alert. There was a customer in his shop, a man staring at lengths of sample frame wood on Jonathan's wall. But Jonathan was speaking in English.

Reeves said, 'I'm coming to Paris tomorrow and I'd like to see you. I have something for you – you know.' Reeves sounded as calm as usual.

Simone wanted Jonathan to go to her parents' home in Nemours tomorrow. 'Can we make it in the evening or – around six p.m., say? I've got a long lunch.'

'Oh, sure, I understand. French Sunday lunches! Sure, around six. I'll be at the Hotel Cayré. That's on Raspail.'

Jonathan had heard of the hotel. He said he would try to be there by 6 or 7 p.m. 'There're fewer trains on Sunday.'

Reeves said not to worry. 'See you tomorrow.'

Reeves was bringing some money, evidently. Jonathan gave his attention to the man who wanted a frame.

Simone looked marvellous on Sunday in the new suit. Jonathan asked her, before they left for the Foussadiers, not to say that he was being paid anything by the German doctors.

'I'm not a fool!' Simone declared with such quick duplicity Jonathan was amused, and felt that Simone really was more with him than with her parents. Often Jonathan felt the opposite.

'Even today,' Simone said at the Foussadiers, 'Jon has to go to Paris to talk to a colleague of the Germans.'

It was a particularly cheerful Sunday lunch. Jonathan and Simone had brought a bottle of Johnny Walker.

Jonathan got the 4.49 p.m. train from Fontainebleau, because there had been no train convenient from St Pierre-Nemours, and arrived in Paris around 5.30 p.m. He took the Métro. There was a Métro stop right beside the hotel.

Reeves had left a message for Jonathan to be sent up to his room. Reeves was in shirt-sleeves, and had apparently been lying on the bed reading newspapers. 'Hello, Jonathan! How is life? . . . Sit down – somewhere. I have something to show you.' He went to his suitcase. 'This – as a starter.' Reeves held up a square white envelope, and took a typewritten page from it and handed it to Jonathan.

The letter was in English, addressed to the Swiss Bank Corporation, and it was signed by Ernst Hildesheim. The letter requested a bank account to be opened in the name of Jonathan Trevanny, and gave Jonathan's shop address in Fontainebleau, and said that a cheque for eighty thousand marks was enclosed. The letter was a carbon, but it was signed.

'Who's Hildesheim?' Jonathan asked, meanwhile thinking that the German mark was worth about one and six-tenths French franc, so that eighty thousand marks would convert to something over a hundred and twenty thousand French francs.

'A businessman of Hamburg – for whom I've done a few favours. Hildesheim's not under any kind of surveillance and this won't appear on his company books, so nothing for him to worry about. He sent a personal cheque. The point is, Jonathan, this money has been deposited in your name, posted yesterday from Hamburg, so you'll be getting your private number next week. That's a hundred and twenty-eight thousand French francs.' Reeves didn't smile, but he had an air of satisfaction. He reached for a box on the writing-table. 'Dutch cigar? They're very good.'

Because the cigars were something different, Jonathan took one, smiling. 'Thanks.' He puffed it alight from the match that Reeves held. 'Thanks also for the money.' It was not quite a third, Jonathan realized. It wasn't a half. But Jonathan couldn't say this.

'Nice start, yes. The casino boys in Hamburg are quite pleased. The other Mafia who're cruising around, a couple of the Genotti family, claim they don't know anything about Salvatore Bianca's death, but of course they would say that. What we want to do now is knock off a Genotti as if in retaliation for Bianca. And we want to get a big shot, a *capo* – a chief just under the boss, you know? There's one named Vito Marcangelo who travels nearly every week-end from Munich to Paris. He has a girl friend in Paris. He's the chief of the dope business in Munich – at least for his family there. Munich by the way is even more active than Marseille now, as far as dope goes . . .'

Jonathan listened uneasily, waiting for an opening in which he could say that he didn't care to take on another job. Jonathan's thoughts had changed in the last forty-eight hours. And it was curious, too, how Reeves' very presence stripped Jonathan of a sense of daring – maybe made the deed more real. Then there was the fact that he had, apparently, a hundred and twenty-eight thousand francs in Switzerland already. Jonathan had sat down on the edge of an armchair.

'. . . on a moving train, a day train, the Mozart Express.'

Jonathan shook his head. 'Sorry, Reeves. I really don't think I'm up to it.' Reeves could block the cheque in marks, Jonathan thought suddenly. Reeves could simply cable Hildesheim. Well, so be it.

Reeves looked crestfallen. 'Oh. Well – so am I sorry. Really. We'll just have to find another man – if you don't do it. And – I'm afraid he'll get the better part of the money too.' Reeves shook his head, puffed his cigar and stared out the window for a moment. Then he bent and gripped Jonathan's shoulder firmly. 'Jon, the first part went so well.'

Jonathan sat back, and Reeves released him. Jonathan squirmed, like someone forced to make an apology. 'Yes, but – to shoot somebody on a train?' Jonathan could see himself nabbed at once, unable to escape anywhere.

'Not a shooting, no. We couldn't have the noise. I was thinking of a garrotte.'

Jonathan could hardly believe his ears.

Reeves said calmly. 'It's a Mafia method. A slender cord, silent – A noose! And you pull it tight. That's all.'

Jonathan thought of his fingers touching a warm neck. It was revolting. 'Absolutely out of the question. I couldn't.'

Reeves took a breath, going into another gear, shifting. 'This man is well guarded, two bodyguards as a rule. But on a train – people get bored sitting and walk in the aisle a bit, or they go to the bog once or twice, or the dining-car, maybe alone. It might not work, Jonathan, you might not – find the occasion, but you could try. – Then there's pushing, just pushing him out the door. Those doors can open when the train's moving, you know. But he'd yell – and it might not kill him either.'

Ludicrous, Jonathan thought. But he didn't feel like laughing. Reeves dreamed on silently, looking up at the ceiling. Jonathan was thinking that if he were caught as a murderer or in an attempt at murder, Simone wouldn't touch any of the money from it. She'd be appalled, ashamed. 'I simply cannot help you,' Jonathan said. He stood up.

'But – you could at least *ride* the train. If the right moment doesn't present itself, we'll just have to think of something else, another *capo* maybe, another method. But we'd love to get this guy! He's going to move from dope to the Hamburg casinos – organizing – that's the rumour, anyway.' Reeves said on another note, 'Would you try a gun, Jon?'

Jonathan shook his head. 'I haven't the nerve, for God's sake. On a train? No.'

'Look at this garrotte!' Reeves pulled his left hand quickly from his trousers pocket.

He held what looked like a thin, whitish string. The end slipped through a loop, and was prevented from going all the way through by a small lump at the end of the cord. Reeves tossed it round the bedpost and pulled, jerking the cord to one side.

'You see? Nylon. Strong as wire almost. No one can even grunt more than once –' Reeves broke off.

Jonathan was disgusted. One would have to touch the victim with the other hand – somehow. And wouldn't it take about three minutes?

Reeves seemed to give it up. He strolled to a window and turned. 'Think about it. You can ring me up or I'll ring you in a couple of days. Marcangelo usually leaves Munich noonish Fridays. It would be ideal if it could be done next week-end.'

Jonathan drifted towards the door. He put his cigar out in an ashtray on the bed-table.

Reeves was looking at him shrewdly, yet he might have been gazing far behind him, thinking already of someone else for the job. His long scar looked, as it did in certain lights, thicker than it was. The scar had probably given him an inferiority complex with women, Jonathan thought. Yet how long had he had it? Maybe just two years, one couldn't tell.

'Like a drink downstairs?'

'No, thanks,' Jonathan said.

'Oh, I have a book to show you!' Reeves went to his suitcase again, and pulled a book with a bright red jacket from a back corner. 'Take a look. Keep it. It's a wonderful piece of journalism. Documentary. You'll see the kind of people we're dealing with. But they're flesh and blood like everyone else. Vulnerable, I mean.'

The book was called *The Grim Reapers: The Anatomy of Organized Crime in America*.

'I'll telephone you Wednesday,' Reeves said. 'You'd come to Munich Thursday, spend the night, I'd be there at some hotel also, then you'd return Friday night to Paris by train.'

Jonathan's hand was on the door-knob, and now he turned it. 'Sorry, Reeves, but I'm afraid it's no go. Bye-bye.'

Jonathan walked out of the hotel and directly across the street to the Métro. On the platform, awaiting a train, he read the blurb on the book-jacket. On the back of the jacket were police photographs, front and profile, of six or eight unpleasant-looking men with downturned mouths, faces loose and grim at once, all with dark, staring eyes. It was curious, the similarity of their expressions, whether the faces were plump or lean. There was a section of five or six pages of photographs in the book. The chapters were titled by American cities – Detroit, New York, New Orleans, Chicago, and at the back of the book, besides an index, was a section of Mafia families like family trees, except that these people were all contemporaries: bosses, sub-bosses, lieutenants, button men, the latter numbering fifty or sixty in the case of the Genovese family of which Jonathan had heard.

The names were real, and in many cases addresses were given in New York and New Jersey. Jonathan browsed in the book on the train to Fontainebleau. There was 'Icepick Willie' Alderman, of whom Reeves had spoken in Hamburg, who killed his victims by bending over their shoulder as if to speak to them and sticking an icepick through their eardrum. 'Icepick Willie' was photographed, grinning, among the Las Vegas gambling fraternity of half a dozen men with Italian names and a cardinal, a bishop, and a monsignore (their names also were given) after the clergy had 'received a pledge of $7,500 to be spread over five years'. Jonathan closed the book in brief depression, then opened it again after a few minutes of staring out the window. The book held facts, after all, and the facts were fascinating.

Jonathan rode the bus from the Fontainebleau–Avon station to the *place* near the château, and walked up the Rue de France to his shop. He had his shop key with him, and he went in to leave the Mafia book in the seldom-used drawer with the hidden francs before he walked to his house in the Rue St Merry.

9

Tom Ripley had noticed the sign FERMETURE PROVISOIRE
POUR RAISONS DE FAMILLE in the window of Jonathan
Trevanny's shop on a certain Tuesday in April, and had
thought that Trevanny might have gone to Hamburg. Tom
was very curious indeed to know if Trevanny had gone to
Hamburg, but not curious enough to telephone Reeves to ask.
Then on a Thursday morning around 10 a.m. Reeves had rung
from Hamburg and said in a voice tense with repressed
jubilation :

'Well, Tom, it's done! It's all – Everything's fine. Tom, I thank
you!'

Tom for the nonce had been wordless. Trevanny had really
come through? Heloise had been in the living-room where he
was, so there had been little Tom could say except, 'Good. Glad
to hear it.'

'No need of the phoney doctor's report. Everything went fine!
Last night.'

'So – and – he's coming back home now?'

'Yes. Due tonight.'

Tom had made that conversation short. He had thought of
Reeves' substituting a report of Trevanny's condition that would
be worse than the truth, and Tom had suggested it in jest,
although Reeves was the type to have tried it – a dirty, humour-
less trick, Tom thought. And it hadn't even been necessary. Tom
smiled with amazement. Tom could tell from Reeves' joy that
his intended victim was actually *dead*. Killed by Trevanny. Tom
was indeed surprised. Poor Reeves had so wanted a word of
praise from Tom for his organization of the coup, but Tom
hadn't been able to say anything : Heloise knew quite a bit of
English, and Tom didn't want to take any chances. Tom thought
suddenly of looking at Mme Annette's *Le Parisien Liberé* which

she bought every morning, but Mme Annette was not yet back from her shopping.

'Who was that?' Heloise asked. She was looking over magazines on the coffee-table, weeding out old ones to be thrown away.

'Reeves,' Tom said. 'Nothing of importance.'

Reeves bored Heloise. He had no talent for small talk, and he looked as if he did not enjoy life.

Tom heard Mme Annette's steps crunching briskly on the gravel in front of the house, and he went into the kitchen to meet her. She came in through the side door, and smiled at him.

'You would like some more coffee, M. Tome?' she asked, setting her basket on the wooden table. An artichoke toppled from the peak.

'No, thank you, Mme Annette, I came to have a look at your *Parisien*, if I may. The horses – '

Tom found the item on the second page. There was no photograph. An Italian named Salvatore Bianca, forty-eight, had been shot dead in an underground station in Hamburg. The assassin was unknown. A gun found on the scene was of Italian manufacture. The victim was known to be of the Di Stefano family of Mafiosi of Milan. The account was hardly three inches long. But it might be an interesting beginning, Tom thought. It might lead to much greater things. Jonathan Trevanny, the innocent-looking, positively square Trevanny, had succumbed to the temptation of money (what else?), and committed a successful murder! Tom had once succumbed himself, in the case of Dickie Greenleaf. Could it be that Trevanny was one of *us*? But *us* to Tom was only Tom Ripley. Tom smiled.

Last Sunday, Reeves had rung Tom from Orly in a dejected state, saying that Trevanny was so far declining the job, and could Tom come up with anybody else? Tom had said no. Reeves said he had written Trevanny a letter which would arrive Monday morning, inviting Trevanny to Hamburg for a medical examination. That was when Tom had said, 'If he comes, you could perhaps see that the report is slightly worse.'

Tom might have gone to Fontainebleau on Friday or Saturday to satisfy his curiosity and catch a glimpse of Trevanny in his shop, perhaps bring a drawing to be framed (unless Trevanny was taking the rest of the week off to recuperate), and in fact Tom had intended to go to Fontainebleau Friday for stretchers from Gauthier's shop, but Heloise's parents had been due for the week-end – they had stayed Friday and Saturday nights – and on Friday the household had been in a tizzy preparing for them. Mme Annette was worried, unnecessarily, about her menu, the quality of the fresh *moules* for Friday night, and after Mme Annette had prepared the guest-room to perfection, Heloise had made her change the bedlinen and the bathroom towels, because they all bore Tom's monogram TPR and not the Plissot family's. The Plissots had given the Ripleys two dozen magnificent heavy linen sheets from the family stock as a wedding present, and Heloise thought it only courteous and also diplomatic to use them when the Plissots visited. Mme Annette had suffered a slight slip of memory about this, for which she certainly wasn't reprimanded by either Heloise or Tom. Tom knew the change of bedlinen was also due to the fact that Heloise did not want her parents to be reminded by his monogram that she was married to him when they got into bed. The Plissots were critical and stuffy – a fact made somehow worse by the fact that Arlène Plissot, a slender, still attractive woman of fifty, made a real effort to be informal, tolerant of the young and all that. It just wasn't in her. The week-end had been a real ordeal, in Tom's opinion, and good heavens, if Belle Ombre wasn't a well-run household, then what was? The silver tea-service (another wedding gift of the Plissots) was kept polished to perfection by Mme Annette. Even the birdhouse in the garden was swept of droppings daily as if it were a miniature guesthouse on the property. Everything of wood in the house gleamed and smelled pleasantly of lavender-scented wax that Tom brought over from England. Yet Arlène had said, while stretched out on the bear-skin before the fireplace in a mauve trouser suit, warming her naked feet, 'Wax is not enough for such floors, Heloise. From time to time they need a treatment with linseed oil and white spirit – *warm*, you know, so it soaks better into the wood.'

When the Plissots left on Sunday afternoon after tea, Heloise had snatched her middy top off and flung it at a french window which had given an awful crack because of a heavy pin on the middy, but the glass had not broken.

'Champagne!' Heloise cried, and Tom dashed down to the cellar to fetch it.

They'd had champagne, though the tea things were not cleared away (Mme Annette was for once putting her feet up), and then the telephone had rung.

It was Reeves Minot's voice, sounding downcast. 'I'm at Orly. Just leaving for Hamburg. I saw our mutual friend in Paris today and he says no to the next – the next, you know. There's got to be one more, I know that. I explained that to him.'

'You've paid him something?' Tom watched Heloise waltzing with her champagne glass in hand. She was humming the grand waltz from *Der Rosenkavalier*.

'Yes, about a third, and I think that's not bad. I've put it in Switzerland for him.'

Tom thought he recalled a promised sum of nearly five hundred thousand francs. A third was not munificent, but it was reasonable, Tom supposed. 'You mean another shooting,' Tom said.

Heloise was singing and twirling. 'La-da-da – la-dee-dee . . . '

'No.' Reeves' voice cracked. He said softly, 'It's got to be a garrotte. On a train. I think that's the hitch.'

Tom was shocked. Of course Trevanny wouldn't do it. 'Must it be on a train?'

'I've got a plan . . . '

Reeves always had a plan. Tom listened politely. Reeves' idea sounded dangerous and uncertain. Tom interrupted. 'Maybe our friend has had enough at this stage.'

'No, I think he's interested. But he won't agree – to come to Munich, and we need the job done by next week-end.'

'You've been reading *The Godfather* again, Reeves. Make some arrangement with a gun.'

'A gun makes noise,' Reeves said without a flicker of humour. 'I'm wondering – either I come up with someone else, Tom, or – Jonathan's got to be persuaded.'

Impossible to persuade him, Tom thought, and Tom said rather impatiently, 'There's no better persuasion than money. If that doesn't work, I can't help you.' Tom was unpleasantly reminded of the visit of the Plissots. Would he and Heloise have bent over backwards, strained themselves for nearly three days, if they didn't need the twenty-five thousand francs a year that Jacques Plissot gave Heloise as an allowance?

'I'm afraid if he's paid any more,' Reeves said, 'he really will quit. I've told you, maybe, I can't get it – the rest of the dough – until he does the second job.'

Tom was thinking that Reeves didn't understand Trevanny's type at all. If Trevanny was paid in full, he'd either do the job or return half the money.

'If you think of something in regard to *him*,' Reeves said with apparent difficulty, 'or if you know of anyone else who could do it, telephone me, will you? In the next day or so?'

Tom was glad when they'd hung up. He shook his head quickly, and blinked his eyes. Reeves Minot's ideas often gave Tom the feeling of being befogged by some heavy dream that hadn't even the reality of most dreams.

Heloise hurdled the back of the yellow sofa, one hand gently touching the sofa back, the other holding her glass of champagne, and she landed silently, seated. Elegantly, she lifted her glass to him. '*Grace à toi ce week-end était très réussi, mon trésor!*'

'Thank you, my darling!'

Yes, life was sweet again, they were alone again, they could dine tonight barefoot if they chose. Freedom!

Tom was thinking of Trevanny. Tom didn't really care about Reeves, who always scraped through, or pulled out in the nick of time from a situation that became too dangerous. But Trevanny – there was a bit of a mystery. Tom cast about for a way of making better acquaintance with Trevanny. The situation was difficult, because he knew that Trevanny didn't like him. But there was nothing simpler than taking a picture to Trevanny to frame.

On Tuesday, Tom drove to Fontainebleau and went first to Gauthier's art supply shop to buy stretchers. Gauthier might volunteer some news about Trevanny, something about his Hamburg trip, Tom thought, since ostensibly Trevanny had gone to consult a doctor. Tom made his purchases at Gauthier's, but Gauthier did not mention Trevanny. Just as he was leaving, Tom said:

'And how is our friend – M. Trevanny?'

'*Ah, oui*. He went to Hamburg last week to see a specialist.'
Gauthier's glass eye glared at Tom, while the live eye glistened
and looked a bit sad. 'I understand the news was not good. A
little worse, perhaps, than what his doctor here tells him. But he
is courageous. You know these English, they never show their
real feelings.'

'I'm sorry to hear he's worse,' Tom said.

'Yes, well – so he told me. But he carries on.'

Tom put his stretchers in his car, and took a portfolio from
the back seat. He had brought a watercolour for Trevanny to
frame. His conversation with Trevanny might not go well today,
Tom thought, but the fact that he would have to pick up his
picture at some future date would ensure that he had a second
chance to see Trevanny. Tom walked to the Rue des Sablons, and
went into the little shop. Trevanny was discussing a frame with
a woman, holding a strip of wood against the top of an etching.
He glanced at Tom, and Tom was sure Trevanny recognized
him.

'It may look heavy now, but with a white mat – ' Trevanny
was saying. Trevanny's accent was quite good.

Tom looked for some change in Trevanny – a sign of anxiety,
perhaps – but so far he saw none. At last it was Tom's turn.
'*Bonjour*. Good morning. Tom Ripley,' Tom said, smiling. 'I was
at your house in – in February, wasn't it? Your wife's birthday.'

'Oh, yes.'

Tom could see in Trevanny's face that his attitude hadn't
changed since that night in February when he had said, 'Oh, yes,
I've heard of you.' Tom opened his portfolio. 'I have a watercolour. Done by my wife. I thought perhaps a narrow dark-
brown frame, a mat – say, two and a half inches at the widest,
at the bottom.'

Trevanny gave his attention to the watercolour which lay on
the notched, sleek-worn counter between them.

The picture was mainly green and purple, Heloise's free
interpretation of a corner of Belle Ombre backgrounded by the
pine woods in winter. It was not bad, Tom thought, because
Heloise had known when to stop. She had no idea Tom had
saved it, and to see it framed was going to be a pleasant surprise
for her, Tom hoped.

'Something like this, perhaps,' Trevanny said, pulling down a length of wood from a shelf where a confusion of pieces stuck out. He laid it above the picture at a distance that the mat would take up.

'I think that's nice, yes.'

'Mat off-white or white? Such as this?'

Tom made his decision. Trevanny printed Tom's name and address carefully on a pad. Tom gave his telephone number too.

What to say now? Trevanny's coolness was almost palpable. Tom knew Trevanny would decline, but felt he had nothing to lose, so he said, 'Perhaps you and your wife would come to my house for a drink some time. Villeperce isn't far. Bring your little boy, too.'

'Thanks. I have no car,' Trevanny said with a polite smile. 'We don't go out very much, I'm afraid.'

'A car's no problem. I could fetch you. And of course count on having some dinner with us too.' The words tumbled out of Tom. Now Trevanny shoved his hands into the pockets of his coat sweater, and shifted on his feet as if his will were shifting. Tom sensed that Trevanny was curious about him

'My wife's shy,' said Trevanny, smiling for the first time. 'She doesn't speak much English.'

'Neither does my wife, really. She's French too, you know. However – if my house is too far away, what's the matter with a *pastis* now? Aren't you about to close?'

Trevanny was. It was a little after noon.

They walked to a bar-restaurant at the corner of Rue de France and Rue St Merry. Trevanny had stopped at a bakery to buy bread. He ordered a draft beer, and Tom had the same. Tom put a ten-franc note on the counter.

'How did you happen to come to France?' Tom asked.

Trevanny told Tom about starting an antique shop in France with an English chum. 'And you?' asked Trevanny.

'Oh, my wife likes it here. And so do I. I can't think of a more pleasant life really. I can travel if I wish. I have lots of free time – leisure you'd call it. Gardening and painting. I paint like a Sunday painter, but I enjoy it. – Whenever I feel like it, I go to London for a couple of weeks.' That was cards on the table, in a way, naïve, harmless. Except that Trevanny might wonder where the money came from. Tom thought it probable that Trevanny had heard the Dickie Greenleaf story, forgotten most of it as most people did, except that certain things stayed in the memory, like Dickie Greenleaf's 'mysterious disappearance', though later Dickie's suicide had been accepted as fact. Possibly Trevanny knew that Tom got some income from what Dickie Greenleaf had left in his will (a will that Tom had forged), because this had been in the papers. Then there'd been the Derwatt affair last year, not so much 'Derwatt' in the French papers as the strange disappearance of Thomas Murchison, the American who had been a guest at Tom's home.

'Sound's a pleasant life,' Trevanny remarked dryly, and wiped foam from his upper lip.

Trevanny wanted to ask him something, Tom felt. What? Tom was wondering whether, for all his English cool, Trevanny could suffer a fit of conscience and either tell his wife or go to the police and confess? Tom thought he was right in assuming Trevanny hadn't and wouldn't tell his wife what he had done. Just five days ago Trevanny had pulled a trigger and killed a man. Of course Reeves would have given Trevanny pep-talks, morale-building lectures on the viciousness of the Mafia and the positive good Trevanny or anybody would do by eliminating one of them. Then Tom thought of the garrotte. No, he could not see Trevanny using a garrotte. How did Trevanny feel about the killing he had done? Or had he had time to feel anything yet? Maybe not. Trevanny lit a Gitane. He had large hands. He was the type who could wear old clothes, unpressed trousers, and still have the air of a gentleman. And he had rugged good looks that he himself seemed quite unaware of.

'Do you happen to know,' said Trevanny, looking at Tom with his calm blue eyes, 'an American called Reeves Minot?'

'No,' Tom said. 'Lives here in Fontainebleau?'

'No. But he travels a lot, I think.'

'No.' Tom drank his beer.

'I'd better push off. My wife's expecting me.'

They went out. They had to go in different directions.

'Thanks for the beer,' Trevanny said.

'A pleasure!'

Tom walked to his car which was in the parking area in front of the Hôtel de l'Aigle Noir, and drove off for Villeperce. He was thinking about Trevanny, thinking that he was a rather disappointed man, disappointed in his present situation. Surely Trevanny had had aspirations in his youth. Tom remembered Trevanny's wife, an attractive woman who looked steady and devoted, the kind of woman who would never push her husband to better his situation, never nag at him to earn more money. In her way, Trevanny's wife was probably as upright and decent as Trevanny himself. Yet Trevanny had succumbed to Reeves' proposal. That meant that Trevanny was a man who could be pushed or pulled in any direction, if one did it intelligently.

Mme Annette greeted Tom with the message that Heloise would be a little late, because she had found an English *commode de bateau* in an antique shop in Chilly-en-Bière, had signed a cheque for it, but had to accompany the antique man to the bank. 'She will be home with the commode at any minute!' said Mme Annette, her blue eyes sparkling. 'She asks you to wait lunch for her, M. Tome.'

'But of course!' said Tom just as cheerily. The bank account was going to be slightly overdrawn, he thought, which was why Heloise had to go to the bank and talk to someone – and how would she manage that during the lunch period when the bank was closed? And Mme Annette was joyous because still another piece of furniture was entering the house which she could get to work on with her indefatigable waxing. Heloise had been looking for a nautical, brassbound chest of drawers for Tom for months. It was a whim of hers to see a *commode de bateau* in his room.

Tom decided to seize the moment and try Reeves, and he ran up to his room. It was 1.22 p.m. Belle Ombre had two new dial telephones since about three months, and one no longer had to get a long-distance number through the operator.

Reeves' housekeeper answered, and Tom used his German and asked if Herr Minot was in. He was.

'Reeves, hello! Tom. I can't talk long. I just wanted to say I've seen our friend. Had a drink with him . . . In a bar in Fontainebleau. I think –' Tom was standing up, tense, staring through the window at the trees across the road, at the empty blue sky. He was not sure what he wanted to say, except that he wanted to tell Reeves to keep trying. 'I don't know but I think it might work with him. It's only a hunch. But try again with him.'

'Yes?' said Reeves, hanging on his words as if he were an oracle that never failed.

'When do you expect to see him?'

'Well, I'm hoping he'll come Thursday to Munich. Day after tomorrow. I'm trying to persuade him to consult another doctor there. Then – on Friday the train leaves around two-ten from Munich to Paris, you know.'

Tom had once taken the Mozart Express, boarding it at Salzburg. 'I would say, give him a choice of a gun and – the other thing, but advise him not to use the gun.'

'I did *try* that!' Reeves said. 'But you think – he might still come around, eh?'

Tom heard a car, two cars, roll on to the gravel in front of the house. It was no doubt Heloise with the antique dealer. 'I've got to sign off, Reeves. Right now.'

Later that day, alone in his room, Tom examined more closely the handsome commode which had been installed between his two front windows. The chest was of oak, low and solid, with shining brass corners and countersunk brass drawer pulls. The polished wood looked alive, as if animated by the hands of the maker, or maybe by the hands of the captain or captains or officers who had used it. A couple of shiny, darkish dents in the wood were like the odd scars that every living thing acquired in the course of life. An oval plaque of silver was set into the top, and on it was engraved in scrolly letters Capt. Archibald L. Partridge, Plymouth, 1734, and in much smaller letters the name of the carpenter, which Tom thought a nice touch of pride.

IO

On Wednesday, as Reeves had promised, he telephoned Jonathan at his shop. Jonathan was unusually busy and had to ask Reeves to ring back just after noon.

Reeves did ring back, and after his usual courtesies, asked if Jonathan would be able to come to Munich the following day.

'There are doctors in Munich too, you know, very good ones. I have one in mind, Dr Max Schroeder. I've found out he could see you early Friday, around eight in the morning. All I have to do is confirm it. If you – '

'All right,' said Jonathan, who had anticipated that the conversation would go exactly like this. 'Very good, Reeves. I'll see about my ticket – '

'One way, Jonathan. – Well, that's up to you.'

Jonathan knew. 'When I find out the plane time, I'll ring you back.'

'I know the times. There's a plane leaving Orly at one-fifteen p.m. direct to Munich, if you can make it.'

'All right. I'll aim for that.'

'If I don't hear from you, I'll assume you're on it. I'll meet you at the town terminus as before.'

Absent-mindedly, Jonathan went to his sink, smoothed his hair with both hands, then reached for his mac. It was raining a little and rather chilly. Jonathan had made his decision yesterday. He would go through the same movements again, visit a doctor in Munich this time, and he would board the train The dubious part to Jonathan was his own nerve. Just how far would he be able to go? He walked out of his shop and locked the door with his key.

Jonathan bumped into a dustbin on the pavement, and realized that he was trudging along instead of walking. He raised his head a little. He'd demand to have a gun as well as the noose, and if he balked at using the noose because of a failure of nerve (which Jonathan fully expected), and he used the gun, then that was that. Jonathan would make an arrangement with Reeves: if he used the gun, if it was obvious that he was going to be caught, then he would use the next bullet or two for himself. That way he could never possibly betray Reeves and the other people Reeves was connected with. For this, Reeves would pay the rest of the money to Simone. Jonathan realized that his corpse couldn't be taken for that of an Italian, but he supposed it was possible that the Di Stefano family could have hired a non-Italian killer.

Jonathan said to Simone, 'I had a telephone call from the Hamburg doctor this morning. He wants me to go to Munich tomorrow.'

'Oh? So soon?'

Jonathan remembered he had told Simone it might be a fortnight before the doctors wanted to see him again. He had said Dr Wentzel had given him some pills whose result he would want to check. There had in fact been a conversation about pills with Dr Wentzel — there was nothing really to do with leukaemia except try to slow it up with pills — but Dr Wentzel had not given him any. Jonathan was sure Dr Wentzel would have given him pills if he had seen him a second time. 'There's another doctor in Munich — someone called Schroeder — Dr Wentzel wants me to see.'

'Where is Munich?' asked Georges.

'In Germany,' Jonathan said.

'How long will you be gone?' Simone asked.

'Probably — till Saturday morning,' Jonathan said, thinking that the train might come in so late Friday night, there wouldn't be a train out of Paris to Fontainebleau.

'And what about the shop? Would you like me to be there tomorrow morning? And Friday morning? — What time must you leave tomorrow?'

'There's a plane at one-fifteen. Yes, darling, it would be a help if you could look in tomorrow morning and Friday morning — even for an hour. There'll be a couple of people calling for pictures.' Jonathan stabbed his knife gently into a piece of Camembert which he had taken and didn't want.

'You're worried, Jon?'

'Not really. – No, on the contrary, any news I get ought to be slightly better news.' Polite cheerfulness, Jonathan thought, and it was really rubbish. The doctors couldn't do anything against time. He glanced at his son who looked a bit puzzled, but not puzzled enough to ask another question, and Jonathan realized that Georges had been overhearing such conversations since he could understand speech. Georges had been told, 'Your father has a germ. Like a cold. It makes him tired sometimes. But you cannot catch it. Nobody can catch it, so it is not going to hurt you.'

'Will you sleep at the hospital?' Simone asked.

Jonathan didn't understand what she meant at first. 'No. Dr Wentzel – his secretary said they'd booked a hotel for me.'

Jonathan left the house the next morning just after 9 a.m., in order to catch the 9.42 a.m. to Paris, because the next train later would have made him too late for Orly. He had bought his ticket, one-way, the preceding afternoon, and he had also put another thousand francs into the account at the Société Générale, and five hundred in his wallet, which left two thousand five hundred in the drawer in his shop. He had also removed *The Grim Reapers* from the drawer and stuck it into his suitcase to give back to Reeves.

Just before 5 p.m., Jonathan got off the bus which had brought him to the Munich city terminus. It was a sunny day, the temperature pleasant. There were a few sturdy, middle-aged men in leather shorts and green jackets, and a hurdy-gurdy played on the pavement. He saw Reeves trotting towards him.

'I'm a little late, sorry!' Reeves said. 'How are you, Jonathan?'

'Quite well, thank you,' Jonathan said, smiling.

'I've got you a hotel room. We'll get a taxi now. I'm in a different hotel, but I'll come up with you and we'll talk.'

They got into a taxi. Reeves talked about Munich. He talked as if he really knew the city and liked it, not as if he were talking out of nervousness. Reeves had a map, and pointed out 'the English Garden', which their taxi was not going to pass, and the section bordering the river Isar, where Reeves told him his appointment was tomorrow morning at 8 a.m. Both their hotels were in the central area, Reeves said. The taxi stopped at a hotel, and a boy in dark red uniform opened the taxi door.

Jonathan registered. The lobby had lots of modern stained-glass panels depicting German knights and troubadours. Jonathan was pleasantly aware that he felt unusually well and therefore cheerful. Was it a prelude to some awful news tomorrow, some awful catastrophe? It struck Jonathan as insane to feel cheerful, and he cautioned himself, as he might if he were on the verge of taking a drink too many.

Reeves came with him up to his room. The bellhop was just leaving, having deposited Jonathan's suitcase. Jonathan stuck his topcoat on a hook in the hall, as he might have done at home.

'Tomorrow morning – even this afternoon we might get you a new topcoat,' Reeves said, looking with a somewhat pained expression at Jonathan's.

'Oh?' Jonathan had to admit his coat was pretty shabby. He smiled a little, unresentful. At least he'd brought his good suit, his rather new black shoes. He hung up the blue suit.

'After all, you'll be in first class on the train,' Reeves said. He walked to the door and slid the button which made it impossible for anyone outside to enter 'I've got the gun. Another Italian gun, a little different. I couldn't get a silencer but I thought – to tell you the truth – a silencer wouldn't make all that much difference.'

Jonathan understood. He looked at the small gun that Reeves had pulled from some pocket, and felt for an instant empty, stupid. To fire this gun at all meant that he'd have to shoot himself immediately afterward. That was the only meaning the gun had for him.

'And this, of course,' said Reeves, pulling the garrotte from his pocket.

In the brighter light of Munich, the cord had a pallid, fleshlike colour.

'Try it on the – the back of that chair,' Reeves said.

Jonathan took the cord and dropped its loop over a projection at the back corner of a chair. He pulled it indifferently until it was tight. He was not even disgusted now, he merely felt blank. Would the average person, he wondered, finding the cord in his pocket or anywhere, know at once what it was? Probably not, Jonathan thought.

'You must jerk it, of course,' said Reeves, solemnly, 'and keep it tight.'

Jonathan felt suddenly annoyed, started to say something ill-tempered and checked himself. He took the cord off the chair, and was about to drop it on the bed, when Reeves said:

'Keep that in your pocket. Or the pocket of whatever suit you're going to wear tomorrow.'

Jonathan started to put it in the pocket of the trousers he was wearing, then went and stuck it in a pocket of the trousers of his blue suit.

'And these two pictures I'd like to show you.' Reeves took an envelope from his inside jacket pocket. The unsealed white envelope held two photographs, one glossy and the size of a postcard, the other a neatly clipped newspaper picture folded twice. 'Vito Marcangelo.'

Jonathan looked at the glossy photograph, which was cracked in a couple of places. It showed a man with a round head and face, heavy curvaceous lips, with wavy black hair. A streak of grey at either temple gave an impression of steam spewing from his head.

'He's about five six,' Reeves said. 'His hair is still grey there, he doesn't touch it up. And here he is partying.'

The newspaper photograph was of three men and a couple of women standing behind a dinner-table. An inked arrow pointed to a short, laughing man with a grey blaze at his temple. The caption was in German.

Reeves took the pictures back. 'Let's go down for the topcoat. Something'll be open. By the way the safety on that gun works as on the other gun. It's loaded with six bullets. I'll put it in here, all right?' Reeves took the gun from the foot of the bed, and put it in a corner of Jonathan's suitcase. 'Briennerstrasse's very good for shopping,' Reeves said as they rode down in the lift.

They walked. Jonathan had left his topcoat in his hotel room.

Jonathan chose a dark green tweed. Who was paying for it? That didn't seem to matter much. Jonathan also thought that he might have only about twenty-four hours to wear it. Reeves insisted on paying for the coat, though Jonathan said he could pay Reeves back when he changed some francs into marks.

'No, no, my pleasure,' said Reeves, jerking his head a little, which was sometimes his equivalent of a smile.

Jonathan wore the coat out of the shop. Reeves pointed out things to him as they walked – Odeonsplatz, the beginning of Ludwigstrasse which Reeves said went on to Schwabing, the district where Thomas Mann had had his house. They walked to the Englischer Garten, then took a taxi to a beerhall. Jonathan would have preferred tea. He realized that Reeves was trying to make him relax. Jonathan felt relaxed enough, and was not even worried about what Dr Max Schroeder would say tomorrow morning. Rather, whatever Dr Schroeder would say simply wouldn't matter.

They dined in a noisy restaurant in Schwabing, and Reeves informed him that practically everyone in the place was 'an artist or a writer'. Jonathan was amused by Reeves. Jonathan felt a bit swimmy in the head from all the beer, and now they were drinking Gumpoldsdinger.

Before midnight, Jonathan stood in his hotel room in his pyjamas. He had just had a shower. The telephone would ring at 7.15 tomorrow morning, followed at once by a continental breakfast. Jonathan sat down at the writing-table, took some notepaper from the drawer and addressed an envelope to Simone. Then he remembered he'd be home day after tomorrow, even perhaps tomorrow night late. He crumpled the envelope and tossed it into the waste-basket. Tonight during dinner he had said to Reeves, 'Do you know a man called Tom Ripley?' Reeves had looked blank and said, 'No. Why?' Jonathan got into bed and pressed a button which, conveniently, extinguished all the lights, including the one in the bathroom. Had he taken his pills to-night? Yes. Just before his shower. He'd put the pill bottle in his jacket pocket, so he could show them to Dr Schroeder tomorrow, in case the doctor was interested.

Reeves had asked, 'Did the Swiss bank write you yet?' They hadn't, but a letter from them might well have come this morn-ing to his shop, Jonathan thought. Would Simone open it? The chances were fifty-fifty, Jonathan thought, depending on how busy she was in the shop. The Swiss letter would confirm a deposit of eighty thousand marks, and there'd probably be cards for him to sign as samples of his signature. The envelope, Jonathan supposed, would have no return address on it, or nothing identifiable as a bank. Since he was returning Saturday, Simone might leave any letters unopened. Fifty-fifty, he thought again, and slid gently into sleep.

In the hospital the next morning the atmosphere seemed strictly routine and curiously informal. Reeves was present the whole time, and Jonathan could tell, though the conversation was all in German, that Reeves did not tell Dr Schroeder about a previous examination in Hamburg. The Hamburg report was now in the charge of Dr Perrier in Fontainebleau, who must by now have sent it to the Ebberle-Valent Laboratoire, as he had promised to do.

Again a nurse spoke perfect English. Dr Max Schroeder was about fifty, with black hair modishly down to his shirt collar.

'He says more or less,' Reeves told Jonathan, 'that it is a classic case with – not so cheerful predictions for the future.'

No, there was nothing new for Jonathan. Not even the message that the results of the examination would be ready for Jonathan tomorrow morning.

It was nearly 11 a.m. when Jonathan and Reeves walked out of the hospital. They walked along an embankment of the Isar, where there were children in prams, stone apartment buildings, a pharmacy, a grocery shop, all the appurtenances of living of which Jonathan felt not in the least a part that morning. He had to remember even to breathe. Today was going to be a day of failure, he thought. He wanted to plunge into the river and possibly drown, or become a fish. Reeves' presence and his sporadic talking irked him. He managed not to hear Reeves finally. Jonathan felt that he was not going to kill anyone today, not by the string in his pocket, not by the gun either.

'Shouldn't I think about getting my suitcase,' Jonathan interrupted, 'if the train's at two something?'

They found a taxi.

Almost beside the hotel there was a shop window of twinkling objects, glowing with gold and silver lights like a German Christmas tree. Jonathan drifted towards the window. It was mostly tourist trinkets, he saw with disappointment, but then he noticed a gyroscope poised at a slant against its square box.

'I want to buy something for my son,' Jonathan said, and went into the shop. He pointed and said, '*Bitte*', and acquired the gyroscope without noticing the price. He had changed two hundred francs at the hotel that morning.

Jonathan had already packed, so all he had to do was close his suitcase. He took it down himself. Reeves stuck a hundred-mark note into Jonathan's hand, and asked him to pay the hotel bill, because it might look odd if Reeves paid it. Money had ceased to matter to Jonathan.

They were early at the station. In the buffet, Jonathan didn't want anything to eat, only coffee.

So Reeves ordered coffee. 'You'll have to make the opportunity yourself, I realize, Jon. It may not work out, I know, but this man we *want* . . . Stay near the restaurant car. Smoke a cigarette, stand at the end of the carriage next to the restaurant car, for instance . . . '

Jonathan had a second coffee. Reeves bought a *Daily Telegraph* and a paperback for Jonathan to take with him.

Then the train pulled in, daintily clicking on the rails, sleek grey and blue – the Mozart Express. Reeves was looking for Marcangelo, who was supposed to board now with at least two bodyguards. There were perhaps sixty people getting on all along the platform, and as many getting off. Reeves grabbed Jonathan's arm and pointed. Jonathan was standing with suitcase in hand by the carriage he was supposed to enter, according to his ticket. Jonathan saw – or did he? – the group of three men that Reeves was talking about, three shortish men in hats climbing the steps two carriages away from Jonathan's and more towards the front of the train.

'It's him. I saw the grey in his hair even,' Reeves said. 'Now where's the restaurant car?' He stepped back to see better, trotted towards the front of the train, and came back. 'It's the one in front of Marcangelo's.'

The train's departure was being announced in French now.

'You've got the gun in your pocket?' Reeves asked.

Jonathan nodded. Reeves had reminded him, when he went up to his hotel room for his suitcase, to put it in his pocket. 'See that my wife gets the money, whatever happens to me.'

'That's a promise.' Reeves patted his arm.

The whistle blew for a second time, and doors banged. Jonathan got on the train and didn't look back at Reeves who he knew would be following him with his eyes. Jonathan found his seat. There were only two other people in the compartment, which was for eight passengers. The upholstery was dark red plush. Jonathan put his suitcase on an overhead rack, then his new coat, folded inside out. A young man entered the compartment, and hung out of the window, talking to someone in German. Jonathan's other companions were a middle-aged man sunk in what looked like office papers, and a neat little woman wearing a small hat and reading a novel. Jonathan's seat was next to the businessman, who had the window seat facing the way the train was moving. Jonathan opened his *Telegraph*.

It was 2.11 p.m.

Jonathan watched the outskirts of Munich glide past, office buildings, onion towers. Opposite Jonathan were three framed photographs – a château somewhere, a lake with a couple of swans, some snow-topped Alps. The train purred over smooth rails and rocked gently. Jonathan half closed his eyes. By locking his fingers and putting his elbows on the armrests, he could almost doze. There was time, time to make up his mind, change his mind, change back again. Marcangelo was going to Paris like him, and the train didn't arrive until 11.7 p.m. tonight. A stop came at Strassburg around 6.30 p.m., he remembered Reeves saying. A few minutes later, Jonathan came awake and realized there was a thin but regular traffic of people in the aisle beyond the glass-doored compartment. A man came partway into the compartment with a trolley of sandwiches, bottles of beer and wine. The young man bought a beer. A stocky man stood smoking a pipe in the aisle, and from time to time pushed himself against the window to let others pass him.

No harm in strolling past Marcangelo's compartment, as if *en route* to the restaurant car, Jonathan thought, just to size up the situation a bit, but it took Jonathan several minutes to muster his initiative, during which time he smoked a Gitane. He put the ashes into the metal receptacle fixed under the window, careful not to drop any on the knees of the man reading office papers.

At last Jonathan got up and walked forward. The door at the end of the carriage was sticky to open. There was another pair of doors before he reached Marcangelo's carriage. Jonathan walked slowly, bracing himself against the gentle but irregular swaying of the train, glancing into each compartment. Marcangelo's was instantly recognizable, because Marcangelo was facing Jonathan in a centre seat, asleep with hands folded across his abdomen, jowls sunk into his collar, the grey streak at the temple flowing back and up. Jonathan had a quick impression of two other Italian types leaning towards each other, talking and gesticulating. There was no one else in the compartment Jonathan thought. He went on to the end of the carriage and on to the platform, where he lit another cigarette and stood looking out the window. This end of the carriage had a W.C., which now showed a red tag in its circular lock, indicating that it was occupied. Another man, bald and slender, stood by the opposite window, perhaps waiting for the W.C. The idea of trying to kill anyone here was absurd, because there were bound to be witnesses. Or even if only killer and victim were on the platform, wouldn't someone very likely appear in a matter of seconds? The train was not at all noisy, and if a man cried out, even with the garrotte already around his neck, wouldn't the people in the first compartment hear him?

A man and a woman came out of the restaurant car, and went into the carriage aisle, not closing the doors, though a white-jacketed waiter at once did this.

Jonathan walked back in the direction of his own carriage, and glanced once more into Marcangelo's compartment, but very briefly. Marcangelo was smoking a cigarette, leaning forward fatly, talking.

If it was done, it ought to be done before Strassburg, Jonathan thought. He imagined quite a lot of people getting on at Strassburg to go to Paris. But maybe in this he was wrong. In about half an hour, he thought, he ought to put on his topcoat and go and stand on the platform at the end of Marcangelo's carriage and wait. And suppose Marcangelo used the loo at the *other* end of his carriage? There were loos at both ends. And suppose he didn't go to the loo at all? That was possible, even though it wasn't likely. And suppose the Italians simply didn't choose to patronize the restaurant car? No, they would logically go to the restaurant car, but they'd go all together, too. If he couldn't do anything, Reeves would simply have to make another plan, a better one, Jonathan thought. But Marcangelo, or someone comparable, would have to be killed, by him, if he was to collect any more money.

Just before 4 p.m., Jonathan forced himself to get up, to haul down his topcoat carefully. In the aisle, he put on the topcoat with its heavy right-hand pocket, and went with his paperback to stand on the platform at the end of Marcangelo's carriage.

II

When Jonathan passed the Italians' compartment, not glancing in this time, he had seen out of the corner of his eye a confusion of figures, men pulling down a suitcase, or perhaps struggling playfully. He had heard laughter.

A minute later, Jonathan stood leaning against a metal-framed map of Central Europe, facing the half-glass door of the corridor. Through the glass, Jonathan saw a man approaching, bumping the door open. This man looked like one of Marcangelo's bodyguards, dark-haired, in his thirties, with the sour expression and the sturdy build that ensured he would one day look like a disgruntled toad. Jonathan recalled the photographs on the jacket of *The Grim Reapers*. The man went straight to the W.C. door and entered. Jonathan continued to look at his open paperback. After a very short time, the man reappeared and went back into the corridor.

Jonathan found that he had been holding his breath. Suppose it had been Marcangelo, wouldn't it have been a perfect opportunity, with no one passing from the carriage or the restaurant car? Jonathan realized he would've stood just where he was, pretending to read, if it *had* been Marcangelo. Jonathan's right hand, in his pocket, pushed the safety on and off the little gun. After all, what was the risk? What was the loss? Merely his own life.

Marcangelo might come lumbering forward at any minute, push the door open, and then – It could be like before, in the German underground. Couldn't it? Then a bullet for himself. But Jonathan imagined firing at Marcangelo, then tossing the gun at once out the door by the W.C., or out the door's window which looked as if it opened, then walking casually into the restaurant car, sitting down and ordering something.

It was quite impossible.

I'll order something now, Jonathan thought, and went into the restaurant car, where there were plenty of free tables. On one side, the tables were for four people, on the other side for two. Jonathan took one of the smaller tables. A waiter came, Jonathan ordered a beer, then quickly changed it to wine.

'*Weisswein, bitte,*' Jonathan said.

A cold quarter-bottle of Riesling appeared. The *cluckety-cluck* of the train sounded more muffled and luxurious here. The window was bigger, yet more private somehow, making the forest – the Black Forest? – look spectacularly rich and verdant. There were endless tall pines, as if Germany had so many it did not need to cut any down for any purpose. Not a scrap of débris or paper was to be seen, nor was any human figure to be seen caring for it, which was equally surprising to Jonathan. When did the Germans do their tidying? Jonathan tried to summon courage from the wine. Somewhere along the line he had lost his momentum, and it was just a matter of getting it back. He drank off the last of the wine as if it were an obligatory toast, paid his bill, and pulled on his coat, which he had laid on the chair opposite. He would stand on the platform until Marcangelo appeared, and whether Marcangelo was alone or with two body-guards, he would shoot.

Jonathan tugged at the carriage door, sliding it open. He was back in the prison of the platform, leaning against the map again, looking at the stupid paperback . . . *David had wondered, did Elaine suspect? Desperate now, David went over the events of* . . . Jonathan's eyes moved over the print like an illiterate's. He remembered something he'd thought of before, days ago. Simone would refuse the money, if she knew how he had got it, and of course she'd know how he had got it, if he shot himself on the train. He wondered if Simone could be persuaded by Reeves, by somebody, convinced – that what he had done wasn't exactly like murder. Jonathan almost laughed. It was quite hope-less. And what was he doing standing here? He could walk straight ahead now, back to his seat.

A figure was approaching, and Jonathan looked up. Then he blinked. The man coming towards him was Tom Ripley.

Ripley pushed open the half-glass door, smiling a little. 'Jona-than,' he said softly. 'Give me the thing, would you? – The garrotte.' He stood sideways to Jonathan, looking out the window.

Jonathan felt suddenly blank with shock. Whose side was Tom Ripley on? Marcangelo's? Then Jonathan started at the sight of three men approaching in the corridor.

Tom moved a bit closer to Jonathan to get out of their way.

The men were talking in German, and they went on into the restaurant car.

Tom said over his shoulder to Jonathan, 'The string. We'll give it a try, all right?'

Jonathan understood, or partly understood. Ripley was a friend of Reeves. He knew Reeves' plan. Jonathan was wadding the garrotte up in his left-hand trousers pocket. He pulled his hand out and gave the garrotte into Tom's willing hand. Jonathan looked away from Tom, and was aware of a sense of relief.

Tom pushed the garrotte into the right-hand pocket of his jacket. 'Stay there, because I might need you.' Tom went over to the W.C., saw it was empty, and went in.

Tom locked the toilet door. The garrotte wasn't even through its loop. Tom adjusted it for action, and put it carefully into the right-hand pocket of his jacket. He smiled a little. Jonathan had gone pale as a sheet! Tom had rung up Reeves the day before yesterday, and Reeves had told him Jonathan was coming but would probably hold out for a gun. Jonathan must have a gun now, Tom thought, but Tom considered a gun impossible in such conditions.

Stepping on the water pedal. Tom wet his hands, shook them, and passed his palms over his face. He was feeling a bit nervous himself. His first Mafia effort!

Tom had felt that Jonathan might botch this job, and having got Trevanny into this, Tom thought it behooved him to try to help him out. So Tom had flown to Salzburg yesterday, in order to board the train today. Tom had asked Reeves what Marcangelo looked like, but rather casually, and Tom didn't think Reeves suspected that he was going to be on the train. On the contrary, Tom had told Reeves that he thought his scheme was hare-brained, and had told Reeves that he might let Jonathan off with half the money and find someone else for the second job, if he wanted to make a success of it. But not Reeves. Reeves was like a small boy playing a game he had invented himself, a rather obsessive game with severe rules – for other people. Tom wanted to help Trevanny, and what a great cause it was! Killing a big shot Mafioso! Maybe even two Mafiosi!

Tom hated the Mafia, hated their loan-sharking, their blackmail, their bloody church, their cowardliness in forever delegating their dirty work to underlings, so that the law couldn't get its hands on the bigger bastards among them, never get them behind bars except on charges of income tax evasion or some other triviality. The Mafiosi made Tom feel almost virtuous by comparison. At this thought, Tom laughed out loud, a laugh which rang in the tiny metal-and-tile room in which he stood. (He was aware too that he just might be keeping Marcangelo himself waiting outside the door.) Yes, there were people more dishonest, more corrupt, decidedly more ruthless than himself, and these were the Mafiosi – that charming, squabbling batch of families which the Italian–American League claimed did not exist, claimed were a figment of fiction-writers' imagination. Why, the church itself with its bishops making blood liquefy at the festival of San Gennaro, and little girls seeing visions of the Virgin Mary, all *this* was more real than the Mafia! Yes, indeed! Tom rinsed his mouth and spat and ran water into the basin and let it drain. Then he went out.

There was no one but Jonathan Trevanny on the platform, Jonathan now smoking a cigarette, but he at once dropped the cigarette like a soldier who wanted to appear more efficient under the eyes of a superior officer. Tom gave him a reassuring smile, and faced the side window by Jonathan.

'Did they go by, by any chance?' Tom had not wanted to peer through the two doors into the restaurant car.

'No.'

'We may have to wait till after Strassburg, but I hope not.'

A woman was emerging from the restaurant car, having trouble with the doors, and Tom sprang to open the second for her.

'*Danke schön,*' she said.

'*Bitte,*' Tom replied.

Tom drifted to the other side of the platform and pulled a

Herald-Tribune from a pocket of his jacket. It was now 5.11 p.m.
They were to arrive at Strassburg at 6.33 p.m. Tom supposed the
Italians had had a big lunch, and were not going to go into the
restaurant car.

A man went into the lavatory.

Jonathan was looking down at his book, but Tom's glance
made Jonathan look at him, and Tom smiled once more. When
the man came out, Tom moved over towards Jonathan. There
were two men standing in the aisle of the carriage, several yards
away, one smoking a cigar, both looking out the window and
paying no attention to him and Jonathan.

'I'll try to get him *in* the loo,' Tom said. 'Then we'll have to
heave him out the door.' Tom jerked his head to indicate the
door on the lavatory side. 'If I'm in the loo with him, knock
twice on the door when the coast is clear. Then we'll give him
the old heave-ho as fast as poss.' Very casually Tom lit a Gauloise,
then slowly and deliberately yawned.

Jonathan's panic, which had reached a peak when Tom had
been in the W.C., was subsiding a little. Tom wanted to go
through with it. Just why he did was beyond Jonathan's power
to imagine just now. Jonathan also had a feeling that Tom might
intend to botch the thing, and leave Jonathan holding the bag.
And yet, why? More likely Tom Ripley wanted a cut of the
money, maybe all the rest of it. At that moment, Jonathan
simply didn't care. It didn't matter. Now Tom himself looked a
bit worried, Jonathan thought. He was leaning against the wall
opposite the W.C. door, newspaper in hand, but he wasn't
reading.

Then Jonathan saw two men approaching. The second man
was Marcangelo. The first man was not one of the Italians.
Jonathan glanced at Tom – who at once looked at him – and
Jonathan nodded once.

The first man looked around on the platform, saw the W.C.
and made for it. Marcangelo passed in front of Jonathan, saw
that the W.C. was occupied, and turned back and returned to the
carriage aisle. Jonathan saw Tom grin and make a sweeping
gesture with his right arm, as if to say, 'Dammit, the fish got
away!'

Marcangelo was in plain view of Jonathan, waiting just a

few feet away in the aisle, looking out the window. It occurred to Jonathan that Marcangelo's guards, who were in the middle of the carriage, wouldn't know that Marcangelo had had to wait, so that this extra time would arouse their anxiety sooner if Marcangelo didn't come back. Jonathan nodded slightly at Tom, which he hoped Tom would understand to mean that Marcangelo was waiting near by.

The man in the loo came out and returned to the carriage.

Now Marcangelo approached, and Jonathan gave a glance at Tom, but Tom was sunk in his newspaper.

Tom was aware that the dumpy figure entering the platform was Marcangelo again, but he did not look up from his newspaper. Just in front of Tom, Marcangelo opened the door of the W.C., and Tom sprang forward like a person who was determined to get into the toilet first, but at the same time he flipped the garrotte over the head of Marcangelo whose cry Tom hoped he stifled as he dragged him, with a jerk of the garrotte like a boxer's right cross, into the little room and closed the door. Tom yanked the garrotte viciously – one of Marcangelo's own weapons in his prime, Tom supposed – and Tom saw the nylon disappear in the flesh of the neck. Tom gave it another whirl behind the man's head and pulled still tighter. With his left hand Tom flicked the lever that locked the door. Marcangelo's gurgle stopped, his tongue began to protrude from the awful wet mouth, his eyes closed in misery, then opened in horror, and began to have the blank, what's-happening-to-me stare of the dying. Lower false teeth clattered to the tiles. Tom was nearly cutting his own thumb and the side of his forefinger because of the force he was exerting on the string, but he felt it a pain worth enduring. Marcangelo had slumped to the floor, but the garrotte, or rather Tom, was holding him in more or less a seated position. Marcangelo was now unconscious, Tom thought, and it was impossible for him to be breathing at all. Tom picked up the teeth, and dropped them into the toilet, and managed to step on the pedal which dumped the pan. He wiped his fingers with disgust on Marcangelo's padded shoulder.

Jonathan had seen the flick of the latch that changed the colour from green to red. The silence was alarming to Jonathan. How long would it last? What was happening? How much time had passed? Jonathan kept glancing through the glass half of the door into the carriage.

A man came from the restaurant car, started for the toilet, and seeing that it was occupied, went on into the carriage.

Jonathan was thinking that Marcangelo's friends would appear at any moment, if Marcangelo was in the least long in getting back to his compartment. Now the coast was clear, and was it time to knock? There *must* have been time for Marcangelo to die. Jonathan went and rapped twice on the door.

Tom stepped calmly out, closed the door and surveyed the situation, and a woman in a reddish tweed suit entered the platform just then – a smallish, middle-aged woman who was plainly headed for the toilet. The indicator was now showing green.

'Sorry,' Tom said to her. 'Someone – a friend of mine is being sick in there, I'm afraid.'

'*Bitte?*'

'*Mein Freund ist da drinnen ziemlich krank,*' Tom said with an apologetic smile. '*Entschuldigen Sie, gnädige Frau. Er kommt sofort heraus.*'

She nodded and smiled, and went back into the carriage.

'Okay, give me a hand!' Tom whispered to Jonathan, and started for the W.C.

'Another one's coming,' Jonathan said. 'One of the Italians.'

'Oh, Christ.' The Italian might simply wait on the platform, Tom thought, if he went into the loo and locked the door.

The Italian, a sallow chap of about thirty, gave Jonathan and Tom a look, saw that the lavatory said *libre*, then went into the restaurant car, no doubt to see if Marcangelo was there.

Tom said to Jonathan, 'Can you bash him with the gun after I hit him?'

Jonathan nodded. The gun was small, but Jonathan's adrenalin was at last stirring.

'As if your life depended on it,' Tom added. 'Maybe it does.'

The bodyguard came back from the restaurant car, moving more quickly. Tom was on the Italian's left, and pulled him by the shirtfront suddenly, out of view of the restaurant car's doors, and hit him in the jaw. Tom followed this with a left fist in the man's abdomen, and Jonathan cracked the Italian on the back of the head with the gun butt.

'The door!' Tom said, jerking his head, trying to catch the Italian who was falling forward.

The man was not unconscious, his arms flailed weakly, but Jonathan already had the side door open, and Tom's instinct was to get him out without spending a second on another blow. The noise of the train wheels came with a sudden roar. They pushed, kicked and poured the bodyguard out, and Tom lost his balance and would have toppled out, if not for Jonathan catching him by his jacket tails. *Bang* went the door shut again.

Jonathan pushed his fingers through his tousled hair.

Tom motioned for Jonathan to go to the other side of the platform, where he could see down the aisle. Jonathan went, and Tom could see him making an effort to collect himself and look like the ordinary passenger again.

Tom raised his eyebrows in a question, and Jonathan nodded, and Tom nipped into the W.C. and swung the latch, trusting that Jonathan would have the wit to knock again when it was safe. Marcangelo lay crumpled on the floor, head next to the basin pedestal, his face pale now with a touch of blue in it. Tom looked away from him, heard the rustle of doors outside – the restaurant car doors – and then a welcome two knocks. This time Tom opened the door just a crack.

'Looks all right,' Jonathan said.

Tom kicked the door open past Marcangelo's shoes which the door bumped, and signalled for Jonathan to open the side door of the train. But in fact they worked together, Jonathan having to help Tom with some of Marcangelo's weight before the side door was in a fully open position. The door tended to close because of the direction of the train. They tumbled Marcangelo through it head-first, heels over head, and Tom, giving him a final kick, didn't touch him at all, because his body had already fallen clear on to a cinder bank so close to Tom that he could see individual ashes and blades of grass. Now Tom held Jonathan's right arm while Jonathan reached for the door's lever and caught it.

Tom pulled the toilet door shut, breathless, trying to assume a calm air. 'Go back to your seat and get off at Strassburg,' he said. 'They'll be looking at everyone on this train.' He gave

Jonathan a nervous pat on the arm. 'Good luck, my friend.' Tom watched Jonathan open the door that went into the carriage aisle.

Then Tom started to enter the restaurant car, but a party of four was coming out, and Tom had to step aside while they waddled, talked and laughed through the two doors. Tom at last entered and took the first vacant table. He sat down in a chair facing the door he had just come through. He was expecting the second bodyguard at any moment. He drew the menu towards him and casually studied it. Cole slaw. Tongue salad. Gulaschsuppe . . . The menu was in French, English and German.

Jonathan, walking down the aisle of Marcangelo's carriage, came face to face with the second Italian bodyguard who rudely bumped into him in getting past. Jonathan was glad he felt a bit dazed, otherwise he might have reacted with alarm at the physical contact. The train gave one whistle followed by two shorter ones. Did that mean something? Jonathan got back to his seat and sat down without removing his overcoat, careful not to glance at any of the four people in the compartment. His watch said 5.31 p.m. It seemed more than an hour since he had looked at his watch and it had been a couple of minutes past 5 p.m. Jonathan squirmed, closed his eyes, cleared his throat, imagining the bodyguard and Marcangelo, having rolled under the train wheels, being chewed into various bits. Or maybe they hadn't rolled under. Was the bodyguard even dead? Maybe he'd be rescued and would describe him and Tom Ripley with accuracy. Why had Tom Ripley helped him? Or should he call it help? What did Ripley want out of it? He was now under Ripley's thumb, he realized. Ripley probably wanted only money, however. Or was he due for worse? Some kind of blackmail? Blackmail had a lot of forms.

Should he try to get a plane from Strassburg to Paris tonight, or stay at a hotel in Strassburg? Which was safer? And safer from what, the Mafia or the police? Wouldn't some passenger, looking out the window, have seen one body, maybe two, falling beside the train? Or had the two bodies fallen too close to the train to be seen? If anybody had seen anything, the train wouldn't have stopped, but word could be radioed, Jonathan supposed. Jonathan was on the alert for a train guard in the aisle, for any sign of agitation, but he didn't see any.

At that moment, having ordered Gulaschsuppe and a bottle of Carlsbad, Tom was looking at his newspaper which he had propped against a mustard pot, and nibbling a crisp roll. And he was amused by the anxious Italian who had waited patiently outside the occupied loo, until to the Italian's surprise a woman had emerged. Now the bodyguard was for the second time peering down the dining-car through the two glass doors. And here he came, still trying to keep his cool, looking for his *capo* or his thug chum or both, walking the whole length of the car as if he might find Marcangelo sprawled under one of the tables or chatting with the chef at the other end of the car.

Tom had not lifted his eyes as the Italian came through, but Tom had felt his glance. Now Tom risked a look over his shoulder, such as a man who was expecting his food might give, and saw the bodyguard – a blondish, crinkly-haired type in a chalk-stripe suit, broad purple tie – talking with a waiter at the back of the car. The busy waiter was shaking his head and pushing past him with his tray. The bodyguard bustled down the aisle between the tables again and went out.

Tom's paprika-red soup arrived with the beer. Tom was hungry, as he had had only a small breakfast in his Salzburg hotel – not the Goldener Hirsch this time, because the staff knew him there. Tom had flown to Salzburg instead of Munich, not wanting to encounter Reeves and Jonathan Trevanny at the railway station. He'd had time in Salzburg to buy a green leather jacket with green felt trim for Heloise, which he intended to hide away until her birthday in October. He had told Heloise he was going to Paris for one night, maybe two, to see some art exhibits, and since Tom did this now and then, staying at the Inter-Continental or the Ritz or the Pont Royal, Heloise had not been surprised. Tom in fact varied his hotels, so that if he told Heloise he was in Paris when he wasn't, she wouldn't be alarmed at not finding him at, say, the Inter-Continental, if she telephoned. He had also bought his ticket at Orly, instead of at the travel agencies at Fontainebleau or Moret where he was known, and he had used his false passport provided by Reeves last year: Rober Fiedler Mackay, American, engineer, born in Salt Lake

City, no wife. It had occurred to Tom that the Mafia could get the passenger list of the train with a bit of effort. Was he on the Mafia's list of interesting people? Tom hesitated to attribute such an honour to himself, but some of Marcangelo's family might have noticed his name in the newspapers. Not recruitable material, not promising as extortion victim either, but still a man on the borderline of the law.

But this Mafia bodyguard, or button man, hadn't given Tom as long a look as he'd given a husky young man in a leather jacket across the aisle from Tom. Perhaps all was well.

Jonathan Trevanny would need some reassuring. Trevanny no doubt thought he wanted money, that he was intending to blackmail him somehow. Tom had to laugh a little (but he was still looking at his newspaper and might have been reading Art Buchwald) at the memory of Trevanny's face when Tom had walked on to the platform, and at that funny moment when Trevanny had realized that he meant to help him Tom had done some thinking in Villeperce, and decided to lend a hand with the nasty garrotting, so that Jonathan could at least collect the money that had been promised. Tom was vaguely ashamed of himself, in fact, for having got Jonathan into it, and so coming to Jonathan's aid relieved a bit of Tom's guilt. Yes, if all went well, Trevanny would be a lucky and much happier man, Tom was thinking, and Tom believed in positive thinking. Don't hope, *think* the best, and things would work out for the best, Tom felt. He would have to see Trevanny again to explain a few things, and above all Trevanny should take full credit for the Marcangelo murder in order to collect the rest of the money from Reeves. He and Trevanny mustn't be seen to be chummy, that was a vital point. They mustn't *be* chummy, at all. (Tom wondered now what was happening to Trevanny, if the second bodyguard was cruising the whole train?) The dear old Mafia would try to track the killer down, the killers maybe. The Mafia often took years, but they never gave up. Even if the man they wanted fled to South America, the Mafia might get him, Tom knew. But it seemed to Tom that Reeves Minot was in more danger than either himself or Trevanny at the moment.

He'd try to ring Trevanny tomorrow morning in his shop. Or tomorrow afternoon, in case Trevanny didn't make it to Paris tonight. Tom lit a Gauloise and glanced at the woman in the reddish tweed suit, whom he and Trevanny had seen on the platform, who was now dreamily eating a dainty salad of lettuce and cucumber. Tom felt euphoric.

When Jonathan got off at Strassburg, he imagined that there were more police than usual in evidence, six perhaps instead of the usual two or three. One police officer seemed to be examining a man's papers. Or had the man simply asked a direction, and the cop was consulting a guidebook? Jonathan walked straight out of the station with his suitcase. He had decided to stay the night in Strassburg which, for no real reason, seemed a safer place than Paris tonight. The remaining bodyguard was probably going on to Paris to join his friends – unless by some chance the bodyguard was at this moment tailing him, ready to plug him in the back. Jonathan felt a light sweat breaking out, and he was suddenly aware of being tired. He let his suitcase down on a kerb at a street intersection, and gazed around at unfamiliar buildings. The scene was busy with pedestrians and cars. It was 6.40 p.m., no doubt the Strassburg rush hour. Jonathan thought of registering under another name. If he wrote a false name plus a false card or identity number, no one would ask to see his real card. Then he realized that a false name would make him even more uneasy. Jonathan was becoming aware of what he had done. He suffered a brief nausea. Then he picked up his suitcase and trudged on. The gun weighed heavily in his overcoat pocket. He was afraid to drop it down a street drain, or into a rubbish bin. Jonathan saw himself getting all the way to Paris and into his own house with the little gun still in his pocket.

12

Tom, having left the green Renault station-wagon near the Porte d'Italie in Paris, got home to Belle Ombre a little before 1 a.m. Saturday. There was no light visible at the front of the house, but when Tom climbed the stairs with his suitcase, he was delighted to see that there was a light in Heloise's room in the back left corner. He went in to see her.

'Back finally! How was Paris? What did you do?' Heloise was in green pyjamas with a pink satin eiderdown pulled up to her waist.

'Ah, I chose a bad film tonight.' Tom saw that the book she was reading was one he had bought, on the French socialist movement. That would not improve relations with her father, Tom thought. Often Heloise came out with very leftist remarks, principles which she had no idea of practising. But Tom felt he was slowly pushing her to the left. Push with one hand, take with the other, Tom thought.

'Did you see Noëlle?' Heloise asked.

'No. Why?'

'She was having a dinner-party – tonight. I think. She needed one more man. Of course she invited us both, but I told her you were probably at the Ritz and to telephone you.'

'I was at the Crillon this time,' Tom said, pleasantly aware of the scent of Heloise's cologne mingled with Nivea. And he was unpleasantly aware of his own filth after the train ride. 'Is everything all right here?'

'Very all right,' said Heloise in a manner that sounded seductive, though Tom knew she didn't mean it that way. She meant she had had a happy and ordinary day and she was happy herself.

'I feel like a shower. See you in ten minutes.' Tom went to his own room, where he had a real shower in the tub, not the telephone-type shower of Heloise's bathroom.

A few minutes later – Heloise's Austrian jacket having been tucked away in a bottom drawer under sweaters – Tom was dozing in bed beside Heloise, too tired to look at *L'Express* any longer. He was wondering if *L'Express* might have a picture of one of the two Mafiosi, or both, beside the railway track in next weeks' edition? Was that bodyguard dead? Tom devoutly hoped he had fallen under the rails somehow, because Tom was afraid he hadn't been dead when they tossed him out. Tom recalled Jonathan pulling him back when he'd been about to fall out, and with his eyes closed Tom winced at the memory. Trevanny had saved his life, or at least saved him from an awful fall, and possibly from having a foot cut off by the train wheels.

Tom slept well, and got up around 8.30 a.m., before Heloise was awake. He had coffee downstairs in the living-room, and in spite of his curiosity didn't switch on the radio for the 9 a.m. news. He took a stroll around the garden, gazed with some pride at the strawberry patch which he had recently snipped and weeded, and stared at three burlap sacks of dahlia roots that had been kept over the winter and were due for planting. Tom was thinking of trying Trevanny by telephone this afternoon. The sooner he saw Trevanny, the better for Trevanny's peace of mind. Tom wondered if Jonathan had also noticed the blondish bodyguard who had been in such a tizzy? Tom had passed him in an aisle when he had been making his way from the restaurant car back to his carriage, three carriages back, the bodyguard looking ready to explode with frustration, and Tom had had a great desire to say in his best gutter Italian, 'You'll get the sack if this kind of work keeps up, eh?'

Mme Annette returned before 11 a.m. from her morning shopping and, hearing her close the side door into the kitchen, Tom went in to have a look at *Le Parisien Liberé*.

'The horses,' Tom said with a smile, picking up the newspaper.

'Ah *oui*! You have a bet, M. Tome?'

Mme Annette knew he didn't bet. 'No, I want to see how a friend made out.'

Tom found what he was looking for at the bottom of page

one, a short item about three inches long. Italian garrotted. Another gravely wounded. The garrotted man was identified as Vito Marcangelo, fifty-two, of Milan. Tom was more interested in the gravely wounded Filippo Turoli, thirty-one who had also been pushed from the train and suffered multiple concussions, broken ribs and a damaged arm that might require amputation in a hospital of Strassburg. Turoli was said to be in a coma and in critical condition. The report went on to say that a passenger had seen one body on the train embankment and alerted a train official, but not before kilometres had been covered by the luxurious Mozart Express, which had been going à *pleine vitesse* towards Strassburg. Then two bodies had been discovered by the rescue team. It was estimated that four minutes had elapsed between the fall of each body, and police were actively pursuing their inquiries.

Obviously there would be more on the subject, with photographs probably, in later editions, Tom thought. That was a nice Gallic touch of detection, the four minutes, like a problem in arithmetic for children also, Tom thought. If a train is going at one hundred kilometres per hour, and one Mafioso is tossed out, and a second Mafioso is found tossed out six and two-thirds of a kilometre distant from the first Mafioso, how much time has elapsed between the tossing out of each Mafioso? Answer: four minutes. There was no mention of the second bodyguard who was evidently keeping his mouth shut and lodging no complaints about the service on the Mozart Express.

But the bodyguard Turoli wasn't dead. And Tom realized that Turoli had perhaps had a look at him before Tom hit him in the jaw, had some idea of him. He might be able to describe him or identify him, if he ever saw Tom again. But Turoli had probably not taken in Jonathan at all, since Jonathan had hit him from behind.

Around 3.30 p.m., when Heloise had gone off to visit Agnès Grais on the other side of Villeperce, Tom looked up Trevanny's shop number in Fontainebleau, and found that he had it correct in his memory.

Trevanny answered.

'Hello. This is Tom Ripley. Um-m – about my picture – Are you alone just now?'

'Yes.'

'I'd like to see you. I think it's important. Can you meet me, say – after you close today? Around seven? I can – '

'Yes.' Trevanny sounded as tense as a cat.

'Suppose I hold my car around the Salamandre bar? You know the bar I mean on the Rue Grande?'

'Yes, I know it.'

'Then we'll drive somewhere and have a talk. Quarter to seven?'

'Right,' said Trevanny as if through his teeth.

Trevanny was going to be pleasantly surprised, Tom thought as he hung up.

A little later that afternoon, when Tom was in his atelier, Heloise telephoned.

'Hello, Tom! I am not coming home, because Agnès and I are going to cook something wonderful and we want you to come. Antoine is here, you know. It's Saturday! So come around seven-thirty, all right?'

'How is eight, darling? I'm working a little.'

'*Tu travailles?*'

Tom smiled. 'I'm sketching. I'll be there at eight.'

Antoine Grais was an architect with a wife and two small children. Tom looked forward to a pleasant, relaxing evening with his neighbours. He drove off for Fontainebleau early so that he could buy a plant – he chose a camellia – as a present for the Grais, and give this as an excuse for being a little late, in case he was.

In Fontainebleau Tom also bought a *France-Soir* for the latest news about Turoli. There was nothing about any change in his condition, but the paper did say that the two Italians were believed to be members of the Genotti family of Mafia, and might have been victims of a rival gang. That at least would please Reeves, Tom thought, as that was Reeves' objective. Tom found a vacant spot at the kerb a few yards from the Salamandre. He looked through his back window and saw Trevanny walking towards him, in his rather slow stride, then Trevanny caught sight of Tom's car. Trevanny was wearing a mac of impressive decrepitude.

'Hello!' Tom said, opening the door. 'Get in and we'll go to Avon – or somewhere.'

Trevanny got in, barely mumbling a hello.

Avon was a twin town with Fontainebleau, though smaller. Tom drove down the slope towards the Fontainebleau-Avon railway station and bore to the right on the curve that led into Avon.

'Everything all right?' Tom asked pleasantly.

'Yes,' Trevanny said.

'You've seen the papers, I suppose.'

'Yes.'

'That bodyguard isn't dead.'

'I know.' Jonathan had imagined, since 8 a.m. that morning when he had seen the papers in Strassburg, that Turoli was going to come out of his coma at any moment and give a description of him and of Tom Ripley, the two men on the platform.

'You got back to Paris last night?'

'No I – I stayed in Strassburg and got a plane this morning.'

'No trouble in Strassburg? No sign of that second bodyguard?'

'No,' Jonathan said.

Tom was driving slowly, looking for a quiet spot. He slid up to a kerb in a little street of two-storey houses, stopped, and switched off his lights. 'I think,' Tom said, pulling out his cigarettes, 'considering the papers haven't reported clues – not the right ones anyway – we did a rather good job. That comatose bodyguard is the only rub.' Tom offered Jonathan a cigarette, but Jonathan took his own. 'Have you heard from Reeves?' Tom asked.

'Yes. This afternoon. Before you rang.' Reeves had rung this morning and Simone had answered. *Someone in Hamburg. An American*, Simone had said. That was also making Jonathan nervous, simply the fact that Simone had spoken with Reeves, although Reeves hadn't given his name.

'I hope he's not being sticky about the money,' Tom said. 'I prodded him, you know. He ought to come up with all of it right away.'

And how much would you like, Jonathan wanted to ask, but decided to let Ripley get to it himself.

Tom smiled and slumped behind the wheel. 'You're probably thinking that I want some of the – forty thousand quid isn't it? But I don't.'

'Oh. – Frankly I was thinking you wanted some. Yes.'

'That's why I wanted to see you today. One of the reasons. The other reason is to ask if you're worried –' Jonathan's tension was making Tom feel awkward, almost tongue-tied. He gave a laugh. 'Of course you're worried! But there're worries and worries. I might be able to help – that is if you talk to me.'

What *did* he want, Jonathan wondered. He surely wanted something. 'I don't quite understand, I suppose, why you were on the train.'

'Because it was a pleasure! A pleasure for me to eliminate, or help to eliminate such people as those two yesterday. Simple as that! Also a pleasure for me to help you put a little money in your pocket. – However, I meant worried about what we did – in any way. It's hard for me to put into words. Maybe because I'm not at all worried. Not yet anyway.'

Jonathan felt off balance. Tom Ripley was being evasive – somehow – or joking. Jonathan still felt a hostility towards Ripley, a wariness of him. And now it was too late. Yesterday on the train, seeing Ripley about to take over the job, Jonathan might have said, 'All right, it's all yours,' and walked off, back to his seat. That would not have erased the Hamburg affair which Ripley knew about, but – Yesterday the money hadn't been the motivation. Jonathan had simply been in a panic, even before Ripley had arrived. Now Jonathan felt he couldn't find the right weapon for his defence. 'I gather it was you,' Jonathan said, 'who put out the story that I was on my last legs. You gave my name to Reeves.'

'Yes,' Tom said a little contritely but firmly. 'But it was a choice, wasn't it? You could've said no to Reeves' idea.' Tom waited, but Jonathan didn't answer. 'However, the situation is considerably better now, I trust. Isn't it? I hope you're not any-where near dying, and you've got quite a bit of dough – lolly, you'd call it.'

Jonathan saw Tom's face light up with his innocent-looking American smile. No one, seeing Tom Ripley's face now, would imagine that he could kill anyone, garrotte someone, and yet he'd done just that about twenty-four hours ago. 'You have a habit of playing practical jokes?' Jonathan asked with a smile.

'No. No, certainly not. This might be the first time.'

'And you want – nothing at all.'

'I can't think of anything I want from you. Not even friendship, because that'd be dangerous.'

Jonathan squirmed. He made himself stop drumming his fingers on a matchbox.

Tom could imagine what he was thinking, that he was under Tom Ripley's thumb, in a way, whether Ripley wanted anything or not. Tom said, 'You're no more in my grip than I am in yours. I did the garrotting, didn't I? You could as well say something against me as I against you. Think of it that way.'

'True,' Jonathan said.

'If there's one thing I'd like to do it's protect you.'

Now Jonathan laughed and Ripley didn't.

'Of course it may not be necessary. Let's hope not. The trouble is always other people. Ha!' Tom stared through the windshield for an instant. 'For instance, your wife. What've you told her about the money coming in?'

That was a problem, real, tangible and unsolved. 'I said I was being paid something by the German doctors. That they're making tests – using me.'

'Not bad,' Tom said musingly, 'but maybe we can think of something better. Because obviously you can't account for the whole sum like that, and you both may as well enjoy it. – How about somebody dying in your family? In England? A recluse cousin, for instance.'

Jonathan smiled and glanced at Tom. 'I've thought of that, but frankly there isn't anybody.'

Tom could see that Jonathan wasn't in the habit of inventing. Tom could have invented something for Heloise, for example, if he'd suddenly come into a great deal of money. He would create an eccentric recluse tucked away in Santa Fe or Sausalito all these years, a third cousin of his mother's, something like that, and embroider the personage with details remembered from a brief meeting in Boston when Tom had been a small boy, orphaned as Tom really had been. Little had he known that this cousin had a heart of gold. 'Still it ought to be easy with your family so far away in England. We'll think about it,' Tom added, when he saw that Jonathan was about to say something in the negative. Tom looked at his watch. 'I'm afraid I'm due for dinner, and I suppose you are too. Ah, one more thing, the gun. A small matter, but did you get rid of it?'

The gun was in the pocket of the raincoat Jonathan was wearing. 'I've got it now. I'd very much like to get rid of it.'

Tom extended his hand. 'Let's have it. One thing out of the way.' Trevanny handed it to him, and Tom stuck it into the glove compartment. 'Never used, so it's not too dangerous, but I'll get rid of it because it's Italian.' Tom paused for thought. There must be something else, and now was the time to think of it, because he did not intend to see Jonathan again. Then it came to him. 'By the way, I will assume that you tell Reeves you did this job alone. Reeves doesn't know I was on the train. It's much better that way.'

Jonathan had rather assumed the opposite, and took a moment to digest this. 'I thought you were a rather good friend of Reeves.'

'Oh, we're friendly. Not too. We keep a distance.' In a way Tom was thinking out loud, and also trying to say the right thing in order not to scare Trevanny, in order to make Trevanny feel more sure of himself. It was difficult. 'No one knows I was on that train but you. I bought my ticket under another name. In fact I was using a false passport. I realized you were having trouble with the garrotte idea. I spoke with Reeves on the telephone.' Tom started his motor and put on the lights. 'Reeves is a bit cracked.'

'How so?'

A motorcycle with a strong headlight came roaring round the corner and passed them, drowning out the car's hum for a moment.

'He plays games.' Tom said. 'He's mainly a fence, as you may know, receives goods, passes them on. It's as silly as spy games, but at least Reeves hasn't been caught yet – caught and released and all that. I understand he's doing quite well in Hamburg, but

I haven't seen his place there. – He shouldn't be dabbling in *this* sort of thing. Not his dish.'

Jonathan had been imagining Tom Ripley a frequent visitor at Reeves Minot's place in Hamburg. He remembered Fritz turning up with a small package at Reeves' that night. Jewellery? Dope? Jonathan watched the familiar viaduct, then the dark green trees near the railway station come into view, their tops bright under the street lights. Only Tom Ripley next to him was unfamiliar. Jonathan's fear rose afresh. 'If I may ask – how did you come to pick on me?'

Tom was just then making the difficult turn left at the top of the hill into the Avenue Franklin Roosevelt, and had to pause for oncoming traffic. 'For a petty reason, I'm sorry to say. That night in February at your party – you said something I didn't like.' Now Tom was clear of traffic. 'You said, "Yes, I've heard of you," in a rather nasty way.'

Jonathan remembered. He also remembered he'd been feeling particularly tired and consequently bloody-minded that evening. So for a slight rudeness, Ripley had got him into the mess he was in now. Rather, he'd got himself into it, Jonathan reminded himself.

'You won't have to see me again,' Tom said. 'The job has been a success. I think, if we don't hear anything from that body-guard.' Should he say 'I'm sorry' to Jonathan? To hell with it, Tom thought. 'And from a moral point of view, I trust you don't reproach yourself. Those men were murderers also. They often murder innocent people. So we took the law into our own hands. The Mafia would be the first to agree that people should take the law into their own hands. That's their cornerstone.' Tom turned right into the Rue de France. 'I won't take you all the way to your door.'

'Any place here. Thanks very much.'

'I'll try to send a friend to pick up my picture.' Tom stopped his car.

Jonathan got out. 'As you like.'

'Do ring me if you're in straits,' Tom said with a smile.

At least Jonathan smiled back, as if he were amused.

Jonathan walked towards the Rue St Merry, and in the next seconds began to feel better – relieved. Much of his relief was due to the fact that Ripley didn't seem to be worried – not by the bodyguard still alive, not by the fact they'd both stood for what seemed an unlikely length of time on that platform in the train. And the money situation – that was as incredible as the rest of it.

Jonathan slowed his steps as he approached the Sherlock Holmes house, though he knew he was later than usual. The signature cards from the Swiss bank had come to his shop yesterday, Simone had not opened the letter, and Jonathan had signed the cards and put them into the post at once that afternoon. He had a four-figure number for his account which he had thought he would remember, but which he had already forgotten. Simone had accepted his second visit to Germany to see a specialist, but there wouldn't be any more visits, and Jonathan would have to account for the money – not all of it but a good deal of extra money, for instance – by stories of injections, pills, and perhaps he'd have to make another trip or two to Germany just to substantiate his story that the doctors were continuing their tests. It was difficult, not at all Jonathan's style. He was hoping that some better explanation might occur to him, but he knew it wouldn't unless he racked his brains to think of one.

'You're late,' Simone said as he came in. She was in the living-room with Georges, picture books spread all over the sofa.

'Customers,' Jonathan said, and flung his mac on a hook. The absence of the gun's weight was a relief. He smiled at his son. 'And how are you, Pebble Boy? What're you up to?' Jonathan spoke in English.

Georges grinned like a little blond pumpkin. One front tooth had vanished while Jonathan had been on the Munich trip. 'I am weeding,' Georges said.

'Reading. You weed in the garden. Unless of course you have a speech defect.'

'Wot's a peach defect?'

Worms, for example. But it could go on for ever. What's worms? A town in Germany. 'Speech defect – like when you st-stutter. B-b-bégayer – that's a –'

'Oh Jon, look at this,' Simone said, reaching for a newspaper. 'I didn't notice it at lunch. Look. Two men – no, one man was killed on the train from Germany to Paris yesterday. Murdered and pushed off the train! Do you think that was the train you were on?'

Jonathan looked at the photograph of the dead man on the slope of ground, looked at the account of it as if he had not seen it before . . . *garrotted* . . . *an arm of the second victim may require amputation* . . . 'Yes – the Mozart Express. I didn't notice anything on the train. But then there were about thirty carriages.' Jonathan had told Simone he had come in too late last night to make the last train to Fontainebleau, and that he had stayed at a small hotel in Paris.

'The Mafia,' Simone said, shaking her head. 'They must've had a compartment with the blinds drawn to do that garrotting. Ugh!' She got up to go to the kitchen.

Jonathan glanced at Georges, who was bent over an Astérix picture book at that instant. Jonathan would not have wanted to explain what garrotting meant.

That evening, though he felt a bit tense, Tom was in the best of spirits at the Grais's. Antoine and Agnès Grais lived in a round stone house with a turret, surrounded by climbing roses. Antoine was in his late thirties, neat and rather severe, master in his own house and tremendously ambitious. He worked in a modest studio in Paris all week, and came to the country at weekends to join his family, and knocked himself out further with gardening. Tom knew that Antoine considered him lazy, because if Tom's garden was equally neat, what miracle was it, since Tom had nothing else to do all day? The spectacular dish that Agnès and Heloise had created was a lobster casserole with a great variety of sea-food in the rice, and a choice of two sauces to go with it.

'I've thought of a wonderful way to start a forest fire,' Tom said musingly when they were having coffee. 'Especially good down in South of France, where there're so many dry trees in summer. You fix a hand lens in a pine tree, you could do it even in winter, and then when the summer comes, the sun shines through it and the magnifying glass starts a little blaze in the pine needles. You place it near the house of somebody you dislike, of course and – snap, crackle and pop! – the whole thing goes up in blazes! The police or the insurance people wouldn't very likely find the hand lens in all the charred wood and even if they did – Perfect, isn't it?'

Antoine chuckled grudgingly, while the women gave appreciative shrieks of horror.

'If that happens to my property down South, I will know who did it!' said Antoine in his deep baritone.

The Grais owned a small property near Cannes which they let in July and August when rents were highest, and used themselves in the other summer months.

Mainly, however, Tom was thinking of Jonathan Trevanny. A stiff, repressed kind of fellow, but basically decent He was going to need some more assistance – Tom hoped merely moral assistance.

13

Because of Vincent Turoli's uncertain state, Tom drove to Fontainebleau on Sunday to buy the London papers, the *Observer* and the *Sunday Times*, which he usually bought from the Villeperce *journaux-tabac* on Monday morning. The news kiosk in Fontainebleau was in front of the Hôtel de l'Aigle Noir. Tom glanced around for Trevanny, who probably bought the London Sundays habitually too, but he didn't see him. It was 11 a.m., and perhaps Trevanny already had the papers. Tom got into his car and looked at the *Observer* first. It had nothing about the train incident. Tom wasn't sure the English papers would bother reporting the story, but he looked into the *Sunday Times* and found an item on page three, one short column which Tom fell upon eagerly. The writer had given it a light touch: ' . . . It must have been an exceptionally fast Mafia job . . . Vincent Turoli of the Genotti family, one arm missing, one eye damaged, regained consciousness early on Saturday, and his condition is improving so rapidly he may soon be flown to a Milan hospital. But if he knows anything, he is not talking.' That was no news to Tom, that he wasn't talking, but plainly he was going to live. That was unfortunate. Tom was thinking that Turoli had probably already given a description of him to his chums. Turoli would have been visited in Strassburg by family members. Important Mafiosi in the hospital were protected day and night by guards, and maybe Turoli would get this treatment too, Tom thought, as soon as the idea of eliminating Turoli crossed his mind. Tom recalled the Mafia-guarded hospitalization of Joe Colombo, head of the Profaci family, in New York. Despite overwhelming evidence to the contrary, Colombo denied that he was a member of the Mafia or that the Mafia existed. Nurses had had to step over the legs of bodyguards sleeping in the halls when Colombo had been in. Best not to think about getting rid of Turoli. He had probably already talked about a man in his thirties, with brown hair, a little over average height, who had socked him in the jaw and the stomach, and there must have been another man behind him too, because he had got a crack on the back of the head. The question was would Turoli be absolutely sure if he spotted him again, and Tom thought there was a good chance of this. Oddly Turoli, if he had seen him, might recall Jonathan a little more clearly, simply because Jonathan didn't look like everyone else, was taller and blonder than most people. Turoli of course would compare notes with the second bodyguard who was alive and well.

'Darling,' Heloise said when Tom walked into the living-room, 'how would you like to go on a cruise on the Nile.'

Tom's thoughts were so far away, he had to think for a moment what the Nile was and where. Heloise was barefoot on the sofa, browsing in travel brochures. Periodically she received a slew of them from an agency in Moret, sent on the agency's initiative, because Heloise was such a good customer. 'I don't know. Egypt – '

'Doesn't this look *séduisant*?' She showed Tom a picture of a little boat called the *Isis* which rather resembled a Mississippi steamboat, sailing past a reedy shore.

'Yes. It does.'

'Or somewhere else. If you don't want to go anywhere, I will see how Noëlle feels,' she said, returning to the brochures.

Spring was stirring in Heloise's blood. Tickling her feet. They had not been anywhere since just after Christmas, when they'd had a rather pleasant time on a yacht, sailing from Marseille to Portofino and back. The owners of the yacht, friends of Noëlle and rather elderly, had had a house in Portofino. Just now Tom didn't want to go anywhere, but he didn't say this to Heloise.

It was a quiet and pleasant Sunday, and Tom made two good preparatory sketches of Mme Annette at her ironing board. She ironed in the kitchen on Sunday afternoons, watching her TV which she wheeled into position against the cupboards. There was nothing more domestic, more French, Tom thought, than Mme Annette's sturdy little figure bent over her iron on a Sunday afternoon. He wanted to capture the spirit of this on canvas – the very pale orange of the kitchen wall in sunlight, and delicate blue-lavender of a certain dress of Mme Annette's that set off so well her fine blue eyes.

Then the telephone rang just after 10 p.m., when Tom and Heloise were lying in front of the fireplace, looking at the Sunday papers. Tom answered.

It was Reeves, sounding extremely upset. The connection was bad.

'Can you hold on? I'll try it from upstairs,' Tom said.

Reeves said he would, and Tom went running up the stairs, saying to Heloise, 'Reeves! A lousy connection!' Not that the telephone was necessarily better upstairs, but Tom wanted to be alone for this.

Reeves said, 'I said my *flat*. In Hamburg. It was *bombed* today.'

'What? My God!'

'I'm ringing you from Amsterdam.'

'Were you hurt?' Tom asked.

'*No!*' Reeves shouted, his voice cracking. 'That's the miracle. I just happened to be out around 5 p.m. So was Gaby because she doesn't work Sundays. These guys, they – must've tossed a bomb through the *window*. Quite a feat. The people below heard a car rush up and rush away after a minute, then two minutes later an *awful* explosion – which knocked all the pictures off their walls, too.'

'Look – how much are they on to?'

'I thought I better get elsewhere for my health. I was out of town in less than an hour.'

'How did they *find out*?' Tom yelled into the telephone.

'I dunno. I really dunno. They might've got something out of Fritz, because Fritz failed to keep a *date* with me today. I sure hope old Fritz is okay. But he doesn't know – you know, our friend's name. I always called him Paul when he was here. An Englishman, I said, so Fritz thinks he lives in England. I honestly think they're doing this on suspicion, Tom. I think our plan has essentially *worked*.'

Good old optimistic Reeves, with his flat bombed, his possessions lost, his plan was a success. 'Listen, Reeves, what about – What are you doing with your stuff in Hamburg? Your papers, for instance?'

'Strongbox at the bank,' Reeves said promptly. 'I can have

those sent. Anyway what papers? If you're worried – I just have *one* little address book and that's always on me. I'm sure as hell sorry to lose a lot of records and paintings I've got there, but the police said they'd protect everything they could. Naturally they questioned me – nicely of course, for a few minutes, but I explained I was in a state of shock, damn near true, and I had to go somewhere for a while. They know where I am.'

'Do the police suspect the Mafia?'

'Didn't say so if they did. Tom old boy, I'll ring you again tomorrow maybe. Take my number, will you?'

Half reluctantly, though he realized he might need it for some reason, Tom took down Reeves' hotel name, the Zuyder Zee, and its number.

'Our mutual friend sure did one hell of a good job, even if that second bastard is still alive. For a fellow who's anaemic – ' Reeves broke off with a laugh that was almost hysterical.

'You've paid him in full now?'

'Did that yesterday,' said Reeves.

'So you don't need him any more, I suppose.'

'No. We've got the police interested here. I mean in Hamburg. That's what we wanted. I heard more Mafia have *arrived*. So that's – '

Abruptly they were cut off. Tom felt a swift annoyance, a sense of stupidity, as he stood there with the buzzing, dead telephone in his hand. He hung up and stood in his room for a few seconds, wondering if Reeves would ring back, thinking he probably wouldn't, trying to digest the news. From what Tom knew of the Mafia, he thought they might leave it at that, bombing Reeves' flat. They might not be out for Reeves' life. But evidently the Mafia knew that Reeves had had something to do with the killings, so the idea of creating the impression of rival Mafia gang-war had failed. On the other hand, the Hamburg police would make an extra effort to clear the Mafia out of the town, out of private gambling clubs, too. Like everything Reeves did, or dabbled in, this situation was vague, Tom thought. The verdict ought to be: not quite successful.

The only happy fact was that Trevanny had his money. He should be informed of that by Tuesday or Wednesday. Good news from Switzerland!

The next days were quiet. No more telephone calls and no letter from Reeves Minot. Nothing in the newspapers about Vincent Turoli in the hospital at Strassburg or Milan, and Tom also bought the Paris *Herald-Tribune* and the London *Daily Telegraph* in Fontainebleau. Tom planted his dahlias, a three-hour job one afternoon, because he had them in smaller packages within the burlap bags, labelled for colour, and he tried to plan his colour patches as carefully as if he were imagining a canvas. Heloise spent three nights at Chantilly, where her parents had their home, because her mother was undergoing a minor operation for a tumour somewhere, which luckily turned out to be benign. Mme Annette, thinking Tom was lonely, comforted him with American food which she had learned to prepare to please him : spareribs with barbecue sauce, clam chowder and fried chicken. Tom wondered from time to time about his own safety. In the peaceful atmosphere of Villeperce, this sleepy, rather proper little village, and through the tall iron gates of Belle Ombre which appeared to guard the castle-like house but actually didn't – anyone might scale them – a murderer might arrive, Tom thought, one of the Mafia boys who would knock on the door or ring the bell, push past Mme Annette, dash up the stairs and plug Tom. It would take the police from Moret a good fifteen minutes to get here, probably, assuming Mme Annette could telephone them at once. A neighbour hearing a shot or two might assume a hunter was trying his luck with owls, and probably wouldn't attempt to investigate.

During the time that Heloise was in Chantilly, Tom decided to acquire a harpsichord for Belle Ombre – for himself, too, of course and possibly for Heloise. Once, somewhere, he had heard her playing some simple ditty on a piano. Where? When? He suspected she was a victim of childhood lessons, and knowing her parents Tom assumed they had knocked any joy out of her endeavours. Anyway, a harpsichord might cost a goodly sum (it would be cheaper to buy it in London, of course, but not with the 100 per cent tax the French would demand for bringing it in), but a harpsichord certainly came in the category of cultural acquisitions, so Tom did not reproach himself for the desire. A harpsichord was not a swimming pool. Tom telephoned an antique dealer in Paris whom he knew fairly well, and though the man dealt only in furniture, he was able to give Tom the name of a reliable place in Paris where he might buy a harpsichord.

Tom went up to Paris and spent a whole day listening to harpsichord lore from the dealer, looking at instruments, trying them out with timid chords, and making his decision. The gem he chose, of beige wood embellished with gold-leaf here and there, cost more than ten thousand francs, and would be delivered on Wednesday, 26 April, along with the tuner who would at once have to get to work, because the instrument would have been disturbed by the move.

This purchase gave Tom a heady lift, made him feel invincible as he walked back to his Renault, impervious to the eye and maybe even the bullets of the Mafia.

And Belle Ombre had not been bombed. Villeperce's tree-bordered, unpavemented streets looked as quiet as ever. No strange characters loitered. Heloise returned in a good mood on Friday, and there was the surprise for her for Tom to look forward to, the arrival of the large and delicately handled crate containing the harpsichord on Wednesday. It was going to be more fun than Christmas.

Tom did not tell Mme Annette about the harpsichord either. But on Monday he said, 'Mme Annette, I have a request. On Wednesday we have a special guest coming for lunch, maybe for dinner too. Let's have something nice.'

Mme Annette's blue eyes lit up. She liked nothing better than extra effort, extra trouble, if it was in the cooking department. *'Un vrai gourmet?'* she asked hopefully.

'I would think so,' Tom replied. 'Now you reflect. I am not going to tell you what to prepare. Let it be a surprise for Mme Heloise also.'

Mme Annette smiled mischievously. One would have thought she had been given a present too.

14

The gyroscope Jonathan bought for Georges in Munich turned out to be the most appreciated toy Jonathan had ever given his son. Its magic remained, every time Georges pulled it from its square box where Jonathan insisted that he keep it.

'Careful not to drop it!' Jonathan said, lying on his stomach on the living-room floor. 'It's a delicate instrument.'

The gyroscope was forcing Georges to learn some new English words, because in his own absorption, Jonathan didn't bother speaking French. The wonderful wheel spun on the tip of Georges' finger, or leaned sideways from the top of a plastic castle turret – the latter a resurrected object from Georges' toy box, pressed into service instead of the Eiffel Tower shown on the pink page of instructions for the gyroscope.

'A larger gyroscope,' Jonathan said, 'keeps ships from rolling on the sea.' Jonathan did a fairly good job of explaining, and thought if he fixed the gyroscope inside a toy boat in a bath-tub of tossing water, he might be able to illustrate what he meant. 'Big ships have three gyroscopes going at once, for instance.'

'Jon, the sofa.' Simone was standing in the living-room doorway. 'You didn't tell me what you think. Dark green?'

Jonathan rolled over on the floor, propped on his elbows. In his eyes the beautiful gyroscope still spun and kept its miraculous balance. Simone meant for the re-covering of the sofa. 'What I think is that we should buy a new sofa,' Jonathan said, getting up. 'I saw an advertisement today for a black Chesterfield for five thousand francs. I'll bet I can get the same thing for three thousand five hundred, if I look around.'

'Three thousand five hundred *new* francs?'

Jonathan had known she would be shocked. 'Consider it an investment. We can afford it.' Jonathan did know of an antique dealer some five kilometres out of town who dealt in nothing but large, well-restored pieces of furniture. Up to now he hadn't been able to think of buying anything from this shop.

'A Chesterfield would be magnificent – but don't go overboard, Jon. You're on a spree!'

Jonathan had talked today about buying a television set, too. 'I won't go on a spree,' he said calmly. 'I wouldn't be such a fool.'

Simone beckoned him into the hall, as if she wanted to be out of Georges' hearing. Jonathan embraced her. Her hair got mussed against the hanging coats. She whispered in his ear :

'All *right*. But when is your next trip to Germany?'

She didn't like the idea of his trips. He had told her they were trying new pills, that Perrier was giving them to him, that though he might stay in the same condition, there was a chance the condition would improve, and certainly it wouldn't get worse. Because of the money Jonathan said he was being paid, Simone didn't believe that he wasn't taking a risk of some kind. And even so, Jonathan hadn't told her how much money, the sum now in the Swiss Bank Corporation in Zürich. Simone knew only that there was six thousand francs or so in the Société Générale in Fontainebleau, instead of their usual four to six hundred – which sometimes went down to two hundred, if they paid a mortgage instalment.

'I'd love a new sofa. But are you sure it's the best thing to buy now? At such a price? Don't forget the mortgage.'

'Darling, how could I? – Bloody mortgage!' He laughed. He wanted to pay off the mortgage at a whack. 'All right, I'll be careful. I promise.'

Jonathan knew he had to think of a better story, or elaborate on the story he'd already told. But for the moment he preferred to relax, to enjoy merely the thought of his new fortune – because spending any of it wasn't easy. And he could still die within a month. The three dozen pills that Dr Schroeder of Munich had given him, pills that Jonathan was now taking at the rate of two a day, were not going to save his life or wreak any great change. A sense of security might be a fantasy of sorts, but wasn't it as real as anything else while it lasted? What else was there? What else was happiness but a mental attitude?

And there was the other unknown, the fact that the bodyguard called Turoli was still alive.

On 29 April, a Sunday evening, Jonathan and Simone went to a concert of Schubert and Mozart played by a string quartet at the Fontainebleau Theatre. Jonathan had bought the most expensive tickets, and had wanted to take Georges, who could behave well if he were sufficiently cautioned beforehand, but Simone had been against it. She was more embarrassed than Jonathan, if Georges was not the model child. 'In another year, yes,' said Simone.

During the interval they went into the big foyer where one could smoke. It was full of familiar faces, among them Pierre Gauthier the art dealer, who to Jonathan's surprise was sporting a wing collar and black tie.

'You are an embellishment of the music this evening, madame!' he said to Simone, with an admiring look at her Chinese-red dress.

Simone acknowledged the compliment gracefully. She did look especially well and happy, Jonathan thought. Gauthier was alone. Jonathan suddenly remembered that his wife had died a few years ago, before Jonathan had really become acquainted with him.

'All of Fontainebleau is here tonight!' said Gauthier, making an effort to speak above the hubbub. His good eye roved over the scores of people in the domed hall, and his bald head shone under the grey-and-black hair he had carefully combed over it. 'Shall we have a coffee afterwards? In the café across the street?' Gauthier asked. 'I shall be pleased to invite you.'

Simone and Jonathan were about to say yes, when Gauthier stiffened a little. Jonathan followed Gauthier's glance and saw Tom Ripley in a group of four or five, only three yards away. Ripley's eyes met Jonathan's and he nodded. Ripley looked as if he might come over to say hello, and at the same time Gauthier sidled to the left, leaving. Simone turned her head to see who both Jonathan and Gauthier had been looking at.

'*Tout à l'heure, peut-être!*' said Gauthier.

Simone looked at Jonathan and her eyebrows went up a little.

Ripley stood out, not so much because he was rather tall as because he looked un-French with his brown hair touched with gold under the chandeliers' lights. He wore a plum-coloured satin jacket. The striking blonde girl who seemed to be wearing no make-up at all must be his wife.

'So?' Simone said. 'Who is that one?'

Jonathan knew she meant Ripley. Jonathan's heart was beating faster. 'I don't know. I've seen him before but I don't know his name.'

'He was at our house – that man,' Simone said. 'I remember him. Gauthier doesn't like him?'

A bell rang, the signal for people to return to their seats.

'I don't know. Why?'

'Because he seemed to want to get away!' Simone said, as if the fact was obvious.

The pleasure of the music had vanished for Jonathan. Where was Tom Ripley sitting? In one of the boxes? Jonathan did not look up at the boxes. Ripley might have been across the aisle from him, for all Jonathan knew. He realized that it wasn't Ripley's presence that had spoilt the evening, but Simone's reaction. And Simone's reaction had been caused, Jonathan knew also, by his own uneasiness at seeing Ripley. Jonathan deliberately tried to relax in his seat, propped his chin on his fingers, knowing all the while that his efforts were not deceiving Simone. Like a lot of other people, she had heard stories about Tom Ripley (even though at this moment she might not recall his name), and she was perhaps going to connect Tom Ripley with – with what? At the moment, Jonathan really didn't know. But he dreaded what would come. He reproached himself for having shown his nervousness so plainly, so naïvely. Jonathan realized he was in a mess, a very dangerous situation, and that he had to play it calmly, if he possibly could. He had to be an actor. A little different from his effort to succeed on the stage when he'd been younger. This situation was quite real. Or if one liked, quite phoney. Jonathan had never before tried to be phoney with Simone.

'Let's try to find Gauthier,' Jonathan said when they were moving up the aisle. The applause was still pattering around them, gathering itself into the co-ordinated palm-pounding of a French audience which wanted still another encore.

But somehow they didn't find Gauthier. Jonathan missed

Simone's reply. She did not seem interested in finding Gauthier. They had the baby-sitter – a girl who lived in their street – at home with Georges. It was almost 11 p.m. Jonathan did not look for Tom Ripley and did not see him.

On Sunday, Jonathan and Simone had lunch in Nemours with Simone's parents and her brother Gérard and his wife. As usual, there was television after lunch, which Jonathan and Gérard did not watch.

'That's excellent that the *boches* are subsidizing you for being one of their guinea-pigs!' Gérard said with one of his rare laughs. 'That is, if they don't do you any harm.' He had come out with this in rapid slang, and it was the first thing he had said that really caught Jonathan's attention.

They were both smoking cigars. Jonathan had bought a box at a tabac in Nemours. 'Yes. Lots of pills. Their idea is to attack with eight or ten drugs all at once. Confuse the enemy, you know. It also makes it more difficult for the enemy cells to become immune.' Jonathan rambled on quite well in this vein, half-convinced he was inventing it as he went along, half recollecting it as a proposed method for combating leukaemia that he had read about months ago. 'Of course there's no guarantee. There could be side-effects, which is why they're willing to pay me a bit of money for going through with it.'

'What kind of side-effects?'

'Maybe – a decrease in blood-congealing level.' Jonathan was getting better and better at the meaningless phrases, and his attentive listener inspired him. 'Nausea – not that I've noticed any so far. Then of course they don't know all the side-effects as yet. They're running a risk. So am I.'

'And if it succeeds? If they call it a success?'

'A couple of more years of life,' Jonathan said pleasantly.

On Monday morning, Jonathan and Simone drove with a neighbour, Irène Pliesse – the woman who kept Georges every afternoon after school until Simone could fetch him – to the antique dealer on the outskirts of Fontainebleau where Jonathan thought he might find a sofa. Irène Pliesse was easy-going, large-boned, and had always struck Jonathan as rather masculine, though perhaps she wasn't in the least. She was the mother of two small children and her house in Fontainebleau was more than commonly full of frilly doilies and organdy curtains. At any rate, she was generous with her time and her car, and had often volunteered to drive the Trevannys to Nemours on the Sundays when they went, but Simone with characteristic scrupulousness had never once accepted, because Nemours was a regular family affair. Therefore the pleasure of using Irène Pliesse's services for the sofa-hunting was an unguilty one, and Irène took as much interest in the purchase as if the sofa was to be in her own home.

There was a choice of two Chesterfields, both with old frames and both recently covered in new black leather. Jonathan and Simone preferred the larger one, and Jonathan managed to knock the price down five hundred to three thousand francs. Jonathan knew it was a bargain, because he had seen the same sized sofa advertised, with a picture of it, for five thousand. Now this vast sum, three thousand, nearly one months' earnings of himself and Simone combined, seemed positively trifling. It was amazing, Jonathan thought, how quickly one could adjust to having a little money.

Even Irène, whose house looked opulent compared to the Trevannys', was impressed by the sofa. And Jonathan noticed that Simone didn't at once know what to say to pass it off smoothly.

'Jon had a little windfall from a relative in England. Not much but – we wanted to get something really nice with it.'

Irène nodded.

All was well, Jonathan thought.

The next evening, before dinner, Simone said, 'I dropped in to say hello to Gauthier today.'

Jonathan felt at once on guard, because of Simone's tone of voice. He was drinking a scotch and water and looking at the evening paper. 'Oh, yes?'

'Jon – wasn't it this M. Ripley who told Gauthier that – that you hadn't long to live?' Simone spoke softly, though Georges was upstairs, probably in his room.

Had Gauthier admitted it, when Simone asked him a direct question? Jonathan didn't know how Gauthier would behave, being asked a direct question – and Simone could be gently persistent until she got her answer. 'Gauthier told me,' Jonathan began, 'that – Well, as I told you, he wouldn't say who told him. So I don't know.'

Simone looked at him. She was sitting on the handsome black Chesterfield sofa, which had since yesterday transformed their living-room. It was due to Ripley, Jonathan was thinking, that Simone was sitting where she was. It didn't help Jonathan's state of mind.

'Gauthier told you it was Ripley?' Jonathan asked with an air of surprise.

'Oh, he wouldn't say. But I simply asked him – was it M. Ripley. I described Ripley, the man we saw at the concert. Gauthier knew whom I meant. You seem to know too – his name.' Simone sipped her Cinzano.

Jonathan fancied her hand shook slightly. 'It could be, of course,' Jonathan said with a shrug. 'Don't forget, Gauthier told me whoever told him – ' Jonathan gave a laugh. 'All this tale-bearing! Anyway Gauthier said, whoever it was – the man said he could have been mistaken, that things got exaggerated. – Darling, it really is best forgotten. It's silly to blame strangers. Silly to make too much out of it.'

'Yes, but – ' Simone tilted her head. Her lips twisted somewhat bitterly, in a way Jonathan had seen only once or twice before. 'The curious thing is, it *was* Ripley. I know that. Not that Gauthier said it, no. He didn't. But I could tell . . . Jon?'

'Yes, dear.'

'It's because – Ripley is very close to being a crook. Maybe he is a crook. Lots of crooks are not caught, you know. That is the reason I ask. I ask *you*. Are you – All this money, Jon – Are you getting it by any chance, somehow, from this M. Ripley?'

Jonathan made himself look straight at Simone. He felt that he had to protect what he already had, and it wasn't *so* connected with Ripley that it would be a lie if he said it wasn't. 'How could I? For what, darling?'

'Just because he is a crook! Who knows for what? What has he got to do with these German doctors? Are they really doctors you are talking about?' She was beginning to sound hysterical. The colour had risen to her cheeks.

Jonathan frowned. 'Darling, Perrier has my two reports!'

'There is something very dangerous about the tests, Jon, or

they wouldn't pay you so much, isn't that true? – I have the feeling you're not telling me the whole truth.'

Jonathan laughed a little. 'What could Tom Ripley, that do-nothing – He's an American, anyway. What could he have to do with German doctors?'

'You saw the German doctors because you were afraid you were going to die soon. And it was Ripley – I am pretty sure – who started the story you were going to die soon.'

Georges was bumping his way down the stairs, talking to some toy that he was dragging down. Georges in his dream-world, but he was a·presence, just a few yards away, and it rattled Jonathan. He found it incredible that Simone had discovered so much, and his impulse was to deny all of it, at any cost.

Simone was waiting for him to say something.

Jonathan said, 'I don't know who it was told Gauthier.'

Georges was standing at the door. Now his arrival was a relief for Jonathan. It effectively stopped the conversation. Georges was asking a question about a tree outside his window. Jonathan didn't listen, and let Simone answer.

During dinner, Jonathan had the feeling Simone did not quite believe him, that she wanted to believe him, but couldn't. Yet Simone (maybe because of Georges) was almost her usual self. She wasn't sulking or cool. But the atmosphere for Jonathan was uncomfortable. And it was going to continue, he realized, unless he could come up with some more specific reason for extra money from the German hospitals. Jonathan hated the idea of lying, exaggerating the danger for himself in order to account for the money.

It even crossed Jonathan's mind that Simone would speak to Tom Ripley himself. Mightn't she telephone him? Make an appointment to see him? Jonathan dismissed that idea. Simone didn't like Tom Ripley. She would not want to come anywhere near him.

That same week, Tom Ripley came into Jonathan's shop. His picture had been ready for several days. Jonathan had a customer in his shop when Ripley arrived, and Ripley proceeded to look over some ready-made frames that leaned against a wall, obviously content to wait till Jonathan should be free. At last the customer left.

'Morning,' Tom said pleasantly. 'It wasn't so easy after all to get someone to pick up my picture, so I thought I'd come myself.'

'Yes, fine. It's ready,' Jonathan said, and went to the back of his shop to get it. It was wrapped in brown paper, but the paper was not tied, and it was labelled RIPLEY, the label fastened with scotch tape to the paper. Jonathan carried it to his counter. 'Like to see it?'

Tom was pleased with it. He held it at arm's length. 'That's great. Very nice. What do I owe you?'

'Ninety francs.'

Tom pulled his billfold out. 'Is everything all right?'

Jonathan was aware that he took a couple of breaths before he answered. 'Since you ask – ' He took the hundred-franc note with a polite nod, pulled out his cash drawer and got the change. 'My wife – ' Jonathan looked at the door, and was glad to see that no one was approaching at the moment. 'My wife spoke to Gauthier. He didn't tell her that you started that story about my – demise. But my wife seems to have guessed it. I really don't know how. Intuition.'

Tom had foreseen this happening. He was aware of his reputation, that many people mistrusted him, avoided him. Tom had often thought that his ego could have been shattered long ago – the ego of the average person would have been shattered – except for the fact that people, once they got to know him, once they came to Belle Ombre and spent an evening, liked him and Heloise well enough, and the Ripleys were invited back. 'And what did you say to your wife?'

Jonathan tried to speak quickly, because there might not be much time. 'What I've said from the start, that Gauthier always refused to tell me who started the story. That's true.'

Tom knew. Gauthier had gallantly refused to tell his name. 'Well, keep cool. If we don't see each other – Sorry about the other night at the concert,' Tom added with a smile.

'Yes. But – it's unfortunate. The worst is, she associates you – she's trying to – with the money we've got now Not that I've told her how much it is.'

Tom had thought of that too. It *was* irritating. 'I won't bring you any more pictures to frame.'

A man with a large canvas on a stretcher was struggling through the door.

'*Bon, m'sieur!*' Tom said, waving his free hand. '*Merci. Bonsoir.*'

Tom went out. If Trevanny was seriously worried, Tom thought, Trevanny could telephone him. Tom had already said that at least once. It was unfortunate, troublesome for Trevanny, that his wife suspected that he had started the nasty rumour. On the other hand, that wasn't easily connected with money from hospitals in Hamburg and Munich, still less connected with the murder of two Mafiosi.

On Sunday morning, when Simone was hanging laundry on the garden line, and Jonathan and Georges were making a stone border, the doorbell rang.

It was one of their neighbours, a woman of about sixty whose name Jonathan wasn't sure of – Delattre? Delambre? She looked distressed.

'Excuse me, M. Trevanny.'

'Come in,' said Jonathan.

'It is M. Gauthier. Have you heard the news?'

'No.'

'He was hit last night by a car. He is dead.'

'Dead? – Here in Fontainebleau?'

'He was coming home around midnight from an evening with a friend, someone in the Rue de la Paroisse. You know M. Gauthier lives in the Rue de la République just off the Avenue Franklin Roosevelt. It was that crossroads with the little triangle of green where there is a traffic light. Someone saw the people who did it, two boys in a car. They didn't stop. They went through a red light and hit M. Gauthier and *didn't stop!*'

'Good lord! – Won't you sit down, Mm –'

Simone had come into the hall. 'Ah *bonjour*, Mme Delattre!' she said.

'Simone, Gauthier is dead,' Jonathan said. 'Run over by a hit-and-run driver.'

'Two boys,' said Mme Delattre. 'They didn't stop!'

Simone gasped. 'When?'

'Last night. He was dead when they got him to the hospital here. Around midnight.'

'Won't you come in and sit down, Mme Delattre?' Simone asked.

'No, no, thank you. I must be off to see a friend. Mme Mockers. I am not sure if she knows yet. We all knew him so well, you know?' She was near tears, and set her shopping basket down for a moment to wipe her eyes.

Simone pressed her hand. 'Thank you for coming to tell us, Mme Delattre. That was kind of you.'

'The funeral is on Monday,' Mme Delattre said. 'At St Louis.' Then she departed.

The news somehow didn't register on Jonathan. 'What's her name?'

'Mme *Delattre*. Her husband's a plumber,' Simone said, as if, of course, Jonathan should know.

Delattre wasn't the plumber they used. Gauthier dead. What would happen to his shop, Jonathan wondered. He found himself staring at Simone. They were standing in the narrow front hall.

'Dead,' Simone said. She put her hand out and gripped Jonathan's wrist, not looking at him. 'We should go to the funeral on Monday, you know.'

'Of course.' A Catholic funeral. It was all in French now, not Latin. He imagined all the neighbours, faces familiar and unfamiliar, in the cool church full of candles.

'Hit-and-run,' Simone said. She walked stiffly down the hall, and looked back over her shoulder at Jonathan. 'It's really shocking.'

Jonathan followed her through the kitchen, out into the garden. It was good to get back into sunlight.

Simone had finished hanging her washing. She straightened some things on the line, then picked up the empty basket. 'Hit-and-run. – Do you really think so, Jon?'

'That's what she said.' They were both talking softly. Jonathan still felt a bit dazed, but he knew what Simone was thinking.

She came a step closer, carrying the basket. Then she beckoned him towards the steps that led to the little porch, as if neighbours on the other side of the garden wall might hear them. 'Do you think he could've been killed purposely? By someone hired to kill him?'

'Why?'

'Because perhaps he knew something. That's why. Isn't it possible? – Why should an innocent person be struck down like that – accidentally?'

'Because – these things happen sometimes,' Jonathan said.

Simone shook her head. 'You don't think possibly that M. Ripley had something to do with it?'

Jonathan saw an irrational anger in her. 'Absolutely not. I certainly don't think so.' Jonathan could have bet his life that Tom Ripley hadn't had anything to do with it. He started to say that, but it would've sounded a bit strong – and if he wanted to look at it in another way, a rather comical bet.

Simone started to pass him and enter the house, but she stopped close to him. 'It's true Gauthier didn't tell me anything definite, Jon, but he might have known something. I think he did. – I have the feeling he was killed on purpose.'

Simone was simply shocked, Jonathan thought, like himself. She was putting into words ideas that she hadn't thought out. He followed her into the kitchen. 'Known something about what?'

Simone was putting the basket away in the corner cupboard. 'That's just it. I don't know.'

15

The funeral service for Pierre Gauthier took place at 10 a.m. Monday in the church of St Louis, the main church of Fontainebleau. The church was filled, and people stood even on the pavement outside where the two black automobiles waited dismally – one a shiny hearse, the other a boxlike bus to carry the family relations and friends who had no car of their own. Gauthier was a widower without children. He perhaps had a brother or sister, maybe therefore some nieces or nephews. Jonathan hoped so. The funeral seemed a lonely thing, despite all the people.

'Do you know he lost his glass eye on the street?' a man next to Jonathan whispered to him in church. 'It fell out when he was hit.'

'Oh?' Jonathan shook his head in sympathy. The man who had spoken to him was a shopkeeper. Jonathan knew his face, but could not connect him with any shop. Jonathan could see clearly Gauthier's glass eye on the black tar road, maybe crushed by a car wheel by now, maybe found in the gutter by some curious children. What did the back of a glass eye look like?

Candles twinkled yellow-like, barely illuminating the church's dreary grey walls. It was an overcast day. The priest intoned in French the formal phrases. Gauthier's coffin stood short and thick in front of the altar. At least, if Gauthier had little family, he had many friends. Several women, a few men, were wiping away tears. And other people were murmuring to each other, as if their own exchanges could give them more comfort than the rote the priest was reciting.

There were some soft bells, like chimes.

Jonathan looked to his right, at the people in the rows of chairs across the aisle, and his eyes were caught by the profile of Tom Ripley. Ripley was looking straight ahead towards the priest who was speaking again, and he seemed to be following the ceremony with concentration. His face stood out among the faces of the French. Or did it? Was it merely because he knew Tom Ripley? Why had Ripley troubled to come? In the next instant Jonathan wondered if Tom Ripley might be putting on an act by coming? If, as Simone suspected, he really had had something to do with Gauthier's death, even arranged it and paid for it?

When the people all stood up to file out of the church, Jonathan tried to avoid Tom Ripley, and he thought the best way to succeed in this was not to try to avoid him, above all not to glance another time in his direction. But on the steps in front of the church, Tom Ripley suddenly dashed up at one side of Jonathan and Simone and greeted them.

'Good morning!' Ripley said in French. He wore a black muffler around his neck, a dark blue raincoat. 'Bonjour, madame. I'm glad to see you both. You were friends of M. Gauthier, I think.'

They were all walking slowly down the steps, because of the dense crowd, so slowly it was hard to keep one's balance.

'Oui,' Jonathan replied. 'He was one of our neighbourhood shopkeepers, you know. A very nice man.'

Tom nodded. 'I haven't seen the papers this morning. A friend in Moret rang me – and told me. Have the police any idea who did it?'

'I haven't heard,' Jonathan said. 'Just "two boys". Did you hear anything else, Simone?'

Simone shook her head which was covered in a dark scarf. 'No. Not a thing.'

Tom nodded. 'I was hoping you might've heard something – living closer than I do.'

Tom Ripley seemed genuinely concerned, Jonathan thought, not just putting on a show for them.

'I must buy a paper. – Are you going to the cemetery?' Tom asked.

'No, we're not,' said Jonathan.

Tom nodded. They had all now reached the pavement level. 'Nor am I. I'll miss old Gauthier. It's too bad. – Very nice to have seen you.' With a quick smile, Ripley went away.

Jonathan and Simone walked on, around the corner of the church into the Rue de la Paroisse, the direction of their house. Neighbours nodded to them, gave them brief smiles, and some said, 'Good morning, Madame, M'sieur,' in a way they wouldn't have done on ordinary mornings. Car motors started up, ready to follow the hearse to the cemetery – which Jonathan recalled was just behind the Fontainebleau Hospital where he had so often gone for transfusions.

'*Bonjour*, M. Trevanny! Et Madame!' It was Dr Perrier, sprightly as ever, and almost as beaming as usual. He pumped Jonathan's hand, at the same time making a small bow to Simone. 'What a dreadful thing, eh? . . . No, no, no, no, they haven't found the boys at all. But someone said it was a Paris licence on the car. A black D.S. That's all they know . . . And how are you feeling, M. Trevanny?' Dr Perrier's smile was confident.

'About the same,' Jonathan said. 'No complaints.' He was glad that Dr Perrier took off at once, because Jonathan was aware that Simone knew he was supposed to be seeing Dr Perrier rather frequently now for pills and injections, though he hadn't been to Perrier since at least a fortnight, when he had delivered Dr Schroeder's report that had come to him at his shop.

'We must buy a paper,' said Simone.

'Up at the corner,' Jonathan said.

They bought a paper, and Jonathan stood on a pavement still a bit crowded with people dispersing from Gauthier's service, and read about 'the disgraceful and wanton act of young hoodlums' which had taken place late Saturday evening in a street of Fontainebleau. Simone looked over his shoulder. The week-end paper had not had time to print the story, so this was the first account they had seen. Someone had seen a large, dark car with at least two young men in it, but no mention was made of a Paris licence number. The car had gone on in the direction of Paris, but had vanished by the time police tried to give pursuit.

'It *is* shocking,' said Simone. 'It isn't often, you know, that there are hit-and-run drivers in France . . .'

Jonathan detected a note of chauvinism.

'That's what makes me suspect – ' She shrugged. 'Of course I could be completely wrong. But it is quite in character if this type Ripley makes an appearance at M. Gauthier's funeral service!'

'He – ' Jonathan stopped. He had been going to say that Tom Ripley had certainly seemed concerned that morning, and also that he bought his art supplies at Gauthier's shop, but Jonathan realized that he was not supposed to know this. 'What do you mean by "in character"?'

Simone shrugged again, and Jonathan knew she was in a mood in which she might refuse to say another word on the subject. 'I think it is just possible this Ripley found out from M. Gauthier that I spoke with him, asking him who started this story about you. I told you I thought it was Ripley, even though M. Gauthier wouldn't say so. And now – this – the *very* mysterious death of M. Gauthier.'

Jonathan was silent. They were nearing the Rue St Merry. 'But that story, darling – it couldn't possibly be worth killing a man for. Be reasonable.'

Simone suddenly remembered they needed something for lunch. She went into a charcuterie, and Jonathan waited on the pavement. For a few seconds Jonathan realized – in a different way, as if he saw it through Simone's eyes – what he had done in killing one man by gunshot, and by helping to kill another. Jonathan had rationalized it by telling himself that the two men had been gunmen themselves, murderers. Simone, of course, wouldn't see it that way. They were human life, after all. Simone was sufficiently upset because Tom Ripley might have hired someone to kill Gauthier – just might have. If she knew that her own husband had pulled a trigger – Or was he influenced at the moment by the funeral service he had just been to? The service had after all been about the sanctity of human life, despite saying that the next world was even better. Jonathan smiled ironically. It was the word *sanctity* –

Simone came out of the charcuterie, awkwardly holding little packages, because she hadn't her shopping net with her. Jonathan took a couple of them. They walked on.

Sanctity. Jonathan had given the Mafia book back to Reeves. If he ever had serious qualms about what he had done, all he needed to do was remember some of the murderers he had read about.

Nevertheless, Jonathan felt apprehensive as he climbed the steps of the house behind Simone. It was because Simone was now so hostile towards Ripley. Simone hadn't cared for Pierre Gauthier all this much, to be so affected by his death. Her attitude was composed of a sixth sense, conventional morality and wifely protectiveness. She believed that Ripley had started the story about his dying soon, and Jonathan foresaw that nothing would shake her, because no other person could easily be substituted as a source of the story, especially now that Gauthier was dead, and couldn't back Jonathan up if he tried to invent another person.

Tom shed his black muffler in his car, and drove southward towards Moret and home. It was a pity about Simone's hostility, that Simone suspected he had arranged Gauthier's death. Tom lit a cigarette with the lighter from his dashboard He was in the red Alfa-Romeo, and felt tempted to go fast, but he held his speed back prudently.

Gauthier's death had been an accident, Tom was sure. A nasty, unfortunate thing, but still an accident, unless Gauthier was mixed up in stranger things than Tom knew about.

A big magpie swooped across the road, beautiful against a background of a pale green weeping willow. The sun had begun to come out. Tom thought of stopping in Moret to buy something – there seemed always something that Mme Annette needed or might like – but today he couldn't recall anything that she'd asked for, and he didn't really feel like stopping. It was his usual framer in Moret who had rung him yesterday to tell him about Gauthier. Tom must have mentioned to him at some point that he bought his paints at Gauthier's in Fontainebleau. Tom let his foot down on the accelerator and passed a truck, then two speeding Citroëns, and soon he was at the turn-off to Villeperce.

'Ah, Tome, you had a long-distance telephone call,' Heloise said when he came into the living-room.

'From where?' But Tom knew. It was probably Reeves.

'Germany, I think.' Heloise went back to the harpsichord,

which now had a place of honour near the french windows.

Tom recognized a Bach *chaconne* whose treble she was reading. 'They'll ring back?' he asked.

Heloise turned her head and her long blonde hair swung out. 'I don't know, *chéri*. It was only the operator I spoke to, because they wanted person-to-person. There it is!' she said as the telephone rang on her last words.

Tom dashed upstairs to his room.

The operator ascertained that he was M. Ripley, then Reeves' voice said:

'Hello, Tom. Can you talk?' Reeves sounded calmer than the last time.

'Yes. You're in Amsterdam?'

'Yeah, and I have a little news you won't find in the newspaper that I thought you might like to hear. That bodyguard died. You know, the one they took to Milan.'

'Who said he died?'

'Well, I heard it from one of my friends in Hamburg. A usually reliable friend.'

It was the kind of story the Mafia might put out, Tom thought. He would believe it when he saw the corpse. 'Anything else?'

'I thought it might be good news for our mutual friend, that this guy is dead. You know.'

'Sure. I do understand, Reeves. And how are you?'

'Oh, still alive.' Reeves forced the sound of a laugh. 'Also I'm arranging for my things to be sent to Amsterdam. I like it here. I feel much safer than in Hamburg, I can tell you that. Oh, there is one thing. My friend Fritz. He telephoned me, got my number from Gaby. He's now with his cousin in some little town near Hamburg. But he got beaten up, lost a couple of teeth, poor guy. Those swine beat him up for what they could get out of him . . .'

That was close to home, Tom thought, and felt a pang of sympathy for this unknown Fritz – Reeves' driver, or package-runner.

'Fritz never knew our friend as anything else but "Paul",' Reeves went on. 'Also Fritz gave them an opposite description, black hair, short and plump, but I'm afraid they might not believe him. Fritz did pretty well, considering he was getting the treatment. He said he stuck to his story – the way our friend looks, and that's all he knows about him. *I'm* the one in a mess, I think.'

That was certainly true, Tom thought, because the Italians knew what Reeves looked like, all right. 'Very interesting news. I don't think we should talk all day, my friend. What're you really worried about?'

Reeves' sigh was audible. 'Getting my things here. But I sent Gaby some money, and she's going to get things shipped. I've written my bank and all that. I'm even growing a beard. And of course I'm using a – another name.'

Tom had supposed Reeves would be using another name, with one of his false passports. 'And what's your name?'

'Andrew Lucas – of Virginia,' Reeves said, with a 'Hah' by way of a laugh. 'By the way, have you seen our mutual friend?'

'No. Why should I? – Well, Andy, let me know how things go.' Tom was sure Reeves would ring if he were in trouble, if it was the kind of trouble in which he was still able to ring, because Reeves thought Tom Ripley could pull him out of anything. But mainly for Trevanny's sake, Tom wanted to know if Reeves was in trouble.

'I'll do that, Tom. Oh, one more thing! A Di Stefano man was plugged in Hamburg! Saturday night. You might see it in the papers and you might not. But the Genotti family must've got him. That's what we wanted . . .'

Reeves at last signed off.

If the Mafia got to Reeves in Amsterdam, Tom was thinking, they'd torture some facts out of him. Tom doubted if Reeves could stand up as well as Fritz apparently had done. Tom wondered which family, the Di Stefanos or the Genottis, had got hold of Fritz? Fritz probably knew only about the first operation, the shooting in Hamburg. That victim had been merely a button man. The Genottis would be far more livid: they had lost a capo, and, it was said now, a button man or bodyguard. Didn't both families know by now that the murders had started with Reeves and the Hamburg casino boys, and not through family warfare? Were they finished with Reeves? Tom felt quite incapable of protecting Reeves, if he should need protection. If it was only one man they were up against, how easy it would be! But the Mafia were beyond count.

Reeves had said at the last that he had been ringing from a post office. That was at least safer than if he had rung from his hotel. Tom was thinking about Reeves' first call. Hadn't that been from the hotel called the Zuyder Zee? Tom thought so.

Harpsichord notes came purely from below stairs, a message from another century. Tom went down the stairs. Heloise would want him to tell her about the funeral service, say something about it, though when he had asked her if she wanted to go with him, she had said that funeral services depressed her.

Jonathan stood in his living-room, gazing out the front window. It was just after 12 noon. He had turned on the portable radio for the noonday news, and now it was playing pop music. Simone was in the garden with Georges, who had stayed in the house alone while he and Simone went to the funeral service. On the radio a man's voice sang 'runnin' on along . . . runnin' on along . . . ' and Jonathan watched a young dog that looked like an Alsatian loping after two small boys on the opposite pavement. Jonathan had a sense of the temporariness of everything, of life of all kinds – not only of the dog and the two boys, but of the houses behind them, a sense that everything would perish, crumble finally, shapes destroyed and even forgotten. Jonathan thought of Gauthier in his coffin being lowered into the ground perhaps at this moment, and then he didn't think about Gauthier again but about himself. He hadn't the energy of the dog that had trotted past. If he'd had any prime, he felt past it. It was too late, and Jonathan felt that he hadn't the energy to enjoy what was left of his life, now that he had a little wherewithal to enjoy it. He ought to close up his shop, sell it or give it away, what did it matter? Yet on second thought he couldn't simply squander the money with Simone, because what would she and Georges have when he died? Forty thousand quid wasn't a fortune. His ears were ringing. Calmly Jonathan took deep, slow breaths. He made an effort to raise the window in front of him, and found he hadn't the strength. He turned to face the centre of the room, his legs heavy and nearly uncontrollable. The ringing in his ears had completely drowned the music

He came to, sweating and cool, on the living-room floor.

Simone was on her knees beside him, lightly passing a damp towel across his forehead, down his face.

'Darling, I just *found* you! How are you? – Georges, it is all right. Papa is *all right*!' But Simone sounded frightened.

Jonathan put his head down again on the carpet.

'Some water?'

Jonathan managed to sip from the glass she held. He lay back again. 'I think I might have to lie here all afternoon!' His voice warred with the ringing in his ears.

'Let me straighten this.' Simone pulled at his jacket which was bunched under him.

Something slipped out of a pocket. He saw Simone pick up something, then she looked back at him with concern, and Jonathan kept his eyes open, focusing on the ceiling, because things were worse if he closed his eyes. Minutes passed, minutes of silence. Jonathan was not worried, because he knew he would hang on, that this wasn't death, merely a faint. Maybe first cousin to death, but death wouldn't come quite like this. Death would probably have a sweeter, more seductive pull, like a wave sweeping out from a shore, sucking hard at the legs of a swimmer who'd already ventured too far, and who mysteriously had lost his will to struggle. Simone went away, urging Georges out with her, then returned with a cup of hot tea

'This has a lot of sugar. It will do you good. Do you want me to telephone Dr Perrier?'

'Oh no, darling. Thanks.' After some sips of the tea, Jonathan got himself to the sofa and sat down.

'Jon, what's this?' Simone asked, holding up the little blue book that was the Swiss bank's passbook.

'Oh – that – ' Jonathan shook his head, trying to make himself more alert.

'It's a bankbook. Isn't it?'

'Well – yes.' The sum was in six figures, more than four hundred thousand francs, which were indicated by an 'f' after them. He also knew that Simone had looked into the little book in all innocence, assuming it was a record of some household purchase, some kind of record they had in common.

'It says francs. French francs? – Where did you get it? What *is* it, Jon?'

The sum was in French francs. 'Darling, that's sort of an advance – from the German doctors.'

'But – ' Simone looked at a loss. 'It's French *francs*, isn't it? This sum!' She laughed a little, nervously.

Jonathan's face was suddenly warm. 'I told you where I got it, Simone. Naturally – I know it's a biggish sum. I didn't want to tell you at once. I – '

Simone laid the little blue book carefully on top of his wallet on the low table in front of the sofa. Then she pulled the chair from in front of the writing-table and sat down on it, sideways, holding to its back with one hand. 'Jon – '

Georges suddenly appeared in the hall doorway, and Simone got up with determination and turned him by the shoulders. 'Chou-chou, papa and I are talking. Now leave us alone for a minute.' She came back and said quietly, 'Jon, I don't believe you.'

Jonathan heard a trembling in her voice. It wasn't only the sum of money, startling though it was, but also his secrecy lately – the trips to Germany. 'Well – you've got to believe me,' Jonathan said. Some strength had returned. He stood up. 'It's an advance. They don't think I'm going to be able to use it. I won't have time. But you can.'

Simone did not respond to his laugh. 'It's in your name. – Jon, whatever you are doing, you are not telling me the truth.' And she waited, just those few seconds when he might have told her the truth, but he didn't speak.

Simone left the room.

And lunch was a sort of duty. They barely talked. Jonathan could see that Georges was puzzled. Jonathan could foresee the days ahead – Simone perhaps not questioning him again, just coolly waiting for him to tell the truth, or to explain – somehow. Long silences in the house, no more love-making, no more affection or laughter. He had to come up with something else, something better. Even if he said he ran the risk of dying under the German doctors' treatment, was it logical that they'd paid him this much? Not really. Jonathan realized that his life wasn't worth as much as the lives of two Mafiosi.

16

Friday morning was lovely with light rain alternating with sunlight every half-hour or so, just the thing for the garden, Tom thought. Heloise had driven up to Paris, because there was a dress sale at a certain boutique in the Faubourg St-Honoré, and Tom felt sure she would come back also with a scarf or something more important from Hermès as well. Tom sat at the harpsichord, playing the base of a Goldberg variation, trying to get the fingering in his head and in his hand. He had bought a few music books in Paris the same day he had acquired the harpsichord. Tom knew how the variation should sound, because he had Landowska's recording. As he was going over it for the third or fourth time and feeling that he had made progress, the telephone jangled.

'Hello?' said Tom.

' 'Ello – ah – to whom am I speaking, please?' a man's voice asked in French.

Tom, more slowly than usual, felt an unease. 'You wished to speak to whom?' he asked with equal politeness.

'M. Anquetin?'

'No, this is not his house,' said Tom, and put the telephone back in its cradle.

The man's accent had been perfect – hadn't it? But then the Italians would get a Frenchman to make the call, or an Italian whose French accent was perfect. Or was he over anxious? Frowning, Tom turned to face the harpsichord and the windows, and shoved his hands into his back pockets. Had the Genotti family found Reeves in his hotel, and were they checking all the telephone numbers Reeves had called? If so, this caller wouldn't be satisfied with his answer. An ordinary person would have said, 'You are mistaken, this is so-and-so's residence.' Sunlight came through the windows slowly, like something liquid pouring between the red curtains on to the rug. The sunlight was like an arpeggio that Tom could almost hear – this time Chopin, perhaps. Tom realized that he was afraid to ring Reeves in Amsterdam and ask what was happening. The call hadn't sounded like a long-distance call, but it wasn't always possible to tell. It could have come from Paris. Or Amsterdam. Or Milan. Tom had an unlisted number. The operator wouldn't give his name or address, but from the exchange – 424 – it would be easy for the man who had the number to find the district, if he cared to. It was part of the Fontainebleau area. Tom knew it wouldn't be impossible for the Mafia to find out that Tom Ripley lived in this area, in Villeperce even, because the Derwatt affair had been in the newspapers, Tom's photograph also, just six months ago. Much depended, of course, on the second bodyguard, alive and uninjured, who had walked the train in search of his capo and his colleague. This one might remember Tom's face from the restaurant car.

Tom was again on the Goldberg variation base when the telephone rang a second time. Ten minutes had passed, he thought, since the first call. This time he was going to say it was the house of Robert Wilson. There was no concealing his American accent.

'*Oui*,' Tom said in a bored tone.

'Hello – '

'Yes. Hello,' Tom said, recognizing Jonathan Trevanny's voice.

'I'd like to see you,' Jonathan said, 'if you've got some time.'

'Yes, of course. – Today?'

'If you could, yes. I can't – I don't want to make it around the lunch hour, if you don't mind. Later today?'

'Sevenish?'

'Even six-thirty. Can you come to Fontainebleau?'

Tom agreed to meet Jonathan at the Salamandre Bar. Tom could guess what it was about: Jonathan couldn't explain the money properly to his wife. Jonathan sounded worried, but not desperate.

At 6 p.m., Tom took the Renault, because Heloise was not back with the Alfa. Heloise had telephoned to say she was going to have cocktails with Noëlle, and might also have dinner with her. And she had bought a beautiful suitcase at Hermès, because it had been on sale. Heloise thought that the more she bought at sales, the more she was being economical, and positively virtuous.

Tom found Jonathan already in the Salamandre, standing at the counter drinking dark beer – probably good old Whitbread's ale, Tom thought. The place was unusually busy and noisy this evening, and Tom supposed it would be all right to talk at the counter. Tom nodded and smiled in greeting, and ordered the same dark beer for himself.

Jonathan told him what had happened. Simone had seen the Swiss bankbook. Jonathan had told her it was an advance from the German doctors, and that he was running a risk in taking their drugs, and that this was a kind of payment for his life.

'But she doesn't really believe me.' Jonathan smiled. 'She's even suggested I impersonated somebody in Germany to get an inheritance for a gang of crooks – something like that – and that this is my cut. Or that I've borne false witness for something.' Jonathan gave a laugh. He actually had to shout to be heard, but he was sure no one was listening in the vicinity, or could understand if they did. Three barmen were working frantically behind the counter, pouring Pernods and red wine and drawing glasses of lager from the tap.

'I can understand,' Tom said, glancing at the noisy fray around him. He was still concerned about the telephone call he had got that morning, which hadn't been repeated in the afternoon. He had even looked around Belle Ombre and Villeperce, as he drove out at 6 p.m., for any strange figures on the streets. It was odd how one finally knew everybody in the village, by their figures, even at a distance, so that a newcomer at once caught the eye. Tom had even been afraid, a little, when he started the motor of the Renault. Fixing dynamite to the ignition was a favourite Mafia prank. 'We'll have to think!' Tom shouted, earnestly.

Jonathan nodded and quaffed his beer. 'Funny she's suggested nearly everything I might've done short of murder!'

Tom put his foot on the rail and tried to think in all the din. He looked at a pocket of Jonathan's old corduroy jacket where a rip had been neatly mended, no doubt by Simone. Tom said in sudden desperation, 'I wonder what's the matter with telling her the truth? After all, these Mafiosi, these *morpions* – '

Jonathan shook his head. 'I've thought of that. Simone – she's a Catholic. *That* – ' Being regularly on the pill was a kind of concession for Simone to have made. Jonathan saw the Catholic retreat as a slow one: they didn't want to be seen to be routed, even if they gave in here and there. Georges was being raised as a Catholic, inevitable in this country, but Jonathan tried to make Georges see that it wasn't the only religion in the world, tried to make him understand that he would be free to make his own choice when he grew a little older, and his efforts had so far not been opposed by Simone 'It's so different for her,' Jonathan shouted, now getting used to the noise and almost liking its protective wall. 'It'd be really a shock – something she couldn't forgive, you know. Human life and all that.'

'Human! Ha-ha!'

'The thing is,' Jonathan said, serious again, 'it's almost like my whole marriage. I mean, as if my marriage itself was at stake. He looked at Tom, who was trying to follow him. 'What a hell of a place to talk about something serious!' Jonathan began again with determination, 'Things are not the same between us, to put it mildly. And I don't see how they're going to get any better. I was simply hoping you might have an idea – as to what I should do or say. On the other hand, I don't know why you *should*. It's my problem.'

Tom was thinking they might find a quieter place, or sit in his car. But would he be able to think any better in a quieter place? 'I will try to get an idea!' Tom yelled. Why did everyone – even Jonathan – suppose that he could come up with an idea for them? Tom often thought he had a hard enough time trying to steer a course for himself. His own welfare often required ideas, those inspirations that came sometimes while he was under the shower, or gardening, those gifts of the gods that were presented only after his own anxious pondering. A single person hadn't the mental equipment to take on the problems of another and maintain the same degree of excellence, Tom thought. Then Tom reflected that his own welfare was tied up with Jonathan's after all, and if Jonathan cracked up – but Tom couldn't imagine Jonathan saying to anyone that Tom had been on the train with him, helping him. There shouldn't be any need to say that, and Jonathan as a matter of principle wouldn't. *How does one suddenly acquire about ninety-two thousand dollars?* That was the problem. It was the question Simone was asking Jonathan.

'If we could only make a double-barrelled thing out of it,' Tom said finally.

'What do you mean?'

'Something added to the sum the doctors might have paid you. – How about a *bet*? One doctor has bet another in Germany, and they've both deposited the money with you, a sort of trust fund – I mean it's in *trust* with you. That could account for – let's say fifty thousand dollars of it, more than half. Or are you thinking in francs? Um-m – more than two hundred and fifty thousand francs, perhaps.'

Jonathan smiled. The idea was amusing, but rather wild. 'Another beer?'

'Sure,' said Tom, and lit a Gauloise. 'Look. You might say to Simone that – that because the bet seemed so frivolous, or ruthless or whatever, you hadn't wanted to tell her, but there's a bet on your life. One doctor has bet that you'll live – a full life span, for instance. That would leave you and Simone with a little more than two hundred thousand francs of your own – which by the way I hope you've already begun to enjoy!'

Tock! Tock! A hectic barman set down Tom's fresh glass and bottle. Jonathan was already on his second.

'We've bought a sofa – much needed,' Jonathan said. 'We could treat ourselves to a telly too. Your idea *is* better than nothing. Thank you.'

A stocky man of about sixty greeted Jonathan with a brief handshake and walked on towards the back of the bar with no glance at Tom. Tom stared at two blonde girls who were being chatted up by a trio of boys in bell-bottom trousers standing by their table. A roly-poly old dog with skinny legs looked miserably up at Tom as he waited on his leash for his master to finish his *petit rouge*.

'Heard from Reeves lately?' Tom asked.

'Lately – not in about a month, I think.'

Then Jonathan didn't know about Reeves' flat being bombed,

and Tom saw no reason to tell him. It would only shake his morale.

'Have you? Is he all right?'

Tom said casually, 'I really don't know,' as if Reeves was not in the habit of writing or telephoning. Tom felt suddenly ill-at-ease, as if eyes were on him. 'Let's take off, shall we?' He beckoned to the barman to take his two ten-franc notes, though Jonathan had pulled out his money also. 'My car's outside to the right.'

On the pavement, Jonathan began awkwardly, 'You feel you're all right yourself? Nothing to worry about?'

Now they were beside his car. 'I'm the worrying type. You'd never think so, would you? I try to think of the worst before it happens. Not quite the same as being pessimistic.' Tom smiled. 'You going home? I'll drop you off.'

Jonathan got into the car.

When Tom got in and closed the door, he at once had a sense of privacy, as if they were in a room in his own house. And how long would his house be safe? Tom had an unpleasant vision of the ubiquitous Mafia, like black cockroaches darting everywhere, coming from everywhere. If he fled his house, getting Heloise and Mme Annette out before him or with him, the Mafia might simply set fire to Belle Ombre. Tom thought of the harpsichord burning, or going up in pieces from a bomb. Tom admitted that he had a love of house and home usually found only in women.

'I'm in more danger than you, if that bodyguard, the second one, can identify my face. I've had a few pictures in the newspapers, that's the trouble,' Tom said.

Jonathan knew. 'I apologize for asking to see you today. I'm afraid I'm awfully worried about my wife. It's because – how *we* get along is the most important thing in my life. It's the first time I've ever tried to deceive her about anything, you see. And I've rather failed – so it's shattering to me. But – you were a help. Thanks.'

'Yes. It's all right this time,' Tom said pleasantly. He meant their seeing each other this evening. 'But it occurs to me – ' Tom opened the glove compartment, and took out the Italian gun. 'I think you ought to have this handy. In your shop, for instance.'

'Really? – To tell you the truth, I'm afraid I'd be hopeless in a shoot-out.'

'It's better than nothing. If someone comes into your shop who looks odd – Haven't you got a drawer just behind your counter?'

A tingle went up Jonathan's spine, because he'd had a dream a few nights ago of exactly that : a Mafia gunman coming into his shop and shooting him point-blank in the face. 'But why do you think I'll need it? There's some reason, isn't there?'

Suddenly Tom thought, why not tell Jonathan? It might inspire him to more caution. At the same time Tom knew that caution wasn't of much help. It also occurred to Tom that Jonathan would be safer if he took his wife and child away on a trip for a while. 'Yes, I had a telephone call today that bothered me. A man who sounded French, but that doesn't mean anything. He asked for some French name. It may not mean anything and yet I can't be sure. Because as soon as I open my mouth, I sound like an American, and he may have been verifying – ' Tom trailed off. 'To fill you in further, Reeves' place in Hamburg was bombed – I suppose it was around the middle of April.'

'His flat. Good God! Was he injured?'

'No one was in the place at the time. But Reeves went to Amsterdam in a hurry. He's still there as far as I know, under another name.'

Jonathan thought of Reeves' flat being looked over for names and addresses, of his and maybe Tom Ripley's also being found. 'Then how much does the enemy know?'

'Oh, Reeves says he has all his important papers under control. They got hold of Fritz – I suppose you know Fritz – and beat him up a bit, but according to Reeves, Fritz was heroic. He gave them an opposite description of you – you being the man Reeves hired, or somebody hired.' Tom sighed. 'I'm assuming they suspect Reeves and a few casino club men – only.' He glanced at Jonathan's wide eyes. Jonathan didn't look so much frightened as jolted.

'Good Christ!' Jonathan whispered. 'Do you suppose they got hold of my address – or our addresses?'

'No,' Tom said, smiling, 'or they'd have been here already, I can tell you that.' Tom wanted to get home. He turned on the ignition and manoeuvred himself into the traffic of the Rue Grande.

'Then – assuming the man who phoned you was one of them, how did he get your number?'

'Now we enter the realm of guesswork,' Tom said, getting his car into the clear at last. He was still smiling. Yes, it was dangerous, and this time he wasn't getting a penny out of it, not even protecting his own money, which was what he had done at least in the Derwatt near-fiasco. 'Maybe because Reeves was stupid enough to ring me from Amsterdam. I'm toying with the possibility that the Mafia boys might've traced him to Amsterdam, because for one thing he's having his housekeeper send his possessions there. Pretty stupid move, so soon,' Tom said as if in parentheses. 'I'm wondering, you see, if – even if Reeves got out of his Amsterdam hotel, the Mafia boys didn't check on the phone calls he made. In which case my number might be there. By the way, he didn't ring you, I trust, when he was in Amsterdam. You're sure?'

'The last call I had was from Hamburg, I know.' Jonathan remembered Reeves' cheerful voice, telling him his money, all of it, would be deposited at once in the Swiss bank. Jonathan was worried about the bulge of the gun in his pocket. 'Sorry, but I'd better go to my shop first to get rid of this gun. Drop me anywhere here.'

Tom pulled up to a kerb. 'Take it easy. If you're seriously – alarmed about anything, go ahead and ring me. I mean that.'

Jonathan gave an awkward smile, because he felt scared. 'Or if I can be of help – do the same.'

Tom drove on.

Jonathan walked towards his shop, one hand in his pocket supporting the weight of the gun. He put the gun into his cash drawer which slid under the heavy counter. Tom was right, the gun was better than nothing, and Jonathan knew he had another advantage: he didn't care much about his own life. It wouldn't be like Tom Ripley getting shot or whatever, losing his life while in the best of health, and for literally nothing, it seemed to Jonathan.

If a man walked into his shop with intent to shoot him, and if he was lucky enough to be able to shoot the man first, it would be the end of the game, anyway. Jonathan didn't need Tom Ripley to tell him that. The gunshot would bring people, the police, the dead man would be identified, and the question would be asked, 'Why should a Mafia man want to shoot at Jonathan Trevanny?' The train journey would be the next thing exposed, because the police would ask his movements in the last weeks, would want to see his passport. He'd be finished.

Jonathan locked his shop door and walked on towards the Rue St Merry. He was thinking of Reeves' flat bombed, all those books, the records, the paintings. He was thinking of Fritz who had guided him to the button man called Salvatore Bianca, of Fritz beaten up and not betraying him.

It was nearly 7.30 p.m., and Simone was in the kitchen. '*Bonsoir!*' Jonathan said, smiling.

'*Bonsoir*,' Simone said. She turned the oven down, then straightened and removed her apron. 'And what were you doing with M. Ripley this evening?'

Jonathan's face tingled a little. Where had she seen them? When he'd got out of Tom's car? 'He came to talk about some framing,' Jonathan said. 'So we had a beer. It was near closing time.'

'Oh?' She looked at Jonathan, not moving. 'I see.'

Jonathan hung his jacket in the hall. Georges was coming down the stairs to greet him, saying something about his hover-craft. Georges was assembling a model Jonathan had bought for him, and it was a little too complicated for him. Jonathan swung him up over his shoulder. 'We'll have a look at it after dinner, all right?'

The atmosphere did not improve. They had a delicious purée of vegetable soup, made in a six-hundred-franc mixer that Jonathan had just bought: it made fruit juices and pulverized almost everything, including some chicken bones. Jonathan tried without success to talk about other things. Simone could soon bring any subject to a halt. It wasn't impossible, Jonathan was thinking, that Tom Ripley should want him to frame some pictures. After all, Tom had said he painted. Jonathan said:

'Ripley is interested in framing several things. I might have to go to his house to look at them.'

'Oh?' in the same tone. Then she said something pleasant to Georges.

Jonathan disliked Simone when she was like this, and hated himself for disliking her. He had been going to plunge into the explanation – the bet explanation – of the sum of money in the Swiss bank. That evening, he simply couldn't.

17

After dropping Jonathan, Tom had an impulse to stop at a bar-café and ring his house. He wanted to know if all was well, and if Heloise was home. To his great relief Heloise answered.

'*Oui, chéri*, I just got home. Where are you? No, I had only a drink with Noëlle.'

'Heloise, my pet, let's do something nice tonight. Maybe the Grais or the Berthelins are free . . . I know it's late to ask anyone for dinner, but for after dinner. Maybe the Cleggs . . . Yes, I feel like seeing some people.' Tom said he would be home in fifteen minutes.

Tom drove fast, but carefully. He felt curiously shaky about tonight. He was wondering about any telephone calls that Mme Annette might have got since he left the house.

Heloise, or Mme Annette, had put the front light on at Belle Ombre, though the dusk had not yet fallen. A big Citroën cruised slowly past, just before Tom turned into his gates, and Tom looked at it: dark blue, lumbering on the slightly uneven road, with a licence plate ending in 75, meaning a Paris car. There had been two people in it at least. Was it casing Belle Ombre? He was probably over anxious.

'Hello, Tome! *Les* Clegg can come for a quick drink, and *les* Grais can come for dinner, because Antoine didn't go to Paris today. Does that please you?' Heloise kissed his cheek. 'Where were you? Look at the suitcase! – I admit it's not very big –'

Tom looked at the dark purple suitcase with a red canvas band around it. The clasps and the lock appeared to be brass. The purple leather looked like kid, and perhaps was. 'Yes. It really *is* pretty.' It really was, like their harpsichord, or like his *commode de bateau* upstairs.

'And look – inside.' Heloise opened it. 'Really str-rong,' she said in English.

Tom stooped and kissed her hair. 'Darling, it's lovely. We can celebrate the suitcase – and the harpsichord. The Cleggs and the Grais haven't seen the harpsichord, have they? No ... How is Noëlle?'

'Tome, something is making you nervous,' Heloise said in a soft voice, in case Mme Annette might hear.

'No,' said Tom. 'I just feel like seeing some people. I had a very quiet day. Ah, Mme Annette, bonsoir! People tonight. Two for dinner. Can you manage?'

Mme Annette had just arrived with the bar cart. 'Mais oui, M. Tome. It will have to be à la fortune du pot, but I shall try a ragoût – my Normandy style, if you remember ...'

Tom didn't listen to her ingredients – there was beef, veal and kidney, because she'd had time to pop out to the butcher's this evening, and it was not going to be pot-luck at all, Tom was sure. But Tom had to wait until she finished. Then he said, 'By the way, Mme Annette, were there any telephone calls since six when I left?'

'No, M. Tome.' With expertise Mme Annette extracted the cork of a small bottle of champagne.

'None at all? Not even a wrong number?'

'Non, M. Tome.' Mme Annette poured champagne carefully into a wide glass for Heloise.

Heloise was watching him. But Tom decided to persist, rather than go into the kitchen to speak with Mme Annette. Or should he not go into the kitchen? Yes. That was quite easy. When Mme Annette went back to the kitchen, Tom said to Heloise, 'I think I'll get a beer.' Mme Annette had left him to make his own drink, as Tom often preferred to do.

In the kitchen, Mme Annette had her dinner in full swing, vegetables washed and ready, and something already boiling on the stove. 'Madame,' Tom said, 'it's very important – today. Are you quite sure nobody telephoned at all? Even somebody – even by error?'

This seemed to jog her memory, to Tom's alarm. 'Ah, oui, the telephone rang around six-thirty. A man asked for – some other name I can't recall, M. Tome. Then he hung up. An error, M. Tome.'

'What did you say to him?'

'I said it was not the residence of the person he wanted.'

'You told him it was the Ripley residence?'

'Oh no, M. Tome. I simply said it was not the right number. I thought that was the correct thing to do.'

Tom beamed at her. It had been the correct thing to do. Tom had reproached himself for going off at 6 p.m. today without asking Mme Annette not to give his name under any circumstances, and she'd handled everything properly on her own initiative. 'Excellent. That's always the correct thing to do,' Tom said with admiration. 'That's why I have an unlisted number, in order to have a little privacy, *n'est-ce pas?*'

'*Bien sûr,*' said Mme Annette, as if it were the most natural thing in the world.

Tom went back to the living-room, forgetting all about beer. He poured a scotch for himself. He was not much reassured, however. If it had been a Mafioso looking for him, he might be doubly suspicious because two people at this house had refrained from giving the name of the proprietor. Tom wondered if some checking was going on in Milan or Amsterdam or perhaps Hamburg? Didn't Tom Ripley live in Villeperce? Couldn't this 424 number be a Villeperce number? Yes, indeed. Fontainebleau numbers began with 422, but 424 was an area southward, including Villeperce.

'What is worrying you, Tome?' Heloise asked.

'Nothing, darling. – What's happening with your cruise plans? Have you seen anything you like?'

'Ah, yes! Something which is not *casse-pied* swank, just nice and simple. A cruise from Venice around the Mediterranean, including Turkey. Fifteen days – and one doesn't have to dress for dinner. How does that sound, Tome? Every three weeks during May and June, for instance, the boat leaves.'

'I'm not much in the mood at the moment. Ask Noëlle if she'd go with you. It would do you good.'

Tom went upstairs to his room. He opened the bottom drawer of his bigger chest of drawers. On top was Heloise's green jacket from Salzburg. At the back on the bottom of the drawer lay a Luger which Tom had acquired just three months ago from Reeves, oddly enough, not directly from Reeves but from a man whom Tom had had to meet in Paris in order to get something the man was delivering, something that Tom had had to hold for a month before posting it. As a favour, as a kind of payment really, Tom had requested a Luger, and it had been given him – a 7·65 mm with two little boxes of ammunition. Tom verified that the gun was loaded, then he went to his closet and looked at his French-made hunting rifle. It was loaded also, with the safety on it. It was the Luger he would need in case of trouble, Tom supposed, tonight or tomorrow or tomorrow night. Tom looked out the two windows of his room, which gave in two directions. He was looking for cruising cars with dimmed lights, but he didn't see any. It was already dark.

A car approached with a determined air from the left: this was the dear, harmless Cleggs, and they turned in smartly through the gates of Belle Ombre. Tom went down to welcome them.

The Cleggs – Howard, fiftyish, an Englishman and his English wife Rosemary – stayed for two drinks, and the Grais joined them. Clegg, a retired lawyer, retired because of a heart condition, nevertheless was more animated than anyone else. His grey, neatly cut hair, seasoned tweed jacket and grey flannels, lent the air of country stability that Tom needed. Clegg, standing with his back to the curtained front window, scotch in hand, telling a funny story – What could happen tonight to shatter this rural conviviality? Tom had left his room light on, and he had turned on the bedside lamp in Heloise's room also. The two cars were parked carelessly on the gravel. Tom wanted his house to present the picture of a party in progress, a party bigger than it was. Not that this would really stop the Mafia boys, if they chose to toss a bomb, Tom knew, and therefore he was putting his friends in danger, perhaps. But Tom had the feeling the Mafia would prefer a quiet assassination for him: get him alone and then attack, maybe without a gun, just a sudden beating up that would be fatal. The Mafia could do it on the streets of Villeperce, and be away before the townspeople knew what had happened.

Rosemary Clegg, slim and beautiful in a middle-aged way, was promising Heloise some kind of plant that she and Howard had just brought back from England.

'Are you intending to set any fires this summer?' Antoine Grais asked.

'Not really my dish,' Tom said, smiling. 'Come out and take a look at the greenhouse-to-be.'

Tom and Antoine walked out the french windows and down the steps on to the lawn, Tom with a flashlight. The foundation had been laid with cement, the pieces for the steel frame were stacked alongside, doing the lawn no good, and the workmen hadn't been around for a week. Tom had been warned by one of the villagers about this crew : they had so much work this summer, they hopped from one job to the next, trying to please everybody, or at least keep a lot of people on the hook.

'That's coming along, I think,' said Antoine finally.

Tom had consulted Antoine as to the best type of greenhouse, paid him for his services, and Antoine had also been able to get the materials for him at a professional discount, or anyway more cheaply than the mason would have got them. Tom found himself glancing towards the lane through the woods behind Antoine, where there were no lights at all, certainly no car lights now.

But by 11 p.m., after dinner when the four of them were drinking coffee and Bénédictine, Tom made up his mind to get both Heloise and Mme Annette out of the house by tomorrow. Heloise would be the easier. He'd persuade her to stay with Noëlle for a few days – Noëlle and her husband had a very large flat in Neuilly – or to stay with her parents. Mme Annette had a sister in Lyon, and fortunately the sister had a telephone, so something might be arranged quickly. And the explanation? Tom shrank from the idea of putting on an act of crotchetyness, such as, 'I must be alone for a few days', and if he admitted that there was danger, Heloise and Mme Annette would be alarmed. They'd want to alert the police.

Tom approached Heloise that evening, as they were getting ready for bed. 'My dear,' he said in English, 'I have a feeling something awful is going to happen, and I don't want you here. It's a matter of your safety. Also I would like Mme Annette to leave tomorrow for a few days – so I hope, darling, you can help me persuade her to visit her sister.'

Heloise, propped up on pale blue pillows, frowned a little and set down the yoghurt she was eating. '*What* is happening that is awful? – Tome, you must tell me.'

'No.' Tom shook his head, then he laughed. 'And maybe I'm only anxious. Maybe it's for nothing. But there's no harm in playing it safe, is there?'

'I don't want a lot of words, Tome. What has happened? Something with Reeves! It is that, isn't it?'

'In a way.' It was a lot better than saying it was the Mafia.

'Where is he?'

'Oh, he's in Amsterdam, I think.'

'Doesn't he live in Germany?'

'Yes, but he's doing some work in Amsterdam.'

'But who else is involved? Why are you worried? — What have you done, Tome?'

'Why, nothing, darling!' It was Tom's usual answer under the circumstances. He wasn't even ashamed of it.

'Then you're trying to protect Reeves?'

'He's done me a few favours. But I want to protect you now — and us, and Belle Ombre. Not Reeves. So you must let me try, darling.'

'Belle Ombre?'

Tom smiled and said calmly, 'I don't want any disturbance at Belle Ombre. I don't want anything broken, not a pane of glass. You must trust me, I'm trying to avoid anything violent — or dangerous!'

Heloise blinked her eyes and said in a slightly piqued tone, 'All right, Tome.'

He knew that Heloise would ask no more questions, not unless there was an accusation by the police, or a Mafia corpse to account for to her. A few minutes later, they were both smiling, and Tom slept in her bed that night. How much worse it must be for Jonathan Trevanny, Tom thought — not that Simone appeared difficult, prying or neurotic in the least, but Jonathan was not in the habit of doing anything out of the ordinary, not even of telling white lies. It must be, as Jonathan had said, shattering if his wife had begun to mistrust him. And because of the money, it was natural that Simone would think of crime, of something shameful that Jonathan couldn't admit.

In the morning, Heloise and Tom spoke to Mme Annette to-gether. Heloise had had her tea upstairs, and Tom was drinking a second coffee in the living-room.

'M. Tome says he wants to be alone and think and paint for a few days,' said Heloise.

They had decided this was best after all. 'And a little vacation wouldn't do you any harm, Mme Annette. A little one before the big one in August,' Tom added, though Mme Annette, sturdy and lively as always, looked in the best of form.

'But if you wish, Madame et M'sieur, of course. That is the big thing, is it not?' She was smiling, her blue eyes not exactly twinkling now, but she was agreeable.

Mme Annette at once agreed to ring her sister Marie-Odile in Lyon.

The post came at 9.30 a.m. In it was a square, white envelope with a Swiss stamp, the address printed – Reeves' printing, Tom suspected – and no return address. Tom wanted to open it in the living-room, but Heloise was talking with Mme Annette about driving her to Paris for the train to Lyon, so Tom went up to his room. The letter said :

May 11

Dear Tom,

I am in Ascona. Had to leave Amsterdam because of a near thing in my hotel, but have managed to put my belongings in store in Amsterdam. God, I wish they would lay off! I am here in this pretty town, known as Ralph Platt, staying at an inn up the hill called Die Drei Baeren – cosy? At least it is very out of the way and family pension style. Wishing the very best to you and Heloise,

As ever,

R.

Tom crushed the letter in his hand, then shredded it into his wastebasket. It was exactly as bad as Tom had thought : the Mafia had caught up with him at Amsterdam, and had doubtless got Tom's telephone number by checking all the numbers Reeves had called. Tom wondered what the near thing at the hotel had been? He swore to himself, not for the first time, that he'd never have anything to do with Reeves Minot in future. In this case, all he'd provided was an idea for Reeves. That should have been harmless, and it was harmless. Tom realized his mistake had been to try to help Jonathan Trevanny. And of course Reeves didn't know that, or Reeves wouldn't have been stupid enough to ring him at Belle Ombre.

He wanted Jonathan Trevanny to come to Belle Ombre by this evening, even this afternoon, though he knew Jonathan worked on Saturday. If anything happened, the situation could be more easily handled by two people, at front and back of the house, for instance, because one person couldn't be everywhere. And who else had he to call on but Jonathan? Jonathan wasn't a promising fighter, and yet in a crisis he might come through, just as he had on the train. He'd done all right there, and had also, Tom remembered, yanked him back to safety when he'd been surely going to fall out the train door. He wanted Jonathan to stay the night, and he'd have to fetch him, too, because there was no bus, and Tom didn't want him to take a taxi, in view of what might happen tonight, didn't want any taxi-driver to recall that he'd driven a man from Fontainebleau to Villeperce, a rather unusual distance.

'You will telephone me tonight, Tome?' Heloise asked. She was packing a big suitcase in her room. She was going first to her family.

'Yes, my love. Around seven-thirty?' He knew Heloise's parents dined promptly at 8 p.m. 'I'll ring and say "All is well", probably.'

'Is it only tonight you are worried about?'

It wasn't, but Tom didn't want to say so. 'I think so.'

When Heloise and Mme Annette were ready to leave around 11 a.m., Tom managed to enter the garage first, before he even helped them with their luggage, though Mme Annette had the old French school idea that she should carry the luggage of both in instalments, simply because she was a servant. Tom looked under the hood of the Alfa. The motor presented the familiar picture of metal and wires. He started the motor. No explosion. Tom had gone out and padlocked the garage doors last evening before dinner, but Tom believed anything when it came to the Mafia. They'd pick a padlock and snap it shut again.

'We will be in touch, Mme Annette,' Tom said, kissing her cheek. 'Enjoy yourself!'

'Bye-bye, Tome! Ring me tonight! And take care!' Heloise shouted.

Tom grinned as he waved good-bye. He could tell that Heloise wasn't very worried. That was all to the good.

Tom then went into his house to telephone Jonathan.

18

The morning had been a rough one for Jonathan. Simone had said, in a pleasant enough tone, because she was then helping Georges tug himself into a turtle-neck sweater:

'I don't see how this ambience can go on for ever, Jon. Do you?'

Simone and Georges had to leave for Georges' school in a couple of minutes. It was almost 8.15 a.m.

'No, I don't. And about that Swiss sum – ' Jonathan determined to plunge on, now. He spoke quickly, hoping Georges wouldn't grasp all of it. 'They've made a bet, if you must know. I'm holding the take for both of them. So that – '

'*Who?*' Simone looked as puzzled and angry as ever.

'The doctors,' Jonathan said. 'They're trying a new treatment – one is – and somebody's betting against him. Another doctor. I thought you'd think it rather macabre, so I wasn't going to tell you about it. But that means there's really only about two hundred thousand, less now, belonging to us. They're paying me that, the Hamburg people, for trying out their pills.'

Jonathan could see that she tried, and couldn't believe him. 'It's absurd!' she said. 'All that money, Jon! For a *bet?*'

Georges looked up at her.

Jonathan glanced at his son and wet his lips.

'Do you know what I think, and I don't care if Georges hears me! I think you are holding – concealing dishonest money for this dishonest type Tom Ripley. And of course he's paying you a little, letting you have a little of it for doing him the favour!'

Jonathan realized he was trembling, and set his bowl of *café au lait* down on the kitchen table. Both he and Simone were standing. 'Couldn't Ripley conceal his own money himself in Switzerland?' Jonathan's instinct was to go to her and grasp her by the shoulders, tell her that she had to believe him. But he knew quite well she'd push him back. So he simply stood up straighter and said, 'I can't help it if you don't believe me. That's the way it is.' Jonathan had had a transfusion last Monday afternoon, the day he had fainted. Simone had gone to the hospital with him, and then he had gone by himself afterward to Dr Perrier, whom he'd had to ring earlier to make the appointment for the transfusion for him. Dr Perrier had wanted to see him as a matter of routine. But Jonathan had told Simone that Dr Perrier had given him more of the medicaments sent by the Hamburg doctor. The Hamburg doctor, Wentzel, hadn't sent pills, but the pills he recommended were available in France, and Jonathan had a supply at home now. It was the Hamburg doctor Jonathan had decided should be betting 'for' and the Munich doctor who should be betting 'against', but he hadn't got that far with Simone as yet.

'But I *don't* believe you,' Simone said, her voice gentle and also sinister. 'Come along, Georges, we've got to go.'

Jonathan blinked, and watched Simone and Georges go up the hall towards the front door. Georges picked up his satchel of books, and perhaps startled by the heated conversation, forgot to say good-bye to Jonathan, and Jonathan was silent too.

Since it was Saturday, Jonathan's shop was busy. The telephone rang several times. Around 11 a.m., the voice on the other end of the telephone was Tom Ripley's.

'I'd like to see you today. It's rather important,' Tom said. 'Are you able to talk now?'

'Not really.' There was a man at the counter in front of Jonathan, waiting to pay for his picture which lay wrapped between them.

'I'm sorry to bother you on a Saturday. But I'm wondering how soon you could get to my house – and stay the evening?'

Jonathan was jolted for a second. Close the shop. Inform Simone. Inform her what? 'Of course I can. Yes.'

'How soon? I'll pick you up. Say at twelve noon? Or is that too soon?'

'No. I'll make it.'

'Pick you up at your shop. Or on the street there. One other thing – bring the gun.' Tom hung up.

Jonathan attended to the people in his shop, and while there was still someone in his shop, he stuck the FERME sign in his door. He wondered what had happened to Tom Ripley since yesterday? Simone was home that morning, but she was more often out than in on Saturday mornings, because she did marketing and chores like going to the dry cleaners. Jonathan decided to write Simone a note and push it through the letter slot in the front door. Jonathan had the note written by 11.40 a.m., and went off with it, up the Rue de la Paroisse, the quickest way, where there was a fifty-fifty chance of encountering Simone, but he didn't. He stuck the note through the slot marked LETTRES, and walked back quickly the way he had come. He had written:

My dear,

Won't be home for lunch or dinner and have closed the shop. Chance of a big job some distance away and am being taken there by car.

                                                                            J.

It was inexplicit, not at all like him. And yet, how could things get any worse than they'd been that morning?

Jonathan went into his shop again, grabbed his old mac, and stuck the Italian gun into its pocket. When he went out on the pavement again, Tom's green Renault was approaching. Tom opened the door, barely stopping, and Jonathan got in.

'Morning!' Tom said. 'How are things?'

'At home?' Jonathan was, despite himself, glancing about for Simone who might be anywhere on the streets here. 'Not very good, I'm afraid.'

Tom could imagine. 'But you're feeling all right?'

'Yes, thanks.'

Tom made the right turn by the Prisunic into the Rue Grande. 'I had another telephone call,' Tom said, 'rather my housekeeper did. Same as before, a wrong number, and she didn't tell him whose house it was, but it's made me nervous. By the way I've sent my housekeeper and also my wife away. I have a hunch something might happen. So I called on you to hold the fort with me. I have no one else to ask. I'm afraid to ask the police to keep a watch. If they were to find a couple of the Mafia around my house, there'd be unpleasant inquiries as to why they were there, of course.'

Jonathan knew that.

'We're not at my house yet,' Tom went on, passing the Monument now and entering the road that led towards Villeperce, 'so there's time for you to change your mind. I'll drive you back gladly and you needn't apologize if you don't want to join me. There may be danger and there may not. But it's easier for two people to be on the look-out there than for one.'

'Yes.' Jonathan felt curiously paralysed.

'It's just that I don't want to leave my house.' Tom was driving rather fast. 'I don't want it to go up in smoke or be blown up like Reeves' place. Reeves by the way is now in Ascona. They tracked him to Amsterdam and he had to run.'

'Oh?' Jonathan experienced a few seconds of panic, of nausea. He felt that everything was collapsing. 'You've – Have you seen anything odd around your house?'

'Not really.' Tom's voice was cool. His cigarette stuck up at a jaunty angle.

Jonathan was thinking, he *could* pull out. Now. Just say to Tom he didn't feel up to it, that he might well faint if it came to the crunch. He could go home and be safe. Jonathan took a deep breath and lowered the window a bit more. He'd be a bastard if he did that, a coward and a shit. He might at least try. He owed it to Tom Ripley. And why should he be so concerned about his own safety? Why suddenly now? Jonathan smiled a little, feeling better. 'I told Simone about the bet on my life. It didn't go down too well.'

'What did she say?'

'The same thing. She doesn't believe me. What's worse, she saw me with you yesterday – somewhere. Now she's thinking I'm holding some money for you – in my name. Dishonest money, you know.'

'Yes.' Tom saw the situation. But it didn't seem important compared to what might happen to Belle Ombre, to himself and maybe Jonathan too. 'I'm no hero, you know,' Tom said out of the blue. 'If the Mafia got me and tried to beat some facts out of me, I doubt if I'd be as brave as Fritz.'

Jonathan was silent. He sensed that Tom was feeling as queasy as he himself had a few seconds ago.

It was a particularly fine day, the air liquid with summer, the sunlight brilliant. It was a shame to have to work on such a day, to have to be indoors as Simone would be this afternoon. She didn't have to work any more, of course. Jonathan had wanted to say that to her for the past couple of weeks.

They were entering Villeperce now, a quiet village of the kind that would have perhaps only one butcher's and one bakery.

'That's Belle Ombre,' Tom said, nodding towards a domed tower that showed above some poplars.

They had driven perhaps half a kilometre from the village. The houses on the road were far apart and large. Belle Ombre looked like a small château, its lines classic and sturdy, but softened by four rounded corner towers which came all the way down to the grass. There were iron gates, and Tom had to get out and open them with a huge key he had taken from the glove compartment. Then they rolled on to the gravel in front of the garage.

'What a beautiful place!' Jonathan said.

Tom nodded and smiled. 'A wedding present from my wife's parents, mainly. And every time I arrive lately, I'm delighted to see that it's still standing. Please come in!'

Tom had a key for the front door, too.

'Not used to locking up,' Tom said. 'Usually my housekeeper's here.'

Jonathan walked into a wide foyer paved with white marble, then into a square living-room – two rugs, a big fireplace, a comfortable-looking yellow satin sofa. And a harpsichord stood beside french windows. The furniture was all good, Jonathan saw, and it was well cared for.

'Take off your mac,' Tom said. For the moment, he felt relieved – Belle Ombre was quiet, and he hadn't seen anything out of the ordinary in the village. He went to the hall table and took his Luger from the drawer. Jonathan watched him, and Tom smiled. 'Yes, I'm going to carry this thing all day, hence these old trousers. Big pockets. I can see why some people prefer shoulder-holsters.' Tom pushed the gun into a pocket of his trousers. 'Do the same with yours, if you don't mind.'

Jonathan did.

Tom was thinking of his rifle upstairs. He was sorry to get

down to business so quickly, but he thought it might be for the best. 'Come up. I want to show you something.'

They climbed the stairway, and Tom took Jonathan into his room. Jonathan at once noticed the *commode de bateau* and went over for a closer look.

'A recent present from my wife – Look – ' Tom was holding his rifle. 'There's this. For long range. Fairly accurate, but not like an army rifle, of course. I want you to look out this front window.'

Jonathan did. There was a nineteenth-century three-storey house across the road, set well back and more than half-obscured by trees. Trees bordered the road on either side in a haphazard way. Jonathan was imagining a car pausing on the road outside the house gates, and that was what Tom was talking about: the rifle would be more accurate than a pistol.

'Of course it depends on what they do,' Tom said. 'If they intend to throw an incendiary bomb, for instance. Then the rifle will be the thing to use. Of course there are back windows too. And side windows. Come this way.'

Tom led Jonathan into Heloise's room, which had a window giving on the back lawn. Here were denser trees beyond the lawn, and poplars bordering the lawn on the right.

'There's a lane going through those woods. You can faintly see it on the left. And in my atelier – ' Tom went into the hall and opened a door on the left. This room had windows on the back lawn and in the direction in which the village of Villeperce lay, but only cypresses and poplars and the tiles of a small house were visible. 'We might keep a look-out on both sides of the house, not that we have to stay glued to the windows but – The other important point is, I want the enemy to think I'm alone here. If you – '

The telephone was ringing. Tom thought for a moment that he wouldn't answer it, then that he might learn something if he did. He took it in his room.

'*Oui?*'

'M. Ripley?' said a Frenchwoman's voice. '*Ici*, Mme Trevanny. Is my husband there by any chance?'

She sounded very tense.

'Your husband? *Mais non*, madame!' Tom said with astonishment in his voice.

'*Merci, m'sieur. Excusez-moi.*' She hung up.

Tom sighed. Jonathan was indeed having troubles.

Jonathan was standing in the doorway. 'My wife.'

'Yes,' Tom said. 'I'm sorry. I said you weren't here. You can send a *pneu*, if you like. Or telephone. Maybe she's in your shop.'

'No, no, I doubt that.' But she could be, because she had a key. It was only a quarter past 1 p.m. How else could Simone have obtained his number, Tom thought, if not from Jonathan's notation in his shop? 'Or if you like, I'll drive you back now to Fontainebleau. It's really up to you, Jonathan.'

'No,' Jonathan said. 'Thanks.' Renunciation, Jonathan thought. Simone had known Tom was lying.

'I apologize for lying just now. You can always blame me. I doubt if I can sink any lower in your wife's mind anyway.' Tom at that moment didn't give a damn, didn't have the time or the inclination to sympathize with Simone. Jonathan wasn't saying anything. 'Let's go down and see what the kitchen has to offer.'

Tom drew the curtains in his room almost closed, but open enough so that one could see out without stirring the curtains. He did the same in Heloise's room, and also downstairs in the living-room. Mme Annette's quarters he decided to let alone. They had windows on the lane side and the back lawn.

There was plenty of Mme Annette's delicious ragoût of last evening. The window over the kitchen sink had no curtains, and Tom made Jonathan sit out of view at the kitchen table, with a scotch and water.

'What a shame we can't potter in the garden this afternoon,' Tom said, washing lettuce at the sink. He had a compulsion to glance out the window at every passing car. Only two cars had passed in the last ten minutes.

Jonathan had noticed that both garage doors were wide open. Tom's car was parked on the gravel in front of the house. It was so quiet, any footstep would be heard on the gravel, Jonathan thought.

'And I can't turn on any music, because I might drown out some other noise. What a bore,' Tom said.

Though neither ate much, they spent a long time at the table in the dining area off the living-room. Tom made coffee. Since there was nothing substantial for dinner that evening, Tom telephoned the Villeperce butcher and asked for a good steak for two.

'Oh, Mme Annette is taking a short holiday,' Tom said in response to the butcher's question. The Ripleys were such good customers, Tom had no hesitation in asking the butcher to pick up some lettuce and a nice vegetable of some kind at the grocery next door.

The very audible crunching of tyres on gravel half an hour later announced the arrival of the butcher's van. Tom had jumped to his feet. He paid the genial butcher's boy, who was wearing a blood-spattered apron, and tipped him. Jonathan was now looking at some books on furniture, and seemed quite content, so Tom went upstairs to pass some time by tidying his atelier, a room which Mme Annette never touched.

A telephone call just before 5 p.m. came like a scream in the silent, a muffled scream to Tom, because he had dared to go out in the garden and was messing about with the secateurs. Tom ran into the house, though he knew Jonathan wouldn't touch the telephone. Jonathan was still lounging on the sofa, surrounded by books.

The call was from Heloise. She was very happy because she had rung Noëlle, and a friend of Noëlle's Jules Grifaud, an interior decorator, had bought a chalet in Switzerland, and was inviting Noëlle and her to drive there with him and keep him company for a week or so while he arranged his things in the house.

'The country around is so beautiful,' Heloise said. 'And we can also help him . . . '

It sounded deadly to Tom, but if Heloise was enthusiastic, that was what mattered. He had known she wouldn't go on that Adriatic cruise, like an ordinary tourist.

'Are you all right, darling? . . . What are you doing?'

'Oh – a little gardening . . . Yes, everything is *very* tranquil.'

19

Around 7.30 p.m., when Tom was standing at the front window
of his living-room, he saw the dark-blue Citroën – the same one
he'd seen that morning, he thought – cruise past the house, this
time at a faster speed, but still not as fast as the usual car which
intended to get somewhere. Was it the same? In the dusk,
colours were deceiving – the difference between blue and green.
But the car had been a convertible with a dirty white upper
trim, like the one this morning. Tom looked at the gates of Belle
Ombre, which he had left'ajar, but which the butcher's boy had
closed. Tom decided to leave them closed, but not locked. They
creaked a little.

'What's up?' Jonathan asked. He was drinking coffee. He
hadn't wanted tea. Tom's unease was making him uneasy, and
as far as he had been able to find out, Tom had no real reason
to be so anxious.

'I think I saw the same car as I saw this morning. A dark-blue
Citroën. The one this morning had a Paris plate. I know most of
the cars around here, and only two or three people have cars
with Paris plates.'

'Could you see the licence now?' It looked dark to Jonathan,
and he had a lamp on beside him.

'No – I'm going to get the rifle.' Tom went upstairs as if borne
on wings, and returned at once with the rifle. He had left no
lights on upstairs. He said to Jonathan, 'I definitely don't want to
use a gun if I can avoid it, because of the noise. It's not the
hunting season, and a gunshot might bring the neighbours – or
someone might investigate. Jonathan –'

Jonathan was on his feet. 'Yes?'

'You might have to wield this rifle like a club.' Tom illustrated,
so that the weightiest part of it, the butt, could be used to best

effect. 'You can see how it works, in case you have to shoot with it. Safety's on now.' Tom showed him.

But they're not here, Jonathan was thinking. And at the same time he was feeling odd and unreal, as he had felt in Hamburg and in Munich, when he had known that his targets were real, and that they would materialize.

Tom was calculating how much time it would take the Citroën to cruise or drive around the circular road that led back to the village. They could of course turn at some convenient place on the road and come straight back. 'If anyone comes to the door,' Tom said, 'I have the feeling I'm going to be plugged when I open the door. That would be the simplest for them, you see. Then the fellow with the gun jumps into the waiting car and off they go.'

Tom was a bit overwrought, Jonathan thought, but he listened carefully.

'Another possibility is a bomb through that window,' Tom said, gesturing towards the front window. 'Same as Reeves had. So if you're – um – agreeable – Sorry, but I'm not used to discussing my plans. I usually play it by ear. But if you're willing, would you hide yourself in the shrubbery to the right of the door here – it's thicker on the right – and clout anyone who walks up and rings the doorbell? They may not ring the doorbell, but I'll be watching with the Luger for signs of bomb throwing. Clout him fast if he's at the door, because he'll be fast. He'll have a gun in his pocket, and all he wants is a clear view of me.' Tom went to the fireplace, where he had meant to light a fire and forgot, and took one of the third-of-a-log pieces from the wood basket. This he put on the floor to the right of the front door. It was not as heavy as the amethyst vase on the wooden chest by the door, but much easier to handle.

'How about,' Jonathan said, 'if *I* open the door? If they know what you look like, as you say, they'll see I'm not you and – '

'No.' Tom was surprised by Jonathan's courageous offer. 'First, they might not wait to see, just fire. And if they did look at you, and you said I don't live here, or I'm not in, they'd only push in and see or – ' Tom gave it up with a laugh, imagining the Mafia blasting Jonathan in the stomach and pushing him into the house at the same time. 'I think you should take up the post by the door now, if you're willing. I don't know how long you'll have to stay there, but I can always bring you refreshments.'

'Sure.' Jonathan took the rifle from Tom and went out. The road in front of the house was quiet. Jonathan stood in the shadow of the house, and practised a swing with the rifle, high up so as to catch a man standing on the steps in the head.

'Good,' Tom said. 'Would you care for a scotch now by any chance? You can leave the glass in the bushes. Doesn't matter if it breaks.'

Jonathan smiled. 'No, thanks.' He crept into the shrubbery – cypress-like bushes four feet high, and laurel also. It was very dark where Jonathan was, and he felt absolutely concealed. Tom had closed the door.

Jonathan sat on the ground, his knees under his chin, and the rifle alongside near his right hand. He wondered if this could last for an hour? Longer? Or was it even a game Tom was playing. Jonathan couldn't believe it was entirely a game. Tom wasn't out of his head, and he believed something might happen tonight, and that small possibility made it wise to take precautions. Then as a car approached, Jonathan felt a start of real fear, an impulse to run straight into the house. The car went by at a fast clip. Jonathan hadn't even a glimpse of it through the bushes and the house gates. He leaned a shoulder against a slender trunk of something and began to feel sleepy. Five minutes later, he lay at full length on his back, but still quite awake, beginning to feel the chill of the earth penetrating his shoulder-blades. If the telephone rang again, it might well be Simone. He wondered if she would, in some frenzy of temper, come to Tom's house in a taxi? Or would she ring her brother Gérard in Nemours and ask him to bring her in his car? A bit more likely. Jonathan stopped thinking about that possibility, because it was so awful. Ludicrous. Unthinkable. How would he explain lying outside the house in the shrubbery, even if he concealed the rifle?

Jonathan heard the house door opening. He had been dozing. 'Take this blanket,' Tom whispered. The road was empty, and Tom stepped out with a steamer rug and handed it to Jonathan. 'Put it under you. That ground must be awful.' Tom's own whispering made him realize that the Mafia boys might sneak up on foot. He hadn't thought of that before. He went back into the house without another word to Jonathan.

Tom went up the stairs, and in the dark surveyed the situation from the windows, front and back. All looked calm. A street light glowed brightly, but without extending its light very far, on the road about a hundred yards to the left in the direction of the village. None of its light fell in front of Belle Ombre, as Tom knew well. It was extremely silent, but that was normal. Even the footsteps of a man walking on the road might have been heard through the closed windows, Tom thought. He wished he could put on some music. He was about to turn from the window, when he heard the faint *crunch-crunch-crunch* of someone walking on the dirt road, and then he saw a not very strong flashlight beam, moving from the right towards Belle Ombre. Tom felt sure this wasn't a person who would turn in at Belle Ombre, and the figure didn't, but went on and was lost to view before it reached the street light. Male or female, Tom couldn't tell.

Jonathan was perhaps hungry. That couldn't be helped. Tom was hungry, too. But of course it could be helped. Tom went down the stairs, still in the dark, his fingertips on the banister, and into the kitchen – the living-room and kitchen were lighted – and made some caviare canapes. The caviare was left over from last night, in its jar in the fridge, so the job was quick. Tom was bringing the plate for Jonathan, when he heard the purr of a car. The car went past Belle Ombre from left to right, and stopped. Then there was the feeble click of a car door, the sound of a car door when it hadn't quite closed. Tom set the plate down on the wooden chest by the door, and pulled out his gun.

Steps crunched firmly, at a polite-sounding pace, on the road, then the gravel. This wasn't a bomb-thrower, Tom thought. The doorbell rang. Tom waited a few seconds, then said in French, 'Who is it?'

'I would like to ask a direction, please,' the man's voice said with a perfect French accent.

Jonathan had been crouching with the rifle since the approach of footsteps, and now he leapt out of the bushes just as he heard Tom slide the bolt of the door. The man was two steps up from

Jonathan, but Jonathan was almost as tall nevertheless, and he swung his rifle butt with all his power at the man's head – which had turned just slightly towards Jonathan, because the man must have heard him. Jonathan's blow caught him behind the left ear, just under the hat-brim. The man swayed, bumped the left side of the doorway, and dropped.

Tom opened the door and dragged him by the feet into the house, Jonathan helping, lifting the man's shoulders. Then Jonathan recovered the rifle and came in the door, which Tom closed softly. Tom picked up the piece of firewood and walloped the man's blondish head with it. The man's hat had fallen off and lay upside down on the marble floor. Tom extended his hand for the rifle, and Jonathan handed it to him. Tom came down with the steel butt of it on the man's temple.

Jonathan couldn't believe his eyes. Blood flowed on to the white marble. This was the husky bodyguard with crinkly blond hair who had been so upset on the train.

'Got that bastard!' Tom whispered with satisfaction. 'This is that bodyguard. Look at the gun!'

A gun had fallen half out of the man's right side jacket pocket.

'Farther into the living-room,' Tom said, and they hauled and pushed the man across the floor. 'Mind the rug with that blood!' Tom kicked the rug out of the way. 'Next guy's due in a minute, no doubt. Bound to be two, maybe three.'

Tom took a handkerchief – lavender, monogrammed – from the man's breast pocket and tidied a splotch of blood on the floor near the door. He kicked the man's hat and sent it flying over the body, and it fell near the hall door to the kitchen. Then Tom bolted the front door, holding his left hand over the bolt so it would not make a noise. 'Next one might not be so easy,' he whispered.

There were footsteps on gravel. The bell rang – nervously twice.

Tom laughed without making a sound, and pulled his Luger. He motioned for Jonathan to take his gun also. Tom was suddenly convulsed, and doubled over to repress his mirth, then straightened and grinned at Jonathan, and wiped the tears from his eyes.

Jonathan didn't smile.

The bell rang again, a long steady peal.

Jonathan saw Tom's face change in a split-second. Tom frowned, grimaced, as if he didn't know what he should do.

'Don't use the gun,' Tom whispered, 'unless you have to.' His left hand was extended towards the door.

Tom was going to open the door and fire, Jonathan supposed, or cover the man.

Then steps crunched again. The man outside was walking towards the window behind Jonathan, a window now quite covered by the curtains. Jonathan edged away from the window.

'Angy? – *Angy!*' the man's voice whispered.

'Ask him at the door what he wants,' Tom whispered. 'Talk in English – as if you were the butler. Let him in. I'll have him covered. – Can you do it?'

Jonathan didn't care to think whether he could or not. Now there was a knocking, then another ring of the bell. 'Who is it, please?' Jonathan called to the door.

'*Je – je voudrais demander mon chemin, s'il vous plaît.*' The accent was not so good.

Tom smirked.

'Whom did you wish to speak to, sir?' Jonathan asked.

'*Une direction! – S'il vous plaît!*' the voice yelled. Desperation had entered in.

Tom and Jonathan exchanged a glance, and Tom gestured for Jonathan to open the door. Tom was immediately to the left of the door to anyone standing outside, but out of sight if the door were opened.

Jonathan slid the bolt, turned the knob of the automatic lock, and opened the door partway, fully expecting a bullet in his abdomen, but he stood tall and stiffly with his right hand in his jacket pocket on the gun.

The somewhat shorter Italian, wearing a hat like the other man, also had his hand in his pocket and was plainly surprised to see a tall man in ordinary clothes in front of him.

'Sir?' Jonathan noticed that the man's left jacket sleeve was empty.

As the man took a step inside the house, Tom poked him in the side with his Luger.

'Give me your gun!' Tom said in Italian.

Jonathan's gun was also pointed at him now. The man heaved his jacket pocket up as if to fire, and Tom pushed him in the face with his left hand. The man didn't fire. The Italian looked paralysed at finding himself suddenly so close to Tom Ripley.

'Reeply!' the Italian said, in a tone of mingled terror, surprise, and maybe triumph.

'Oh, never mind that and give us the gun!' Tom said in English, poking the man again in the ribs and knocking the door shut with his foot.

The Italian got the idea, at least. He dropped the gun on the floor, when Tom indicated that was what he wanted. Then the Italian saw his chum on the floor yards away, and started, wide-eyed.

'Bolt the door,' Tom said to Jonathan. Then Tom said in Italian, 'Any more of you?'

The Italian shook his head vigorously, which meant nothing, Tom thought. Tom saw that his arm was in a sling under his jacket. So much for the newspaper reports.

'Cover him while I do this,' Tom said, beginning to frisk the Italian. 'Off with your jacket!' Tom took the man's hat off and threw it in Angy's direction.

The Italian let his jacket slide off and drop. His shoulder-holster was empty. There were no weapons in his pockets.

'Angy –' said the Italian.

'Angy è *morto*,' Tom said. 'So will you be, if you don't do what we say. You want to die? What's your name? – What's your *name*?'

'Lippo. Filippo.'

'Lippo. Keep your hands up and don't move. Your hand. Go stand over there.' He motioned for Lippo to go stand by the dead man. Lippo lifted his good right arm. 'Cover him, Jon, I want to have a look at their car.'

With his Luger ready, Tom went out and turned right on the road, approaching the car cautiously. He could hear the motor. The car was at the side of the road with parking lights on. Tom stopped and closed his eyes for a few seconds, then opened them wide, trying to see if there was any movement at the sides of the car or behind the back window. He advanced slowly and steadily, expecting possibly a shot from the car Silence. Could they have sent only two men? Tom hadn't brought a torch in his nervousness. With his gun pointed at someone who might be crouched in the front seat, Tom opened the left-side door. The interior light came on. The car was empty. Tom closed the door enough to shut the light off, stooped, and listened. He didn't hear anything. Tom trotted back and opened the gates of Belle Ombre, then went back to the car and backed it in on to the gravel. A car passed just then on the road, coming from the village direction. Tom turned off the ignition and the parking lights. He knocked and announced himself to Jonathan.

'It seems this is all of them,' Tom said.

Jonathan was standing where Tom had seen him last, pointing his gun at Lippo, who now had his good arm down and hanging a little out from his side.

Tom smiled at Jonathan, then at Lippo. 'All alone now, Lippo? Because if you're lying, it's *finito* for you, you get me?'

Mafia pride seemed to be returning to Lippo, and he merely narrowed his eyes at Tom.

'*Risponde*, you . . . !'

'*Si!*' said Lippo, angry and scared.

'Getting tired, Jonathan? Sit down.' Tom pulled up a yellow upholstered chair for him. 'You can sit down, too, if you want to,' Tom said to Lippo. 'Sit next to your pal.' Tom spoke in Italian. His slang was returning.

But Lippo remained standing. He was a bit over thirty, Tom supposed, about five feet ten, with round but strong shoulders and a paunch already starting, hopelessly dumb, not capo material. He had straight black hair, a pale olive face that was now faintly green.

'Remember me from the train? A little bit?' Tom asked, smiling. He glanced at the blond hulk on the floor. 'If you behave well, Lippo, you won't end up like Angy. All right?' Tom put his hands on his hips, and smiled at Jonathan. 'Suppose we have a gin and tonic for fortification? You're all right, Jonathan?' Jonathan's colour had returned, Tom saw.

Jonathan nodded with a tense smile. 'Yep.'

Tom went into the kitchen. While he was pulling out the ice tray, the telephone rang. 'Never mind the phone, Jonathan!'

'Right!' Jonathan had a feeling it was Simone again. It was now 9.45 p.m.

Tom was wondering how to force Lippo to get his chums off his trail. The telephone rang eight times and stopped. Tom had unconsciously counted the rings. He went into the living-room with a tray of two glasses, ice, and an open tonic bottle. The gin was on the bar cart near the dining-table.

Tom handed Jonathan his drink and said, 'Cheers!' He turned to Lippo. 'Where's your headquarters, Lippo? Milano?'

Lippo chose to maintain an insolent silence. What a bore. Lippo would have to be beaten up a little. Tom glanced with distaste at the splotch of drying blood under Angy's head, set his glass down on the wooden chest by the door, and went back to the kitchen. He wet a sturdy floor-cloth – called a *torchon* by Mme Annette – and mopped up the blood from Mme Annette's waxed parquet. Tom pushed aside Angy's head with his foot, and stuck the cloth under it. No more blood was coming, Tom thought. With sudden inspiration, Tom searched Angy's pockets more thoroughly, trousers, jacket. He found cigarettes, a lighter, small change. A wallet in the breast pocket, which he left. There was a wadded handkerchief in a hip pocket, and when Tom pulled it out, a garrotte came with it. 'Look!' Tom said to Jonathan. 'Just what I was wanting! Ah, these Mafia rosaries!' Tom held it up and laughed with pleasure. 'For you, Lippo, if you're not a good boy,' Tom said in Italian. 'After all, we don't want to make any noise with guns, do we?'

Jonathan looked at the floor for a few seconds as Tom strolled towards Lippo. Tom was whirling the garrotte around one finger.

'You are of the distinguished Genotti family, *non è vero*, Lippo?'

Lippo hesitated, but very briefly, as if it only flitted across his mind to deny it. '*Si*,' he said firmly, with a trace of *vergogna*.

Tom was amused. Strength in number, in togetherness, the families had. Alone like this one, they turned yellow, or green. Tom was sorry about Lippo's arm, but he wasn't torturing him yet, and Tom knew the tortures the Mafia put its victims to if they didn't come across with money or services – yanked toe-nails and teeth, cigarette burns. 'How many men have you killed, Lippo?'

'*Nessuno!*' cried Lippo.

'No one,' Tom said to Jonathan. 'Ha, ha.' Tom went to rinse his hands in the little loo opposite the front door. Then he finished his drink, picked up the piece of log beside the front door, and approached Lippo with it. 'Lippo, you're going to telephone your boss tonight. Maybe your new capo, eh? Where is he tonight? Milano? Monaco di Bavaria?' Tom gave Lippo a swat over the head with the wood, just to show he meant business, but the blow was fairly hard, because Tom was nervous.

'Stop it!' yelled Lippo, staggering up from a near collapse, one hand pitifully on top of his head. 'Me a guy with one arm?' he shrieked, talking like himself now, the gutter Italian of Naples, Tom thought, though it could have been of Milan, because Tom was not an expert.

'*Sissi!* And two against one even!' Tom replied. 'We don't play fair, eh? Is that your complaint?' Tom called him something unspeakable, and turned on his heel to get a cigarette. 'Why don't you pray to the Virgin Mary?' Tom said over his shoulder. 'Another thing,' he said to Lippo in English, 'no more shouting or you'll get this over your head in no time flat!' He came down with the piece of firewood in the air – *whish!* – to show what he meant. 'This is what killed Angy.'

Lippo blinked, his mouth slightly open. He was breathing shallowly and audibly.

Jonathan had finished his drink. He was holding the gun pointed at Lippo, holding it in two hands, because the gun had become heavy. He was not at all sure he could hit Lippo if he had to fire it, and anyway Tom was frequently between him and Lippo. Now Tom was shaking the Italian by his belt. Jonathan couldn't understand all of what Tom was saying, some of it being in clipped Italian, the rest in French and in English. Tom was mostly muttering, but his voice finally rose in anger, and he shoved the Italian back and turned round. The Italian had hardly said anything.

Tom went to the radio, pressed a couple of buttons, and a 'cello concerto came on. Tom made the volume medium. Then he made sure the front curtains were completely closed. 'Isn't this dreary,' Tom said apologetically to Jonathan. 'Sordid. He won't tell me where his boss is, so I've got to hit him a bit. Naturally he's as afraid of his boss as he is of me.' Tom gave Jonathan a quick smile, and went and changed the music. He found some pop. Then he picked up the wood with determination.

Lippo brushed the first blow aside, but Tom bashed him in the temple with a backhand stroke. Lippo had yelped, and now he cried, 'No! Lasciame!'

'Your boss's number!' Tom yelled.

Crack! That was a swat at Lippo's middle, which caught the hand Lippo had put there to protect himself. Glass particles fell on the floor. Lippo wore his watch on his right wrist, the watch must have been shattered, and Lippo held his hand in pain against his abdomen, while he looked at the glass on the floor. He gasped for breath.

Tom waited. The log was poised.

'Milano!' Lippo said.

'All right, you're going to –'

Jonathan missed the rest.

Tom was pointing to the telephone. Then Tom went to the table near the front windows where the telephone was and got a pencil and paper. He was asking the Italian the number in Milan.

Lippo gave a number and Tom wrote it down.

Then Tom made a longer speech, after which he turned to Jonathan and said, 'I've told this guy he's going to be garrotted if he doesn't ring his boss and tell him what I want him to say.' Tom adjusted the garrotte for action, and as he turned to face Lippo, the sound of a car came from the road, the sound of a car stopping at the gates.

Jonathan stood up, thinking it was either Italian reinforcements or Simone in Gérard's car. Jonathan didn't know which would be the worse fate, both seeming a death of sorts at that moment.

Tom didn't want to part the curtains to look out. The motor purred on. Lippo's face showed no change, no sign of relief that Tom could see.

Then the car moved on, towards the right. Tom looked between the curtains. The car was going on, very much on, and all was well, unless the car had let out a few men to hide in the bushes and fire through the windows. Tom listened for several seconds. It might have been the Grais, Tom thought, might have been the Grais who had telephoned a few minutes ago, and maybe they'd seen the strange car on the gravel inside the gates, and decided to go on, thinking the Ripleys had visitors.

'Now, Lippo,' Tom said calmly, 'you're going to telephone your boss, and I'm going to listen with this little gadget.' Tom picked up the round earpiece that was clipped to the back of his telephone, which the French employed for the second ear to augment the sound. 'And if anything doesn't sound *perfect* to me,' Tom continued in French now, which he could see the Italian understood, 'I won't hesitate to pull this suddenly tight, you see?' Tom illustrated with the noose around his wrist, then he walked towards Lippo and flipped the garrotte over Lippo's head.

Lippo jerked back a little in surprise, then Tom led him forward like a dog on a leash towards the telephone. He pushed Lippo down in the chair there, so Tom was in a position to apply strength on the garrotte.

'Now I'll get the number for you, collect, I'm afraid. You will say you are in France, and you and Angy think you are being followed. You will say you have seen Tom Ripley, and Angy says he is not the man you were looking for. Right? Understand? Any funny words, code words and – this – ' Tom tightened the garrotte, but not so tight that it disappeared into Lippo's neck.

'*Sissi!*' said Lippo, staring in terror from Tom to the telephone.

Tom dialled the operator, and asked for the long-distance operator, for Milan, Italy. When the operator asked for his number, as French operators always did, Tom gave it.

'From whom?' asked the operator.

'Lippo. Just Lippo,' Tom replied. Then he gave the number. The operator said she would ring Tom back. He said to Lippo, 'If this turns out to be a corner grocery or one of your girl friends, I'll choke you just the same! *Capish?*'

Lippo squirmed, looking as if he were desperate to try something by way of escape, but as if he didn't know what, as yet.

The telephone rang.

Tom motioned for Lippo to pick the telephone up. Tom took the earpiece and listened. The operator was saying that the call would be accepted.

'Pronto?' a male voice said at the other end.

Lippo held the telephone with his right hand to his left ear. 'Pronto. Lippo here. Luigi!'

'*Si*,' said the other voice.

'Listen, I – ' Lippo's shirt was sticking to his back with sweat. 'We saw – '

Tom jerked the garrotte a little to make Lippo get on with it.

'You are in France, no? With Angy?' the other voice said with some impatience. '*Allora* – what's the matter?'

'Nothing. I – We saw this fellow. Angy says he is not the man ...No...'

'And you think you are being followed,' Tom whispered, because the connection was not good, and he hadn't any fear that the man in Milan could hear him.

'And we think – maybe we're being followed.'

'Followed by *who*?' asked Milan sharply.

'I dunno. So what the —— should we do?' Lippo asked, in fluent argot with a word Tom didn't understand Lippo sounded genuinely scared now.

Tom's ribs tensed with laughter, and he glanced at Jonathan who was still dutifully covering Lippo with his gun. Tom could understand not quite all of what Lippo was saying, but Lippo didn't seem to be pulling any tricks.

'Return?' said Lippo.

'*Si!*' said Luigi. 'Abandon the car! Take a taxi to the nearest airport! Where are you now?'

'Tell him you've got to hang up,' Tom whispered, gesturing.

'Got to sign off. *Rivederch*, Luigi,' said Lippo and hung up. He looked up at Tom with eyes like a miserable dog's.

Lippo was finished and he knew it, Tom thought. For once Tom was proud of his reputation. Tom had no intention of sparing Lippo's life. Lippo's family wouldn't have spared anyone's life under the circumstances.

'Stand up, Lippo,' Tom said, smiling. 'Let's see what else you've got in your pockets.'

When Tom started to search him, Lippo's good arm twitched back as if to strike him, but Tom didn't bother ducking. Just nerves, Tom thought. Tom felt coins in one pocket, a crumpled bit of paper which on inspection turned out to be a decrepit strip of Italian tram ticket, then in the hip pocket a garrotte, this one a sportif red-and-white striped cord that reminded Tom of a barber's pole, fine as cat-gut, and Tom thought it was.

'Look at this! Still another!' Tom said to Jonathan, holding up the garrotte as if it were a pretty pebble he had found on a beach.

Jonathan barely glanced at the dangling string. The first garrotte was still around Lippo's neck. Jonathan did not look at the dead man who was hardly two yards from him, one shoe turned inward in an unnatural way on the polished floor, but Jonathan kept seeing the prone figure in the margin of his vision.

'My goodness,' Tom said, looking at his watch. He hadn't realized it was so late, after 10 p.m. It had to be done now, he and Jonathan had to drive hours' distance away and get back before sun-up, if possible. They had to dispose of the corpses some distance from Villeperce. South, of course, in the direction of Italy. South-east, perhaps. It didn't really matter, but Tom preferred south-east. Tom took a deep breath, preparatory to action, but the presence of Jonathan inhibited him. However, Jonathan had seen corpses' removal before, and there was no time to lose. Tom picked up the wood from the floor.

Lippo dodged, flung himself on the floor, or tripped and fell, but Tom came down on his head, and again a second time, with the wood. At the same time, Tom had not put his full strength into it – the thought of not getting more blood on Mme Annette's floors being in the back of his mind.

'He's only unconscious,' Tom said to Jonathan. 'He's got to be finished, and if you don't want to see it – go in the kitchen, perhaps.'

Jonathan had stood up. He definitely didn't want to see it.

'Can you drive?' Tom asked. 'My car, I mean. The Renault.'

'Yes,' Jonathan said. He had a licence from the early days in France with Roy, his chum from England, but the licence was at home.

'We've got to drive tonight. Go in the kitchen.' Tom motioned Jonathan away. Then Tom bent to his task of pulling the garrotte tight, not a pleasant task – the trite phrase crossed his mind – but what about people who hadn't the merciful anaesthetic, unconsciousness? Tom held the cord tight, the cord had disappeared in flesh, and Tom fortified himself with the thought of Vito Marcangelo succumbing on the Mozart Express by the same means : Tom had brought that job off, and this was his second.

He heard a car, tentative on the road, then rolling up, stopping, with a pull of the handbrake.

Tom kept his grip exactly the same on the garrotte. How many seconds had passed? Forty-five? Not more than a minute, unfortunately.

'What's *that*?' Jonathan whispered, coming in from the kitchen.

The motor of the car was still running.

Tom shook his head.

They both heard light footsteps trotting on the gravel, then a knock at the door. Jonathan felt suddenly weak, as if his knees would give way.

'I think it's Simone,' Jonathan said.

Tom desperately hoped that Lippo was dead. Lippo's face looked merely dark pink. Damn him!

The knock came again. 'M. Ripley? – Jon!'

'Ask her who's with her,' Tom said. 'If she's with somebody, we can't open the door. Tell her we're busy.'

'Who are you with, Simone?' Jonathan asked through the closed door.

'No one! – I've told the taxi to wait. What is happening, Jon?'

Jonathan saw that Tom had heard what she said.

'Tell her to get rid of the taxi,' Tom said.

'Pay off the taxi, Simone,' Jonathan called.

'He is paid!'

'Tell him to leave.'

Simone went away towards the road to do this. They heard the taxi drive off. Simone came back, up the steps and this time she didn't knock, only waited.

Tom straightened up from Lippo, leaving the garrotte on him. Tom was wondering if Jonathan could go out and explain to her that she couldn't come into the house? That they had other people? That they would send for another taxi for her? Tom was thinking of the taxi-driver's impressions. Best to have dismissed this one, rather than *not* show signs of letting Simone into a house that plainly had lights and at least one person in it.

'Jon!' she called. 'Will you open the door? I would like to speak with you.'

Tom said softly, 'Can you wait with her outside while I ring for another taxi? Tell her we're talking business with a couple of other people.'

Jonathan nodded, hesitated an instant, then slid back the bolt. He opened the door not widely, intending to slip out himself, but Simone thrust the door against him suddenly. She was in the foyer.

'Jon! I am sorry to – ' Breathless, she glanced around as if looking for Tom Ripley, master of the house, then she saw him, and at the same time saw the two men on the floor. She gave a short cry. Her handbag slipped from her fingers and dropped with a soft thud on the marble. '*Mon dieu!* – What is happening here?'

Jonathan gripped one of her hands tightly. 'Don't look at them. These – '

Simone stood rigid.

Tom walked towards her. 'Good evening, madame. Don't be frightened. These men were invading the house. They are unconscious. We had a bit of trouble! – Jonathan, take Simone into the kitchen.'

Simone didn't walk. She was swaying, and leaned against Jonathan for a moment, then lifted her head and looked at Tom with hysterical eyes. 'They look dead! – Murderers! *C'est épouvantable!* – Jonathan! I cannot believe that it is *you – here*!'

Tom was going to the bar-cart. 'Can Simone take some brandy, do you think?' he called to Jonathan.

'Yes. – We'll go in the kitchen, Simone.' He was prepared to walk between her and the corpses, but she wouldn't move.

Tom, finding the brandy more difficult than the whisky to open, poured whisky into one of the glasses on the cart. He took it to Simone, neat. 'Madame, I realize this is dreadful. These men are of the Mafia – Italians. They came to the house to attack us – me, anyway.' Tom was much relieved to see that she was sipping the whisky, barely grimacing, as if it were medicine that was good for her. 'Jonathan helped me, for which I'm very grateful. Without him – ' Tom stopped. Anger was rising again in Simone.

'Without him? What is he doing here?'

Tom stood straighter. He went into the kitchen himself, think-ing it was the only way to draw her from the living-room. She and Jonathan followed him. 'That I can't explain tonight, Madame Trevanny. Not now. We've got to leave now – with these men. Would you – ' Tom was thinking, had they time, had he time to take her back to Fontainebleau in the Renault, then return to remove the corpses with Jonathan's assistance? No. Tom absolutely didn't want to waste that much time which would mean a good forty minutes. 'Madame, shall I ring for a taxi to take you back to Fontainebleau?'

'I will not leave my husband. I want to know what my husband is doing here – with such filth as you!'

Her fury was directed entirely against him. Tom wished it could all come out now and for ever, in a great burst. He could never deal with angry women – not that he had had to deal with many. To Tom it was a circular chaos, a ring of little fires, and if he successfully extinguished one, the woman's mind leapt to the next. Tom said to Jonathan, 'If Simone could only take a taxi back to Fontainebleau – '

'I know, I know. Simone, it really is best if you go back to our house.'

'Will you come with me?' she asked.

'I – I can't,' Jonathan said, desperate.

'Then you don't want to. You are on his side.'

'If you'll let me talk with you later, darling – '

Jonathan went on in that vein, while Tom thought, perhaps Jonathan wasn't willing, or had changed his mind. Jonathan was getting nowhere with Simone. Tom interrupted:

'Jonathan.' Tom beckoned to him. 'You must excuse us a moment, madame.' Tom spoke with Jonathan in the living-room, in a whisper. 'We've got six hours' work ahead – or I have. I've got to take these two away and dispose of them – and I'd prefer to be back by dawn or before. Are you really willing to help?'

Jonathan felt lost in the sense that he might be lost in the middle of a battle. But the situation seemed already lost in regard to Simone. He could never explain. Going back to Fontainebleau with her would gain him nothing. He had lost Simone, and what else was there to lose? These thoughts flashed in Jonathan's mind like a single image. 'I am willing, yes.'

'Good. – Thanks.' Tom gave a tense smile. 'Surely Simone doesn't want to stay here. She could of course stay in my wife's room. Maybe I can find a sedative. But for Christ's sake, she can't come *with* us.'

'No.' Simone was his responsibility. Jonathan felt powerless either to persuade or command. 'I have *never* been able to tell her – '

'There's some danger,' Tom interrupted, then stopped. There was no time to lose in talking, and he went back into the living-room, felt compelled to glance at Lippo whose face was now bluish, or so Tom thought. At any rate, his clumsy body had that abandoned look of the dead – not even dreamlike or sleep-like, but simply an empty look as if consciousness had departed for ever. Simone was coming in from the kitchen, which Tom had been heading for, and he saw that her glass was empty. He went to the bar-cart and brought the bottle. He poured more into the glass in her hand, though Simone indicated that she didn't want any more. 'You don't have to drink it, madame,' Tom said. 'Since we must leave, I must tell you there is some danger if you stay in this house. I simply don't know if more of these won't turn up.'

'Then I will go with you. I will go with my husband!'

'That you *cannot*, madame.' Tom was firm.

'What are you going to do?'

'I'm not sure, but we have to get rid of these – this carrion!' Tom gestured. '*Charogne!*' he repeated.

'Simone, you have got to take a taxi back to Fontainebleau,' Jonathan said.

'*Non!*'

Jonathan grabbed her wrist, and with his other hand took the glass, so it wouldn't spill. 'You must do as I say. It's your life, it's my life. We cannot stay and argue!'

Tom leapt up the stairs. He found, after nearly a minute's searching, Heloise's little bottle of quarter-grain pheno-barbitols, which she so seldom took that they were at the back of everything in her medicine cabinet. He went down with two in his fingers, and dropped them casually into Simone's glass –

which he had taken from Jonathan – as he topped the glass up with a splash of soda.

Simone drank this. She was sitting on the yellow sofa now. She seemed calmer, though it was too soon for the pills to have taken effect. And Jonathan was on the telephone now, Tom presumed phoning for a taxi. The slender Seine-et-Marne directory was open on the telephone-table. Tom felt a little dazed, the way Simone looked. But Simone looked also stunned with shock.

'Just Belle Ombre, Villeperce,' said Tom when Jonathan glanced at him.

20

While Jonathan and Simone waited for the taxi, both standing in terrible silence near the front door, Tom went out to the garden via the french windows, and from the toolhouse got the jerry can of spare petrol. To Tom's regret it was not full, but it felt three-quarters full. Tom had his torch with him. When he came round the front corner of the house, he heard a car approaching slowly, the taxi, he hoped. Tom, instead of putting the jerry can in the Renault, set it in the laurels, out of sight. He knocked on the front door and was admitted by Jonathan.

'I think the taxi's here,' Tom said.

Tom said good night to Simone, and let Jonathan escort her to the taxi which was waiting beyond the gates. The taxi drove off, and Jonathan came back.

Tom was refastening the french windows. 'Good Christ,' Tom said, not knowing what else to say, and being immensely relieved to find himself alone with Jonathan again. 'I hope Simone isn't too livid. But I can hardly blame her.'

Jonathan shrugged in a dazed way. He tried to speak and couldn't.

Tom realized his state and said, like a captain giving orders to a shaken crew, 'Jonathan, she'll come round.' And she wouldn't ring the police either, because if she did, her husband would be implicated. Tom's fortitude, his sense of purpose was returning. He patted Jonathan's arm as he walked past him. 'Back in a minute.'

Tom got the jerry can from the bushes and put it in the back of his Renault. Then he opened the Italians' Citroën, the interior light came on, and he saw that the fuel gauge registered slightly over half full. That might do: he wanted to drive for more than two hours. The Renault, he knew, had only slightly more than half a tankful, and the bodies were going to be in there.

He and Jonathan hadn't had any dinner. That wasn't wise. Tom went back into the house and said :

'We ought to eat something before this trip.'

Jonathan followed Tom into the kitchen, glad to escape for a few moments from the corpses in the living-room. He washed his hands and face in the kitchen sink. Tom smiled at him. Food, that was the answer – for the moment. He got the steak from the fridge and stuck it under the glowing bars. Then he found a plate, a couple of steak knives and two forks. They sat down finally, eating from the same plate, dipping morsels of steak into a saucer of salt and another of HP. It was excellent steak. Tom had even found a half-full bottle of claret on the kitchen counter. There'd been many a time when he'd dined worse.

'That will do you good,' Tom said, and tossed his knife and fork on to the plate.

The clock in the living-room gave a ping, and Tom knew it was 11.30 p.m.

'Coffee?' asked Tom. 'There's Nescafé.'

'No, thanks.' Neither Jonathan nor Tom had spoken while they had bolted the steak. Now Jonathan said, 'How are we going to do it?'

'Burn them somewhere. In their car,' Tom said. 'It isn't necessary to burn them, but it's rather Mafia-like.'

Jonathan watched Tom rinsing a thermos at the sink, careless now of the fact he stood before an open window. Tom was running the hot water. He tipped some of the jar of Nescafé into the thermos and filled it with steaming water

'Like sugar?' Tom asked. 'I think we'll need it.'

Then Jonathan was helping Tom carry out the blond man, who was now stiffening. Tom was saying something, making a joke. Then Tom said he had changed his mind : both bodies were going into the Citroën.

' . . . even though the Renault,' Tom said between gasps, 'is bigger.'

It was dark in front of the house now, the distant street lamp not even shedding a glow this far. They tumbled the second body on to the first on the back seat of the Citroën convertible, and Tom smiled because Lippo's face seemed to be buried in Angy's neck, but he refrained from comment. He found a couple of newspapers on the floor of the car and spread them over the dead men, tucking them in as best he could. Tom made sure that Jonathan knew how the Renault worked, showed him the turn signals, the headlights and the bright lights.

'Okay, start it. I'll close the house.' Tom went into the house, left one light on in the living-room, came out and closed the front door and double-locked it.

Tom had explained to Jonathan that their first objective was Sens, then Troyes. From Troyes they would go farther eastward. Tom had a map in his car. They would rendezvous first at Sens at the railway station. Tom put the thermos in Jonathan's car.

'You're feeling all right?' Tom asked. 'Don't hesitate to stop and drink some coffee if you feel like it.' Tom waved him a cheerful good-bye. 'Go ahead out first. I want to close the gates. I'll pass you.'

So Jonathan drove out first, Tom closed his gates and pad-locked them, then soon passed Jonathan on the way to Sens, which was only thirty minutes away. Jonathan seemed to be doing all right in the Renault. Tom spoke briefly to him at Sens. At Troyes, they were again to go to the railway station. Tom didn't know the town, and on the road it was dangerous for one car to try to follow another, but the way to 'La Gare' was pretty well marked in every town.

It was about 1 a.m. when Tom got to Troyes. He hadn't seen Jonathan behind him for more than half an hour He went into the station café for a coffee, a second coffee, and kept a look-out through the glass door for the Renault which might pull into the parking area in front of the station. Finally Tom paid and went out, and as he walked towards his own car, his Renault came down the slope into the parking area. Tom gave a wave, and Jonathan saw him.

'You're all right?' Tom asked. Jonathan looked all right to Tom. 'If you want some coffee here, or to use the loo, best go in alone.'

Jonathan didn't want either. Tom persuaded him to drink some coffee out of the thermos. No one was giving them a glance, Tom saw. A train had just come in and ten or fifteen people were heading for their parked cars or to the cars of people who had come to meet them.

'From here we take the National Nineteen,' Tom said. 'We'll aim for Bar – Bar-sur-Aube – and meet again at the railway station. All right?'

Tom started off. The highway became clearer, with very little traffic except two or three elephantine trucks, their rectangular rears outlined in white or red lights, moving forms which might have been blind, Tom felt, blind at least to the two corpses in the back of the Citroën under newspaper, such a tiny cargo compared to theirs. Tom was not going fast now, not more than ninety kilometres or around fifty-five miles per hour. At the Bar railway station he and Jonathan leaned out of their windows to speak with one another.

'Petrol's getting low,' Tom said. 'I want to go beyond Chaumont, so I'm going to pull in at the next petrol station, okay? And you do the same.'

'Right,' said Jonathan.

It was now 2.15 a.m. 'Keep on the old N nineteen. See you at the railway station in Chaumont.'

Tom pulled in at a Total station as he was leaving Bar. He was paying the man, when Jonathan drove in behind him. Tom lit a cigarette and didn't glance at Jonathan. Tom was walking about, stretching his legs. Then he pulled his car a little aside and went to the toilet. It was only forty-two kilometres to Chaumont.

And there Tom arrived at 2.55 a.m. Not even a taxi stood at the railway station, only a few parked and empty cars. There were no more trains tonight. The station bar-café was closed. When Jonathan arrived, Tom approached the Renault on foot, and said:

'Follow me. I'm going to look for a quiet spot.'

Jonathan was tired, but his fatigue had switched into another gear: he could have gone on driving for hours more, he felt. The Renault handled tightly and quickly, with the minimum of effort on his part. Jonathan was totally unfamiliar with the country here. That didn't matter. And now it was easy, he merely kept the red taillights of the Citroën in view. Tom was going more slowly, and twice paused tentatively at side roads, then went on. The night was black, the stars not visible, at least not with the glow of the dashboard before him. A couple of cars passed, going in the opposite direction, and one lorry over-took Jonathan. Then Jonathan saw Tom's right indicator pulse, and Tom's car disappeared to the right. Jonathan followed, and barely saw the black gorge that was the road, or lane, when he came to it. It was a dirt road that led at once into forest. The road was narrow, not wide enough for two cars to pass, the kind of road often found in the French countryside, used by farmers or men gathering wood. Bushes scraped delicately at the front fenders, and there were potholes.

Tom's car stopped. They had gone perhaps two hundred yards from the main road in a great curve. Tom had cut his lights, but the interior of the car lit when he opened the door. Tom left the door open, and walked towards Jonathan, waving his arms cheerfully. Jonathan was at that instant cutting his own motor and his lights. The image of Tom's figure in the baggy trousers, green suède jacket, stayed in Jonathan's eyes for a moment as if Tom had been composed of light. Jonathan blinked.

Then Tom was beside Jonathan's window. 'It'll be over in a couple of minutes. Back your car about fifteen feet. You know how to reverse?'

Jonathan started the car. The car had backing lights. When he stopped, Tom opened the second door of the Renault and pulled out the jerry can. Tom had his torch.

Tom poured petrol on to the newspapers over the two corpses, then on their clothing. Tom splashed some on the roof, then the upholstery – unfortunately plastic, not cloth – of the front seat also. Tom looked up, straight up where the branches of the trees almost closed together above the road – young leaves, not yet in their fullness of summer. A few would get singed, but it was for a worthy cause. Tom shook the last drops from the jerry can on to the floor of the car where there was rubbish, the remains of a sandwich, an old road map.

Jonathan was walking slowly towards him.

'Here we go,' Tom said softly, and struck a match. He had left the front door of the car open. He flung the match into the back of the car, where the newspapers flared up yellow at once.

Tom stepped back, and grabbed Jonathan's hand as his foot slipped in a depression at the side of the road. 'In the car!' Tom whispered, and trotted towards the Renault. He got into the driver's seat, smiling. The Citroën was taking nicely. The roof had started to burn in one central, thin yellow flame, like a candle.

Jonathan got in on the other side.

Tom started his motor. He was breathing a little hard, but it soon became laughter. 'I think that's all *right*. Don't you? I think that's just great!'

The Renault's lights burst forward, diminishing the growing holocaust in front of them for an instant. Tom backed, fairly fast, his body twisted so he could see through the back window.

Jonathan stared at the burning car, which completely disappeared as they backed along the curve in the road.

Then Tom straightened out. They were on the main road.

'Can you see it from here?' Tom asked, shooting the car forward.

Jonathan saw a light like that of a glowworm through the trees, then it vanished. Or had he imagined it? 'Not a thing now. No.' For an instant, Jonathan felt frightened by this fact – as if they had failed somehow, as if the fire had died out. But he knew it hadn't. The woods had simply swallowed the fire up, hidden it utterly. And yet, someone would find it. When? How much of it?

Tom laughed. 'It's burning. They'll burn! We're in the clear!'

Jonathan saw Tom glance at his speedometer, which was climbing to a hundred and thirty. Then Tom eased back to a hundred.

Tom was whistling a Neapolitan tune. He felt well, not tired at all, not even in need of a cigarette. Life afforded few pleasures tantamount to disposing of Mafiosi. And yet –

'And yet – ' Tom said cheerfully.

'And yet?'

'Disposing of two does so little. Like stepping on two cockroaches when the whole house is full of them. I believe, however, in making the effort, and above all it's nice to let the Mafia know now and then that people can diminish them. Unfortunately in this case they're going to think another family got Lippo and Angy. At least I hope they'll think that.'

Jonathan was now feeling sleepy. He fought against it, forcing himself to sit up, pressing his nails into his palm. My God, he thought, it was going to be hours before they got home – back to Tom's or to his own house. Tom seemed fresh as a daisy, singing now in Italian a tune he'd been whistling before.

> ' . . . papa ne meno
> Como faremo fare l'amor . . . '

Tom was chatting on, about his wife now, who was going to stay with some friends in a chalet in Switzerland. Then Jonathan awakened a little as Tom said:

'Put your head back, Jonathan. No need to stay awake. – You're feeling all right, I hope?'

Jonathan didn't know how he was feeling. He felt a bit weak, but he often felt weak. Jonathan was afraid to think about what had just happened, about what was happening, flesh and bone being burnt, smouldering on hours from now. Sadness came over Jonathan suddenly, like an eclipse. He wished he could erase the last few hours, cut them out of his memory. Yet he had been there, he had acted, he had helped. Jonathan put his head back and fell half asleep. Tom was talking cheerfully, casually, as if he were having a conversation with someone who now and then replied to him. Jonathan had in fact never known Tom in such good spirits. Jonathan was wondering what he was going to say to Simone? Merely to be aware of that problem exhausted him.

'Masses sung in English, you know,' Tom was saying, 'I find simply embarrassing. Somehow one gives the English-speaking people credit for believing what they're saying, so a mass in English . . . you feel either the choir has lost its mind or they're a pack of liars. Don't you agree? Sir John Stainer . . . '

Jonathan woke up when the car stopped. Tom had pulled on to the edge of the road. Smiling, Tom was sipping coffee from the thermos cup. He offered some to Jonathan. Jonathan drank a little. Then they drove on.

Dawn came over a village that Jonathan had never seen before. The light had awakened Jonathan.

212

'We're only twenty minutes from home!' Tom said brightly.

Jonathan murmured something, and half shut his eyes again. Now Tom was talking about the harpsichord, his harpsichord.

'The thing about Bach is that he's instantly civilizing. Just a phrase . . .'

21

Jonathan opened his eyes, thinking he had heard harpsichord music. Yes. It wasn't a dream. He hadn't really been asleep. The music came from downstairs. It faltered, recommenced. A sarabande, perhaps. Jonathan lifted his arm wearily and looked at his wristwatch: 8.38 a.m. What was Simone doing now? What was she *thinking*?

Exhaustion sucked at Jonathan's will. He sank deeper into the pillow, retreating. He'd taken a warm shower, put on pyjamas at Tom's insistence. Tom had given him a new toothbrush and said, 'Get a couple of hours' sleep, anyway. It's terribly early.' That had been around 7 a.m. He had to get up. He had to do something about Simone, had to speak to her. But Jonathan lay limp, listening to the single notes of the harpsichord.

Now Tom was fingering the bass of something, and it sounded correct, the deepest notes a harpsichord could pluck. As Tom had said, *instantly civilizing*. Jonathan forced himself up, out of the pale blue sheets and the darker blue woollen blanket. He staggered, and with an effort stood straight as he walked towards the door. Jonathan went down the stairs barefoot.

Tom was reading the notes from a music book propped in front of him. Now the treble entered, and sunlight came through the slightly parted curtains at the french windows on to Tom's left shoulder, picking out the gold pattern in his black dressing-gown.

'Tom?'

Tom turned at once and got up. 'Yes?'

Jonathan felt worse, seeing Tom's alarmed face. The next thing Jonathan knew, he was on the yellow sofa, and Tom was wiping his face with a wet cloth, a dishtowel.

'Tea? Or a brandy? . . . Have you got any pills you take?'

Jonathan felt awful, he knew the feeling, and the only thing that helped was a transfusion. It hadn't been so long since he'd had one. The trouble now was that he felt worse than he usually did. Was it only from losing a night's sleep?

'What?' Tom said.

'I'm afraid I'd better get to the hospital.'

'We'll go,' said Tom. He went away and came back with a stemmed glass. 'This is brandy and water, if you feel like it. Stay there. I'll just be a minute.'

Jonathan closed his eyes. He had the wet towel over his forehead, down one cheek, and felt chilly and too tired to move. It seemed only a minute until Tom was back, dressed. Tom had brought Jonathan's clothing.

'Matter of fact, if you put on your shoes and my topcoat, you won't have to dress,' Tom said.

Jonathan followed this advice. They were in the Renault again, heading for Fontainebleau, and Jonathan's clothes were folded neatly between them. Tom was asking him if he knew exactly where they should go when they got to the hospital, if he could get a transfusion right away.

'I've got to speak with Simone,' Jonathan said.

'We'll do that – or you will. Don't worry about that now.'

'Could you bring her?' Jonathan asked.

'Yes,' said Tom firmly. He hadn't been worried about Jonathan until that instant. Simone would hate the sight of him, but she would come to see her husband, either with Tom or on her own. 'You still have no phone at your house?'

'No.'

Tom spoke to a receptionist in the hospital. She greeted Jonathan as if she knew him. Tom held Jonathan's arm. When Tom had seen Jonathan into the charge of the proper doctor, Tom said, 'I'll have Simone come, Jonathan. Don't worry.' To the receptionist, who was in nurse's uniform, Tom said, 'Do you think a transfusion will do it?'

She nodded pleasantly, and Tom left it at that, not knowing whether she knew what she was talking about or not. He wished he'd asked the doctor. Tom got into his car and drove to the Rue St Merry. He was able to park a few yards from the house, and he got out and walked towards the stone steps with the black handrails. He'd had no sleep, was in slight need of a shave, but at least he had a message that might be of interest to Mme Trevanny. He rang the bell.

There was no answer. Tom rang again, and looked on the pavement for Simone. It was Sunday. No market in Fontaine-bleau, but she might well be out buying something at 9.50 a.m., or might be at church with Georges.

Tom went down the steps slowly, and as he reached the pavement, he saw Simone walking towards him, Georges beside her. Simone had a shopping basket over her forearm.

'*Bonjour*, madame,' Tom said politely, in the face of her bristling hostility. He continued, 'I only wanted to bring you news of your husband. – *Bonjour*, Georges.'

'I want nothing from you,' Simone said, 'except to know where my husband is.'

Georges stared at Tom alertly and neutrally. He had eyes and brows like his father. 'He is all right, I think, madame, but he is – ' Tom hated saying it on the street. 'He is in the hospital for the moment. A transfusion, I think.'

Simone looked both exasperated and furious – as if Tom were to blame for it.

'May I please speak with you inside your house, madame. It is so much easier.'

After an instant's hesitation, Simone agreed to this, out of curiosity, Tom felt. She unlocked the door with a key which she produced from her coat pocket. It wasn't a new coat, Tom noticed. 'What has happened to him?' she asked when they were in the little hall.

Tom took a breath and spoke calmly. 'We had to drive nearly all night. I think he is merely tired. But – of course I thought you would want to know. I've just brought him to the hospital now. He's able to walk. I do think he's not in danger.'

'Papa! I want to see papa!' Georges said rather petulantly, as if he had asked for papa last evening too.

Simone had set her basket down. '*What* have you done to my husband? He is not the same man I knew – since he met *you*, m'sieur! If you see him again, I – I will –'

It seemed only the presence of her son that kept her from saying that she would kill him, Tom thought.

She said with bitter control of herself, 'Why is he in your power?'

'He is not in my power and never was. And I think now the job is finished,' Tom said. 'It's quite impossible to explain now.'

'What job?' Simone asked. And before Tom could open his mouth, she continued, 'M'sieur, you are a crook, and you corrupt other people! What sort of blackmail have you subjected him to? And why?'

Blackmail – the French word *chantage* – was so off the beam, Tom stammered as he began to reply. 'Madame, no one is taking money from Jonathan. Or anything from him. Quite the contrary. And he has done nothing to give people power over him.' Tom spoke with genuine conviction, and he certainly had to, because Simone looked the picture of wifely virtue, probity, her fine eyes flashing, and her brows concentrated against him, powerful as the Winged Victory of Samothrace. 'We have spent the night cleaning things up.' Tom felt shabby saying that. His more eloquent French had suddenly deserted him. His words were no match for the virtuous helpmeet who stood before him.

'Cleaning what up?' She stooped to pick up her basket. 'M'sieur, I will be grateful if you leave this house. I thank you for informing me where my husband is.'

Tom nodded. 'I would also be happy to take you and Georges to the hospital, if you like. My car is just outside.'

'*Merci, non.*' She was standing midway in the hall, looking back, waiting for him to leave. 'Come, Georges.'

Tom let himself out. He got into his car, thought of going to the hospital to ask how Jonathan was, because it would be at least ten minutes before Simone could get there either by taxi or on foot. But Tom decided to telephone from his house. He drove home. And once home, he decided not to telephone. By now Simone might be there. Hadn't Jonathan said the transfusion took several hours? Tom hoped it wasn't a crisis, that it wasn't the beginning of the end.

He turned on France Musique for company, opened his curtains wider to the sunlight, and tidied the kitchen. He poured a glass of milk, went upstairs and got into pyjamas again and went to bed. He could shave when he woke up.

Tom hoped that Jonathan could straighten things out with

Simone. But it was the same old problem: how did the Mafia get tied up, how could they possibly be tied up with two German doctors?

This unsolvable problem began to make Tom sleepy. And Reeves. What was happening to Reeves in Ascona? Madcap Reeves. Tom still had a lurking affection for him. Reeves was now and then maladroit, but his crazy heart was in the right place.

Simone sat beside the flat bed, more wheels than bed, on which Jonathan lay taking in blood through a tube in his arm. Jonathan as usual avoided looking at the jar of blood. Simone was grim. She had spoken with the nurse out of Jonathan's hearing. Jonathan thought his condition now wasn't serious (assuming Simone had heard anything), or Simone would have been more concerned about him, kinder. Jonathan was propped on a pillow, and there was a white blanket pulled up to his waist for warmth.

'And you're wearing that man's pyjamas,' Simone said.

'Darling, I had to wear something – to sleep in. It must've been six in the morning when we got back – ' Jonathan broke off, feeling hopeless and tired. Simone had told him that Tom had called at the house to tell her where he was. Simone's reaction had been anger. Jonathan had never seen her so grim. She detested Tom as if he were Landru or Svengali. 'Where's Georges?' Jonathan asked.

'I telephoned Gérard. He and Yvonne are coming to the house at ten-thirty. Georges will let them in.'

They would wait for Simone, Jonathan thought, then they would all go to Nemours for Sunday lunch. 'They want me to stay here till at least three, I know,' Jonathan said. 'The tests, you know.' He knew she knew, probably another marrow sample would be taken, which required only ten or fifteen minutes, but there were always other tests, urine, the spleen-feeling. Jonathan still did not feel well, and he didn't know what to expect. Simone's hardness further upset him.

'I cannot understand. I cannot,' she said. 'Jon, why do you see this monster?'

Tom was not really such a monster. But how to explain?

Jonathan tried again. 'Do you realize that last night – those men were killers? They had guns, they had garrottes. *Tu comprends, garrottes.* – They came to Tom's house.'

'And why were you there?'

Gone was the excuse of paintings that Tom wanted framed. One didn't help Tom kill people, help him get rid of corpses, because one was going to frame a few pictures. And what was the favour Tom Ripley had done him to make him cooperate so? Jonathan closed his eyes, gathering strength, trying to think.

'Madame – ' That was the nurse's voice.

Jonathan heard the nurse telling Simone that she should not tire her husband. 'I promise you that I will explain, Simone.'

Simone had stood up. 'I think you cannot explain. I think you are afraid to. This man has trapped you – and why? For money. He pays you. But why? – You want me to think that you are a criminal too? Like that monster?'

The nurse had gone away and couldn't hear. Jonathan looked at Simone through half-closed eyes, desperate. wordless, defeated, for the moment. Couldn't he make her see, some time, that it was not so black and white as she thought? But Jonathan felt a chill of fear, a premonition of failure, like death.

And Simone was leaving, as if on a final word – *her* word, *her* attitude. At the doorway she blew him a kiss, but perfunctorily, like a person in church genuflecting barely, without thinking, as he passed some object. She was gone. The day ahead stretched like a bad dream to come. The hospital might decide to keep him overnight. Jonathan closed his eyes and moved his head from side to side.

They were almost finished with the tests by 1 p.m.

'You have been under a strain, haven't you, m'sieur?' asked a young doctor. 'Any unusual exertions?' Unexpectedly, he laughed. 'Moving house? Or too much gardening?'

Jonathan smiled politely. He was feeling a little better. Suddenly Jonathan laughed too, but not at what the doctor had said. Suppose it had been the beginning of the end, this morning's collapse? Jonathan was pleased with himself because he had pulled through it without losing his nerve. Maybe he could do that one day with the real thing. They let him walk down a corridor for the final test, the spleen palpation.

'M. Trevanny? There is a telephone call for you,' a nurse said. 'Since you are so near – ' She motioned towards a desk and a telephone, which was off the hook.

Jonathan felt sure it was Tom. 'Hello?'

'Jonathan, hello. Tom. How is everything? . . . Can't be too bad if you're on your feet now . . . That's fine.' Tom sounded really pleased.

'Simone was here. Thank you,' Jonathan said. 'But she's – ' Even though they were talking in English, Jonathan couldn't get the words out.

'You had a tough time, I can understand.' Platitudes. Tom at his end heard the anxiety in Jonathan's voice. 'I did my best this morning, but do you want me to – to try to talk with her again?'

Jonathan moistened his lips. 'I don't know. It's not of course that she – ' He'd been going to say 'threatened anything', such as taking Georges and leaving him. 'I don't know if you *can* do anything. She's so – '

Tom understood. 'Suppose I try? I will. Courage, Jonathan! You're going home today?'

'I'm not sure. I think so. By the way, Simone is with her family in Nemours for lunch today.'

Tom said he wouldn't try to see her till about 5 p.m. If Jonathan was home then, that would be fine.

It was a bit awkward for Tom, Simone's not having a telephone. On the other hand, if there'd been a telephone, she would probably have given him a firm 'No' if he asked if he might come to see her. Tom bought flowers, yellow forced dahlias, from a vendor near the château in Fontainebleau, as he had nothing presentable as yet from his own garden. Tom rang the Trevanny doorbell at 5.20 p.m.

There were steps, then Simone's voice, '*Qui est-ce?*'

'Tom Ripley.'

A delay.

Then Simone opened the door with a stony face.

'Good afternoon – *bonjour, encore,*' Tom said. 'Could I speak with you for a few minutes, madame? Has Jonathan returned?'

'He will be home at seven. He is having another transfusion.' Simone replied.

'Oh?' Tom boldly took a step into the house, not knowing if Simone would flare up or not. 'I brought these for your house, madame.' He presented the flowers with a smile. 'And Georges. *Bonjour*, Georges.' Tom extended his hand, and the child took it, smiling up at him. Tom had thought of bringing sweets for Georges, but he hadn't wanted to overdo it.

'What is it you want?' Simone asked. She had given Tom a cool '*Merci*' in regard to the flowers.

'I definitely must explain. I must explain last night. That is why I am here, madame.'

'You mean – you can explain?'

Tom returned her cynical smile with a fresh and open one. 'As much as anyone can explain the Mafia. Of course! Yes! Come to think of it, I could have bought them off – I suppose. What else do they want except money? However, in this case I'm not so sure, because they had a special grudge against me.'

Simone was interested. But this fact did not diminish her antipathy to Tom. She had taken a step back from him.

'Can't we go into your living-room – perhaps?'

Simone led the way. Georges followed them, gazing fixedly at Tom. Simone motioned Tom to the sofa. Tom sat down on the Chesterfield, gently slapped its black leather and started to pay Simone a compliment on it and didn't.

'Yes, a special grudge,' Tom resumed. 'I – You see, I happened – just happened to be on the same train as your husband when he was returning from a visit to Munich recently. You remember.'

'Yes.'

'Muniche!' said Georges, his face lighting up as if in anticipation of a story.

Tom smiled back at him. 'Muniche. – *Alors*, on this train – for reasons of my own – I will not hesitate to tell you, madame, that sometimes I take the law into my own hands just as much as the Mafia do. The difference is, I don't blackmail honest people, I don't need protection money from people who wouldn't need protection if not for my threats.' It was so abstract, Tom was sure Georges was not following it, despite Georges' intense gaze at Tom.

'What're you getting at?' Simone asked.

'At the fact that I killed one of those beasts on the train, and nearly killed the other – pushed him out – and Jonathan was there and saw me. You see – ' Tom was only briefly daunted by the shock in Simone's face, by her fearful glance at Georges who was following the story avidly, and perhaps thought that 'beasts' were indeed animals, or maybe that Tom was making it up as he went along. 'You see, I had time to explain the situation to Jonathan. We were on the platform – on the moving train. Jonathan kept a look-out for me, that's all he did. But I'm grateful. He helped. And I hope you see, Madame Trevanny, that it was for a good cause. Look at the way the French police are fighting the Mafia down in Marseille, the drug merchants. Look at the way *everyone* is fighting the Mafia! Trying to. But one must expect dangerous retaliations from them, you know that. So that's what happened last night. I –' Did he dare say he had asked for Jonathan's help? Yes. 'It was entirely my fault that Jonathan was at my house, because I asked him if he would be willing to help me again.'

Simone looked puzzled, and highly suspicious. 'For money, of course.'

Tom had expected this, and remained calm. 'No. No, madame.' It was a matter of honour, Tom started to say, but that didn't completely make sense, even to him. Friendship, but Simone wouldn't like that. 'It was kindness on Jonathan's part. Kindness and courage. You shouldn't reproach him.'

Simone shook her head slowly, disbelieving. 'My husband is not a police agent, m'sieur. Why don't you tell me the truth?'

'But I am,' Tom said simply, opening his hands.

Simone sat tensely in the armchair, her fingers working together now. 'Very recently,' she said, 'my husband has received quite a bit of money. Are you saying that that has nothing to do with you?'

Tom leaned back on the sofa and crossed his feet at the ankles. He was wearing his oldest, nearly worn-out desert boots. 'Ah, yes. He told me a little about that,' Tom said with a smile. 'The German doctors are making a bet together, and they've entrusted the take to Jonathan. Isn't that right? I thought he'd told you.'

Simone merely listened, waiting for more.

'In addition, Jonathan told me they'd given him a bonus – or prize money. After all they are using him to experiment on.'

'He also told me there was no – no real danger in the drugs, so why should he be paid?' She shook her head and laughed briefly. 'No, m'sieur.'

Tom was silent. His face showed disappointment, and he meant it to. 'There are stranger things, madame. I'm simply telling you what Jonathan told me. I have no reason to think it isn't true.'

That was the end of it. Simone stirred restlessly in her chair, then stood up. She had a lovely face, clear, handsome eyes and brows, an intelligent mouth that could be soft or stern. Just now it was stern. She gave him a polite smile. 'And what do you know about the death of M. Gauthier? Anything? I understand you often bought things at his shop.'

Tom had stood up, and he faced this, at least, with a clear conscience. 'I know that he was run over, madame, by a hit-and-run driver.'

'That is all you know?' Simone's voice was a little higher pitched, and it trembled.

'I know that it was an accident.' Tom wished that he hadn't to speak in French. He felt he was being blunt. 'That accident makes no sense. If you think I – that I had anything to do with it, madame – then perhaps you will tell me for what purpose. Really, madame – ' Tom glanced at Georges, who was now reaching for a toy on the floor. Gauthier's death was like something in a Greek tragedy. But no, Greek tragedies had reasons for everything.

Her mouth twitched a little, bitterly. 'I trust you won't have need of Jonathan again?'

'I won't call on him if I do,' Tom said pleasantly. 'How is – '

'I would think,' she interrupted, 'the people to call on are the police. Don't you agree? Or perhaps you are already in the secret police? Of America, perhaps?'

Her sarcasm had very deep roots, Tom realized. He was never going to succeed with Simone. Tom smiled a little, though he felt slightly wounded. He'd endured worse words in his life, but in this case it was a pity because he had so wanted to convince

Simone. 'No, that I am not. I get into scrapes now and then, as I think you know.'

'Yes. I know.'

'Scrapes, what is scrapes?' Georges piped up, his blond head turning from Tom to his mother. He was on his feet, very near them.

Tom had used the word *pétrins* – which he'd had to grope for.

'Sh-h, Georges,' said his mother.

'But in this case, you must admit to take on the Mafia is not a bad thing.' Whose side are you on, Tom wanted to ask, but that would be rubbing it in.

'M. Ripley, you are an extremely sinister personage. That is all I know. I would be most grateful if you left both me and my husband alone.'

Tom's flowers lay on the hall table, waterless.

'How is Jonathan now?' Tom asked in the hall. 'I hope he's better.' Tom was even afraid to say he hoped Jonathan would be home tonight, lest Simone think he intended to use him again.

'I think he is all right – better. Good-bye, M. Ripley.'

'Good-bye and thank you,' Tom said. '*Au revoir*, Georges.' Tom patted the boy's head, and Georges smiled.

Tom went out to his car. Gauthier! A familiar face, a neighbourhood face, now gone. It piqued Tom that Simone thought he had had something to do with it, had arranged it, even though Jonathan had told him days ago that Simone thought this. My God, the taint! Well, yes, he had the taint, all right. Worse, he had killed people. True. Dickie Greenleaf. *That* was the taint, the real crime. Hot-headedness of youth. Nonsense! It had been greed, jealousy, resentment of Dickie. And of course Dickie's death – rather his murder – had caused Tom to kill the American slob called Freddie Miles. Long past, all that. But he had done it, yes. The law half-suspected it. But they couldn't prove it. The story had crept through the public, the public mind, like ink creeping through a blotter. Tom was ashamed. A youthful, dreadful mistake. A fatal mistake, one might think, it was just that he had had amazing luck afterwards. He'd survived it, physically speaking. And surely his – murder since then, Murchison for instance, had most certainly been done to protect others as much as himself.

Simone was shocked – what woman wouldn't have been – at seeing two corpses on the floor when she walked into Belle Ombre last night. But hadn't he been protecting her husband as well as himself? If the Mafia had caught him and tortured him, wouldn't he have come out with the name and address of Jonathan Trevanny?

This made Tom think of Reeves Minot. How was he faring? Tom thought he ought to ring him. Tom found himself staring with a frown at the handle of his car door. His door was not even locked, and his keys, in Tom's usual style, were hanging in the dashboard.

22

The evidence of the marrow test, which a doctor took in mid-afternoon Sunday, was not good, and they wanted to keep Jonathan overnight and give him the treatment called Vincaines-tine, which was a complete change of blood, and which Jonathan had had before.

Simone came to see him just after 7 p.m. They had told Jonathan that she had telephoned earlier. But whoever had spoken to her had not told her that he had to stay overnight, and Simone was surprised.

'So – tomorrow,' she said, and seemed not to find any more words.

Jonathan lay with his head a little raised by pillows. Tom's pyjamas had been changed for a loose garment, and he had a tube in both arms. Jonathan felt a terrible distance between Simone and himself. Or was he imagining it? 'Tomorrow morning, I suppose. Don't trouble to come here, my dear, I'll get a taxi. – How was the afternoon? How's your family?'

Simone ignored the question. 'Your friend M. Ripley paid a visit to me this afternoon.'

'Oh, yes?'

'He is so – absolutely full of lies, it is hard to know even what smallest part to believe. Maybe none of it.' Simone glanced behind her, but there was no one. Jonathan's was one of many beds in the ward, not all of them occupied, but the ones on either side of Jonathan were occupied, and one man had a visitor.

They couldn't easily talk.

'Georges will be disappointed that you don't come back to-night,' Simone said.

Then she left.

Jonathan went home the next morning, Monday, around 10 a.m. Simone was at home, ironing some of Georges' clothing.

'Are you feeling all right? . . . Did they give you breakfast? . . . Would you like some coffee? Or tea?'

Jonathan felt much better – one always did just after a Vincainestine, until his disease got to work and ruined the blood again, he thought. He wanted only a bath. He had a bath, then put on different clothes, old beige corduroy trousers, two sweaters because the morning was cool, or perhaps he was feeling the chill more than usually. Simone was ironing in a short-sleeved woollen dress. The morning newspaper, the *Figaro*, lay folded on the kitchen table with its front page outermost, as usual, but it was obvious from the looseness of the paper that Simone had looked at it.

Jonathan picked up the paper, and since Simone did not look up from her ironing, he walked into the living-room. He found a two-column item in a bottom corner of the second page.

TWO CORPSES INCINERATED IN CAR

The dateline was 14 May, Chaumont. A farmer named René Gault, fifty-five, had found the still-smoking Citroën early on Sunday morning, and had at once alerted the police. The still unburnt papers in the wallets of the dead men identified them as Angelo Lippari, thirty-three, contractor, and Filippo Turoli, thirty-one, salesman, both of Milan. Lippari had died of skull fractures, Turoli of unknown causes, though he was believed to have been unconscious or dead when the car was set alight. There were no clues at the moment, and police were making investigations.

The garrotte had been completely burnt, Jonathan supposed, and evidently Lippo so badly burnt that the signs of garrotting had been destroyed.

Simone came into the doorway with folded clothing in her hands. 'So? I saw it too. The two Italians.'

'Yes.'

'And you helped M. Ripley to do that. That is what you called "cleaning up".'

Jonathan said nothing. He gave a sigh, sat down on the luxuriously squeaking Chesterfield sofa, but he sat up rather straight, lest Simone think he was retreating on grounds of weakness. 'Something had to be done with them.'

227

'And you simply had to help,' she said. 'Jon – now that Georges is not here – I think we should talk about this.' She put the clothes on top of the waist-high bookcase by the door, and sat down on the edge of the armchair. 'You are not telling me the truth, and neither is M. Ripley. I am wondering what else you are going to be obliged to do for him.' On the last words, her voice rose with hysteria.

'Nothing.' Jonathan did feel sure of that. And if Tom asked him to do anything else, he could quite simply refuse. At that moment, it seemed quite simple to Jonathan. He had to hold on to Simone at any cost. She was worth more than Tom Ripley, more than anything Tom could offer him.

'It is beyond my understanding. You knew what you were doing – last night. You helped to kill those men, didn't you?' Her voice dropped, and it trembled.

'It was a matter of protecting – what had gone before.'

'Ah, yes, M. Ripley explained. By accident you were on the same train as he was, coming from Munich, is that right? And you – assisted him in – in *killing* two people?'

'Mafia,' Jonathan said. What *had* Tom told her?

'You – an ordinary passenger, assist a murderer? You expect me to believe that, Jon?'

Jonathan was silent, trying to think, miserable. The answer was no. *You don't seem to realize they were Mafia*, Jonathan wanted to repeat. *They were attacking Tom Ripley*. Another lie, at least in regard to the train. Jonathan pressed his lips together, and sat back on the generous sofa. 'I don't expect you to believe it. I have only two things to say, this is the end of it, and the men we killed were criminals and murderers themselves. You must admit that.'

'Are you a secret police agent in your spare time? – *Why* are you being paid for this, Jon? You – a killer!' She stood up with her hands clenched. 'You are a stranger to me. I have never known you before now.'

'Oh, Simone,' Jonathan said, standing up too.

'I cannot like you and I cannot love you.'

Jonathan blinked. She had said that in English.

She continued in French: 'You are leaving out something, I know. And I don't even want to know what it is. Do you understand? It is some horrible connection with M. Ripley, that odious personage – and I wonder what,' she added with the bitter sarcasm again. 'Plainly it is something too disgusting for you to tell me, I shouldn't wonder. You've no doubt covered up some other crime for him, and for this you're being paid, for this you're in his power. Very well, I don't want –'

'I am not in his power! You'll see!'

'I've seen enough!' She went out, taking the clothes with her, and climbed the stairs.

When it came time for lunch, Simone said she wasn't hungry. Jonathan made himself a boiled egg. Then he went to his shop, and kept the FERME sign in the door, because he was not officially open on Mondays. Nothing had changed since Saturday noon. He could see that Simone hadn't been in Jonathan suddenly thought of the Italian gun, usually in a drawer, now at Tom Ripley's. Jonathan cut one frame, cut the glass for it, but lost heart when it came to driving the nails in. What was he to do about Simone? What if he told her the whole story, just as it had been? Jonathan knew, however, that he was up against a Catholic attitude about taking human life. Not to mention that Simone would consider the original proposition to him 'Fantastic! – Disgusting!' Curious that the Mafia was a hundred per cent Catholic, and they didn't mind about human life. But he, Simone's husband, was different. He shouldn't take human life. And if he told her it was a 'mistake' on his part, that he regretted it – Hopeless. First of all, he didn't particularly believe it had been a mistake, so why tell another lie?

Jonathan went with more determination back to his worktable, and got the glue and nails in the picture frame, and sealed it neatly with brown paper on the back. He clipped the owner's name to the picture wire. Then he looked over his orders to be filled, and tackled one more picture, which like the other needed no mat. He went on working until 6 p.m. Then he bought bread and wine, and some ham slices from a charcuterie, enough for dinner for the three of them in case Simone hadn't done any shopping.

Simone said, 'I am in terror that the police will knock on the door at any moment, wanting to see you.'

Jonathan, setting the table, said nothing for a few seconds. 'They will not. Why should they?'

'There is no such thing as no clues. They will find M. Ripley, and he will tell them about you.'

Jonathan was sure she hadn't eaten all day. He found some left-over potatoes – mashed potatoes – in the fridge, and went about preparing the dinner himself. Georges came down from his room.

'What did they do to you in the hospital, papa?'

'I have completely new blood,' Jonathan replied with a smile, flexing his arms. 'Think of that. All new blood – oh, at least eight litres of it.'

'How much is that?' Georges spread his arms also.

'Eight times this bottle,' said Jonathan. 'That's what took all night.'

Though Jonathan made an effort, he couldn't lift the gloom, the silence of Simone. She poked at her food and said nothing. Georges couldn't understand. Jonathan's efforts, failing, embarrassed him, and over coffee he too was silent, not able even to chat with Georges.

Jonathan wondered if she had spoken with her brother Gérard. He steered Georges into the living-room to watch the television, the new set which had arrived a few days ago. The programmes – there were only two channels – weren't interesting for kids at this hour, but Jonathan hoped he would stay with one of them for a while.

'Did you talk to Gérard by any chance?' Jonathan asked, not able to repress the question.

'Of course not. Do you think I could possibly tell him – this?' She was smoking a cigarette, a rare thing for her. She glanced at the doorway to the hall, to be sure Georges was not coming back. 'Jon – I think we should make some arrangement to separate.'

On the television, a French politician was speaking about *syndicats*, trade unions.

Jonathan sat down again in his chair. 'Darling, I do know – It's a shock to you. Will you let a few days pass? I know, somehow, I can make you understand. Really.' Jonathan spoke with utmost conviction, and yet he realized he was not convinced himself, not at all. It was like an instinctive clinging to life, Jonathan thought, his clinging to Simone.

'Yes, of course you think that. But I know myself. I am not an emotional young girl, you know.' Her eyes looked straight at him, hardly angry now, only determined, and distant. 'I am not interested in all your money now, not any of it. I can make my own way – with Georges.'

'Oh, Georges – my God, Simone, I'll support Georges!' Jonathan could hardly believe they were saying these words. He got up, drew Simone up from her chair a little roughly, and some coffee spilled out of her cup into the saucer. Jonathan embraced her, would have kissed her, but she squirmed away.

'*Non!*' She put her cigarette out, and started clearing the table. 'I am sorry to say also that I don't want to sleep in the same bed with you.'

'Oh, yes, I assumed that.' And you'll go to church tomorrow and say a prayer for my soul, Jonathan thought. 'Simone, you must let a little time go by. Don't say things now that you don't mean.'

'I will not change. Ask M. Ripley. I think he knows.'

Georges came back. Television was forgotten, and he looked at them both with puzzlement.

Jonathan touched Georges' head with his fingertips as he went into the hall. Jonathan had thought to go up to the bedroom – but it wasn't their bedroom any more, and anyway what would he do up there? The television droned on. Jonathan turned in a circle in the hall, then took his raincoat and a muffler, and went out. He walked to the Rue de France and turned left and at the end of the street went into the bar-café on the corner. He wanted to telephone Tom Ripley. He remembered Tom's number.

'Hello?' Tom said.

'Jonathan.'

'How are you? . . . I telephoned the hospital, I heard you stayed the night. You're out now?'

'Oh, yes, this morning. I –' Jonathan gasped.

'What's the matter?'

'Could I see you for a few minutes? If you think it's safe. I'm – I suppose I could get a taxi. Surely.'

'Where are you?'

'The corner bar – the new one near the Aigle Noir.'

'I could pick you up. No?' Tom suspected Jonathan had had a bad scene with Simone.

'I'll walk towards the Monument. I want to walk a little. I'll see you there.'

Jonathan felt at once better. It was spurious, no doubt, it was postponing the situation with Simone, but for the moment that didn't matter. He felt like a tortured man momentarily relieved of the torture, and he was grateful for a few moments of the relief. Jonathan lit a cigarette and walked slowly, because it would take Tom nearly fifteen minutes. Jonathan went into the Bar des Sports, just beyond the Hôtel de l'Aigle Noir, and ordered a beer. He tried not to think at all. Then one thought rose to the surface on its own : Simone *would* come round. As soon as he thought consciously about this, he feared that she wouldn't. He was alone now. Jonathan knew he was alone, that even Georges was more than half cut off from him now, because surely Simone was going to keep Georges, but Jonathan was aware that he didn't yet realize it fully. That would take days. Feelings were slower than thoughts. Sometimes.

Tom's dark Renault in a thin stream of other cars came out of the darkness of the woods into the light around the Obelisque, the Monument. It was a little past 8 p.m. Jonathan was on the corner, on the left side of the road, and Tom's right. Tom would have to make the complete circle to regain his road homeward – if they went to Tom's. Jonathan preferred Tom's house to a bar. Tom stopped and unlatched the door.

'Evening!' Tom said.

'Evening,' Jonathan replied, pulling the door shut, and at once Tom moved off. 'Can we go to your place? I don't feel like a crowded bar.'

'Sure.'

'I've had a bad evening. And day, I'm afraid.'

'So I thought. Simone?'

'It seems she's finished. Who can blame her?' Jonathan felt awkward, started to take a cigarette, and found even that purposeless, so he didn't.

'I tried my best,' Tom said. He was concentrating on driving as fast as possible without bringing down a motor-cycle cop, some of whom lurked in the woods at the edge of the road here.

'Oh, it's the money – it's the corpses, good Christ! As for the money, I said I was holding the stake for the Germans, you know.' It was suddenly ludicrous to Jonathan, the money, the bet also. The money was so concrete in a way, so tangible, so useful, and yet not nearly so tangible or meaningful as the two dead men that Simone had seen. Tom was driving quite fast. Jonathan felt unconcerned whether they hit a tree or bounced off the road. 'To put it simply,' Jonathan went on, 'it's the dead men. The fact that I helped – or did it. I don't think she's going to change.' What profiteth it a man – Jonathan could have laughed. He hadn't gained the whole world, nor had he lost his soul. Anyway, Jonathan didn't believe in a soul. Self-respect was more like it. He hadn't lost his self-respect, only Simone. Simone was morale, however, and wasn't morale self-respect?

Tom did not think Simone was going to change towards Jonathan either, but he said nothing. Maybe he could talk at home, and yet what else could he say? Words of comfort, words of hope, of reconciliation, when he didn't really believe there'd be one? And yet who knew about women? Sometimes they appeared to have stronger moral attitudes than men, and at other times – especially as to political skulduggery and the political swine they could sometimes marry – it seemed to Tom that women were more flexible, more capable of double-think than men. Unfortunately, Simone presented a picture of inflexible rectitude. Hadn't Jonathan said she was a church-goer too? But Tom's thoughts were equally on Reeves Minot now. Reeves was nervous, for no very strong reason that Tom could see. Suddenly Tom was at the turn-off at Villeperce, guiding the car slowly through the familiar, quiet streets.

And there was Belle Ombre behind the tall poplars, a light glowing above the doorway – all intact.

Tom had just made coffee, and Jonathan said he would join him in a cup. Tom heated the coffee a bit, and brought it with the brandy bottle to the coffee-table.

'Speaking of problems,' Tom said, 'Reeves wants to come to France. I phoned him today from Sens. He's in Ascona staying at a hotel called The Three Bears.'

'I remember,' Jonathan said.

'He imagines he's being spied on – by people in the street. I tried to tell him – our enemies don't waste time with that sort of thing. He should know. I tried to discourage him from coming even to Paris. Certainly not to my place, here. I wouldn't call Belle Ombre the safest spot in the world, would you? Naturally, I couldn't even hint at Saturday night, which might've reassured Reeves. I mean, we at least got rid of the two people who saw us on the train. I'm not sure how long the peace and quiet will last.' Tom hitched forward, elbows on his knees, and glanced at the silent windows. 'Reeves doesn't know anything about Saturday night, or didn't say anything, anyway. Might not even connect it, if he reads the papers. I suppose you saw the papers today?'

'Yes,' Jonathan said.

'No clues. Nothing on the radio tonight either, but the TV boys gave it a spot. No clues.' Tom smiled, and reached for one of his small cigars. He extended the box to Jonathan, but Jonathan shook his head. 'What's equally good news, not a question from the townsfolk here. I bought bread and went to the butcher's today – on foot, taking my time – just to see. And around seven-thirty p.m. Howard Clegg arrived, one of my neighbours, bringing me a big plastic sack of horse manure from one of his farmer friends where he buys a rabbit now and then.' Tom puffed on his cigar and relaxed with a laugh. 'It was Howard who stopped his car outside Saturday night, remember? He thought we had guests, Heloise and I, and that it mightn't be the time to deliver horse manure.' Tom rambled on, trying to fill in the time, while Jonathan, he hoped, lost a little of his tension. 'I told him Heloise was away for a few days, and I said I'd been entertaining some friends from Paris, hence the Paris car outside. I think that went down very well.'

The clock on the mantel struck nine, with pure little pings.

'However, back to Reeves,' Tom said. 'I thought of writing him, saying I had some grounds for thinking the situation had improved, but two things stopped me. Reeves might leave Ascona at any hour now, and second, things haven't improved for him, if the wogs still want to get him. He's using the name Ralph Platt now, but they know his real name and what he looks like.

There's nothing for Reeves but Brazil, if the Mafia still wants to get him. And even Brazil – ' Tom smiled, but not happily now.

'But isn't he rather used to it?' Jonathan asked.

'Like this? No. – Very few people, I suppose, get used to the Mafia and live to talk about it. They may live, but not very comfortably.'

But Reeves had brought it on himself, Jonathan was thinking. And Reeves had drawn him into it. No, he'd walked into it of his own free will, let himself be persuaded – for money. And it was Tom Ripley who had – at least tried to help him collect that money, even if it had been Tom's idea from the start, this deadly game. Jonathan's mind spun back to those minutes on the train between Munich and Strassburg.

'I *am* sorry about Simone,' Tom said. Jonathan's long, cramped figure, hunched over his coffee cup, seemed to illustrate failure, like a statue. 'What does she want to do?'

'Oh – ' Jonathan shrugged. 'She talks about a separation. Taking Georges, of course. She has a brother, Gérard, in Nemours. I don't know what she'll say to him – or to her family there. She's absolutely shocked, you see. And ashamed.'

'I do understand.' So is Heloise ashamed, Tom thought, but Heloise was more capable of double-think. Heloise knew he dabbled in murder, crime – yet was it crime? At least recently, with the Derwatt thing, and now the accursed Mafia? Tom brushed the moral question aside for the moment, and at the same time found himself flicking a bit of ash off his knee. What was Jonathan going to do with himself? Without Simone, he'd have no morale at all. Tom wondered if he should try talking to Simone again? But his memory of yesterday's interview discouraged him. Tom didn't fancy trying again with Simone.

'I am finished,' Jonathan said.

Tom started to speak, and Jonathan interrupted:

'You know I'm finished with Simone – or she is with me. Then there's the old business of how long will I live anyway? Why drag it on? So Tom – ' Jonathan stood up. 'If I can be of service, even suicidal, I'm at your disposal.'

Tom smiled. 'Brandy?'

'Yes, a little. Thanks.'

Tom poured it. 'I've spent the last few minutes trying to

explain why I think – I *think* we're over the hump. That is with the wogs. Of course we're not out of the woods if they catch Reeves – and torture him. He might talk about both of us.'

Jonathan had thought of that. It simply didn't matter much to him, but of course it mattered to Tom. Tom wanted to stay alive. 'Can I be of any service? As a decoy, perhaps? A sacrifice?' Jonathan laughed.

'I don't want any decoys,' Tom said

'Didn't you say once the Mafia might want a certain amount of blood, as revenge?'

Tom had certainly thought it, but he wasn't sure if he had said it. 'If we do nothing – they may get Reeves and finish him,' Tom said. 'This is called letting nature take its course. I didn't put this idea – assassinating Mafiosi – into Reeves' head, and neither did you.'

Tom's cool attitude took the wind out of Jonathan's sails a little. He sat down. 'And what about Fritz? Any news? I remember Fritz well.' Jonathan smiled, as if recollecting halcyon days, Fritz arriving at Reeves' flat in Hamburg, cap in hand, with a friendly smile and the efficient little pistol.

Tom had to think for a moment who Fritz was : the factotum, the taxi-driver-messenger in Hamburg. 'No. Let's hope Fritz has returned to his folks in the country, as Reeves said. I hope he's staying there. Maybe they're finished with Fritz.' Tom stood up. 'Jonathan, you've got to go home tonight and face the music.'

'I know.' Tom had, however, made him feel better. Tom was realistic, even about Simone. 'Funny, the problem isn't the Mafia any more, it's Simone – for me.'

Tom knew. 'I'll go with you, if you like. Try to talk with her again.'

Jonathan shrugged again. He was on his feet now, restless. He glanced at the painting that Tom had said was called *Man in Chair*, by Derwatt, over the fireplace. He was reminded of Reeves' flat, with another Derwatt over the fireplace, maybe destroyed now. 'I think I'll be sleeping on the Chesterfield tonight – whatever happens,' Jonathan said.

Tom thought of turning on the news. It wasn't the right time to get anything, though, not even to get Italy. 'What do you think? Simone can always forbid me the door. Unless you think it'll make it worse for you if I'm with you.'

'Things could not be worse. – All right. I'd like you to come, yes. But what'll we say?'

Tom pushed his hands into the pockets of his old grey flannels. In his right pocket was the small Italian gun which Jonathan had carried on the train. Tom had slept with it under his pillow since Saturday night. Yes, what to say? Tom usually relied on inspiration of the moment, but hadn't he already shot his bolt with Simone? What other brilliant facet of the problem could he come up with, to dazzle her eyes, her brain, and make her see things their way? 'The only thing to do,' Tom said thoughtfully, 'is try and convince her of the safety of everything – now. I admit that's hard to do. That's hurdling the corpses all right. But much of her trouble is anxiety, you know.'

'Well – are things safe?' Jonathan asked. 'We can't be sure, can we? – It's Reeves, I suppose.'

23

They were in Fontainebleau at 10 p.m. Jonathan led the way up the front steps, knocked, then put his key into the lock. But the door was bolted inside.

'Who is it?' Simone called.

'Jon.'

She slid the bolt. 'Oh, Jon – I was worried!'

That sounded hopeful, Tom thought.

In the next second, Simone saw Tom, and her expression changed.

'Yes – Tom's with me. Can't we come in?'

She looked on the brink of saying no, then she stepped back a little stiffly. Jonathan and Tom went in.

'Good evening, madame,' Tom said.

In the living-room the television was on, some sewing – what looked like a repair on a coat lining – lay on the black leather sofa, and Georges was playing with a toy truck on the floor. The picture of domestic calm, Tom thought. He said hello to Georges.

'Do sit down, Tom,' said Jonathan.

But Tom didn't, because Simone showed no sign of sitting.

'And what is the reason for this visit?' she asked Tom.

'Madame, I – ' Tom stammered on, 'I've come to take all the blame on myself, and to try to persuade you to – to be a little kinder to your husband.'

'You are telling me that my husband – ' She was suddenly aware of Georges, and with an air of nervous exasperation took him by the hand. 'Georges, you must go upstairs. Do you hear me? Please, darling.'

Georges went to the doorway, looked back, then entered the hall and mounted the stairs, reluctantly.

'*Dépêche-toi!*' Simone yelled at him, then closed the living-room door. 'You are telling me,' she resumed, 'that my husband knows nothing about these – events, until he just walked in on them. That this sordid money comes from a bet between doctors!'

Tom took a breath. 'The blame is mine. Perhaps – Jon made a mistake in helping me. But can't that be forgiven? He is your husband – '

'He has become a criminal. Perhaps this is your charming influence, but it is a fact. Is it not?'

Jonathan sat down in the armchair.

Tom decided to take one end of the sofa – until Simone ordered him out of the house. Bravely, Tom started again. 'Jon came to see me tonight to discuss this, madame. He is most upset. Marriage – is a sacred thing, you know that well. His life, his courage would be quite destroyed if he lost your affections. You surely realize that. And you should think also of your son, who needs his father.'

Simone was a little affected by Tom's words, but she replied, 'Yes, a father. A real father to respect. I agree!'

Tom heard footsteps on the stone steps, and looked quickly at Jonathan.

'Expecting someone?' Jonathan asked Simone. She had probably telephoned Gérard, he thought.

She shook her head. 'No.'

Tom and Jonathan jumped up.

'Bolt the door again,' Tom whispered in English to Jonathan. 'Ask who it is.'

A neighbour, Jonathan thought as he went to the door. He slid the bolt quietly shut. *'Qui est-ce, s'il vous plaît?'*

'M. Trevanny?'

Jonathan didn't recognize the man's voice, and looked over his shoulder at Tom in the hall.

There'd be more than one, Tom thought.

'Now what?' asked Simone.

Tom put his finger to his lips. Then, not caring what Simone's reaction might be, Tom went down the hall towards the kitchen, which had a light on. Simone was following him. Tom looked around for something heavy. He still had one garrotte in his hip pocket, and of course it wouldn't be necessary if the caller was a neighbour.

'What're you doing?' Simone asked.

Tom was opening a narrow yellow door in a corner of the kitchen. It was a broom closet, and here he saw what he might need, a hammer, and besides that a chisel, plus several innocuous mops and brooms. 'I might be more useful here,' Tom said, picking up the hammer. He was expecting a shot through the door, the sound of the front door being assaulted by shoulders from outside, perhaps. Then he heard the faint click of the bolt being slid – open. Was Jonathan mad?

Simone at once started off boldly into the hall, and Tom heard her gasp. There was a scuffling sound in the hall, then the door slammed shut.

'Mme Trevanny?' said a man's voice.

Simone's cry was shut off before it became a real cry. The sounds came up the hall now towards the kitchen.

Simone appeared, sliding on the heels of her shoes, manhandled by a thick fellow in a dark suit, who had his hand over her mouth. Tom, to the left of the man as he entered the kitchen, stepped out and hit him with the hammer just below his hatbrim in the back of the neck. The man was by no means unconscious, but he released Simone, and straightened up a little, so that Tom had an opportunity to bash him on the nose, and this Tom followed – the man's hat having fallen off – by a blow on the forehead, straightforward and true, as if he had been an ox in a slaughter-house. The man's legs sank under him.

Simone got to her feet, and Tom drew her towards the broom closet corner, which was concealed from the hall. As far as Tom knew, there was only one other man in the house, and the silence made Tom think of the garrotte. With his hammer, Tom went up the hall towards the front door. Quiet as he tried to be, he was still heard by the Italian in the living-room, who had Jonathan on the floor. It was indeed the old garrotte again. Tom sprang at him with the hammer raised. The Italian – in a grey suit, grey hat – released the garrotte and was pulling his gun from a shoulder-holster when Tom hit him in the cheek-bone. More accurate than a tennis racket, the hammer! The man, who had not quite stood up, lurched forward, and Tom removed his hat quickly with his left hand and with his right came down again with the hammer.

Crack! Little Leviathan's dark eyes closed, his pink lips relaxed, and he thudded to the floor.

Tom knelt beside Jonathan. The nylon cord was already well into Jonathan's flesh. Tom turned Jonathan's head this way and that, trying to get at the cord to loosen it. Jonathan's teeth were bared, and he was trying with his own fingers, but feebly.

Simone was suddenly beside them, holding something that looked like a letter-opener. She pried with the point of it into the side of Jonathan's neck. The string loosened.

Tom lost his balance on his heels, sat down on the floor, and sprang up again. He yanked the curtains of the front window shut. There had been a gap of six inches between them. Tom thought that a minute and a half had passed since the Italians had come in. He picked up the hammer from the floor, went to the front door and bolted it again. There was no sound from outside, except for the normal-sounding steps of someone walking past on the pavement, and the hum of a passing car.

'Jon,' said Simone.

Jonathan coughed and rubbed his neck. He was trying to sit up.

The porcine man in grey lay motionless, with his head propped by accident against a leg of the armchair. Tom tightened his grip on the hammer, and started to give the man one more blow, but hesitated, because there was already some blood on the carpet. But Tom thought the man was still alive.

'Pig,' Tom murmured, and pulled the man up a little by his shirt front and flamboyant tie, and smashed the hammer head into his left temple.

Georges stood wide-eyed in the doorway.

Simone had brought Jonathan a glass of water. She was kneeling beside him. 'Go *away*, Georges!' she said. 'Papa is all right! Go in the – Go upstairs, Georges!'

But Georges didn't. He stood there, fascinated by a scene that was perhaps unsurpassed on the television. By the same token, he wasn't taking it too seriously. His eyes were wide, absorbing it all, but he was not terrified.

Jonathan got to the sofa, helped by Tom and Simone. He was sitting up, and Simone had a wet towel for his face. 'I'm really all right,' Jonathan mumbled.

Tom was still listening for footsteps, front or back. Of all times, Tom thought, when he'd meant to create a peaceable impression on Simone! 'Madame, is the garden passageway locked?'

'Yes,' said Simone.

And Tom remembered ornamental spikes along the top of the iron door. He said in English to Jonathan, 'There's probably at least one more of them in a car outside.' Tom supposed Simone understood this, but he couldn't tell from her face. She was looking at Jonathan, who seemed to be quite out of danger, and then she went to Georges who was still in the doorway

'Georges! Will you – !' She shooed him upstairs again, carried him half-way up the stairway, and spanked his bottom once. 'Go into your room and close the door!'

Simone was being splendid, Tom thought. It would be a matter of seconds until another man, just as at Belle Ombre, came to the door, Tom supposed. Tom tried to imagine what the man in the car would be thinking : from the absence of noise, of screams, of gunshots, the waiting man or men probably supposed that everything had gone as planned. They must be expecting their two chums to come out the door at any moment, mission accomplished, the Trevannys garrotted or beaten to death. Reeves must have talked, Tom thought, must have told them Jonathan's name and address. Tom had a wild idea of Jonathan and himself putting on the Italians' hats, making a dash out the door to the Italians' car (if any), and taking them by surprise with – the one small gun. But he couldn't ask Jonathan to do that.

'Jonathan, I'd better go out before it's too late,' Tom said.

'Too late – how?' Jonathan had wiped his face with the wet towel, and some blond hair stood on end above his forehead.

'Before they come to the door. They'll be suspicious if their chums don't come out.' If the Italians saw the situation here, they'd blast the three of them with guns and make a getaway in their car, Tom was thinking. Tom went to the window and stooped, looking out just above the sill level. He listened for a car motor idling somewhere, looked for a car stationed with parking lights on. Parking was permitted on the opposite side of the street today. Tom saw it – maybe it – to the left, some twelve yards away diagonally. The big car's parking lights were on, but Tom could not be sure the motor was, because of the hum of other noises on the street.

Jonathan was up, walking towards Tom.

'I think I see them, Tom said.

'What should we do?'

Tom was thinking of what he would do alone, stay in the house and try to shoot anyone who broke in the door. 'There's Simone and Georges to consider. We don't want a fight in here. I think we should rush them – outside. Otherwise they'll rush us here, and it'll be guns if they break in. – I can do it, Jon.'

Jonathan felt a sudden rage, a desire to guard his house and home. 'All right – we'll go together!'

'What are you going to do, Jon?' Simone asked.

'We think there might be more of them – coming,' Jonathan said in French.

Tom went to the kitchen. He got the hat from the linoleum floor near the dead man, stuck it on his head and found it fell over his ears. Then he suddenly realized that these Italians, both of them, had guns in their shoulder-holsters. Tom took this man's gun from the holster. He went back into the living-room. 'These guns!' he said, reaching for the gun of the man on the floor. The drawn gun was hidden under his jacket. Tom took the man's hat, found that it fitted him better, and handed Jonathan the hat from the kitchen. 'Try this. If we can look like them till we cross the street, it's a slight advantage. Don't come with me, Jon. It's just as good if one person goes out. I just want them to move off!'

'Then I'll go,' Jonathan said. He knew what he had to do: scare them off, and perhaps shoot one first if he could, before he was shot himself.

Tom handed a gun to Simone, the small Italian gun. 'It might be useful, madame.' But she looked shy of taking the gun, and Tom laid the gun on the sofa. The safety was off.

Jonathan pushed the safety off the gun in his hand. 'Could you see how many are in the car?'

'Couldn't see a thing inside.' On his last words, Tom heard someone walking up the front steps, cautiously, with an effort to be silent. Tom jerked his head at Jonathan. 'Bolt the door after us, madame,' he whispered to Simone.

Tom and Jonathan, both wearing hats now, walked up the hall, and Tom slid the bolt and opened the door in the face of the man standing there. At the same time, Tom bumped him and caught him by the arm, turning him back down the stairs again. Jonathan had grabbed his other arm. At a glance, in the near darkness, Tom and Jonathan might have been taken for his two chums, but Tom knew the illusion wouldn't last more than a second or two.

'To the left!' Tom said to Jonathan. The man they held was struggling, but not yet yelling, and his efforts nearly lifted Tom off his feet.

Jonathan had seen the car with its parking lights on, and now he saw the lights come full on, and heard the motor revving. The car backed a little.

'Dump him!' Tom said, and he and Jonathan, like a pair that had rehearsed it, hurled the Italian forward, and his head hit the side of the slowly moving car. Tom was aware of the clatter of the Italian's drawn gun on the street. The car had stopped, and the door in front of Tom was opening: the Mafia boys wanted their chum back, apparently. Tom pulled his gun from his trousers pocket, aimed at the driver, and fired. The driver, with the aid of a man in the back, was trying to get the dazed Italian into the front seat. Tom was afraid to fire again, because a couple of people were running towards them from the Rue de France. And a window opened in one of the houses. Tom saw, or thought he saw, the other back door of the car being opened, someone being pushed out on to the pavement.

One shot came from the back of the car, then a second, just as Jonathan stumbled or walked right in front of Tom. The car was moving off.

Tom saw Jonathan slump forward, and before Tom could catch him, Jonathan fell on the place where the car had been. Damn it, Tom thought, if he'd hit the driver, it must have been only in the arm. The car was gone.

A young man, then a man and woman came trotting up.

'What's happening?'

'He's shot?'

'*Police!*' The last was the cry of a young woman

'Jon!' Tom thought Jonathan had merely tripped, but Jonathan wasn't getting up, and was barely stirring. With the assistance of one of the young men, Tom got Jonathan to the kerb, but he was quite limp.

Jonathan had been shot in the chest, he thought, but he was mainly aware of numbness. There had been a jolt He was going to faint soon, and maybe it was more serious than fainting. People dashed around him, shouting.

Only now did Tom recognize the figure on the sidewalk – Reeves! Reeves was crumpled, apparently trying to recover his breath.

' . . . ambulance!' a Frenchwoman's voice was saying. 'We must call an ambulance!'

'I have a car!' a man cried.

Tom glanced at Jonathan's house windows, and saw the black silhouette of Simone's head as she peered through the curtains. He shouldn't leave her there, Tom thought. He had to get Jonathan to the hospital, and his car would be quicker than any ambulance. 'Reeves! – Hold the fort, I'll be back in one minute. – *Oui, madame*,' Tom said to a woman (now there were five or six people around them), 'I'll take him to the hospital in my car at once!' Tom ran across the street and banged on the house door. 'Simone, it's Tom!'

When Simone opened the door, Tom said :

'Jonathan has been hurt. We must go to the hospital at once. Just take a coat and come. And Georges too!'

Georges was in the hall. Simone didn't waste time with a coat, but she did grope in a coat pocket, in the hall, for her keys, then hurried back towards Tom. 'Hurt? Was he shot?'

'I'm afraid so. My car is to the left. The green one.' His car was twenty feet behind where the Italians' car had been. Simone wanted to go to Jonathan, but Tom assured her that the most useful thing she could do was open the doors of his car, which was unlocked. There were more people, but no policeman as yet, and one officious little man asked Tom who in hell he thought he was, taking charge of everything?

'Stuff yourself!' Tom said in English. He was struggling with Reeves to lift Jonathan in the gentlest way possible. It would have been wiser to have brought the car closer, but having got Jonathan off the ground, they continued, and a couple of people assisted, so after a few steps it was not difficult. They braced Jonathan in a corner of the back seat.

Tom got into his car, dry in the mouth. 'This is Mme Trevanny,' Tom said to Reeves. 'Reeves Minot.'

'How do you do?' said Reeves with his American accent.

Simone got into the back, where Jonathan was. Reeves took Georges in beside him, and Tom pulled out, heading for the Fontainebleau hospital.

'Papa has fainted?' Georges asked.

'*Oui*, Georges.' Simone had begun to weep.

Jonathan heard their voices, but couldn't speak. He couldn't move, not even a finger. He had a grey vision of a sea running out – somewhere on an English coast – sinking, collapsing. He was already far away from Simone whose breast he leaned against – or so he thought But Tom was alive. Tom was driving the car, Jonathan thought, like God himself. Somewhere there had been a bullet, which somehow no longer mattered. This was death now, which he had tried to face before and yet had not faced, tried to prepare and yet hadn't been able to There was no preparation possible, it was merely a surrender, after all. And what he had done, misdone, accomplished, striven for – all seemed absurdity.

Tom passed an ambulance just coming up, wailing. He drove carefully. It was only four or five minutes' drive. The silence among all of them in the car became eerie to Tom. It was as if he and Reeves, Simone, Georges, Jonathan if he was conscious of anything, had been frozen in one second that went on and on.

'This man is *dead*!' said an intern in an astonished voice.

'But – ' Tom didn't believe it. He couldn't get another word out.

Only Simone gave a cry.

They were standing on the concrete at one entrance to the hospital. Jonathan had been put on a stretcher, and two helpers held the stretcher poised, as if they didn't know what to do next.

'Simone, do you want – ' But Tom didn't even know what he had been going to say. And Simone was now running towards

Jonathan who was being borne inside, and Georges followed her. Tom ran after Simone, thinking to get her keys from her, to remove the two corpses from her house, or do *something* with them, then he stopped abruptly and his shoes slid on the concrete. The police would be at the Trevanny house before he was. The police were probably already breaking in, because the people in the street would have told them that the disturbance started from the grey house, that after the shots one person (Tom) had run back to the house, and he and a woman and small boy had come out and got into a car.

Simone was now disappearing round a corner, following the stretcher of Jonathan. It was as if Tom saw her already in a funeral procession. Tom turned and walked back to Reeves.

'We take off,' Tom said, 'while we can.' He wanted to take off before someone asked questions or made a note of his licence number.

He and Reeves got into Tom's car. Tom drove off, towards the Monument and home.

'Jonathan's *dead* — do you think?' Reeves asked.

'Yes. Well – you heard the intern.'

Reeves slumped and rubbed his eyes.

It wasn't sinking in, Tom thought, not to either of them. Tom was apprehensive lest a car from the hospital be trailing him, even a police car. One didn't deposit a dead man and drive off with no questions asked. What was Simone going to say? They'd excuse her for not saying anything this evening, perhaps, but tomorrow? 'And you, my friend,' Tom said, his throat hoarse. 'No bones broken, no teeth knocked out?' He'd talked, Tom remembered, and maybe at once.

'Only cigarette burns,' Reeves said in a humble voice, as if burns were nothing compared to a bullet. Reeves had an inch-long beard, reddish.

'I suppose you know what's at the Trevanny's house – two dead men.'

'Oh. Good. – Yes, of course I know. They're missing. They never came back.'

'I'd have gone by the house to do something, try to, but the police must be there now.' A siren behind Tom made him grip the wheel in sudden panic, but it turned out to be a white ambulance with a blue light on its roof, which passed Tom at the Monument, and whisked away in a quick right turn towards Paris. Tom wished it might have been Jonathan, being taken to a Paris hospital where they were better able to deal with him. Tom thought that Jonathan had deliberately stepped between him and a man's gun in the car. Was he wrong? No one overtook them, or sirened them to a stop, in the drive to Villeperce. Reeves had fallen asleep against the door, but he woke up when the car stopped.

'This is home sweet home,' Tom said.

They got out in the garage, and Tom locked the garage, then opened his house door with a key. All was serene. It was rather unbelievable.

'Do you want to flop on the sofa while I make some tea?' Tom asked. 'Tea is what we need.'

They had tea and whisky, more tea than whisky. Reeves, with his usual apologetic manner, asked Tom if he had any anti-burn ointment, and Tom produced something from the downstairs loo medicine cabinet, and Reeves retired there to dress his wounds, which he said were all on his stomach. Tom lit a cigar, not so much because he craved a cigar as because a cigar gave him a sense of stability, perhaps illusory, but it was the illusion, the attitude towards problems that counted. One simply had to have a confident attitude.

When Reeves came into the living-room, he took note of the harpsichord.

'Yes,' Tom said. 'A new acquisition. I'm going to see about taking lessons in Fontainebleau – or somewhere. Maybe Heloise will take lessons too. We can't go on twiddling on the thing like a pair of monkeys.' Tom felt curiously angry, not against Reeves, not against anything specific. 'Tell me what happened in Ascona.'

Reeves sipped his tea and whisky again, silent for a few seconds like a man who had to drag himself back inch by inch from another world. 'I'm thinking about Jonathan. Dead. – I didn't want that, you know.'

Tom recrossed his legs. He was thinking about Jonathan too. 'About Ascona. What did happen there?'

'Oh. Well, I told you I thought they'd spotted me. Then a couple of nights ago – yes – one of these fellows approached me on the street. Young fellow, summer sports clothes, looked like an Italian tourist. He said in English "Get your suitcase packed and check out. We'll be waiting." Natch, I – I knew what the alternative was – I mean if I'd decided to pack my suitcase and run. This was around seven p.m. Sunday. Yesterday?'

'Yesterday was Sunday, yes.'

Reeves stared at the coffee-table, but he sat upright, one hand delicately against his midriff, where perhaps the burns were. 'By the way, I never took my suitcase. It's still in the lobby of the hotel in Ascona. They just beckoned me out the door and said "Leave it".'

'You can telephone the hotel,' Tom said, 'from Fontainebleau, for instance.'

'Yes. So – they kept asking me questions. They wanted to know the master-mind of it all. I told them there wasn't any. Couldn't have been *me*, a master-mind!' Reeves laughed weakly. 'I wasn't going to say *you*, Tom. Anyway it wasn't you who wanted to keep the Mafia out of Hamburg. So then – the cigarette burns started. They asked me who'd been on the train. I'm afraid I didn't do as well as Fritz. Good old Fritz –'

'He's not dead, is he?' asked Tom.

'No. Not that I know of. Anyway to make this disgraceful story short, I told them Jonathan's name – where he lived. I said it – because they were holding me down in the car in some woods somewhere, giving me the cigarette burns. I remember thinking that if I screamed like mad for help, no one would have heard me. Then they started holding my nose, pretending they were going to suffocate me.' Reeves squirmed on the sofa.

Tom could sympathize. 'They didn't mention my name?'

'No.'

Tom wondered if he could dare to believe that his coup with Jonathan had come off. Perhaps the Genotti family really thought that Tom Ripley had been a wrong trail 'These were the Genotti family, I presume.'

'Logically, yes.'

'You don't know?'

'They don't mention the family, Tom, for goodness' sake!'

That was true. 'No mention of Angy – or Lippo? Or a capo called Luigi?'

Reeves thought. 'Luigi – maybe I heard the name. I'm afraid I was scared stiff, Tom –'

Tom sighed. 'Angy and Lippo are the two Jonathan and I did in Saturday night,' Tom said in a soft voice as if someone might overhear him. 'Two of the Genotti family. They came to the house here, and we – They were incinerated in their own car, miles from here. Jonathan was here and he was marvellous. You should see the paper!' Tom added, smiling. 'We made Lippo phone his boss Luigi and tell him that I wasn't the man he wanted. That's why I'm asking you about the Genottis. I'm very interested to know whether it was a success or not.'

Reeves was still trying to remember. 'They didn't mention your name, I know. Killed two of them here. In the house! That's something, Tom!' Reeves sank back on the sofa with a gentle smile, looking as if it were the first time he'd relaxed in days. Perhaps it was.

'However, they know my name,' Tom said. 'I'm not sure whether the two in the car recognized me tonight That's – in the stars.' He was surprised at the phrase coming from his lips. He meant it was fifty-fifty, something like that. 'I mean,' Tom continued on a firmer note, 'I don't know whether their appetites are satisfied by getting Jonathan tonight or not.'

Tom stood up, turning away from Reeves. Jonathan dead. And Jonathan hadn't even needed to go out with Tom to the car. Hadn't Jonathan deliberately stepped in front of him, between him and the pistol pointing from the car? But Tom wasn't quite sure he'd seen a pistol pointing. It had all happened so quickly. Jonathan had never reconciled Simone, never had a word of forgiveness from her – nothing but those few minutes of attention she had given him after he'd been nearly garrotted.

'Reeves, shouldn't you think about turning in? Unless you'd like to eat something first. Are you hungry?'

'I think I'm too bushed to eat, thanks. I'd really like to turn in. Thanks, Tom. I wasn't sure you could put me up.'

Tom laughed. 'Neither was I.' Tom showed Reeves up to the guest-room, apologized for the fact Jonathan had slept for a few hours in the bed, and offered to change the sheets, but Reeves assured him that it didn't matter.

'That bed looks like bliss,' Reeves said, weaving with exhaustion as he started to undress.

Tom was thinking, if the Mafia boys tried another attack to-night, he had the bigger Italian gun, plus his rifle, the Luger also, with a tired Reeves instead of Jonathan. But he didn't think the Mafia would come tonight. They would probably prefer to get a great distance from Fontainebleau. Tom hoped he had wounded the driver, at least, and badly.

The next morning, Tom let Reeves sleep on. Tom sat in his living-room with his coffee, with the radio tuned to a French popular programme which gave the news every hour. Unfortunately it was just after 9 a.m. He wondered what Simone was saying to the police, and what she had said last night? She wouldn't, Tom thought, mention him, because that would expose Jonathan's part in the Mafia killings. Or was he right? Couldn't she say that Tom Ripley had coerced her husband – But how? By what kind of pressure? No, it was more likely that Simone would say, more or less, 'I can't imagine why the Mafia (or the Italians) came to our house.' 'But who was the other man with your husband? The witnesses say there was another man – with an American accent.' Tom hoped none of the bystanders would remark on his accent, but probably they would. 'I don't know,' Simone might say. 'Someone my husband knew. I have forgotten his name . . .'

Things were a bit uncertain, at the moment.

Reeves came down before 10 a.m. Tom made more coffee, and scrambled some eggs for him.

'I must take off for your sake,' Reeves said. 'Can you drive me to – I was thinking of Orly. Also I want to telephone about my suitcase, but not from your house. Could you take me to Fontainebleau?'

'I can take you to Fontainebleau and Orly. Where are you headed?'

'Zürich, I was thinking. Then I could swoop back to Ascona and get my suitcase. But if I telephone the hotel, they might send the suitcase to Zürich care of American Express I'll just say I forgot it!' Reeves laughed a boyish, carefree laugh – or rather, forced it out of himself.

Then there was the money situation. Tom had about thirteen

hundred francs in cash in the house. He said he could easily let Reeves have some for the plane ticket and to change into Swiss francs once he got to Zürich. Reeves had traveller's cheques in his suitcase.

'And your passport?' Tom asked.

'Here.' Reeves patted his breast pocket. 'Both of them. Ralph Platt with the beard and me without. Had the picture taken by a chum in Hamburg, me wearing a phoney beard. Can you imagine the Italians didn't take the passports off me? That's luck, eh?'

It certainly was. Reeves was unkillable, Tom thought, like a slender lizard flitting over stone. Reeves had been kidnapped, cigarette-burnt, intimidated God knew how, dumped, and here he was eating scrambled eggs, both eyes intact, not even his nose broken.

'I'm going back to my own passport. So I'll shave off my beard this morning, take a bath too, if I may. I just came down in a hurry, because I thought I'd slept pretty late.'

Tom telephoned while Reeves was bathing, and found out about planes to Zürich. There were three that day, the first taking off at 1.20 p.m., and the girl at Orly said there would very likely be a single seat available.

24

Tom was at Orly with Reeves a few minutes past noon. He parked his car. Reeves telephoned the hotel Three Bears in Ascona about his suitcase, and the hotel agreed to send it to Zürich. Reeves was not much concerned, not as concerned as Tom would have been if he'd left behind an unlocked suitcase with an interesting address book in it. Reeves would probably recover his suitcase with all its contents undisturbed tomorrow in Zürich. Tom had insisted on Reeves' taking one of his small suitcases with an extra shirt, a sweater, pyjamas, socks and underwear, and Tom's own toothbrush and toothpaste, which Tom thought essential for a suitcase to look normal. Somehow Tom hadn't wanted to give Reeves the new toothbrush that Jonathan had used only once. Tom also gave Reeves a raincoat.

Reeves looked paler without the beard. 'Tom, don't wait to see me off, I'll manage. Thanks infinitely. You saved my life.'

That wasn't quite true, unless the Italians had been going to plug Reeves on the pavement, which Tom doubted. 'If I *don't* hear from you,' Tom said with a smile, 'I'll assume you're all right.'

'Okay, Tom!' A wave of the hand, and he vanished through the glass doors.

Tom got his car and drove homeward, feeling wretched and increasingly sad. He didn't care to try to shake it off by seeing people this evening, not the Grais again, not the Cleggs either. Not even a film in Paris. He'd ring Heloise around 7 p.m., and see if she'd departed on the Swiss jaunt. If she had, her parents would know her telephone number in the Swiss chalet. or some way of reaching her. Heloise always thought of things like that, leaving a telephone number or an address where she could be found.

Then of course he might have a visit from the police, which

would put an end to his efforts to shake off his depression. What could he say to the police, that he had been home all last evening? Tom laughed, and the laugh was a relief. He ought to find out first, of course, what Simone had already said, if he could.

But the police did not come, and Tom made no effort to speak with Simone. Tom suffered his usual apprehension that the police were spending this time in amassing evidence and testimony before they dumped it on him. Tom bought some things for his dinner, practised some finger exercises on the harpsichord. and wrote a friendly note to Mme Annette in care of her sister in Lyon:

My dear Mme Annette,

Belle Ombre misses you painfully. But I hope you are relaxing and enjoying these beautiful days of early summer. Everything is all right here. I will telephone one of these evenings and see how you are. All the best wishes

Affectionately,
Tom

The Paris radio reported a 'shoot-up' in a Fontainebleau street, three men killed, no names given. The Tuesday paper (Tom bought *France-Soir* in Villeperce) had a five-inch-long item: Jonathan Trevanny of Fontainebleau shot dead, and two Italians also shot in Trevanny's house. Tom's eyes glided over their names as though he didn't want to remember them, though he knew they might linger a long time in his memory: Alfiori and Ponti. The Italians had invaded the house for no reason that Mme Simone Trevanny knew, she had told the police. The had rung the doorbell, then burst in. A friend whom Mme Trevanny did not name had aided her husband, and later driven them both, with their small son, to the hospital in Fontainebleau where her husband had been found dead on arrival.

Aided, Tom thought with amusement, in view of the two Mafiosi with their skulls bashed in in the Trevanny house. Pretty handy with a hammer, that friend of the Trevannys, and maybe Trevanny himself, considering they had been up against a total of four men with guns. Tom began to relax, to laugh even – and if there was a little hysteria in the laugh, who could blame him?

He knew that more details were going to come out in the newspapers, and if not the newspapers then via the police themselves – direct to Simone, direct to him, maybe. But Mme Simone was going to try to protect her husband's honour and her nest-egg in Switzerland, Tom believed, otherwise she would have told them a bit more already. She could have mentioned Tom Ripley, and her suspicion of him. The newspapers could have said that Mme Trevanny promised to make a more detailed statement later. But evidently she hadn't.

The funeral of Jonathan Trevanny was to be held Wednesday afternoon, 17 May, at 3 p.m. in the church of St Louis. On Wednesday, Tom wanted to go, but he felt it would have been exactly the wrong thing to do, from Simone's point of view, and after all funerals were for the living, not the dead. Tom spent that time in silence, working in his garden. (He must prod those blasted workmen about the greenhouse.) Tom became more and more convinced that Jonathan had on purpose shielded him from that bullet by stepping in front of him.

Surely the police were going to question Simone in the days to come, demand to know the name of the friend who had aided her husband. Hadn't the Italians, maybe identified by now as the Mafia, been in pursuit of the friend, perhaps, not Jonathan Trevanny? The police would give Simone a few days to recover from her grief, and then they would question her again. Tom could imagine Simone's will strengthened even more in the direction in which she had started : the friend didn't want his name given, he was not a close friend, he had acted in self-defence, as had her husband, and she wanted to forget the whole nightmare.

About a month later, in June, when Heloise was long back from Switzerland, and Tom's speculations on the Trevanny affair had come true – there had been no further statements from Mme Trevanny in the newspapers – Tom saw Simone approaching him on the same pavement in the Rue de France in Fontainebleau. Tom was carrying a heavy urn-like thing for the garden, which he had just bought. Tom was surprised to see Simone, because he had heard that she had already removed herself and her son to Toulouse where she had bought a house. Tom had heard this news via the young and thrusting owner of the new and expensive delicatessen shop into which Gauthier's art supply shop had been converted. So with his arms nearly giving out from the load which he had almost entrusted to the clerk at the florist's, the unpleasant memory of *céleri rémoulade* and herrings-in-cream in his mind instead of the as yet odourless tubes of paint, virgin brushes and canvases that he was used to seeing in Gauthier's premises, plus the belief that Simone was already hundreds of miles away – Tom had the feeling he was seeing a ghost, having a vision. Tom was in shirtsleeves, beginning to crumple, and if not for Simone, he might have set the urn down to rest for a moment. His car was at the next corner. Simone saw him and at once began to glare like a focusing enemy. She paused briefly beside him, and as Tom almost came to a stop also, thinking at least to say '*Bonjour*, madame,' she spat at him. She missed his face, missed him entirely, and plunged on towards the Rue St Merry.

That, perhaps, corresponded to the Mafia revenge. Tom hoped that would be all that there was to it – either from the Mafia or Mme Simone. In fact, the spit was a kind of guarantee, unpleasant to be sure, whether it hit or not. But if Simone hadn't decided to hang on to the money in Switzerland, she wouldn't have bothered spitting and he himself would be in prison. Simone was just a trifle ashamed of herself, Tom thought. In that, she joined much of the rest of the world. Tom felt, in fact, that her conscience would be more at rest than that of her husband, if he were still alive.